The Québec Affair

by Robert Penbrooke

Bibliothèque interculturelle

Montréal ✿

PROMONTORY
P R E S S

Promontory Press
www.promontorypress.com

ISBN: 978-1-927559-04-8

Typeset by One Owl Creative in 12 pt Garamond
Cover design by Marla Thompson of Edge of Water Design

Printed in Canada
0987654321

Disclaimer

THE QUÉBEC AFFAIR is a work of fiction. Names, places, and incidents are the products of the author's imagination, or they are used fictitiously. Any resemblance to actual events, locales, or persons living or dead, is entirely coincidental. Where the names of actual persons, places, or events are mentioned, it is purely to provide historical context for the story, and the interpretation of the significance of any events and setting is taken entirely from the author's imagination.

Dedication

This story is dedicated to my beloved sister, Lesje Juliana Foxon, who attended Emma Willard School for Girls in Troy, New York and the McGill University School of Occupational and Physical Therapy (1956-61) in Montréal. She heard the outline of this story, in its entirety, only weeks before she died of cancer in Cambridge, Massachusetts, in 1987.

Her patient and quiet care for friends and family and her love of all things Canadian were an inspiration to those who knew her. They provide hope that the three great nations of the North American continent, Canada, the U.S., and Mexico, may live in peace and harmony and, by example, be of service to the rest of the world community.

With much love,

Robert Penbrooke
March 3, 2004

Acknowledgements

Although this story is dedicated to my sister, it is my wife Sylvia who deserves the most credit for the patient companionship, hard work, sacrifice, and encouragement over the years that has made the writing of this story possible. We joined in visits to Montréal, the provinces of Québec, Ontario, Prince Edward Island, Nova Scotia, and New Brunswick that only made us wish for more.

Our children and their spouses have provided helpful support ranging from typing drafts, to advice on aircraft, the intricacies of computers, and critical analysis of literary skill. My brother John, a true sportsman and naturalist, has been a model for this adventure.

I must thank Publisher Bennett R. Coles of Promontory Press, Victoria, BC, his editor, Michelle Balfour, his assistant editor, Marg Gilks of Scripta Word Services, Toronto, Ontario, Lisa Fraser of Promontory Press, her assistants, and the Promontory Press marketing team for their advice. Absent their guidance and detailed efforts, this work would not have seen daylight.

Other needed inspiration and encouragement have come from Frank Carnevale, Fran and Jack Coleman, Berjoubhi Esmarian, Terry Graves, and "T" Tirana. Without individually naming them,

I would also like to thank each of my Princeton roommates for rich and rewarding companionship during college years. In their subsequent life's work, they have demonstrated extraordinary leadership beyond those early treasured days together.

My deep thanks, also, to the classmate from Canada who inspired this story in the first place.

The Québec Affair

Part I

QUEBOGGIN

FUSION ENERGY

Exploding inwardly,
Fathoms of light . . .
The prescient dawn.

CDB, Jr.
1976

1

MONDAY, SEPTEMBER 5, 1983

Former CIA Agent, John Thurmond, left the Philadelphia suburb of Buckingham at seven a.m. Sal came outside while he put his overnight bag in the trunk. They embraced and she waved while he disappeared around the bend in the driveway.

He had packed a bite for later in the morning. Carl was still asleep, but Sal had a busy agenda for the day. As an author of children's books, her publisher was forwarding copies of the illustrated text an artist had prepared to attract an older youth audience. She had to write captions for the illustrations.

The traffic northward thinned. Greenstone had finally returned his call Sunday night at five. His meeting with Greenstone would require Q-10 protocols. It looked like Greenstone was still active in the intelligence service, though his mission had evolved. It was important not to have direct contact without coded procedures for identity protection and continued security of meeting places. Greenstone had provided an address in Syracuse, New York: 112 South Alba Street, Apartment 2F. It wouldn't be the location of the meeting itself, but it would be the beginning of John's search.

John had first met Greenstone in late August, 1971. After two months in Reserve Army Basic Artillery Officer training at Fort Sill, Oklahoma, he received an order to report to the long, low buildings housing the post commandant's headquarters. They were located some distance from his tent in the Bachelor Officer's Quarters. It was a hot summer day, with temperatures well above a hundred degrees. He was puzzled at the request, but put on his Class 'A' khaki uniform and reported as ordered.

Captain Greenstone's office was located in one of the few air-conditioned offices on the post. The contrast for John was an unexpected but pleasant shock. Greenstone saluted without getting up and motioned him to a seat in front of his desk.

"John Thurmond?"

"Yes sir." John sat straight in his designated chair.

"I understand you were born in Canada?"

"Yes sir."

"What made you want to join the ROTC and to become an American citizen?"

It was a question he was often asked, so John had his answer ready. "Politics, sir. At the time, I was uneasy with the neutral stance that Canada had taken toward Nationalist China. I felt that isolating Taiwan was unfair, and only plays into Mainland China's ambitions. The situation we face now in Vietnam is a perfect example of the result."

Greenstone muttered his acceptance. "Well, you are entitled to make your own decisions in life, Lieutenant. That said, I'll put your statement on file." The Captain picked up one of the thin, unmarked folders stacked neatly on his desk. "I have here a transcript of your grades at Princeton and your scores in Reserve Officer's Basic Training to date. You majored, as an under-graduate, in physics. But I see from your record that you took labs in quantum mechanics in your last two years."

John blinked, taken aback by the change in topic. "Sir, most people experiment a little before finding what they're suited to."

"Well enough." Greenstone laced his fingers over the manila folder. "Then, to the point: we are looking for someone who fits your profile for a special assignment. It will require intensive training. Are you interested?"

Now he saw where this was going. "That depends, sir. I would like to know about the mission."

"Naturally. There will be a briefing for several candidates in Snowe Hall at sixteen hundred hours tomorrow. I will clear your schedule with Battalion HQ. The meeting will take about an hour and a half. If you are interested, you will receive further instructions."

"Thank you, sir." It was an obvious dismissal, and John rose to leave.

Greenstone didn't smile, but returned his salute crisply. On the way out, John noticed a small plate above the room number on the door, labelled: 'S-2, Central Command'.

That was the only time, except for a few occasions in the officers' mess hall, that he could recall actually meeting Greenstone.

The next afternoon, John had reported to Snowe Hall, and found the first hour devoted to a very thorough questionnaire. A short examination followed, with sections on math, physics, chemistry, English, and foreign language. All the questions were multiple-choice, but with increasing gradients of difficulty.

Growing up in Québec, John had naturally chosen French as a second language. However, he was surprised to see the selections were as varied as Chinese, Arabic, Urdu, Russian, Korean, Burmese, Czech, German, and others. He was intrigued by the scope of it all. The five other candidates seemed intelligent and competent, though none of them came from his training battalion.

An officer collected the paperwork and then introduced two

young men in civilian clothes. They wore drab-coloured suits and neckties, the younger's steel-blue eyes in contrast with his darker companion's. The speakers did not offer their names, but it soon became apparent they were recruiters from the Central Intelligence Agency. They spoke about the agency's responsibilities and the opportunity to work overseas, to focus on the history, culture, and foreign policy of other nations. This was something that had always appealed to John and so, after more questions and a lot of further pre-screening, he had volunteered.

That was twelve years ago. A lot of time had passed in the interval. It was such a far cry from where he was now, leaving suburban Philadelphia at seven in the morning. These days, he had other matters to think about. His wife, their kid, his law firm . . . but, the annoying pressure of unfinished business remained. Now, it seemed, he could finally see this matter through to its end.

John glanced over at the empty passenger seat. It would have been nice to take Sal and Carl on this trip, but obviously, that was out of the question.

As a new agent, he had been assigned to a classified program of complete immersion at the Defence Language Institute in Washington, DC. For fifteen months he spoke, read, wrote, ate, and slept nothing but Chinese. The course progressed through typical tourist and domestic usage, to courses in business, politics, and current events.

It was an intensive process, and John sometimes felt lonely. His contact with his family was limited, and his frequent letters to his girlfriend, Sal, had to stop. He knew she might be disappointed, but his mission called to him in a way that demanded sacrifice. He explained he had been assigned to a special project.

Finally, in the last months of the course—with frequent trips to headquarters in Langley, Virginia—his classified orders were updated and the focus was shifted to atomic energy and briefings on the current state of nuclear fusion research around the world.

Although he completed his officer's basic training after three months at the Institute, his U.S. military status was to be disguised. With his Canadian background, John Thurmond was given an alias, 'Craig Durrand', issued a new Canadian passport, and told he would become a junior assistant to Gordon Ellsworth, a well-known foreign correspondent for the Toronto *Globe and Mail* posted to Beijing.

John was only too aware that Canada held a unique position as a neutral party in the Southeast Asian conflict. It supported mainland China's application for membership in the United Nations very early on. China now sought diplomatic contact with the West, and rewarded Canadian representatives with access to otherwise restricted travel destinations in China. Most importantly, in the case of the *Globe and Mail*, it allowed correspondents to mingle socially with official members of the Chinese government at receptions and certain official functions. This was thought to be a considerable opening to an otherwise closed society.

Gordon Ellsworth was a respected international affairs columnist, who walked a very careful line in his releases to the home office. Ellsworth was willing to promote China's official version of news events, because he felt that even biased information was better than no information. In any case, all reports from China were also edited by several levels of management at the paper's headquarters. Ellsworth also maintained direct contact with important members of the Canadian Ministry in Ottawa through confidential private dispatches, which supplemented their reports from the Canadian legations in Shanghai and Beijing.

John Thurmond's 'Craig Durrand' role was to be the eyes and ears of the *Globe and Mail* at functions that Ellsworth attended. Ellsworth would be engaged in interviewing Party officials, who had all been well-rehearsed in the information they were to release.

John's responsibility, as Ellsworth's junior assistant, was to absorb the background colour and mood of the occasion, listen in on private conversations as best he could, and try to engage participants in 'unofficial' opinions or versions of events. Ellsworth found that this kind of information added essential spice and flavour to his columns. It broadened his readership considerably, and as such, was an important part of his reporting.

Though by no means completely fluent, John, as 'Craig Durrand' could communicate well enough with the average worker to begin to make friends. There were not many westerners in China, and a westerner who spoke Mandarin was a great curiosity among the tradesmen in the immediate vicinity of his apartment.

He rode a bicycle to the *Globe* office each day, and soon noticed that two men would follow him on bicycles at a respectful distance everywhere he went. He became used to them, and would occasionally try tricks to shake them from his tail. It did not bother John that the government was trying to keep tabs on his movements, because his real mission was completely different.

⊕

In the fall of 1974, on special coded notice from the home office, John was ordered to join a group of Canadian industrialists and scientists visiting Beijing University, where China's best students were studying. The CIA had learned that a distinguished Soviet scientist, teaching at the University, wanted to defect to the West. The professor had recently been part of a joint Soviet-Chinese team building a new fusion energy accelerator near Lanzhou in Gansu province. He formerly led research at Soviet sites and the Lop Nor desert atomic testing facility. Although energy for peaceful use was of benefit to the whole world, the underlying science for military applications was so intertwined that it was important for NATO to know what the Chinese and Russians were up to. Arrangements for the scientist's escape were conditioned on his providing some substantial intelligence useful to the Western Allies. In spite of current international treaties governing the sharing of fusion energy research, the information he could provide was seen to be extraordinarily important.

As the day approached, Ellsworth made arrangements with Party officials to have 'Craig' accompany the international group. The visit of the industrialists was well publicized, but Ellsworth himself was scheduled for an important government briefing on agriculture. He had no idea of 'Craig's' secret assignment.

As soon as John left his apartment that day, he felt jumpy—his nerves on razor edge. He walked up the steps to the large building following the group of delegates. The physics laboratory was located on the main campus in a large ornate brick structure built in the 1920s. Its principal feature was a long, wide lecture hall with a high ceiling, clerestory windows, and lab tables for two hundred students. It was surrounded on all sides by smaller private offices.

A major ceremony marked the delegates' arrival at the University. This was the first such international group to visit China in more than eight years. The president of the University and Party officials stood on a podium surrounded by flags, and were given flattering attention from the Chinese press. John counted over thirty TV camera crews and many other local newspaper photographers present.

The leader of the delegation was from Belgium, and the scientific contingent was well-represented by France, Italy, Japan and India, as well as Canadians interested in wheat and paper production. Noticeably absent were any British or Americans. John's instructions were to be alert as they passed through the laboratories. The guided tour would be carefully watched by security personnel and any unusual behaviour noted.

The members of the delegation all seemed to be looking forward to the day's events in a detached way, as if it was some sort of holiday. As the visitors entered the main hall from outdoors, it took John's eyes several minutes to become accustomed to the vast interior. How was he supposed to meet his contact?

At the far end of the empty building, a bearded man with a lab coat and full, dark whiskers crossed the immense lab space several times. He was examining student experiments left on the tables. The crowd of delegates clustered together near the entrance. The tour guide, in high-pitched, broken English, was listing the various departments that used the building.

John was not interested in the guide, but kept a sharp eye on the bearded professor. The man was not western, but not Asian, either. Twice the professor looked toward the crowd, before returning to what John presumed to be his office. It was only a few yards from a water cooler.

As the delegates moved on, John lagged behind the main crowd to refresh himself. The professor came out of his office—his eyes resting on John for a second—then turned on his heels and walked to the exit at the far end of the empty hall. The door slammed shut and the professor was gone.

John felt sweat under his armpits trickle down his ribs. Now was his moment. He had to find out if this man was his target.

Glancing back in the direction the delegates had gone, the coast seemed clear. He stepped inside the professor's office.

A desk took up much of the small room, so he started there. Several letters from 'Moskva' in the Cyrillic alphabet lay on the surface addressed to a Dr. Sergei Spolchelnik. He was in the right place.

The material he was searching for had to be small, but the office space was cluttered. John pushed letters and papers aside—nothing. Outside the office, the halting English lecture of the Chinese woman continued. He looked in the shelves hanging from the wall over the desk. There were Russian and Chinese textbooks, papers in folders, and notebooks. But that was all too bulky to be what he was looking for, and time was running out.

In a wide drawer below the desktop, stuffed with more clutter, John found a small envelope labelled 'Lanzhou'. It had camera negatives inside. When held to the light, it was obvious they were photos of hand-written lab notes. All that John could make out of them were lengthy formulas with footnotes in Russian. But he knew enough about physics to know that he held something important.

Some nineteen individual frames or pages were included on four strips of negative. He quickly inserted these inside his coat pocket, returned the empty envelope, and closed the drawer. Again, he searched the top of the desk and shelves above. There was nothing out-of-order, and no clues to anything else that might have been purposely left. It was time to go.

At the far end of the main lab room, the echo of a male voice rose above the rest. It seemed like the delegates were leaving—he had not a moment to lose.

John stepped carefully to the door and saw the crowd of visitors beginning to thin at the front exit. Among them, he spotted two guards next to the spokesperson. One of the guards looked toward the end of the hall, then at his watch, and turned away to check notes. The other looked toward John, but was distracted by a question from a delegate. John slipped out of the room, took a quick pause at the cooler and rejoined the tour. Neither of the guards reacted, and John let out a shaky sigh.

After more speeches in front of the building, the delegates re-boarded the bus for a visit to a state-run chemical factory. 'Craig Durrand' left the tour to return to his office. He was glad there were no pat-down searches of the delegates. The Party must have thought the delegation too important for such indignities.

Yes, despite John's nerves, the scheme had worked out well. He went home that night to his apartment, secure in the belief that no obstacles remained to prevent him from passing the information back to CIA control.

Unfortunately, the truth proved to be otherwise. The following morning, the local papers screamed that one of the offices at the laboratory had been burglarized. Scientific papers were missing, and the incident coincided with the visit of foreign dignitaries.

John was relieved on one account. The paper mentioned 'scientific papers' and not 'photo negatives'. Maybe it was all a red herring put out by Spolchelnik, to cover his trail in case anyone saw John enter the office. The professor had not been in the lab at the time, but could use the guards as witnesses to verify any intrusion. Absent that, the professor could subsequently claim he had found the misplaced original notes elsewhere, apologize for the oversight, and try to smooth the matter over.

There was still one thing, however, that troubled him. He had not worn gloves, and worried that fingerprints might have been left on the drawer pull. John hoped that whoever followed had smudged the print sufficiently to obscure it. Either way, as a member of the tour, he knew he would be watched.

Now it was up to him to protect the information, and figure some way to get it out of the country.

In the meantime, Ellsworth had a tough time casting the Party's accusations in a positive light for the *Globe and Mail*. It was highly embarrassing to the delegation, and some governments had already protested through their official emissaries. Things quieted down after a while, but a week later, John found his apartment completely ransacked; closets and drawers were left open, his personal effects scattered all over. He had made a point of sewing the filmstrips into the lining of his coat and taking it everywhere he went; but obviously, that was still risky.

John got his first break when matters came to a boiling point in the south. As the North Vietnamese closed in on Saigon, the U.S. put their support in a young officer, Colonel Lon Nol, as head of state of Cambodia.

Lon Nol was opposed by the Chinese-backed Khmer Rouge rebel leader Pol Pot, who used the terribly heavy U.S. bombing of the Cambodian eastern borderlands as an effective recruiting measure among the local farmers. John later learned that Pol Pot had managed to raise a rebel army of nearly one hundred thousand volunteers this way. His tactics were ruthless, and terrified the towns and villages approaching the capital.

In spite of U.S. backing, Col. Lon Nol was fighting a losing campaign, and there were signs that Phnom Penh would soon be overrun. The deposed Cambodian Prince, Norodom Sihanouk, had earlier sought protection in China from Lon Nol and Pol Pot, and now wanted to return to Phnom Penh to participate in negotiations for a cease-fire. Could 'Craig' be a representative for the press corps on the plane? That would get him out of China, and from there he could easily leave Phnom Penh in a hurry, claiming danger to himself. He broached the idea of his inclusion in the press corps to Ellsworth, who was skeptical.

"You'd be headed for a hot spot Craig—you know that, don't you?"

They stood informally in Ellsworth's office. John turned from the window to face his boss directly. "I do, sir, but in March '75, my assignment to this position in Beijing will be up. I'd like to see some real action before I go home. I'm sure there will be a window of opportunity to get away from Phnom Penh. The Chinese won't let Sihanouk hang out to dry. He's got too much history on his side."

"All right, I'll do what I can to get you on the plane, if there is any room, but don't say I didn't warn you."

In the end, 'Craig' was not able to get on the plane with Sihanouk, because Sihanouk didn't go. Pol Pot had proven he was strong enough to succeed against the others, and the Chinese decided that they would back Pol Pot against the Americans and North Vietnamese.

The change meant John had to come up with a new plan, with several stops on the way south. Ellsworth made sure he was given clearance to leave the country, and contacted the French legation in Phnom Penh. It meant John would have to travel part of the way by train, and the rest by air, but being young and adventuresome, he did not hesitate. It was only later that John learned that the Khmer Rouge had stopped a train in a northern province of Cambodia and slaughtered all on board.

A few days before his departure, John went shopping to secure a 'memento' of his stay in China. He found a finely lacquered miniature chest-of-drawers with intricate detail, so unusual in the West, but fairly commonplace in Asia. Its rich, dark, cherry finish would make a nice present for his mother. It had one more feature that made it attractive: each drawer came lined with a thin silken fabric. It would be a perfect place to conceal the precious photo negatives. In his apartment, John carefully peeled back the lining to hide the negatives, and then re-glued them to match the original. He would remove them later, once he got out of China.

On the day of his departure, 'Craig' took a taxi to the train station. En route, he was surprised to see a small red car following at a distance. At the gate, the same two men who had been assigned to shadow him for the last six months went to the ticket counter. John hadn't seen them in days and thought he was well rid of them.

The two men sat in the back seat of the railway coach, pretending not to notice John. He shifted uneasily. Apparently, Spolchelnik was sticking to his original story, and the authorities were following every lead in the loss of the 'scientific papers'. If so, his safety might no longer be protected by treaty outside of China.

The rail trip southward wound through endless rice paddies, villages, and cities until they reached the terminal at Wuhan. At the crowded station, John changed trains and turned west, following the Yangtze into the highlands of Chongqing, where he would meet his plane.

Although Chongqing was in hilly country, the climate was much warmer than Beijing. John saw it as a warning that they were moving into the tropics. Taking a quick taxi from the station to the airport at dawn, he saw his plane sitting on the airfield, ready for departure. He bought rice cakes from a vendor, presented his tickets and identity papers at the gate, and was briskly searched. The thin border patrol saw no need to take a closer look at his tourist purchases, however, and the photo negatives went undiscovered.

Relieved, John found a cramped seat among passengers on the Russian-made turbo-prop that would carry him to Rangoon, Burma. There were no direct flights into Cambodia from China.

Strangely, all signs of his shadowy companions were absent since leaving the train at Wuhan.

The noisy turbo-prop droned ever higher over mountainous peaks in Yunnan Province until crossing the upper Mekong and the border into Burma. Flying low over jungle highlands, they finally reached Rangoon in the early afternoon.

The plane had barely touched the ground when the wall of suffocating heat hit John. He spent exhaustive hours awaiting his second flight into Phnom Penh in a smoke-filled lobby. Rumours that the perimeter of Phnom Penh's only airport was being threatened by Khmer Rouge were widespread. As the threat increased, the cost of tickets rose. Whereas his flight into Phnom Penh was almost empty, flights leaving the Cambodian capital were over-booked, and passengers fought for seats. It was turning ugly.

On landing in Phnom Penh, 'Craig Durrand' went directly from the airport to the French legation. He had not seen anything more of his shadows, but he wasn't going to be fooled twice. He wanted to carry out his role as a *Globe* reporter to completion. He had his Canadian passport, visa, and press credentials at the ready.

Refugees crowded the main road to the city, many on foot and others with small carts. His driver negotiated the road with fierce determination, almost knocking a few of them down.

"Must make big money now," he shouted. "Bad people coming!"

John asked what the driver would do.

"I go to farming—my sister, she has house—I hide from them!"

The legation was almost under siege by French nationals waiting to leave the country and trying to get their affairs in order. At the legation, John talked with a French engineer, who was standing in line with all the rest.

"Yes, m'sieur, the armistice negotiations are supposed to be held at the small hotel near the airport. Troops loyal to Lon Nol and the Americans are holding the perimeter. To bring the negotiators all the way into the city is much too dangerous!"

John asked where he might find accommodations.

"There is a hotel where journalists like you stay, just east of here at the circle on the north end of Norodom Boulevard—it's almost empty now."

John decided he had all the information he needed, and departed on foot, carrying two small bags. The hotel was small by western standards, but met his requirements. He spent the evening removing the negatives from the tiny gift chest and sewing them once more inside his coat lining.

The next day, he inquired at the Cambodian government offices for a pass to cover the truce negotiations for the *Globe and Mail*. The office's skeleton staff, pre-occupied with private discussions, exchanged worried looks. Finally, a thin man in uniform and dark glasses came from an inner office. "Unfortunately sir, the Capital is under martial law, and only Colonel Lon Nol has the power to issue such a permit. You may go to the place where officials are meeting, but you will have to talk with the officers at the gate."

John hired a taxi, setting out at once for the conference centre hotel. Refugees and their belongings filled the road. There were not just one, but three check points.

He got past the first two, but stalled at the third. Barbed wire and military vehicles prevented access to the centre's grounds. When John showed his credentials, the officer was polite. "I'm sorry sir. Negotiations have entered a critical phase, and members are in closed-door session. You cannot pass."

A few sombre journalists, one American and two Australian, stood by the gate. "It doesn't look good, mate. Pol Pot is giving Lon Nol forty-eight hours to quit the city. Then he is going to initiate a full attack. The Soviets and the Americans are outraged, but China is standing firm behind Pol Pot. It looks like the end."

The situation had deteriorated faster than he had expected. John knew he should wait no longer to leave, and went straight to the airport to arrange for a flight to Kuala Lumpur. When he arrived, the line stretched out of the building. His heart sank. It was practically useless to try to get out by air now. He would have to return to the city.

Back once more on Norodom Boulevard, he was surprised to see a black sedan with the two Chinese agents in the circle across the street from his hotel. They were trying to look inconspicuous—but not trying very hard.

This was not good. Instead of going up to his hotel room, he went directly to the French Embassy. Considering his serious intelligence matter, he hoped to speak to someone in authority.

The Embassy lobby was full, and included small children. The desk clerk answered, "I'm sorry, sir, everyone is busy, but I'll see."

After a long delay, one of the legation's mid-level officers came to the front desk. "I think you should talk with Major Louis Xenon, our military liaison officer. He will know what to do. He just left to check forces on the Eastern perimeter. He's still in the parking lot, if you go out that door." He pointed to the end of the hall.

John reacted swiftly, exiting the building just in time to see the Major stopped at the street, trying to turn into traffic. He sprinted across the lot and put his hand on the canvas top of the small military Citroën. "Major! It is very important that I speak to you!"

"Entrez, s'il vous plaît! I have to keep going, but you are welcome to ride with me."

John opened the door and sat down, quite out of breath. "Thank you, sir. I'm glad I caught you. I'm in a difficult situation—this involves your allies, Canada, the U.S., and NATO." He showed the Major his press card, and briefly outlined the story of the Soviet defector and the two Chinese agents shadowing him.

The Frenchman shook his head, not taking his eyes away from the crowded street. "Pardonnez-moi, M'sieur, mais naturellement, you must realize we have an understanding with the Canadian government. Wherever we have legations and they do not, we represent and defend the interests of Canadian nationals like yourself! Of course we will help you, particularly if, as you say, it involves the Soviet defector. How would you like us to assist?"

John had been thinking hard. "I have four strips of photographic negatives, nineteen exposures in all. They are from the would-be-defector as proof of his sincerity and potential value to the Western allies. I am the agent who actually picked up the film, but somehow the transfer was leaked to the Chinese Press and caused an uproar. Now the Chinese government has shortened the list of suspects and some agents have followed me from Beijing to Phnom Penh. They may believe I no longer have the immunity allowed the Canadian press corps."

"I agree, M'sieur Durrand. You are in a dangerous spot. What do you propose to do?"

"I, in turn, have a question for you, Major. How does the French Ambassador react to the impending take-over of the rebel forces? Are you going to stay or will you evacuate?"

"I am afraid, M'sieur Durrand, that Pol Pot does not control his troops well. In fact, many towns have been looted and burned with great loss of civilian life. I suspect it will be the same here. We have been ordered to stay as long as we have French nationals requesting assistance, but the list is drawing down. We may not be here more than a few days—a week at most. We have heavy-lift helicopters in Bangkok, Thailand, on a standby basis waiting for orders to pick us up. We will take anyone who can prove their French citizenship, but some dependents may have to be left behind—we only have limited capacity—it is very sad."

They were approaching a bridge across the Tonle Sap River. Next to and slightly ahead of them, a bus full of soldiers headed toward the front. In the opposite lane, a stream of refugees clogged passage for the vehicles heading into the city.

"Major," John began, "I have a request . . ."

An orange plume engulfed the bus ahead of them. A tremendous concussion followed.

John felt searing heat as the windshield shattered. A secondary explosion lifted the Citroën into the air—John's world spinning madly—as they crashed into the river.

The vehicle lay on its side, in about four feet of water. The canvas top was in shreds, and John was pinned under the weight of the Major. He was able to extract himself from underneath, but the Citroën was settling fast, and the Major was non-responsive. John was barely able to keep both their heads above water. Fortunately, they were only a hundred feet from land. With intense effort, and clutching slimy reeds at every step, John half swam and half pulled himself and the Major to the muddy bank. John lay exhausted for some minutes before he could attend to the Major. The officer's face was bleeding, and his shirt ripped at his left shoulder, but his eyes were open now and he slowly moved his head from one side to another. "Mon Dieu! What happened?"

"The bus—the bus exploded in front of us!"

On the bridge above, the sound of sirens announced the arrival of medical personnel to take care of the wounded. Civilians had rushed to the bridge to try to help and inspect the carnage. One of the multiple arches of the bridge span had been weakened by the blast and had fallen in a great splash, with the Citroën, into the water below. Bodies floated in the river.

"How do you feel?"

"I don't feel too bad." The major gingerly lifted his left arm and inspected the flesh wound. "I'll survive, but my ears are still ringing! 'Sonnez les matines', eh?"

John laughed. They were both totally caked in mud, and it was a while before the Major felt stable enough to get up and walk. When he did so, it was with a noticeable limp.

"Does your leg hurt?"

"Oh no, mon ami! I got that one at Diên Biên Phu! This is a tough region to build a career in!"

John chuckled again. The two made their way back to the road that ran along the bank of the river. The sun was beating down. They were quite a sight: two westerners, one with a bloody face and shirt, limping past the bridge. Only a few among the many onlookers took note of them. The legation was less than a mile away.

The colourful shops and stalls on the riverbank still displayed their wares, but in spite of crowds, few were buying. Some of the shop owners had worried looks and others were boarding up the front openings, usually covered by a curtain or a screen. Small craft filled the river, busy with the desperate commerce that precedes an invasion. A number were assisting in rescuing survivors of the explosion. John assumed none in the bus were still alive.

Major Xenon waved toward the shops. "In two days all this will go. They'll be lucky if they have anything left when the rebels take over."

John shook his head. He was thinking how he himself would manage to escape the capital. "Major? If you had to go overland to the U.S. base in Thailand, how would you do it?"

"I would be very careful. It's a little under three hundred kilometres to the border, but you'll do a lot of back and forth between the villages because of the rivers. The advantage you'll have, if you leave soon, is that the rebels are focussing their forces to take and control the capital, and they'll meet a lot of resistance. Once you get about twenty kilometres away, the rebel's hand will be lighter—although the main roads west will still be guarded."

John frowned, uncertain how he was going to manage all of that in unfamiliar territory.

As if reading his expression, the Major continued, "If you'll pardon me, I have a suggestion for you. I know a man who does odd jobs for us—not official, mind you, and always very expensive—but he will know how to get you to Thailand on back roads. He'll have an armed escort, because he always does, no matter what army is in charge. I think he wants to become a warlord himself."

John nodded. The more he thought about it, the less likely it seemed that he would get through the ordeal unscathed. And still he had to make sure the negatives got out of Cambodia and safely beyond the control of the Chinese.

"Come!" The Major interrupted his thoughts. "I know a little place here where we can sit down and collect ourselves. Incidentally, thank you very much for saving my life back there. I would hate a watery grave."

John smiled. "Thanks for offering—I would like a drink very much!"

Leaving the river and shops, they walked past some of the larger residences for government employees. These, too, would soon be ransacked.

They entered a tiny café immediately next to a walled garden. Even though they were a hideous sight, the manager recognized the Major and welcomed them warmly.

"Please come in, Messieurs. Were you near the bus on the bridge?"

"Yes," said the Major. "The news travels fast! My car was blown into the water. We're lucky to be alive."

The manager was shocked and called his daughter from the back room. "Soo Lin! Get these men some cool drinks, but first get each a nice wet towel so they can clean up a little."

The young girl was shaken by their appearance, but bowed politely, and soon returned with a pitcher of sweet citrus drink, glasses, and towels for each of them: a warm wet one and a dry one.

"Prabang is a good man. He knows what you need before you ask." The Major smiled at the young girl and thanked her. There were no others at the tables.

They sat in the cool darkness for a while, each preoccupied with his own thoughts, staring at the intricate stone floor pattern.

"Tell me, Major, if I give you something that is very valuable, will you carry it to the west and hold it for me? I have a feeling that I haven't seen the last of the Chinese. They may get pretty insistent before they discover I have nothing in my possession."

The Major nodded solemnly. "I would be proud to be of such assistance."

John took a knife from the table and began working on the lining of his jacket. The coat was soaked, but the negatives were undamaged. They had been kept clean by the lining and a cellophane packet. "These are the exposures—I can't tell you exactly what they are for, but our scientists want them badly."

The Major took the filmstrips from the cellophane, held them against the light, and then inserted them, with the cellophane, into a glasses case he carried. "But how will I know where to send these?"

"Give me your military I.D. number. I'll ask for Major Louis Xenon. They'll tell me where you are, and then I'll make arrangements to secure them from you. It's a long shot, I know, but it seems the only way to get the information to the right people!"

"Bien sur, mon ami. Try to contact me as early as you can!"

"Do you think you'll be back in France soon?"

The Major took a sip of his drink, then put the glass down. "A couple of months, perhaps. My tour ends in January. Processing will begin some weeks before that."

"What part of France will you go to?"

"Up North; I like the area around Le Havre. After my parents died, I spent a few years there and found it suited my temperament."

The young girl came back and asked if they wished for more of the citrus drink, but it was time to go. The Major gave her some paper money and she went to the money drawer. "Mm'selle? Please keep the change!"

She smiled and he bowed and then turned to John. "The sad thing is, in weeks, that money will probably be worthless. That's what happened at Diên Biên Phu. When the 'Old' is thrown out, it is replaced by the 'New'."

Refreshed, they made it to the gates of the French mission in ten minutes. When the guard saw the Major, he saluted and waved him on. The Major turned and shook John's hand. "Bonne chance, mon ami! Contact me as soon as you can. I will give instructions and leave the phone number of the man I mentioned in your name at the desk."

"Thank you very much, Major, and good luck to you and your countrymen. May we all meet again, safely!"

John turned back onto the street and in a few blocks was at his hotel. The black sedan was still parked at the opposite corner. One occupant was staring at the front door while the other leaned back in his seat. When John approached, they both sat up, perhaps surprised at his wretched appearance.

John entered the hotel and took the elevator up to his room to take a shower. His luck changed at that point. He never even made it back to the French legation to pick up the warlord's telephone number.

A huge pothole came out of nowhere on the highway and John swerved to avoid it. He had been thinking so deeply about the past, he'd almost forgotten he was driving—he needed to pay attention!

He was just passing Song Mountain in Tully. The Porsche was carrying him further and further north to Syracuse, New York, and Greenstone. In spite of John's wandering thoughts, the car seemed to have a life of its own.

2

He could see that things had changed. John parked by the curb, as the street was empty. 112 South Alba Street was a large framed clapboard residence in a run-down section of Syracuse. Many homes in the area were boarded up and the porch had broken steps flanked by high weeds.

The entry door was ajar, so he stepped cautiously inside. The smell of urine on the floor was unmistakable. Ben's apartment was supposed to be on the second floor, toward the street. Up a creaky flight of stairs, he found the door open. A stained mattress with a tattered blanket, bottles, and newspapers were strewn across the floor.

What was Ben trying to do? The instructions were clear enough, but the condition of this place was awful. John knew Greenstone followed Agency protocol for clandestine meetings, but this was stretching it.

Greenstone had called him, so he did not know what number would reach the old army Captain quickly. What should he be looking for? The newspapers held no clue. There was no closet, unless you could call a small alcove with a filthy sink and toilet a closet. The bottles on the floor were Labatt's Blue Label beer. The only thing that seemed out of place was a capped 16 oz. bottle of Union Spring Water. It was tucked under a flap of the blanket on the bed.

Maybe that was it?

He looked at the label closely. 'Union Spring Water, Union Springs Bottling Co., Union Springs, NY.' He recalled seeing Union Springs on a map of the Finger Lakes, midway up the east shore of Lake Cayuga. It couldn't be much more than a short drive away. He had better keep moving.

The noon sun had warmed the leather seats of the Porsche. Closer to the lake, in the hamlet of Mapleton, he asked for directions.

"The bottling plant? Take Van Liew Road to Spring Street Road. It's on the right, set way back."

He was just about to pull over and ask at a farm house again, when he saw a small sign on the side of the road reading: 'Union Springs Bottling Company'. There was a curving, gravel drive over flat fields leading to some white buildings, partially hidden by pine trees in the distance. If anything, this was a small operation.

He pulled off the road at the entrance. He could use some kind of cover, although Greenstone had not indicated the use of an assumed name. Telling anyone he met that he needed to see Greenstone would have to suffice.

The first of the buildings was a large, white-columned farmhouse, dating from the late 1800s. The driveway formed a circle, and next on the left was a long garage, with eight bays and a dormered apartment above. A few barn-like structures housed equipment, and a low, cement block building in the rear, also painted white, completed the complex. A bulky delivery truck, with the Union Springs Water logo, was standing at the loading dock.

Not sure where to go first, he knocked at the door of the main building. A small, grey-haired woman with a flat expression came to the door.

"Is Mr. Greenstone in?"

"Who may I say is calling?"

"Craig Durrand. I have an appointment."

"One moment please." She turned and went to an inner room where John could hear her speak on the phone. She appeared once more in the doorway. "He will see you now. Please go to the door at this end of the garage. His office is on the second floor." With that, the woman closed the door in his face.

Her reaction was abrupt, but at least he had the satisfaction that he had guessed right on Union Springs.

He walked across the bright gravel driveway toward the garage. The weather had only improved with the day. He noticed the stains and moss on the building's roof, where nearby tall spruces dropped their needles and filled the gutters. He judged the structure to be fifty years old if it was a day. The door was streaked, warped, and not as recently painted as it seemed from a distance. John knocked, and a distant voice from upstairs said, "Come in!"

John entered at the bottom landing, and made his way up a long flight of narrow stairs partly covered by rubber treads. When he reached the top, a man with grey hair rose from his desk and limped toward him, extending his hand.

"Craig Durrand?"

"Yes, sir. And you are Ben Greenstone?"

"That's my name."

"Well, it's been a long time. I was at Fort Sill when you introduced me to some recruiters from the CIA. You may have known me then as Lt. John Thurmond."

"I did? Well, I guess that was a long time ago. What can I do for you, Craig—or should I call you John?"

"John will be fine, sir. I was sent by the U.S. Government to Canada to join one of the Toronto *Globe and Mail's* correspondents in Beijing—"

Greenstone held up his hand. "John, I want to be frank with you. Since you called yesterday, I contacted the Agency, and they were able to fax me a copy of your file. Whatever happened to you when you left Beijing? You seem to have dropped completely out of sight."

John sighed. He had expected this, but it was a long tale. Greenstone gestured to a chair opposite his desk, and seated himself behind it. With the desk, two chairs, and a bank of computer monitors along the far wall, John was amazed at the amount of equipment that was present. There seemed to be every kind of radio, recorder, monitor, and scanner imaginable to fit into the crowded space.

John absently let his gaze skip over them while he settled into the worn leather chair and thought about where to begin.

He started with a brief outline of the year in Beijing, and the events that led him to leave China, his meeting Major Xenon, and the reason he was unable to return to America.

Three horrific weeks after his first meeting with the French liaison officer, John found himself in the steaming jungles of Malaysia. His passport was long gone, along with the rest of his belongings. He wasn't sure how much longer he could survive.

After returning to his hotel in Phnom Penh, he had been surprised in his room by two Soviet agents. Apparently, they were two steps ahead of the Chinese, and while the Russians were persona non grata under the rebel Khmer Rouge, the Soviets had made their way from North Vietnam on intelligence painfully extracted from poor Dr. Spolchelnik.

The Russians did not fool around. John was blindfolded and carried in stifling and insufferable conditions out of Cambodia by private aircraft, first across the Gulf of Siam, then by truck and ox cart down the Malay Peninsula. On reaching an uninhabited coastline, they trekked for miles through fetid swamplands. He was made a beast of burden, forced to carry the large tent and supplies.

When the interrogation finally began, the Russians left him standing hours on end for sleep deprivation. They denied him both food and water. His bare feet and ankles were swollen, and fire ants, leeches, and mosquitoes attacked every area of his exposed skin, causing red blisters and oozing pus. His wrists were raw from chafing ropes that bound them.

To his interrogators, he was expendable. No one knew he was in Malaysia—the Russians could not risk entanglement with the Khmer Rouge. If—when—John died, it would be as an unidentified white male, covered in a trench, overtaken by the jungle environment.

Information from Spolchelnik, however obtained, had pointed to John as the most likely suspect. The Russians were convinced he had taken the secrets, but now his tormentors wanted to know where they were hidden. John's consistent response was, "I have taken nothing. You should look for someone else."

Of the two interrogators, the older, a grey man in his late fifties, had a sadistic desire to burn, beat, and abuse him in every manner possible. The other agent, slightly younger, seemed more polished, occasionally speaking French. He had a curious sort of gallows humour that made John question its origins. Both were given to cruelty, and enjoyed dissecting a live, ground-dwelling jungle fowl in full view, prolonging its agony as long as possible.

After weeks in captivity, John suspected the ordeal was reaching its climax. He had overheard the younger agent mention privately to the older, "We must leave for Saigon a week from now. He won't last much longer—we've tried everything. When he dies of thirst, the jungle can do the rest."

John knew he must act, and soon. He had little strength left, and even that was quickly dwindling.

John memorized every detail of the tent's interior: the exit, where the arms were stored, and where the older slept and the younger dozed.

The following day, in the early morning darkness, he was able to free one hand, then loosen the other. He could barely feel anything; his hands had been burned, bound, and lashed to the centre pole for so long. But, surprising his guards, he pulled the tent pole free from the wet ground and knocked the dozing agent to the floor.

Under the collapsed tent, the two Russians struggled to get out, but John had planned his escape route carefully. While the Russians struggled under the cloth, John methodically clubbed them with the butt-end of one of their rifles. Their resistance finally ceased. The blood-soaked fabric would be a feast for flies.

Though badly weakened by the terrible treatment he had received, John was able to make his way to a fishing village on the coast, and from there to Rupat Island and the small port of Batupanjang. There, he secured a berth on a tramp freighter and worked his way to Java, East Timor, New Guinea and ultimately, New Zealand.

The journey took months. He was far from U.S. influence, and had to make his escape among the poorest citizens in Southeast Asia. The tramp freighter's owners begrudged the very food the seamen ate, let alone any independent idea of self-respect. When John sneaked off the freighter at Wellington, he hid for days, fearing he might be re-captured and dragged back to the vessel by the captain's officers.

As the rusty tramp freighter left the harbour, John finally felt safe enough to approach the Canadian Consulate in Wellington. He needed to arrange for a wire transfer of funds from his family, and renew his Canadian passport. He borrowed money to phone his parents near Sherbrooke, Québec. It was a welcome day when John was able to say, "Hi, Mom. How is everybody in North Hatley?"

Greenstone shifted in his swivel chair. John could tell he wanted to take time to get John's full story; he was no doubt probing to check his background.

"Well, John, what happened next?" Ben asked.

John had heard a clatter on the other end, likely his mother dropping a knife or other kitchen implement. She didn't respond to him directly, but John heard her gasp and then breathlessly call to his father to pick up the other line. "Howard—Howard, it's John!" She gathered herself, and John heard the choked sound of her speaking through her tears. "Where are you, John boy—what have you been doing?"

"I'm in New Zealand, Mom, trying to get passage home." John blinked the blurring from his own eyes. "I need money for a plane ride."

"We hoped you would be evacuated from Saigon, but you were reported missing in action. Oh, John boy, we didn't know what to do . . . are you all right?"

John's parents had received no notice of his real mission. He knew they had suffered for it, but it was better than the knowledge of what had actually transpired.

"I'm fairly okay, Mom, but I'll need a lot of rest."

"Are you injured?"

"Yes, but I'm healing up." That was partially true, at least. But he would carry with him many scars.

His father choked up. "Oh, my boy, take care of yourself—we want to see you so much!"

"Yes, Dad, I will. We can talk a lot more when I get back. Please wire the funds, care of the Embassy, here. They know all about it. I can't wait to see you both—and the rest of the family. I love you!"

"Absolutely, Son." His father was hardly able to get anything else out. John knew they were stunned. The chance of hearing news after a soldier was labelled as MIA was a long shot indeed. Now, John would be coming home at last.

In another week, he was able to fly back across the Pacific to Vancouver and then, with special papers, make his way across Canada to the family farm. John did not bother to check in with CIA control—that would come later, when he was rested, healed, and the trauma had subsided. Now, for the moment, John was just happy to be safely home in North Hatley, among his closest loved ones.

⊕

It was July of 1975 before John finally returned to the family farm. His experience affected him deeply, and it was weeks before he could begin to shake off the trauma of Phnom Penh. He relived the explosion, the rain-soaked nightmare of captivity on the Malay Peninsula, and the torturous ordeal in the equatorial jungle.

After some weeks of convalescence and rest with his parents, he wrote to his CIA contact at headquarters in Langley, Virginia, requesting a meeting for debriefing purposes. It was very unsettling to have his letter returned, unable to be delivered. He then called the main CIA offices in Washington, only to find that the department that handled his mission to Beijing was terminated ten months before, and there was no further information available.

Profoundly frustrated, John fell into a deep depression. He felt puzzled, helpless, and betrayed by the U.S. Government. After some days though, the rhythms of Canadian farm life—time in the fields and anticipation of the fall harvest—began to restore his faith in nature and himself.

One day in mid-August, returning from the fields because his tractor had broken down, John realized he wanted to go back to university and continue his education. He had received good training in the physical sciences, but now the world called for people trained in international law and political activism.

He reviewed law schools where he might be accepted and decided to start by applying to Georgetown University. Making arrangements to visit the campus, and more certain of himself, he tried to reach Sal in Doylestown, Pennsylvania. Her parents were delighted to hear from him, but said she was working in a senator's office in Washington, D.C.

He succeeded in contacting her for the first time in four years. He had no idea the heavy toll his indecisiveness had exacted on her when he joined the Agency. She was hesitant, to say the least, but agreed to meet him at a restaurant for a meal. It was only a start, but John was successful in his application to the law school, and in the following month, took careful steps to heal the breach with Sal. After deep soul-searching, Sal agreed to start over where they left off. John and Sal soon realized they did not want to wait for things to happen. They knew they wanted to share their lives—to face its challenges and joys together, and chose to get married in Doylestown at Christmas time.

Her parents were thrilled, and John's family came down from Sherbrooke and Montréal to celebrate. The couple found an apartment together while John finished law school, and when he passed the Pennsylvania Bar exam, they moved to Buckingham, near New Hope on the Delaware, where they expected their first child. His new firm litigated maritime disputes for major clients.

Yet, with all that had gone right in their lives, there was this annoying pressure of unfinished business. It was more than just the nightmares that plagued him after his experiences in steamy Malaysia. Any reading of the international press indicated dramatic changes in global geopolitics. Threats to developing countries were symptoms of the stresses exerted by NATO and the Warsaw Pact bloc on other nations. Scientific advances in nuclear fusion could become an international powder keg, or release the potential of an enormous energy source for constructive, peaceful purposes.

Over the years, John had approached all manner of contacts at the CIA, the U.S. Departments of State, Defence, and Energy, with no response. The new administration seemed to have different priorities. It appeared his personal involvement with anything to do with fusion research had become 'closed book', at least on an official level.

John tried calling friends he had known in his army days, to no avail. At this point, he was looking for any connection, no matter how minor.

On Saturday, he finally caught a break. It was a warm mid-afternoon in Bucks County. John had just finished the more detailed aspects of the week's work when the phone rang. "Where the hell have you been?" the gruff, familiar voice of an old friend at the other end grumbled. "I called you this morning, and the house was quiet as a tomb."

John noticed, ruefully, there was an indicator blinking on the message machine. He laughed. "Sorry about that. Sal and Carl were out."

"No matter. Last I saw you, you mentioned an Army Captain at Sill involved in intelligence training?"

John perked up. "Yes, I did!"

"Well, I have a buddy who was at Sill years ago, and he mentioned he remembered a Captain Ben Greenstone who was on the training staff. Does that ring any bells?"

"Greenstone. Of course. That's the guy!" John spun around as a wave of recognition hit him; his old Navy friend had finally found something. "Fantastic! How do I make contact with him?"

"I really couldn't say. My buddy left Sill years ago, but there must be some kind of process with the D.O.D. I wouldn't know if he's still active or retired."

"That's wonderful, I have a source. I'll get right on it. Thanks very much for your help; I owe you one."

John put his fist in the air. At last, after all this time, he had something to go on. Greenstone was not his assigned contact, but the only one left who might know something about the mission.

It was extremely important that the information he obtained in Asia should find its way into the hands of trustworthy scientists who could judge its value. In spite of his ongoing frustration with the eight-year delay, he was also all too conscious of the dangers involved. He hadn't given up any information about the negatives to his Russian tormentors, and he certainly wouldn't let his guard down, now that this could be the end of it all.

⊕

Greenstone had to laugh several times during John's long story when he recognized the personal difficulties John had overcome to reach him.

He eyed John carefully, occasionally making notes. When John finished his account, Greenstone said, "Well, I'm glad you finally tried to contact me. I can understand your frustration at the amount of time that has elapsed. Things have changed a lot at the Agency. Because of our new administration, we're still trying to re-start certain projects."

Greenstone's eyes focussed on the computer monitors on the wall behind John's seat. "Excuse me, John; I've got to take a call . . ."

While Greenstone busied himself with his equipment, John got up and walked to the window overlooking the bottling plant. In the end, he was only able to grant the illusion of privacy. John could only hear snatches of it, but he knew Greenstone's current conversation was with someone in Canada.

Greenstone's role seemed to have increased in complexity since he was in S-2 at Ft. Sill all those years before. Was Greenstone still an Army officer? Was he retired, a civilian employee of the Agency? Was he really part of the Agency at all?

"Excuse me for interrupting you." Greenstone entered some data on the keyboard. "That was a man who is coming from Manitoba to meet me this evening. In fact . . ." He turned to study John. Finally, he said, "Tell me, John, can you spend the night? I'd like you to speak with him in person."

John's face creased in a slight frown. "And he is?"

"Someone who will be working with us and the information you have brought over from Asia."

John almost hesitated—but they had not really come to grips with any of the issues. At least, not the two of them alone. It was now or never. "Okay sir," he said.

"Please. Those days are behind me. It's Ben."

"All right, Ben." John paused. "What about . . ." He waved toward the white farmhouse.

"Oh, the Oberchevskys? They run the bottling plant. Oberchevsky comes from Eastern Europe. He was a key operative in the unsuccessful resistance to recent tightening of Soviet control in Latvia. We extracted him at the last minute, and the CIA gave him this position and a yearly stipend, which also helps provide cover for my mission. They are a fairly reserved couple, preferring to keep to themselves. They have been through a lot, but they are trustworthy."

"I did notice that Mrs. Oberchevsky didn't say much."

Ben stared out the window toward the plant. "Now that you mention it, however, I think it would be a good idea if you took a tour of our facility. There are only a few employees, but they may be prone to gossip about any strangers that come to visit. I'll give you a spiel on water quality testing that should allay their suspicions. The employees think I'm the sales manager."

"Then I'll be your potential customer."

"Good man."

Ben rose from his swivel chair and ran through some procedures at his desk, switching on a tape at one of the consoles.

"I have to put the station on auto-pilot for the night." He made a soft noise that John took for a chuckle. "There is a lot that goes on here that does not meet the naked eye."

John nodded, eyeing all the dials, tapes, and little black boxes. Everything in its place.

"Ben, why do you maintain such a shambles at Alba Street?"

This time, John was sure the low noise was Ben's laugh. "You liked that one, did you? Every so often, I have to leave the plant for days or a week at a time, to attend to 'business'. I do not want people following me; so, if they think I'm a recovering alcoholic, falling off the wagon, they may be disgusted, but they will give it no more thought. I put in an appearance now and then at Alba Street, to make it look like an all-night bender, but otherwise, I don't have to account for my whereabouts."

John gave Ben a grim smile. Another misdirection. It seemed plausible, even if a little distasteful.

Ben turned back to his consoles and switched on another tape. Finally he was ready.

John turned to follow, but paused in the office doorway. Tucked between a short-wave radio and the fax machine was an old, black and white photograph in a worn frame. It depicted a young boy beside his dog in the woods, proudly bearing a small rifle.

Ben noticed what had caught John's attention. "That's my brother, Sam. He was killed in the retreat from the Yalu River in the early part of the Korean War. I took that photo." Ben paused over the computer dials. John couldn't see his face. "It was our first coon-hunting trip together. He always was a poor shot. . ."

Ben's voice trailed off, and John decided not to comment. He didn't want to push. At least that part of Ben Greenstone's life seemed real.

Ben cleared his throat abruptly. "Shall we? This should only take a few minutes."

The plant lay-out confirmed in John's mind that it was a small, but well-run, operation. They said their good-byes to the supervisor, and stepped outside onto the drive again. Here, a high enclosure abutted the rear of the farmhouse. Two large, grey-coated dogs stood at attention behind the heavy, chain-link fence. John did not recognize the breed, but they looked formidable.

"What kind of dogs are those?"

Ben barely gave them a second glance. "A special strain of hunting dog, used by the Soviets to track down escaped prisoners in the labour camps. The Oberchevskys brought them over from Europe."

"They look dangerous."

"That's the idea. After dark, Oberchevsky lets them out to run freely for security."

John shuddered. "What keeps them from running off?"

"They're very well trained. The Oberchevskys have had them since birth."

When they reached the garage again, Ben stopped. "Well, I'll leave you to get settled. I have to head over to Keuka Lake to pick up the doctor from Manitoba I mentioned earlier. I shouldn't be more than a few hours."

It was obvious to John that he should accompany Ben. He needed to learn all he could about Greenstone, and evaluate if he could be trusted with the negatives, and the information they contained. So far, John was not totally convinced, but he had to play along until things became clearer.

"I'd like to come with you."

Ben raised a shaggy eyebrow. "Really?"

"No offence, Ben, but I have no idea who this guy is. I'd like to meet him, first hand, before we start discussing things further." And maybe learn a bit more about Ben in the meantime.

Ben stared at John for a discomforting amount of time before curtly nodding. "Fair enough."

Ben strode through the garage entrance, but instead of going up the stairs to his office, turned to the left and went through a door into the garage itself.

There were eight bays available, although only five were occupied, including John's Porsche. A large black van had silver and gold 'Union Spring Water' lettering stenciled on the side. John assumed it belonged to Mr. and Mrs. Oberchevsky. Next was a rusting Ford Mustang, at least ten years old. The third bay held a dark blue Chevy Corsica, and the fourth, a long grey Mercedes six-passenger sedan.

A tall man stood by the black van and stepped forward as soon as Ben opened the door. Dark, and heavily built, his shoulders were unlike anything John had ever seen. The man gave John a half smile as he shook his hand, and John had the distinct feeling that his hand had just come out of a rock crusher.

"Thanks Bruno, we'll take the grey car."

Bruno nodded, and handed Ben a set of keys from a board behind the workbench.

"Would you be kind enough to tell Mrs. Oberchevsky that we'll be back about nine p.m.? I'd like to have supper for three in the small dining room."

Ben eased himself into the driver's seat of the sedan. John walked to the passenger side and got in. Ben waved goodbye to Bruno, the garage door opened, and the Mercedes moved out onto the crushed white gravel driveway. "You may be interested—Bruno used to be an Italian Mafia informant. He had to be relocated here for his own health."

A slight drizzle had started falling. John stared through the pattern of raindrops on the windshield. The inside of the car was extremely quiet, and he became aware of the extraordinary weight of the vehicle. It seemed heavy enough to be able to take a direct hit from an anti-tank missile. The thick glass in the side doors was tinted a dark grey, and the sun, which was just emerging from behind clouds, looked as though it would disappear again.

Speeding south, the digital read-out from the dashboard reflected a pale green light on Greenstone's pallid face. John's eyes glanced at the speedometer, which, more frequently than not, was registering seventy miles an hour. The scenery along the narrow macadam road swept by, but they slowed for villages and cross roads. Ben seemed to know the countryside and all its shortcuts intimately, and passed through Ithaca and Watkin's Glen without difficulty. It was quarter to seven when they reached the village of Wayne.

Ben drove along the lakeshore a few miles, and then onto a short, bumpy, narrow dirt driveway leading through brush and trees to a clearing by the water's edge. Completely hidden from the highway, they came to a small cove with a stony beach. Weeds and brush touched the door on John's side.

When the car rolled to a stop, Ben said, "I got a message that our guest is flying in by float plane from Portage Lake, Québec. He's had a four-hour flight. I thought he'd be coming direct from Winnipeg. We're a little early, so we may as well stay inside the car."

There was a drawn-out silence as they sat waiting. John looked at his watch several times as he took in the surroundings.

A few miles up the lake, a large promontory loomed out of the dusk, which split the northern end of the lake into two forks. Steep forested lower slopes and high upland farm fields covered the central peninsula the entire twenty miles to the north end of the lake.

The sun had set below the hills on the western side. The water was calm, but a fresh breeze had sprung up, and the ripples darkened the reflection of the sky. Temperatures had dropped considerably since their departure. The clearing sky to the west promised a cold night. High clouds, tinged with dull reds and yellows, rapidly receded toward the darker eastern horizon.

John broke the silence. "What is your friend's background?"

"Dr. Vanderstadt is an atomic physicist from South Africa. He was a fellow at the University of Chicago and has since moved to Winnipeg, where he's the director of INS-Manitoba, a high energy research laboratory."

The name Vanderstadt was vaguely familiar to John, but he couldn't place it. Considering the man's field of specialty, there was the obvious connection between the scientist's visit and John's own conference with Greenstone. This was progress, because it demonstrated that Greenstone was taking him seriously, but he was still puzzled at the Canadian's involvement.

"Is there a connection between the fact that Vanderstadt is a physicist working in Canada, and our project?"

"Yes, there certainly is. Originally, there was a joint agreement between the United States, Canada, and other countries, to share information related to nuclear research. Canada has great resources: mineral, hydrocarbon, atomic, and hydro, and an extensive existing power grid that exports large amounts of energy to the United States. The first nuclear reactors in Canada were built by a consortium of U.S., French, British, and Canadian engineering firms. Because the Canadian industry developed after U.S. growth had peaked, Canadian physicists were actually able to make improvements on U.S. and British models. The Japanese and French came in even later. It was when the Chinese wanted to get into the picture that NATO became concerned and asked for international regulation."

John was aware of the arms race, but had not followed developments in the private sector too closely.

Greenstone stared out the window as he spoke, and his tone took on that of a man giving a lecture he had heard many times before. "When the U.S., followed by the French, succeeded in exploding a hydrogen bomb in the Pacific, many nations, including the Soviet Union and India, entered the contest to develop and exploit fusion energy. We had research labs in New Jersey, Oak Ridge, Tennessee, and California working on this. A certain Soviet physicist, the defector you contacted, offered to share private formulas that the Russians developed on a heavy-ion particle accelerator. We were not sure whether the Russians were ahead or behind us, but for security reasons, it was highly important for us to have this data. That is where you came in."

Greenstone was well informed. Prior to his departure for China, John had spent months studying classified aspects of fusion research. The goal was to gain a near endless supply of kinetic energy, in the form of heat, from streams of neutrons released in the continuous, high-temperature reaction. The pressing challenge was how to contain it. With temperatures many times in excess of the interior of the sun, it required huge magnetic fields to hold the hot plasma in check, and special cooling equipment to envelop the containment vessel, using temperatures close to absolute zero.

John swallowed hard. Ben was just restating facts of which he was only too aware. "If what you say is the case, Ben, then why have my contacts in the government been so confoundedly uninformed about the subject? I have tried to be discrete, and not spill the beans about the China mission, but no one here seems to know anything about anything."

"It is a complicated issue, John. We discovered there was a Soviet mole in the project, who was reporting our research results back to Russia's primary security agency in Novosibirsk The KGB is very closely tied to their military research efforts. The Department of Energy and our agency decided the best plan was to shut the entire project down and reconstitute it under another name, elsewhere. The whole thing is so secret we had to abandon equipment and suppliers and build another laboratory. It cost D.O.E. probably three-quarters of a billion dollars in the process, but there was no alternative."

"I see—but I'm surprised that absolutely no one put out feelers to see if I had uncovered anything in China."

"I can understand your concern, John, but we had to be extremely careful. We did not know if you had been compromised, in any way, overseas. You were completely out of touch for four months. We figured you would attempt to reach us if your mission was successful and you had something to share."

John looked hard at Greenstone to try to read what he was thinking. The Captain's unblinking grey eyes revealed nothing. What did Greenstone think he had been doing all this time? He only

tried to follow normal channels. And now his costly and painful mission had, effectively, been put on a back burner for years.
"Well, I guess we'll just have to keep taking one step at a time," he
said, discouraged.

Ben smiled at John's grumblings. "I think you'll like Vanderstadt.
He's a real scientist. He'll be able to put all this into perspective."

They both looked out over the water again without speaking. John
resolved to be patient. The whole thing seemed so risky—but, at the
moment, he could not see any alternative.

Lights were winking on in dwellings, farms, and highways across
the water. A cross breeze caused the dry weeds and brush to strike
the door panel on his side of the car.

Except for that, all was quiet.

Then John saw it, a slow-moving green and white light. It appeared against the base of the promontory, heading south down
the lake. Not far above the water, it moved in a slow arc until it was
directly head-on with Ben's vehicle. About a quarter mile offshore,
it splashed gently to the surface. John could see the wake and outline of silver wings taxiing toward them.

"He's here," Ben murmured and stepped out of the car.

John followed, and wished he had brought a warmer jacket. The
floatplane was a lot larger than it first appeared. He estimated it
could carry five or six passengers with full baggage. The cowling
of the heavy air-cooled engine caught the last light from the west.
From the red Canadian fuselage and wing markings, it looked like
the workhorse of a bush pilot.

The propeller stopped, and the plane ghosted toward shore. Ben
was on hand to guide the floats onto the stony beach. The hatch
opened, and a tall man, with reddish brown hair and a yellow parka, stepped down the ladder. Waving at Ben without comment, he
tossed him a small anchor attached to a line, and carried another up
the bank at an angle to the first. He nodded to John as he walked by.

Once that was secure, he stepped on the floats to get an overnight bag from the cabin and locked the door.

Ben put his hand on John's shoulder. "John, I'd like you to meet Dr. Roeloff Vanderstadt."

The ride back to Union Springs went quickly. Ben explained about John's 'Craig Durrand' role in Beijing, including the fact that he had returned to civilian life a good many years before. The discussion was animated by Vanderstadt's desire to know all about John's mission to China and subsequent misadventures in Southeast Asia. At Ben's concurrence (expressed with a slight nod and the pursing of his lips when Vanderstadt's line of questioning opened), John expanded on details he had given Ben earlier. This was to the delight and keen interest of the Dutch South African.

They pulled onto the long gravel driveway of the Oberchevsky farm as John concluded his story. Vanderstadt had not spoken for some time, but he turned from the front passenger seat now to face him.

"John, you have no idea how important this information is. Our research may have been following a wrong path for years. It has not been a total failure, but the Russians and the Chinese have avoided some of the difficulties we encountered, and they may be months ahead of us by now. What can we do to expedite access to this information?"

The question prompted another glance toward Greenstone, who again nodded. John replied dryly, "I don't have the negatives. They're in Europe."

The doctor was startled. "You don't have the negatives?"

"I haven't had the resources or the immediate need to bring them to the States. They are a dangerous commodity. I don't want the life of my wife or my son jeopardized unnecessarily by having those materials in my possession."

"Well, by God, man, where are they?" Ben's usual placid demeanour was transformed. He outright glared at John from the driver's seat. Taken aback, John didn't know how to respond. Was he correct in worrying about the lengths to which Ben Greenstone would go to have this information?

Dr. Vanderstadt looked at the concern on his face and began again. "John, we urgently need this data. How can we help you get it?"

John did his best to keep his voice measured. "Fortunately, in the past years, I've been able to stay in touch with Col. Louis Xenon, and we have a code that will signal him to meet me at a rendezvous in roughly a month's time."

"Couldn't we arrange to have a courier pick up the material in Europe?" Vanderstadt's question was in earnest.

"I still have no idea of the amount of scrutiny Xenon has received. He is an experienced retired French intelligence agent. I have no idea if any of the Chinese or Soviets have been able to bring him under observation."

Ben Greenstone's bushy eyebrows joined together in a frown. "In my mind, the French probably have all this information, and have shared it with the Swiss . . . It is likely all over the place. So you are telling us, Thurmond, you had no other choice but to give it to Xenon?"

"Absolutely."

Dr. Vanderstadt stayed on point. "How soon can you safely get the materials here?"

"My best guess is a month—possibly more if anything goes wrong. If we can get him safely to this country, then all responsibility for the information can rest with you and the government and the pressure will be off the Colonel."

"Well, don't worry about expenses. We'll make sure all of those are covered." Vanderstadt stared out the window of the car. "This may be the breakthrough we've long awaited—"

Ben interrupted. "John, did you ever hear what happened to the

Russian defector?" His voice still held a measure of controlled ir-
ritation, biting off words as he spoke them.

"No, I assume the Russians finally got to him. It was Russian
agents who gave me such a rough go of it in Malaysia."

"Hmm. Last I heard, the Chinese pulled Dr. Spolchelnik out of
the University of Beijing and the labs in Gansu, but the Russians
managed to get a hold of him and put him under interrogation at
the maximum security KGB facility in Moscow. He hasn't been
heard of since."

Vanderstadt shook his head sadly. "It's an old story, I'm afraid:
the scientist vs. the state."

Ben stepped stiffly out into the cool evening air. "Bruno will bring
your bag over to the house, Roel; John says he can spend the night
with us."

John nodded. He still needed to get to know a lot more about
Vanderstadt and Greenstone. They walked slowly across the driveway to the main house. Though his stomach had been growling
with hunger during the ride back, now he felt ill thinking of Spolchelnik's fate. He was more certain than ever that he had met Dr.
Vanderstadt before.

It was after one a.m. The weather had cleared and a full moon cast
light over the countryside. Mrs. Oberchevsky's strong coffee seemed
to be effective, because no matter how many times he turned over,
John could not sleep. Finally, he got up, crossed to the window and
stared at the hillside rising behind the bottling plant.

The conversation at the dinner table played over in his mind.
Vanderstadt was transparent, but, though John respected Greenstone, he felt the need to keep up his guard. Why did everything
have to go into computers? Why was there such a need for surveillance? Then there was Greenstone's off-hand mention of perimeter

security. Those dogs could tear you limb from limb. What was Ben Greenstone so eager to conceal?

Perhaps it was the coffee or perhaps it was all the unanswered questions, but John could not resist the urge to find out more. He decided to go outside and see if there was anything that Greenstone hadn't shown him during the tour. It was only the grounds that were guarded, after all. Other than the dogs, John hadn't seen anything else for security.

At the foot of the hill, next to the old springhouse, a worn path led up through the woods. John followed that trail and came to a wide clearing on top of the hill. A steel antenna, over a hundred feet tall, guyed by wires to the ground, stood in the centre of the opening. Fastened to the tower at mid-height, an array of microwave dishes and other specialized receptors were suspended. All of it was surrounded by high, chain-link fencing. In the darkness, the whole appearance of the structure was menacing in the extreme.

Powering the array were transformers and an emergency generator in a small control building at the bottom of the tower. Presumably, an underground cable connected to the local power grid and Greenstone's office. So this was how Greenstone obtained his information. From the size of it all, John assumed that Greenstone could continuously monitor not only all U.S. commercial frequencies in the area, but also governmental agencies in both Canada and the United States. He questioned if such a set-up was legal.

He had only moments to speculate on what he had seen. On the far side of the clearing, cautious movement in the high grass spelled danger. With only seconds before the dogs detected his scent, John ran full speed down the path.

He leaped from rock to rock, ignoring the scrapes of branches and brambles. He fell once, sliding painfully along the steep gradient, cutting his hand and ankle. He needed cover quickly. The lead dog charged after him, its rough, silvery back reflecting in the moonlight.

The looming shadow of the old springhouse held a slim chance. Built into the hillside, the mossy structure had padlocked doors.

John yanked one open, the rusting hasp giving way just in time for two snarling beasts to thud against its weathered planks. Barking loudly, their nails scratching furiously at the rotting wood; they left John inside gasping for breath, trembling all over.

With blood trickling down his ankle, he looked around desperately for something to secure the door. He found nothing.

The space, lit by an arched window above the portal, admitted the moon's dim light. A large, semi-circular stone cistern in the centre of the room emitted the faint smell of sulfur dioxide. The base of the cistern was covered by slimy moss, where water trickled into a trench that led to a hole in the floor. John smiled grimly at the scene's association with his agency.

The dogs' fierce barking fell too heavily on the still night air. He was embarrassed—the whole household must be awake by now.

A sharp voice cursed the animals, and they fell immediately silent. The heavy breathing of a large Latvian farmer could be heard as he pulled at the latch and cracked open the doors.

"I'm in here." John said cautiously, fearing he might be shot.

"Who goes der?"

"John Thurmond . . . Craig Durrand!"

"Mein Gott! You vas almost tot! Neffer, neffer be arount here ven dises hunds bis heraus!"

John stepped over the rotting doorsill. The Latvian was around six and a half feet tall, and three hundred pounds if he was an ounce. His rough mix of German and English was sufficient to convey his anger. A heavy face, scowling above a hastily donned flannel shirt and jeans, moved John to explain, "I'm sorry to disturb you, sir, but I couldn't sleep. I didn't mean to cause such an uproar."

The Latvian brought his angry face close to John's. "You are lucky to be a-life!"

John followed Mr. Oberchevsky back to the house, and up the

rear stairs to his room. Greenstone's garage light went on for a moment, then off again. Oberchevsky went to his apartment without further comment. The dogs returned to their patrol when they entered the house.

In the morning, John felt sheepish coming to the breakfast table, where Greenstone and Vanderstadt were already seated. Though Greenstone had certainly been informed of the excursion, he did not mention it. Vanderstadt was unaware and talking about his laboratory. Mrs. Oberchevsky gave John a sharp look when she brought in the eggs and bacon, but otherwise, he escaped questioning.

John enjoyed the breakfast. He had been able to wash his scraped ankle, cover it with a white cotton sock, and even get a little shut-eye before dawn. The coffee was good, and the conversation turned to fusion research.

The doctor spoke first. "So, you were at Princeton's Forrestal Campus when the Symmetric Tokamak was operational?"

"Yes—as an undergraduate in 1970, we were permitted to audit graduate courses at the P.U. Plasma Physics Laboratory, dealing with plasma instability."

"Have you followed the progress on the TFTR—the Tokamak Fusion Test Reactor?

"Yes, I've been back for reunions a couple of times and visited PPPL to see how things are going."

The doctor shifted in his seat and leaned back. "You know, John, in our field, eight years is a lot of time. Whole new experiments have come and gone, and many nations are involved. Though we have made progress, we're still on the edge of this thing. Plasma instability at high temperatures remains the big problem. Andrei Sakharov, the father of fusion research, has been under house arrest in Gorky since 1980."

"I'm sorry Doctor—where is this going?"

"I want you to know the information from your mission remains highly relevant. Sergei Spolchelnik may have paid with his life, but it is important that we know everything we can about what the Russians and Chinese are doing. Is there anything we can do to get your courier safely to North America?"

"I will contact him from Philadelphia with our code," John said. "We have discussed everything, and he knows what to do."

Greenstone, still a little dubious, said, "How and when will you contact me?"

"First, I need to get the negatives back in my hands. Then I'll leave a message for you with my contact number. We can make arrangements from there."

"And the date?

"I can't be specific now, but it should be sometime between mid-October and early November."

Greenstone tapped his empty plate. "What if your communication gets intercepted?"

John forced himself not to sound offended. "I know protocol. We've previously arranged that any communication that I send him will be protected.

Greenstone nodded curtly. "Good."

Though Greenstone fell silent, Vanderstadt remained courteous. John could tell that he was relieved that at least some progress had resulted from the trip. As a scientist, he was evidently one of the original promoters of contact with the Russian defector.

"That's where I met him," John reflected. "At the *Globe and Mail* reception! He sure was tight-lipped about his involvement back then."

As for Greenstone, John sensed that he was annoyed at the delay, but he also was beginning to understand John's own situation. He was obviously well-informed, on many levels, and went to lengths to protect whatever information he did receive.

From what John gathered, Vanderstadt planned to spend more time with Greenstone before departure. John, however, was eager to get home. "Believe me, I'm as impatient as you are to get this transfer behind us. I know from experience that the Soviets play for keeps, and I don't want any unfortunate mistakes. I'm headed to Philadelphia now, and will forward the message to Xenon immediately."

The two older men stood up, and the doctor shook his hand. "Thanks, John, for your help. A lot rides on this information. Let's keep in touch."

They walked him to the front door, where John had left his overnight bag. "Please thank Mr. and Mrs. Oberchevsky for me, won't you?"

Both Greenstone and the doctor smiled—no doubt, his nocturnal misadventures were not as secret as he had hoped.

John left the building, and walked across the white gravel driveway to Greenstone's office.

Bruno was on hand to open the garage doors. The sun was already bright and the air clear as he stepped into his Porsche. The engine responded enthusiastically, as if in response to his thoughts of home.

As he drove south beyond Binghamton, the relaxed atmosphere and clear air reminded him of his family's farm in North Hatley. His childhood there had been a good one. The LeClerc family were tenants living at the farm. Their only son, Philippe, had practically grown up with John. The LeClercs were a poor family with four children, and when his parents decided that he was to attend private school for more individualized instruction, he knew he would rarely get to see Philippe anymore. It was that last day before he left for the fall semester. John played it over so many times in his head.

Philippe had been the one to open the door, inviting him in excitedly. Their fathers were out working on the farm, pulling in the first harvest of potatoes for the year. Mr. LeClerc had a severe stuttering disability from the trauma of fighting in the Normandy Invasion, but he was a hardy labourer.

John could smell something delicious cooking for supper. There was always potato soup on the stove, with leeks or onions and some amazing miracle ingredient that served to uphold the reputation of French home cooking.

"Bonjour, John! I was just going to take this letter over to your father. It's from my grandparents in France. They want to come over and see the family and Annette. They've never been here before."

Annette was Philippe's younger sister. A delicate girl of fourteen, she had contracted a slow-growing form of lung cancer from her parents' incessant smoking. The cough had been growing perceptibly worse in recent months. Philippe and John often took turns reading popular stories to her as she lay with closed eyes on her bed next to the living room.

John had put the letter, written by Philippe's father, into his coat. Mr. LeClerc had always been better with written words rather than speaking them.

They spent the rest of the day playing cards, and spending time with Annette whenever she was awake. It was nearly six when John finally left, saying goodbye to his friends for the summer. He wouldn't see them again until the winter holidays. When he left, it was far too warm outdoors to wear his coat. He put it on a peg in the coat closet when he reached home.

A month later, John was in school in Hawkesbury, Ontario, when he got a call from his father.

"John, Annette LeClerc has passed away—she went to the hospital last Thursday. There was nothing that could be done."

John was shocked. No close relative or friend of his had ever died. He insisted on coming to the funeral service. "Dad, I've got to be there. The family will be devastated."

At the ceremony, there was a cloud over the whole LeClerc family. The older sisters seemed especially affected. John approached his comrade, putting his arm around Philippe's shoulder. "She was our friend—I am so sorry—Annette was such a beautiful person . . ."

Strangely, Philippe moved away. It was clear he did not want to associate with John.

John called after him, "Mon ami, I found out today, by terrible mistake, I never gave Dad the letter from your father. I discovered it today in the jacket I was wearing. Please forgive me. I'm awfully sorry, Philippe, I really am."

In the letter, M'sieur LeClerc had asked John's father if he could borrow enough money to pay for airfares for his wife's parents to come from France to see Annette. He said they would be willing to pay it off with future wages.

John felt heartsick. He remembered how happy Philippe was earlier when he mentioned his grandparents might be coming to Sherbrooke. Philippe's father had taken Mr. Thurmond's silence for a refusal. Now, the visit had never occurred, and Annette had died without their loving presence. Because of John's irresponsibility, Annette and her family had paid the price.

Philippe couldn't speak. Tears slid down his face during the whole service, but now the grief that filled his expression was more than when he was standing above his sister's coffin. He closed his eyes and shook his head. John was not able to speak with him again.

John's parents spent a lot of time with the older LeClercs that afternoon. John learned much later that they arranged for all the LeClerc family to visit France, but irreparable damage had been done. Reparations for that sort of negligence could not be easily made.

From that point on, Philippe turned away. John had to return to school, a sadder and wiser man, but not the better for it. He was not able to return when Philippe graduated valedictorian from the regional high school that year.

The LeClercs moved away, and the last John had heard, Philippe had graduated from university with a degree in economics, and had started his own electrical business. But it had been too long ago, with so much time having passed. He hadn't tried to contact Philippe. The tenant house still stood empty, a sad monument to an earlier, happier time.

When he awoke from his reverie, he had arrived home in Buckingham, a bit more subdued than when he had started. Sal and Carl of course, were glad to see him. That night, after dinner and a game of Chutes and Ladders with Carl, he typed the USGS coordinates of the 'cabine' and 151083 in a simple message to Louis. He took it to the small Buckingham post office the first thing Wednesday morning.

3

Former French Army Lt. Colonel Louis Xenon was sitting on the front steps of L'Auberge des Trois Normands. The early autumn breezes off the French Channel occasionally blew a fine mist from the breakwater over his rugged face. The sun was warm, and he felt comfortable in his heavy knit sweater from the Jersey Islands. A similar cool wind had been blowing off the Atlantic for several days, as a large, high-pressure system approached the north of France from the west.

He stared at the veins on the back of his tanned hands and rubbed strong fingers over them. He had been in retirement from the French military for six years, and had lived here in Le Havre for three. It was a quiet life. He felt he deserved such; between his training as a military officer, the wounds he received in Diên Biên Phu, three years fighting against rebel factions in France and Algeria, and his subsequent assignment as a station officer for the French legation in Phnom Penh, he had rarely had the chance to relax.

And yet, for some reason, he had begun to feel uneasy and anxious for a change. An active man in his late forties, settling into retirement had been welcome, but he wondered if there would be new developments—if there could be a new phase in his life after this.

The sun sank closer to the horizon, and the intense blue of the ocean swells reflected its light. White caps had been present on the waves all day. Le Havre was a busy port, and large container ships were always either outbound or approaching on the horizon. A light freighter, preceded by a fishing vessel, headed northeast up the coast toward Rotterdam.

A few dry leaves from the plane trees near the breakwater scudded across the street and lodged themselves in tangled ferns on either side of the front steps.

In his pocket, Louis had a letter from America. Though it might contain a message he had long awaited, it could also sharply alter the peaceful existence to which he had become accustomed. He decided he would delay opening the letter until suppertime.

As shadows lengthened, the cool breeze became uncomfortable, and he stood up stiffly. He still experienced pain where a bullet had destroyed the cartilage in his left knee, although the flesh wound along his ribs had healed nicely.

He walked up the wooden stair on the outside of the building to his second floor apartment. Most of the boarders took their evening meal downstairs with the owner of the inn, but Louis was a private man, and preferred to take advantage of his somewhat obscure veteran status to eat alone.

Xenon had been at the market earlier in the day, and purchased a fine blue-fish at a stall. He retrieved the fillets from the cooler and laid them out on newspaper. His eyes were blurred from the wind, and his fingers ached, but he soon had a gas flame and butter melting on the stove. He sautéed a savoury sauce, laid the fillets in the liquid, and covered the pan with a tight-fitting lid to poach the fish.

While his dinner cooked, he went to a large armchair and sat down at his desk. He searched in the drawer for a letter opener. It lay neatly next to the 38-calibre pearl-handled revolver kept from his days in the military.

The letter contained no return address, but he recognized the small, disciplined, handwriting of his Canadian friend. It stirred memories, long dormant, of sun-drenched heat on the dusty streets of Phnom Penh. It was before the collapse of Lon Nol's U.S.-aligned puppet government, and the surrounding Khmer Rouge rebel forces were tightening their grip. He could remember a white-faced young man from the Toronto *Globe and Mail*, who rode with him in his Citroën leaving the city. Then, there was the explosion on the Tonle Sap river bridge, as they followed government soldiers crossing in a bus to meet the rebel threat. He had been knocked unconscious, but came to on the river's edge, having been rescued by his young passenger. The bridge's collapse effectively cut off an escape route for worried refugees leaving the city.

The young Canadian, Craig Durrand, burned with the intensity of a man twice his age. In a few short minutes, he convinced Louis of the importance of his mission, and made arrangements for Louis to take the negatives to France.

After some delay, Craig finally contacted him. He claimed that he could not take the negatives back at that time, waiting instead to hear from his superiors first. They had maintained correspondence, off and on, for a number of years. However, the Frenchman had not heard from Craig for a long time now, and wondered what had happened.

When the fish was ready, Louis set the lid aside and laid the steaming fillets on a plate. He carried them back to his desk, and put the plate on top of a book while he opened the letter.

There was no heading, but a series of numbers followed a date and the word 'cabine' in parentheses.

This was the signal. He knew what was required.

He had long since acquired geodetic survey maps of the Eastern Provinces of Canada and New England. He knew it would be up to him to make all the necessary arrangements to be at the proper site on the date of the rendezvous. The word 'cabine' was puzzling, but he figured its meaning would become clearer in due course.

The hot, thick liquid surrounding the fish had cooled only slightly, but the rich, delicious aroma was mouth-watering. He tasted a portion and decided it needed a little salt from the cupboard. Soon the fish had defused its satisfying warmth and savour into his circulation system and his chilled shoulders began to feel normal again.

Settling back in his chair, he reached for his map case and pulled out a heavy roll of thumb-worn maps from around the world. He had a rough idea of the North American continent, but was surprised to see that the latitude and longitude indicated in the letter fell near the summit of a mountain peak in the White Mountains of New Hampshire. He had thought he would be meeting Craig at a location somewhere in Canada.

He allowed his head to rest against the back of the chair and closed his eyes. He had a month to complete the arrangements and get ready to depart. The letter indicated October 15th, but the actual rendezvous would be two weeks later, per plan. They would avoid cities. His training warned him that nothing should be taken for granted. At the outset, he would have to create an excuse for the trip, then make arrangements for travel. Finally, he would have to 'disappear' somewhere along the way so that he could move incognito to the rendezvous.

Each phase required separate planning. By October 29, he needed to be on-site.

In the morning, Louis made an unusual appearance in the dining room downstairs. Most of the workmen had already gone, but some of the regulars were still seated. He poured himself a cup of black coffee and took a croissant, a little white Boursin cheese, and some blueberry preserve to a seat by the corner window. He scanned *Le Journal* for its headlines. He remarked to Mme. Marguerite Du-Bois at the next table, "I see your son has been elected to the borough council."

"Mais oui, M'sieur Xenon! He is quite happy. His wife called me last night!"

"Do you think he will be able to carry forward his agenda?"

"I think he will have a tough time, but he is very persistent, and he has strong support from his constituents."

"I wish him well."

The slightly plump, older woman gestured daintily with her teacup. "And what about you, M'sieur Xenon? What is new with you that brings you down to join us for breakfast?"

"I am planning a vacation, Madame."

"Oh, you are?"

"Yes, to North America. I've always wanted to try sport fishing, and I think I'd better do it soon before I get too old."

One of their fellow boarders, M'sieur Martin Drapeneau, entered the room and took his usual seat next to the pantry door. "Aaah, M'sieur Xenon! What has made you want to join the proletariat again? We have missed you here for some weeks."

"C'est la guerre! In times like these one needs friends." Louis said, attempting a smile.

Mme. DuBois laughed.

M'sieur Drapeneau always had some snide remark for Louis, and it was because of his rather tedious repetitions that Louis preferred to eat alone. Drapeneau was a younger man with a dark sense of humour. Although he was quick-witted and conversant on all the topics of the day, he never seemed to have an actual job, and usually hung around with a rough bunch at the docks and the market place. Whenever Louis approached, Drapeneau would crack some joke under his breath and the ring of his acquaintances would stare at Louis and then explode into laughter.

Louis knew he should not take Drapeneau's pointed barbs lying down. He winked at Mme. DuBois, and she smiled back.

Louis followed up on Martin's remark. "M'sieur Drapeneau, to be honest, I must say that I have missed you too. And it isn't because the economy is going to be improved by hard work!"

With that, as the maid came through the door with fresh coffee, Drapeneau blew a large ring of cigar smoke into the air. "Oh you capitalists are all alike. We can't trust any of you!"

"Sure, sure, M'sieur Drapeneau, and on an Army pension to boot. Where now, in fact, do you get your livelihood, my friend? Do you have some hidden foreign assets?"

Louis had said the words in jest, but he noticed a sudden change in the younger man's face. As Drapeneau stared back at Louis, for a moment it seemed a pugnacious vein of temper had come to the surface, and then it subsided, just as quickly as it had arisen.

"You'll get yours come the Revolution, M'sieur Xenon, you'll get yours!"

Louis shook his head. He did not know where Drapeneau was coming from, but he knew there was a strong distaste. He folded *Le Journal* and laid it on the table. "Goodbye, Mme. DuBois, please give your son my congratulations."

"Oh yes, thank you, M'sieur Xenon. I hope you have a nice trip!"

The next day, Louis went to the travel office at the harbour to order passage. He heard that there would be a cruise liner sailing direct from Le Havre, via Cherbourg and Southampton. It would arrive in Québec on the seventeenth of October. Though he could take a flight directly to Québec from Paris, this was one of the last crossings of the liner, the price was affordable, and the passenger ship's schedule helped to kill time before the rendezvous. Besides, he thought he would enjoy a sea voyage.

He had not been standing in line long, when Drapeneau appeared out of the crowd and sauntered up to him. "So, I understand you are taking a vacation."

"As a matter of fact, yes, Martin. I've wanted to for a long time."

"Where are you planning to go?"

"For some fishing to Québec—the headwaters of the Péribonka— above the Saguenay. Have you heard of it?"

"I can't say I have—I'm not much into fishing."

"You should try it some time."

Louis tried to be friendly, but Martin stared at the ground, toying with a gum wrapper next to his foot. "When are you planning to leave?"

"There's a cruise liner from Le Havre to Québec City leaving October 11th. It's a seven-day passage."

"Au revoir, mon ami . . . don't get lost!" Martin did not smile. In fact, his response was cold. He gestured vaguely and turned on his heels to vanish into the crowd.

Louis had trouble understanding him. Drapeneau was communicative in a one-on-one situation, but any time he was with others, he played the clown. His questions put Louis on guard, though. The message was out. Louis wondered how, in the next weeks, the drama would unfold.

He returned to his apartment at the auberge. He had no fishing gear of his own. He would count on being outfitted by the expedition company he had chartered, but there were some things he wanted to be sure to take.

He went through his map case, and picked out charts he would need, with a few extra, to throw any inquisitive inspector off the scent. He had a pistol permit and did not expect any problems in Canada. He would take warm clothing, and an evening jacket for the ship passage. He had his passport, cash, and account record from Barclays Bank. There would be some hefty expenditure on this mission. And then, of course, there were the photo negatives.

The raison d'être of the whole adventure.

He had purchased a small waterproof case for them in Phnom Penh. He took it from its special hiding place behind a board at the base of his closet. He placed it in a pocket, separate from his cash, in the money belt. He could afford to lose everything else, but not the negatives; those he might have to defend with his life.

After storing everything, Louis finally went to bed. It was late, but he was restless and stared at the ceiling for a long time. He still had twenty-three days before the ship departed. This voyage . . . could it be the beginning of the change for which he had so long been waiting?

MONDAY OCTOBER 3, 1983

Early snowflakes swirled down like birds alighting on a field against the dark forest backdrop at Lac Tamarack, two hundred forty kilometres southwest of Ungava Bay, in northern Québec. Philippe LeClerc sat alone in his second floor office. All was quiet, except for the ticking of a large, gilded, French Empire clock hanging on the wall.

His morning had been busy.

Suzette, his personal secretary, had gone for lunch in the executive dining room. She left a pile of fresh, typed letters for him to sign and a plant-wide report on requirements for environmental remediation at all their facilities. The federal ministry in Ottawa was pressuring the corporation with new requirements for compliance. He would have to review the report carefully.

For a moment, he held his face in his hands, thinning dark hair betraying the pressure he was under as head of Québec-Fermont-Rapide, the huge nuclear-industrial combine just south of Rivière aux Feuilles.

The corporate CFO stuck his head in the door. He handed Philippe the report on cost projections LeClerc had requested. As he left, Philippe signaled he would like the door closed.

Cité des Mélèzes was at the northern terminus of a string of hydro and nuclear facilities, stretching across the province, exploiting the rich resources of the sub-arctic. A railroad had been built, and almost a thousand employees at the Lac Tamarack nuclear plant lived in relative comfort in the new community that had sprung up. Now, retail enterprises and industry were quickly following. Cree and Inuit were finding new employment where traditional hunting grounds were affected by trends toward warmer temperatures. Preliminary surveys were yielding reports of potential deposits of valuable rare-earth minerals along Québec's border with Labrador. It was a time of change.

The primary markets for hydro and nuclear power were many hundreds of miles to the south and west. LeClerc was negotiating feeder upgrades in Ontario, and of course, there were expanding industrial markets in New York State and New England to be served. The East Coast blackout of the mid-60s had caught both Canada and the U.S. by surprise, and taught the critical importance of linking the power grids of the two nations in mutual support. If resource development along the George River was successful, a whole new market for nuclear energy would open up in the north.

Despite all of this, things were not going well. The possible merger with the transmission line giant, TransOntario, was stalled. Environmentalists were objecting to plans for on-site storage at two new plant locations. Some of QFR's special corporate accounts were being probed, and his wife objected more and more to him spending so much time at Lac Tamarack.

Of it all, it was the business with his wife that really bothered him.

His wife, Bethe, lived in their gracious home in Montréal, where social contacts and the urban lifestyle suited her taste. Philippe commuted by corporate jet from Cité des Mélèzes on weekends, and managed to keep the delicate balance of their marriage alive.

He accomplished this, essentially, by staying out of her way and acceding to her demands for luxurious living. Nannies cared for their two young children, who were soon to be changing schools. It was not a happy marriage, but Philippe and Bethe had reached an understanding of sorts. She lived her life and he lived his. She objected to his being away on business matters so often, but he, in turn, felt trapped by the trivialities of the Montréal social scene, which his wife seemed so much to enjoy.

And then of course, there was the other, darker side to Philippe's life. At the core, it was his long-standing annoyance with federal regulatory agencies in Ottawa. The politics of the Prime Minister and the conservative leanings of Parliament had under-cut Québec's aim for greater autonomy and self-regulation. Philippe sensed a continuing current of anti-French sentiment from western Canada. He long felt that Québec, with its strong Francophone heritage and rich resources, could stand alone economically, and did not need to be subservient to the superior attitude and stubbornness of some of the Anglophone provinces.

His secret association with Parti 17 dated back to his days as a graduate electrical engineering student at L'École Polytechnique à L'Université de Québec in Montréal .

After leaving the farm of his childhood near Sherbrooke, his family moved to Laval, and during the Vietnam protests, he led a cell of student activists pressing for French separatism at Laval University. Through them, he was invited to travel to Cuba, and there came under the influence of Marcel Duburier, who in turn, introduced him to Marxists from Europe.

They intrigued the bright and ambitious engineering student with their goal of active infiltration of the corporate and political power structure of the French province. At a future time, when Separatists were able to assume control of the government, they would be ready.

Philippe's alliance with the party was unknown to his wife, and was one of the many wedges that lay between them. But then, his alliance was something of which she certainly would not approve, and would be anathema to many of his friends and corporate associates.

As he grew in corporate responsibility, his party contacts dwindled to two men, known secretly as Number 2 and Number 3.

Number 2, Jean Claude, was an old school Marxist, who had operated on the fringes of the French Canadian labour movement for years. Though he had a history of violence in his youth, he had worked faithfully for Philippe through QFR for many years now.

Number 3 was a younger man, and not an employee of QFR. He was a labour leader from Lachine, who was able to marshal enthusiastic political support for causes dear to the labour party and the Montréal port.

Philippe's role, as Number 1, was to provide financial life-blood for the cell through a blind account, and to develop his own following among certain trusted employees at QFR.

So far, he had been successful, and was proud of the loyal team surrounding him in the ranks of top management and staff at the plant. They had diverse talents, but he felt he could call on them to make personal sacrifices and trusted them to maintain strict confidentiality on party activities. He privately referred to them as his 'kitchen cabinet' and increasingly found more comfort with them at work than at home.

One fly in the ointment was the anticipated arrival of a newcomer from Europe, who seemed to have an agenda of his own. Number 2, a QFR employee and old associate of Philippe's, was excited by a chance 'to stir the pot', and recommended this European, Martin, to Philippe. Philippe thought the newcomer's ideas more of a distraction than a real contribution to growth, and he was worried about the potential effect on party unity.

Just before it opened, he heard a tap on the door. Suzette, his secretary, had returned from lunch. She entered without any further preamble. "Did you see the report?"

"Yes, but I didn't have a chance to read it. I did leave a letter to TransOntario for you, on the recorder. I'd like it in the mail today."

Suzette nodded, her brown hair swinging. She had worked with him since the early days of Parti 17, and was a former student from Long Island University. She had joined the Vietnam protests in Montréal, and needed a job after leaving school. As Philippe's personal secretary, she had followed his rise from his original small engineering firm to the corporate success of QFR. With the company's expanded and growing requirements, she had come to know just about every aspect of the huge combine's operation.

"All right Philippe, but don't forget that report. They called me again today."

He spun around in his chair to look at the clock. It was one-thirty, and he was hungry. "I don't want to miss lunch. I'll read it when I get back."

Suzette nodded, about to head out. She paused at the door. "Oh, your wife called. She said there was a problem with a letter of credit from the bank."

Philippe sighed and rose stiffly from his chair. There was a limit to how much he felt he could handle.

4

Mark Talyard parked his battered VW next to a swiftly flowing stream near the White Mountain National Forest. Rain had fallen during the long drive from Boston and had soaked the dense woods on either side of the narrow access road. An overcast sky muted the otherwise brilliant display of red maple and yellow beech saplings, all struggling for light among the thick conifers crowding the banks of the rocky stream.

Mark had taken a short break, after Columbus Day, from his studies and part-time campus job at Boston University. Now, the moist, fresh air of earth and forest lifted his spirits. His uncle's offer of time at the cabin was a tempting retreat after the first half of the fall semester.

He took a sandwich from his pack and stared at the pristine water pouring over the rocks below. The rain had stopped, and the forecast was for clearing weather.

Satisfied with his simple fare, he drove the remaining distance to the washed out bridge that marked the trailhead to his Uncle

John's cabin.

The bridge was six miles or so below Jason Head. Carrying a rucksack would not be hard until he got several hundred feet below the saddle, where the trail divided between the upper and lower peaks. A series of rock ledges with scrub balsam on the south flank of the mountain spur was a difficult barrier to overcome.

Beyond that, the woods deepened again, and the cabin was sheltered by a spruce grove about a quarter mile up a ridge, west of a small pond near the trail.

He thought about his uncle. John Thurmond had been a godsend to the Talyard boys when their parents died in a collision the week before Mark graduated from high school. His older brother, Bob, was already attending the University of Massachusetts, and the tragedy affected them deeply. John and Sal Thurmond stepped into the breach, and offered financial assistance to the boys to complete their education.

John was the younger brother of Mark's mother, and as the closest of all the Thurmond siblings to him in age, Uncle John had been a role model for Mark. Sometimes his uncle would expand on his Canadian upbringing, and why he chose to go to university in the United States.

Of his time after that, Mark's uncle said very little. Mark knew that something had happened during his years in military service, but he rarely went into detail. Whatever it was had left him deeply scarred. Mark could understand why his uncle would see the need for a secluded retreat like the cabin. It had been really nice of him to let Mark stay there overnight. It was just what he needed for a short break. He knew he would have to return to the University in time for classes on Thursday. He had only one responsibility—open the cabin door. His uncle planned to have a friend visit the cabin over the following weekend, and the friend didn't have a key.

After a two-hour hike from the trailhead, Mark reached the cabin. It was mid-afternoon. Standing on the porch, he noticed a padlock dangling from the door and the staple pried loose from the doorframe.

Disgusted, Mark nudged the cabin door open with his boot. Thanks to his uncle's military background, the building was habitually kept cleaned and well-stocked with emergency supplies.

Now, it was in complete disarray. Benches were unnecessarily pulled out from the table, the door lock was ruined, and ashes on the hearth were left smoking.

Mark sighed heavily, dropping his backpack with a thunk. "Aww, man . . ." He surveyed the room, taking stock of what was missing, misplaced, or broken.

A small scrap of paper, half charred, lay near the hearth under one of the benches. Mark scooped it up. Blue lettering at the top of the sheet read:

Stillman Electric Company, Inc.
South Converse, NH
High Voltage Capacitors and Specialty Ceramics

There was something else written in ballpoint on the note. It started, 'John, if I ever—', but the rest was burned away. Mark tried to rub out some of the char near the edge, to decipher at least that one word, but only succeeded in crumbling more of the paper. He winced at this, but pocketed what he could.

Reluctantly, he picked up his rucksack once more and re-fastened the cabin door, securing the hasp and staple as best he could. His hiking boots crunched across the porch that led to the forested spruce glen below.

He was not prepared to handle something like this. This was supposed to be a vacation—not spent cleaning up after vandals in the middle of the woods.

But still, the mist-shrouded summit, open vistas, and the bracing air of New Hampshire's 'White Mountains' were like tonic. Located in a high pass among the lesser peaks, the small cabin was far enough away from the main hiking trail so that trespassers were a rarity. Out of respect for his uncle, he felt he ought to try to discover who had broken into the building. The warm ashes were evidence the intruder, or intruders, had been there quite recently. If he hurried, he might catch up to them.

Spruce branches cut his face as he churned back down through the soft earth and needles on the steep slope below the cabin. In spite of the cool mist that enveloped that side of the mountain, he felt energized. He found a set of footprints; it looked like just one person. Or maybe the others were just harder to see. A plume of mica schist tailings all but engulfed his boots as he traversed the base of a low cliff close to the upper pond. Whoever it was, they were heading north; Mark remembered there were several access trails on the map he carried.

As he neared the northern exposure, the mist cleared, and the forested canopy changed from spruce and fir to low aspen, their branches bent away from the wind. Only a few isolated yellow leaves remained.

Once on harder terrain, it was difficult to follow the intruders—he was pretty sure there were more than one, now. Why would anyone come up this far? His uncle's cabin was pretty remote. And what about that scrap of paper? He wished he could have seen more of what it said.

He approached the exposed rock overlook, where thickets of mountain cranberry, stunted aspen, and weathered grasses were rooted in scattered pockets. Wind from the west blew into Mark's face as soon as he was beyond the shelter of the trees.

Approaching the north face, a battered signpost showed three trails. The higher peak, called Jason Head, was well above the timberline and almost one mile to the east.

The path leading to Gulf Road was particularly difficult, going ahead almost straight down. Over precipitous rock, it would be dangerous in all seasons but summer and early fall.

A sign to the west pointed to the village of North Godwin, eight miles away.

It was difficult to guess which way the cabin's 'visitors' had gone.

Below and to the left, where the mist parted, he saw a tiny road winding through grey and brown fields. Most of the hardwoods at upper elevations had already lost their leaves—the result of early frosts. The nearest peaks of any height were briefly visible through low, scudding clouds in a dark band, some fifteen to twenty miles away. Many lower, intermediate ridges and valleys separated him from the Presidential Range.

A constant damp breeze blew as Mark surveyed the prospect. The clouds to the north, at eye level, were almost close enough to touch. Mist from various sources carried rapidly up the slope and continued through the pass on the moist breeze. He sought shelter from the wind behind a large boulder and removed a pair of binoculars from his rucksack.

His glasses swept over the woods and gorges that spread out in folded skirts at the foot of the mountain. A hawk wheeled and turned, hundreds of feet below the pass.

He noticed a small field near the outfall of a ravine far to the left. If his eyes had passed a fraction of an inch on either side, he would have missed it, but his binoculars confirmed a tiny, dark convertible parked in an opening at the edge of the trees. They might have taken the Godwin trail!

There was a slim chance he could reach the parking field before the intruders. At this time, he had no better lead. It was this or let the vandals go. It was a tough choice, but he found he would rather take the risk, and help out his uncle, than not make the effort.

Mark rose quickly and shouldered his pack. He would have to

shelve his ideas for the fall break, but committed himself to the new plan. He would pursue the 'visitors' until he got some answers.

Half an hour later, Mark was running down a russet and yellow leaf-covered passage of tall beeches. After threading its way over grassy outcroppings, the exposed path had inserted itself into a denser evergreen forest along the edge of a deep ravine. He could hear the wild coursing of a brook falling in pools over bare rocks. Mighty trunks of toppled Douglas fir and hemlock spanned the stream. In the quiet of the mature forest, it was hard to miss the passage of hikers. Their boots left telltale tracks in the disturbed needles and dark humus along alternate sides of the trail.

Eventually the path leveled, and Mark did less slipping and sliding in his rapid descent. Checking his map, he saw he only had half a mile left to catch up; otherwise, he would miss his opportunity.

He pressed quickly ahead; it was now or never.

He reached a grove of maples that, at its end, formed a screen before a large opening. It opened up into a field, just in time for Mark to see three figures on the far side getting into a small, forest-green Fiat convertible. Two in the party were men, and one was a young woman in brown corduroy pants and leather boots. The younger man in a dark sweater wore a hat that hid his face from view.

Without further ado, the car reversed, wheels spinning, and maneuvered itself through a gate at the end of the mowed field. Mark ran out and just caught sight of the Québec licence plate as it reached the gate. HYG-365. The Fiat quickly pulled ahead, and disappeared down the gravel road and out of sight.

Mark stood with his mouth open, breathing heavily. Suddenly, he had a greater sense of isolation than he did on the mountaintop. He dropped his backpack as he caught his breath. All that, and nothing but a vague description and a licence plate number to show for it. At least he had something he could report to his uncle—even though he had been unable to stop the strangers.

He stepped onto the field to catch his breath and stumbled through the short grass in the waning light. To make matters worse, he was now far below the cabin. He had not the energy, nor desire, to make a return trip up the steep trail in the dark.

His only other option was the daunting hike of eighteen miles around the base of the mountain to the access road and his car. With some luck, on paved roads, he might be able to hitchhike most of the distance from North Godwin to where his car was parked in Cauley.

And so, he began the long walk to the village. The gravel lane led through lower fields, to a narrow macadam road at the bottom of the valley. The remnants of what was once a stone wall separated the road from the fields. Scarlet Virginia creeper and yellow wild grape vines entwined themselves with young saplings and sumac beside it. The heavy sky muted the otherwise brilliant display. "What a contrast to Boston!" he thought.

Forty-five minutes later, his low-cut boots rang on the pavement outside the village. Ahead and around him, the peaks of what had, from above, seemed like small hills now loomed in blue-grey masses. As twilight shrank to a long low band of light in the west, the mountains darkened. There would be heavy frost before morning.

He had not encountered a single car in the two miles from the gravel road. He passed an occasional farm on the highway, each more ramshackle than the last, but here the village of Godwin was tidier in the traditional, New England sense. A few plain residences with modest outbuildings brought him to the main thoroughfare, where clapboarded homes with porches set well back from the sidewalk gave an aura of one-time prosperity. However, the main street proved to be misleading. The entire commerce of the town consisted of a barn-like structure at a gravel crossroad, and a secondary building in the rear that contained either a farm hardware store or a collision shop. Everything was dark, except for single lights in a few houses where inhabitants had retreated to their kitchens.

Approaching the intersection, Mark saw some pickup trucks across a sidewalk, where light streamed up from a basement doorway. A stocky man in overalls came up the steps and grunted as he passed. Tobacco smoke and a heavy scent of beer emanated from the man. Mark decided he might have more luck with those still inside.

He went down stone steps to the open door and peered into the room. Two bare bulbs cast light on a long, upturned feed box that served as a bar. Three men there turned slightly as he entered, and another thinner man, with a green light-shade over his eyes, pulled a towel from below the bar and wiped his hands.

The feeling in the room was anything but welcome. Mark had difficulty forming words in his mouth. "Is there a telephone around here?"

A quick glance through the space told him the answer was negative. The three men turned back to the bar. The bartender continued to rub his hands on the towel. When the silence became embarrassing, Mark turned to go outside.

"You'll find a gas station one mile west of town on the state road."

Mark, still facing the door, paused. "Thanks."

Outside, the air seemed colder than when he had entered. He shifted the heavy rucksack on his shoulders. Another mile or so would not be too bad, although his right shoulder was getting sore.

Soon, he saw the large green letters of an illuminated Hess sign that marked the station. The intersection was otherwise completely dark. He crossed the pavement near the gas island. A young man stepped out of the office.

"We're closing up!" The man was younger than Mark, and seemed pleasant enough.

"It's kind of early, isn't it?"

"Things always shut down here at six p.m. We don't open up again until nine in the morning."

"Don't you get much business here?"

The attendant smiled at him and shook his head. "Not on this side of the mountain. Most people head south if they want to cross over to Bradford."

"Phew! I'm glad I caught you, then. Do you have a telephone?"

The young man gestured to the office, and Mark followed him inside. He found a handset on the desk. "Do you mind if I make a credit card call?"

"Not at all. I've got a few things to take care of outside. I'll be back in a few minutes."

After Mark reached the operator, he got the call through and waited as the phone at the other end rang and rang. After five rings, his brother's wife answered on a recording.

Quickly, Mark poured out the heart of his concerns. He did not want to go through the rigmarole of the credit card again. All too soon, the beep at the other end sounded, and he had to hang up.

The young man came through the door and switched off the great overhead lights on the illuminated sign and gas island outside. "Can I take you anywhere?"

"I was planning to hitch-hike," Mark said.

"There won't be another car through here until morning."

"Well, I need to go all the way down to Cauley."

"No problem, it's on my way." The young man went over to the cash register and rang up the day's receipts. "I'll only be a few minutes."

"Well, thanks a lot, umm . . ."

"Name's Joe."

"Thanks Joe." Mark perused a rack of road maps and post cards next to the display case. "Say, by any chance, did you see a green Fiat go through here? It would've been about four-thirty this afternoon."

"I sure did. They were my last customers. Why?"

"I think they broke into my uncle's cabin."

"What? No way!"

Mark nodded. "I saw them pulling away from the trailhead. It's kind of a remote area."

"Well ain't that a crummy thing to do." Joe closed the till with a clatter. "Don't think I can tell you much. They'd been arguing about something in French."

Well, that fit with the Québec licence plate number Mark saw. "I didn't get all that good a look at him. The driver was a bigger guy, wearing a dark shirt."

Joe nodded. "Navy blue. And you're right. He looked about six feet, and he had dark hair, I think."

"Well thanks, that does help."

"Only wish I could do better." Joe shrugged, and went outside again to lock up the propane rack. Mark could see his outline in the plate glass window.

He glanced at a newspaper that lay folded on the counter in front of him. The Tuesday Cedar Valley Times. Mark thumbed through the pages as he waited for Joe. On the last page, a photo and article caught his eye:

LOCAL MANUFACTURER SEEKS COMMITMENT FROM CANADIAN UTILITY FOR LARGE CAPACITOR ORDER

Stillman Electric Company executives in South Converse, New Hampshire, met on Monday with the director and other representatives of one of Canada's largest electricity suppliers. Their goal was to negotiate the $13,000,000 purchase of special-purpose capacitors for two new nuclear power plants being constructed by QFR in Northern Québec. Following the meeting, Director Philippe LeClerc of Québec-Fermont-Rapide (QFR) Combine Industrielle, Ltd. said that all but a few of the details had been worked out, and that the South Converse plant might be ready to start production as early as March.

"We hope that Stillman Electric can play a valuable role in QFR Nuclear's George River expansion efforts. We will rely on the high quality of workmanship that this community is known for," LeClerc said.

Mark shuffled around in his pocket until he found the scrap of paper. Sure enough, Stillman Electric.

Joe came back inside, but paused on seeing Mark. "Something up?"

"What's Stillman Electric?"

Joe cocked his head. "Stillman . . . oh, uh, it's one of the few large manufacturing companies around here. Yeah, they have a plant, hereabouts. Why, what's up?"

"Something I read in the paper." Mark gestured to the open page. "It matches the letterhead on a scrap of paper left in my uncle's cabin."

"That's strange!" Joe took a close look at the scrap in Mark's hand, and the page he was open to. "Hey, this guy looks a lot like the one from the Fiat."

"Wait. Are you sure?"

"Well, I can't be sure sure, you know, it is kinda a grainy photo, but . . ." Joe shrugged. "Sure looks like him. I wonder how it could be."

"I agree. Do you mind if I take this?" Mark took a penknife and separated the last page from the rest of the paper. "I'd like to send it to my uncle."

The battered Chevy pickup's open windows poured cool air on Mark's shoulders. It was the first opportunity for him to get off his feet since he spotted the intruders from on top of the mountain. He paid attention to the dark road winding through small hamlets as the valley led southward. As they passed through South Converse, he kept looking for the "Stillman Electric" sign. Eventually, he saw the logo with an arrow pointing out of town to the west. Although he would like to have stopped, he sensed that Joe had commitments, and would not appreciate an extra excursion.

In another fifteen minutes, they entered Cauley, where the small

Merry River joined the main branch of the Cedar. The Merry had its source high in a mountain meadow near the summit of Jason Head. It was the one that Mark had parked his car beside. A mill had once operated on its banks, but it appeared abandoned when Mark had driven past earlier. Now, through the willow trees, Mark could see dark waters of the reservoir behind the high stone dam; as though there was some kind of pent-up evil waiting.

"Joe, would you mind driving me up to the trailhead? It's not far from here."

"No problem! I'm glad to help out." He turned left at the main intersection, and they were soon out of the village.

In seven minutes, they reached Mark's VW.

"Thanks for the ride, Joe. Can I give you anything toward your mileage?"

"Naw, that's all right. I enjoyed talking with you."

"Well, I really appreciate the lift."

"Good luck with the cabin!"

Mark stepped out and the battered Chevy spun in a U-turn and disappeared down the dirt road. Mark stared after the fading tail-lights before walking toward his car.

The silence of the forest took over. A spring flood had undermined one of the abutments of the concrete bridge, and its surface tilted menacingly toward the dark stream that passed under it. It hardly seemed a 'merry' river now.

Drawing closer to the car, he stopped short. All four tires were flat. He walked around the vehicle, trying to think who could have played such a dirty trick. What a disaster. There was no way he could fill the tires until morning. The road was much too steep and rough for him to attempt to drive the car into town. He could not afford to pay for four new tires.

He was in a fix, but there was no alternative—he had to live with it. He unlocked the door to the back seat, threw in his rucksack and put a sweater on beneath his parka. He was trying to think what else he needed, when he noticed a small piece of paper under the windshield wiper. He had barely seen it in the dim reflection of the night sky.

"DO NOT INTERFERE" was scrawled in pencil in bold letters. He could barely read the damp paper in the low light. There was nothing else on the sheet. Interfere with what? The guy who did this must be a wacko.

He thought for a few minutes. Though he had been planning on sleeping in the car until he could go back to town and find a garage, he wasn't sure he was comfortable doing so. Some creep had gone through all the trouble of messing with his car and leaving a vague but threatening note. What else was this guy willing to do? He decided to return to the village. He could wait in a booth at the all-night diner until a service station opened in the morning. If he followed the river to the mill, he could save time.

The moon cast long shadows from alders and willows lining the creek. He waded through thick, wet, waist-high meadow grass. Light patches of sumac silhouetted themselves against the woods and the fragrance of lodged goldenrod filled the meadow.

After what he had found at his car, his imagination was overreacting. More than once, as he moved toward the road, he thought for a moment that someone was following him. He repeatedly looked over his shoulder. His path through the silvery wet weeds back to the tree line was clearly defined. The scene was perfectly still. He shook the feeling off. He was just jumpy.

But he couldn't help asking himself: could the incident at the car have anything to do with the problem at the cabin? Why would someone bother to leave a note on his windshield? For that matter, why would a guy that worked for a large corporation like QFR or Stillman Electric consider breaking into a cabin on top of a mountain? Not to mention get involved in something as petty as car vandalism. The pieces just didn't fit.

He reached the rather soggy inlet to the millpond, and went to the right of a patch of tall reeds that blocked access to a high bank along the road. Looking back once more over his shoulder, he was appalled to see a dark figure hastening across the open meadow. The pursuer was several hundred yards from the distant tree line, and was following Mark's path with quick strides.

The appearance of the figure was so abrupt Mark could feel hair rise on the back of his head. He ducked behind the reeds and looked for cover. He could scramble to the road on top of the bank, but at this time, no one would be on the highway on the outskirts of town. He could not tell if the man had a weapon or not.

There was no good hiding place in the meadow, and the wet grass made following him an easy task. He decided taking the road was the safest bet in the end, and struggled up through the brush to the guardrail. Once at the paving, he sprinted along the edge of the reservoir toward the mill. Thick willow trees hid the placid surface of the water.

When he reached the mill, he looked back and saw the dark stranger beginning the difficult ascent of the bank. If Mark continued down the road, he'd be an open target.

He decided on the mill. A narrow door swayed open several feet from a widened gravel shoulder at a bend in the road. He darted inside to escape from view and catch his breath. Brushing cobwebs from his face, Mark reasoned that if the guy did follow him, at least he would have the element of surprise in the shadows.

In total darkness, he stepped back from the doorframe, groping with his hands and feeling the worn floorboards with his feet. He was searching for something to use as a weapon. Under him, water spilled through the decaying spokes of a giant water wheel that had fallen from its trunnions. Dim light at the door was his only guide.

Heavy boots reverberated on the pavement and then made a squishing sound as they crossed the weedy gravel shoulder to the door opening. A huge, heavily muscled figure, with knitted cap and denim jacket, suddenly appeared in the opening. Breathing heavily, the apparition stared directly at Mark.

Alarmed, forgetting that he was unseen, Mark stepped back onto a rotten board. It gave way with a splintering crash.

He plunged through wide-placed floor joists into empty space. As he turned in the air, his temple struck something sharp, and he fell heavily onto a pile of planks. A warm sticky substance flowed over his hand as he lay on the dusty boards. Dazed and badly bruised, the chill, mossy dampness of the mill's ancient stone foundations closed in around him, and he lost consciousness.

Hours later Mark awoke, lying on his stomach. The light was dim, but enough so that he could see the cold, embossed metal plating beneath him. A sound like a large engine roared in his ears. He was surrounded on all sides by wicker baskets.

He tried to move, but painful bruises and a throbbing forehead discouraged him. Frequent buffeting from side to side accompanied the vibration of the metal floor. A plane, maybe? Where was he being taken?

He vaguely remembered the mill at nighttime. There was the big man, then landing on lumber; the pain, the musty smell of rotting beams and planks. Then all went black.

Turning slightly, he found someone had thrown a blanket over him. For uncomfortable minutes, he struggled to roll onto the blanket's edge to get a little protection from the metal floor. He had been taken from the mill, but his wrists were bound with copper wire. The engine droned on endlessly.

In front, he heard two men conversing in low tones. He could barely understand what the men were saying through thick accents.

"We should arrive in Queboggin in two hours."

The other responded in a deeper voice, "Not soon enough for me."

Mark was puzzled. Frenchmen? And what was Queboggin? Was that where was he being taken? Mark could see daylight in the tight storage area of the plane, but there was no sun. The temperature was markedly chilly. He began to shiver uncontrollably.

"How is our passenger doing?" said the first one, probably the pilot. He spoke louder than the other. The other replied sharply, "I'll worry about him. You worry about getting us to the Queboggin meeting."

"Oui, mon ami; I just wish there was somewhere closer we could take him . . . it looks like we are going to get snow."

The air became rougher as the plane's engines strained against a crosswind. Mark could no longer hear the plane's other passenger in the cockpit. He could tell they had started to fly lower, because his ears popped. As the machine droned on, Mark dozed, awoke for what seemed hours, and then fell asleep again.

Thrown roughly against the baskets, he was awakened abruptly when a sharp impact registered through the metal floor. The plane bounced and rolled over an uneven surface, and finally came to a stop.

"Merci Dieu," muttered the second voice.

There was a period of silent activity as the men readied themselves to leave the plane. Mark had to think quickly about what to do when the men confronted him. What were they going to do with him? He decided his best bet was to feign unconsciousness.

A blast of chilled air entered the cabin as the men dropped to the ground. It was much colder outside than in the plane.

The Frenchmen walked away from the craft, and he could not hear their conversation. Then they returned, to begin unloading the baskets. When they reached Mark, they grabbed him by his legs and pulled him roughly across the floor. The big man cantilevered him over his shoulders in a fireman's carry while the other man took the blanket.

"Il a frappé sa tête mal. I hope he survives!"

"Vraiment—it's not that bad. He'll make it."

Mark opened his eyes a crack. Snowflakes drifted down. They were crossing a field surrounded by low birches. There was a large abandoned production facility to the west.

The pilot fumbled with some keys. "Here," he said. "I may have to get fuel."

The man carrying Mark grunted, and snatched the keys.

Mark was whirled around as the big man turned. He could see the outline of the plane, a small Cessna, standing a hundred yards away in the gloom of the falling snow.

A few more strides, and the man stopped at an old shed. Mark could hear the click and scrape of metal as the keys unlocked some sliding doors. The man placed Mark on the blanket, laid directly inside on the dirt floor. Without further ado, the man padlocked the door and returned to the plane.

Mark sprang to his feet, though his head hurt badly. Through the crack between the doors, he caught glimpses of the men carrying large baskets toward the other building. Darkness was approaching, and they would soon return. It looked like the shed was big enough to be a temporary hanger.

His situation was critical. He tried to unbend the twisted coated copper wire wrapped around his wrists, but could find no protruding nail to help. He looked toward the main building. The two men were heading his way. He slumped back down on to the blanket.

Mark heard crunching footsteps over frozen grass. The padlock was removed and the door slid open without any ceremony. The big man came and uncovered Mark's face. He quickly removed the wire from his wrists.

"What were you thinking? We can't leave him out here. He'll freeze!"

"Just help me." The two men put Mark's arms around each of

their necks and half carried, half dragged him a hundred yards or so through the snow-dusted field.

As they passed around the end of the building, Mark saw a dark Chrysler town car nosed in next to the loading dock. A young woman sat in the rear seat, her face close to the window.

A bare-headed man, likely the driver, stood next to the car, smoking. He appeared completely disinterested in Mark and the two men. Mark kept his head low anyway. But as they passed the girl, her eyes met his. Very attractive, she looked up at him in what seemed almost an appeal. He could not help but wonder why she was there.

He was taken inside the large building, and the blanket spread on the floor of an empty closet. The tiny room was a little warmer than outside, but the men had to use flashlights to find their way. When the door closed, the hall and stair soon filled with new arrivals going to the upper floor. What was this place, with so many people?

"What are we going to do with him?" The pilot's voice sounded worried.

"Claude just got in. I want to hear what he has to say."

"Okay. What about the plane? We have to move it under cover, before the snow gets too deep."

"I'm going to stay here with him. Can you handle it?"

Muffled shouts from upstairs obscured the pilot's response. It seemed a loud argument had just erupted. An exasperated voice sounded clearly, "Mère de Dieu, Claude, what were you thinking? Who the hell do you think is going to be responsible?" A quieter stream of unintelligible words followed this proclamation, which were not answered.

Mark's two captors paused in silence; then the gruff man said, "We'd better go upstairs; Claude may need our help."

Mark heard the pair as they left, following the voices to the second floor. He sprang to his feet in the darkness. They had neglected to retie his hands, or fasten the closet door.

In the hallway, he looked both ways—for what good it did him.

It was pitch black.

He crept through the hall, back the way he had been carried. He found the door, and tried the handle. Not locked.

A dim light at the top of the stair startled him. Muffled voices from the top landing became clearer for a moment, before being shut out again. The two men were returning to the ground floor. Heavy boots jarred the top steps.

Mark slipped outdoors as flashlights probed the bottom landing.

The snow outside was falling heavily. Racing toward the shed, he hoped his trail would be obscured by earlier footprints.

He reached the shed's protection, hiding behind its door, still left ajar. He carefully watched the main building, ready to strike off into the woods if there was any serious pursuit. All was silent. Perhaps they had not yet noticed he was missing. He had only a little time until they did.

He stood next to the shed, wondering what to do. He looked toward the plane in the field, and then toward the dim light that showed from the upper windows of the old production facility.

A light breeze carried biting cold from the northwest, reminding Mark that he couldn't stay out here forever. As it was, he was lucky he had added the extra sweater under his coat.

Still, he hesitated. For some reason there was no pursuit. All planes carried logbooks. If he could get that, maybe it would answer some of the many questions regarding this strange night.

After one last nervous look about the field, he sprinted through the snow cover toward the Cessna. The passenger door was unlocked, and he discovered a bound book and maps in a compartment below the instrument panel. These he inserted in a zippered side pocket of his coat, and ran back toward the shed.

Cautiously circling through the low birches beyond, he saw weathered piles of lumber against the snow at the edge of the woods. The building might have been used for cabinet or pallet manufacture. A dirt road led from the parking area and curved out of sight. The girl and the driver had disappeared inside, but the big car remained.

Mark checked each vehicle, but did not know how to hot-wire an ignition. By good fortune, a vintage motorcycle stood against the steps, the engine still warm. Old 'Indians', like this one, were kick-started. It was worth a shot.

He grabbed the handlebars and ran the bike across the lot and down the snowy road beyond. He might not know where he was, but if cars came up it, the old road must lead to a highway. As the building disappeared behind him, he thought he saw lights shining at the loading dock. They were looking for him already.

The road was pitted, rutted, and curved to the right as it descended the hill. He didn't dare turn on the bike until he was well away from the building. His captors might hear him

He wondered about that as he coasted silently through the twists and turns. Who were all those people? Why were they there? And why had they kidnapped him . . . of all strange things? He thought of the girl in the car. She had appeared frightened. He remembered those eyes, pleading silently to him for help. What did a nice girl like her have to do with this clandestine meeting at an abandoned building?

What was going on here?

5

Gelda Vanderstadt sat in the VIA Rail observation car as it snaked its way, with a dozen sleepers, eastward to Montréal. Much of the train's route was across vast stretches of forest. Most of the leaves in the mountains had fallen, and it was only along edges of lakes and rivers that yellow and scarlet offset the uniform light greys and dull browns of forests and agricultural fields. Occasionally, the railway crossed wide valleys, opening up to vistas of the north.

Gelda had been reading notes from a visiting French micro-biology lecturer at McGill University. In the second year of a two-year master's program, she was studying the effects of bacteria on the remediation of toxic waste spills. It was a small program, without government funding, but early experiments showed promise. Her professor had encouraged her to pursue the research, and both positive and negative results were beginning to emerge. She was also a graduate assistant in the University's biology laboratory, and had to translate notes for a test she was giving Wednesday to undergraduates in the department.

Graduates and Undergraduates alike took a fall break to celebrate Thanksgiving, and she had left campus two days early to be with her family in Winnipeg. The time with them had been wonderful. Her younger brother came back from college in California; he had to cut classes because of the earlier national holiday in Canada, but felt it was worth it.

Her father was particularly interested in the news of McGill. He was a physicist, and usually up-to-the-minute on Montréal politics. As director of INS-Manitoba, a high-energy physics lab with many government contracts, half of his work was located in the province of Québec.

It was good to visit with everyone, but finally Gelda had to say goodbye and head to the railway station for the trip back to the University. She arrived in time to board the VIA Rail overnighter to Montréal. Normally, she returned by air, but the twenty-six-hour train trip gave her a change of pace, and a chance to catch up on reading.

While the steward fixed her berth in the sleeper, she took breakfast in the dining car. Fresh-squeezed orange juice, hot oatmeal with real cream, and a poached egg were in marked contrast with her usual meagre off-campus fare.

After breakfast and some time in the observation car, she returned to her roomette to read.

By mid-morning, they had almost crossed Ontario through the beautiful forested mountains of the Algoma district. South of Sudbury, the land opened up, and farmland stretched to the horizon, with isolated barns and small weathered farmhouses dotting the open landscape. It was a tough climate for farmers, but the soil was good and selected crops did well.

The train was scheduled to arrive in Montréal at five after eight that evening. She hoped to have enough time to visit Marie Dionne at the small delicatessen not far from her apartment. They were good friends, and Gelda always enjoyed a chance to chat at the shop after work in the lab.

Arriving in Montréal, she struggled down the platform to the taxi gate with her suitcase. Once the taxi was clear of the worst traffic, they turned off to one of the short, quiet streets that ended in steps at the foot of Mt. Royal Park.

She had been lucky to find an apartment there. A colleague of her father had an eighty-two-year-old mother living in Montréal who needed someone to occupy the top floor of her building. The three-story grey stone house was a formidable sight. However, it had a cozy studio apartment with a tiny kitchen, bedroom, and separate bath; it was all Gelda wanted to make herself at home.

Mrs. Abernathy had a few simple rules: no men, no smoking, and no loud music. Gelda got along well with the elderly lady, and often spent a half hour or so conversing in her parlour.

When she reached the house, she lugged her bags to the third floor and quickly changed into slacks and a heavy sweater to accommodate the chill evening. She left on the run to get to the delicatessen, which closed at nine.

It was two long blocks to Marie's. The shop was narrow, no more than twelve feet wide, and two display windows flanked the front door. Gelda smiled when she saw Marie had put Hallowe'en harvest decorations, mixed with treasures of food specialties from Europe, into the windows over the weekend. Entering, Gelda smelled the aroma of fresh coffee that always brewed in the store.

Marie was wiping a bread knife when Gelda entered. "Hi, Gelda," she said with her native French accent.

"Hi, Marie," Gelda said, out of breath. "I like your window display."

"You do? We worked on it yesterday. How was the time with your family?"

"Oh, wonderful! The weather was perfect. My brother flew home from California."

Marie's brother, Jacques, appeared, carrying a carton up a steep stair from the basement.

"Hello Jacques," Gelda said. Jacques nodded and went into the back room to pick up the phone. Gelda found it hard to get to know Jacques, even though he was usually at the shop; he helped Marie with most of the food preparation. He was shy and a little stand-offish, but Gelda just ascribed it to 'younger brother-itis'. She selected some pasta salad and a thick piece of honey-cured ham for her supper. With a granola bar from the rack, she turned to Marie. "How much do I owe you?"

Gelda took her change. Jacques looked around the corner, his light hair covering one eye, to see if she was still there. Gelda gathered up her groceries. "Oh, I almost forgot—I'm out of milk." She went to a refrigerated case, took out a litre, and gave Marie seventy-five cents.

"Merci bien, Gelda!"

"Bonsoir, Marie! Good-bye, Jacques!"

Outdoors, it was colder. A breeze was coming off the top of Mount Royal. She had paper bags under each arm, and walked briskly toward the park to keep warm. There were streetlights on the hill, but not as many as at Marie's. Her street stopped at the park.

A long, black town car pulled up on her side of the pavement. The driver got out to stand on the sidewalk. It must be nice to afford to hire a chauffeur to go out on the town. But Gelda would need to be finished with her schooling, and the expenses those incurred, before she could even dream of such for herself.

The tall driver smiled at her. She had not gone two steps past before he grabbed both her arms from behind and propelled her quickly to the car's rear door. Her grocery bags fell to the curb and spilled out on the grass. The car door opened from within, and before she could scream, a man inside pulled her into the back seat.

The driver jumped back in the car. As the doors slammed shut, the car made a rapid U-turn. Wheels screeched, but no one had been on the street to witness the abduction. Shocked, upset, and struggling to break free, Gelda demanded to know where she was being taken.

No one answered. After another block, with a heavy French accent, the driver said, "Pardon, Mm'selle; we must cover you up." The man next to her took a grey wool blanket and put it roughly over her head. Gelda protested with shrieks and kicks, but the man was firm, and she was unable to free her arms enough to remove the cover.

The driver appeared to be skilled. The town car swept through the streets. After moments in traffic, and later, the telltale sound of a long bridge, she figured they had crossed the St. Lawrence, heading east. After that, she lost all sense of direction. No one spoke except for occasional references to signs, and that was all in French.

Her mind churned with a dozen questions and vivid scenarios. Where were they taking her? Why? She shook. People disappeared in large cities more often than most would care to admit. It wasn't something she often thought of. And now, unfortunately, she did. What could she do?

Her family would be expecting her call after she arrived in Montréal. But how long would it take them to worry? An hour? Two? Too long for her liking. What could they do to her in that time?

She did not want to think about that. She did not want to become one of many faceless statistics.

She had to stay calm, she reminded herself. Anxiety was not going to solve anything. She had to keep her wits and use her head.

The second man was still beside her in the seat, but now that she had stopped struggling, his grip on her and the blanket had relaxed. But she was in a moving vehicle—she couldn't just run away.

She had to wait for her chance. They kept the blanket on her for a reason. They either didn't want her knowing where they were going, or they didn't want her seen. Maybe both. So they were still in a metropolitan area. The vehicle didn't slow often, but she could occasionally hear other traffic. Meaning they had to stop some time. She decided to make a break for freedom at the next stop light.

She did not have to wait long. As the car came to a halt, she plunged her fist into the man's lap beside her with all her strength. The surprise and pain for him was immediate.

Gelda launched her body toward the door, sweeping her left arm toward the door lock to release it.

The blanket caught under the seat, pulling her up short. It pulled away from her face as she went halfway through the door, kicking her legs to get free. Her blonde hair swept the pavement, only an inch away.

Despite his obvious pain, the man beside her struggled to get her back in the car. The driver swore and jumped out onto the street. Gelda was quickly subdued.

In her brief struggle for freedom, Gelda had seen they were in the right-hand lane of a three-lane boulevard. A red Dodge van was in back, but the young male driver was looking the other way. Her still-wheezing captor, a long scratch on his unshaven face from her nails, quickly covered her head with the blanket again. He locked her arms so she could not move.

The driver, back in his seat, did not wait for the light. He turned right, and sped down side streets, turning left and right at crossings to shake off any pursuit.

After some minutes, the driver guided the vehicle onto what must have been a highway, for they sped up and no longer turned down other streets.

Eventually, he spoke. "Miss Vanderstadt, that was a very stupid move—which you won't repeat. Your best chance of getting out of this whole deal safely is to behave yourself. We have every means to keep you quiet; including painful measures we don't want to take."

Gelda kept silent. They knew her name. She didn't know if that was a good thing or not. Hers was not a random abduction.

She was disappointed at her failure to escape, but had no choice but to look forward to the next opportunity.

When minutes stretched into an hour, and the road became smoother, she began dozing off. The car was not uncomfortable, but her feet were cold. When an hour passed and then two, she began to lose all sense of time as well. It all seemed like such a bad dream. But one she wasn't about to wake up from. What did these men want? They had been after her specifically, if they knew her name. Was it money? Politics? What could give her the upper hand—give her a chance to survive?

Suddenly, the tall driver pulled over. "We're here." He eased the town car into a gravel driveway. Gelda's stomach clenched. Would she figure out what this was all about?

The driver turned off the engine. "Miss Vanderstadt, we are stopping here for a few hours. I advise you to get some rest. We will be leaving very early in the morning. We have a long day ahead. You can take that blanket with you."

She was allowed out, her captors keeping a strong hold on her the whole time. The blanket was removed, and she saw an old, grey farmhouse. Isolated from any main roads, only the decrepit property was within view.

They went inside the building. There was a musty smell and scant furniture, but the house, at least, was heated and clean. "You will be in this room. If you need anything, knock on the door or call. We hope you rest well."

The door closed tight behind her. There were no windows. A lone ceiling light was all that illuminated the place of her captivity. She held the blanket close to her and lay down on a mattress as far from the door as possible.

It was late into the night, or very early into the morning, when the ceiling light came back on. A voice outside the door said, "Time to get up. We're leaving." Groggily, Gelda pulled herself together and was pushed back into the car in under five minutes—again, beside the unshaven men in the rear seat. Her shoulders were chilled under her knitted sweater, but the car warmed up after a few miles, and she dozed off once again.

The driver seemed to know his way, avoiding all of the main provincial routes. They turned south and east and back north again on a whole series of minor roads passing through a number of small villages. Each time they approached a village, Gelda was advised to look straight ahead and keep her eyes closed. She had not been able to identify any of the route signs so far.

This was to be the routine throughout the day. They parked at a hamburger joint at about two o'clock, and the driver took some cash and went inside to pick up an order. She was glad to see the food, having not eaten since her train ride. The money was a disappointment, as it meant they were not paying in any way that could be traced. Not that her parents would know who to look to for her abduction. The burgers settled heavily in Gelda's stomach.

In another forty minutes, she was told to put the blanket over her head again. She did not mind the darkness, but began to get a sense of urgency. They were likely near another city. Could she try and escape once more?

Gelda was pushed down, so that she lay curled on the seat. The man with the scratched face held her down. Disappointment grew. They were not taking any chances she would be seen.

It was more than two hours before the man removed the blanket from her head again and allowed her to sit up. This time they were travelling southwest at high speed through a pine forest. She was really turned around in her sense of direction.

No sooner had the blanket come off than the town car slowed, and in the dim grey twilight, Gelda saw they were turning left onto a narrow, dirt road. As it climbed through woods to higher ground, snowflakes began falling. The driver turned on the wipers, and Gelda could see about two inches of accumulation on the ground.

A steep and twisting mile beyond, they came to a large industrial building with weathered, wood-slab siding. The driver parked the town car next to two smaller vehicles, and the men got out, leaving her in her seat. They talked briefly, out of earshot, and then the driver returned to the car.

"Miss Vanderstadt, you will stay in the car with Antoine. Do not try anything funny. We will return in a moment."

Antoine, it seemed, had no desire to get back in the car with Gelda. He stood outside, bare-headed, smoking a cigarette while the snow melted on his dark overcoat. Gelda judged he was in his early thirties, with an unfriendly face made worse by the large scratch on the side of his neck.

The other men disappeared into a single door next to the loading dock. Gelda became aware of the great silence that blanketed the forest.

She was surprised to hear the sound of a light aircraft approaching from the South. The engine cut out as it drew near, landed and then it started up again to taxi closer to the shed behind the building. Two men appeared, carrying wicker baskets, which they deposited inside and then returned to the field for more.

Not long afterwards, the two came back around the corner, supporting a young man between them. He seemed injured or unconscious, his feet dragging in the snow. As he passed the car, she saw his eyes were open. He stared straight at her. He kept his head down, and her own captor, Antoine, did not seem to notice. Why was the man being carried? Was he being kidnapped too? He was taken inside, and a few minutes later, her driver returned. "You will come in now, Mm'selle."

Antoine opened the door on her side. "We must cover you up again. Be very quiet."

They went into a small, dark hallway and up a long stair, then into a large, lighted space where she was led to a folding chair and told to keep quiet. She heard the sound of cloth rustling, like a curtain or other divider being brushed against, as men passed.

She slowly moved her hands from her sides. The left bumped up against something, even in height with her chair. A low table, or perhaps a cot. A blanket covered the surface.

Someone was speaking; she recognized the voice, as the driver. Another broke in abruptly. His had the same strong accent as her driver's. "Mère de Dieu, Claude, what were you thinking? Who the hell do you think is going to be responsible?" From there it devolved into a major shouting match between two Frenchmen, this new-comer and her driver, Claude. She only caught every other word as the two switched to their native language in the heat of their argument. They seemed to be sensitive to her presence.

Antoine sat on the cot, nervously tapping the floor with his foot. She felt awkward and uncomfortable in the new situation. The discussion dragged on, and settled into petty arguments about who would do what.

She could not be sure, but some distance away—in spite of the voices—she thought she heard a motorcycle engine cough to life. Its lonely sound gradually diminished in the distance. Gelda was left to face her worries by herself.

6

Mark knew there was no time to lose. As soon as they noticed him missing, there would be hot pursuit. He let the bike coast in a straight stretch of snow and stony gravel. Moving at a good clip, he turned on the magneto, released the clutch, and blessedly, the engine roared to life. The bike had no headlight, and the snow hurt his eyelids, but with a few skids in the ruts, he made it out of the woods and onto a macadam highway.

Mark paused at the intersection. The gloom in the southwest provided only the last hint of daylight. He must have been travelling north from the camp. Many car tracks came from the west, but he was not sure he should follow them. Perhaps the safest way to go was toward the east, though he had no idea where the road would lead. He wheeled his bike onto the macadam, facing away from that last glimmer of light. He shook the snow off his jacket and tried to warm his hands under his armpits. The open road would be his worst challenge in the cold.

He had to be extremely careful now, not exceeding twenty miles per hour because of the snow. The road led through long, dark, pine forests, and then onto fields and a great, cultivated plain dropping low in the distance. He could see faint lights, miles away, where a heavy darkness stretched beyond. The wind from the east froze his hands to the grips. They no longer had feeling. The snow plastered his forehead. His eyebrows were caked with ice; he could not move his face. He was going down now and he knew it, but there was no other option. He had to hold out until he reached some kind of shelter.

He had no memory of intervening time. He passed through the night between woods and high banks.

Then, up ahead, he saw lights from a building set back from the road on the right. He tried to slow the bike. It wobbled once in the slush before he lost control of it entirely. It slid sideways across the snowy entrance drive and went into a ditch, throwing him headfirst over the handlebars. With not much snow, he hit hard.

His face stung; he tried to move his arm, so that he could roll over. The pain had him face-first in the slush once more.

It was minutes before he could try again. His shoulder now throbbed angrily; moving, even without his right arm, was laborious, and sent pain shooting through his collarbone.

Dazed, he slowly pulled his legs under him, and with his left elbow in the snow, managed to get up on his knees. He was shaking; from the cold or the pain, he wasn't sure which.

Staggering through low drifts to the house, he attempted to knock, and tried opening the glass storm door with his wrist. Some footsteps came toward the inner door from the other side and opened it gingerly. Mark felt a glow of warmth and light, but when invited inside, tripped on the threshold and fell forward on the floor. It was the last thing he knew for twelve hours.

When he opened his eyes, he was in a small bedroom with blankets piled on top of him. Daylight came in the window from behind a shade. It was warm, and there was a faint smell of kerosene. He was swaddled in a number of light blankets, but when he tried to move his right arm, pain darkened the room once more.

More carefully this time, he flexed the fingers of his hands; there was a burning sensation in both of them. The shin of his right leg hurt. He must have a major bruise, from when he went into the air, over . . . handle bars? Then it came back to him; the motorcycle, riding through the night in the snow, and the farm house. Was that where he was? He needed to get up, and find out his location.

Mark managed to get his legs out of the narrow cot, but when he sat up, he felt faint. He had a horrible feeling in his shoulder. He was still for a moment, and then went stiffly over to the window and looked out. All he could see was a barn with more sheds beyond.

But it was light out. He checked the time. His hands were swathed in bandages, but they didn't cover his watch. Nine forty.

On the bedside table, there was a telephone and a directory for Campbellton, New Brunswick area. He was in New Brunswick? That explained the long, cold ride in the light plane.

He wanted to call his brother in Boston, but needed first to check with the family who had provided refuge, the warm bed, and first-aid.

He opened the door and found a small, grey-haired lady with a printed apron tidying magazines in the adjacent sitting room. In the centre was a large kerosene heater.

She looked up with a surprised expression. Mark bowed. "You were very kind to take me in last night—you saved my life. My name is Mark Talyard, from Boston. I'm sorry, your name is . . .?

"I am Elaine Cody. My husband, Bob, is out in the barn now." She gestured out back. "You were not in good condition when you knocked at our door. We called our neighbour, Dr. Freebury, who lives just down the road. He found your motorcycle in the ditch out front."

Mark shook his head. "Sad to say, I lost control of the bike because of the temperature. I was frozen stiff. If you don't mind, could you please tell me the name of this village?"

"Well, it's not really a village. We're between Kedgwick and St. Quentin. Some folk call it Queboggin, but that is because of an old lumber camp back up in the hills. We're really quite isolated here."

John had heard of neither town nor the camp, but he thanked his lucky stars he had run into the Codys.

Mrs. Cody opened the door to the small kitchen. "Can I give you something to eat? Dr. Freebury will be here soon—he said he would stop by at eleven."

"A little toast would be fine." Mark was confused for a moment, but then noticed the kitchen clock said ten forty-five. They were on Atlantic time.

A red pickup pulled into the farmyard, passing the kitchen window. "Oh, he's here already. Early as always."

A few moments later, the doctor came to the door, stamping snow off his feet on the mat outside. "Hello, Elaine. How's the patient?"

"Hello, Dr. Freebury, Mr. Talyard just woke up."

Mark smiled at the doctor and offered his left hand, still a sight wrapped in linen. "Just call me Mark."

"Not moving that arm, I see. I worried about that."

"Yes, I went over the handlebars of the motorbike I was riding."

"Oh? Well, let's have another look at it. We made sure you were breathing all right last night, and that nothing was out of place. You seemed exhausted. The cold will do that to you."

The doctor gestured for Mark to sit, and started helping him remove his sweater and shirt. It was a painful process. To distract him, the doctor continued talking. "I saw your motorcycle. The whole front frame is bent; you must have taken a real header." The doctor looked for bruises, and felt Mark's shoulder. He gently raised Mark's right arm, and Mark winced in pain.

"I see. You have some older bruises, and a deep laceration on your head as well. We'll have to get some x-rays. You weren't very well dressed to be out riding in that storm!" The doctor's tone was chiding, like Mark had been caught in some foolish prank. But what was he to say? That he was kidnapped out of the mountains in New Hampshire by unknown Frenchmen, and then taken to what Mrs. Cody claimed was an abandoned lumber camp? It sounded ridiculous, even to him. How could something like that even happen?

He began to shiver, though he wasn't cold. Was he? Certainly not like last night. He started to feel sick to his stomach.

Mrs. Cody came in with hot coffee and buttered toast.

The doctor accepted his with a smile, then looked over at Mark with a worried frown. "Young man, you're not looking so good. Elaine, can we get another blanket?"

Mrs. Cody nodded, and left the room.

"I think we had better get you to the hospital for a complete examination. I'll take you over to Campbellton."

Mark nodded slowly. He felt terrible. What was he going to do? Had last night actually happened? His injuries suggested it had.

"Thank you, Elaine." Dr. Freebury wrapped the blanked around Mark, being careful of his right shoulder. "I'm afraid I'm going to have to take your patient from you."

"That's all right, Doctor. I hope you feel better, Mr. Talyard."

"Th-thank you very much, Mrs. Cody. May I pay you something for your trouble?"

"Oh, not at all, Mr. Talyard; I just hope you get well quickly."

"Shall we go, son? Do you have any other belongings?"

Mark shook his head. "C-can I use the phone first? I think I need to call my brother." Or maybe Uncle John. How was he going to explain all of this?

The doctor said, "Mark, I think we better leave right away. I've got commitments I need to take care of. You'll have a good chance to call your family from the hospital."

7

The rendezvous in John's letter, October 15, fell on a Saturday. The overt occasion for the trip to the Adirondacks was a two-day symposium of big maritime insurance company representatives. The timing had been coincidental, but the setting was ideal because Thurmond could break away to meet Xenon on Saturday in New Hampshire without undo attention. The conference would permit informal conversations with some of the litigants in their client's trial.

Sal had been invited by her younger brother and sister-in-law to take the children to a small seaside cottage in Cape May, New Jersey, for a weekend, off-season, and they were looking forward to the change.

It was mid-afternoon and the temperature had risen to the sixties. The coolness of the shadowed grove of hemlocks by the lake was welcome relief after the long drive. And yet, John did not feel relieved. He had just gotten off the phone with his nephew, Mark, who had dropped a bombshell.

John was shaken to his roots. What on earth was happening? Mark had been kidnapped and injured? The boy had claimed it wasn't that bad, but who would do such a thing? Did someone know that Col. Louis Xenon was on his way to New Hampshire?

It was the only reason that John could think of. And that had awful implications. He had no way of warning off the Colonel—he didn't even know how Xenon was planning on getting from Europe to the White Mountains. He had left it entirely up to the Colonel and his experience. It also provided a safeguard against anyone intercepting their communications.

And it appeared someone had. Someone, with connections to either Stillman Electric or QFR Nuclear, had been at the cabin. That same someone had kidnapped his nephew, for no reason other than being at the wrong place at the wrong time. Despite the difference between the 11th and the 15th, Mark had fallen into some kind of trap.

And QFR—how in heaven's name was Philippe LeClerc involved? When Mark had told him about the newspaper clipping, and that Philippe was the head of QFR—one of the two companies involved—John had been shocked yet again. What possible motive would he have of breaking into the cabin? He hadn't spoken with Philippe in years. Or did the connection have nothing to do with John's cabin at all, and only concern the nuclear information? Far too much of his past had come back to haunt him in the past month for him to make any sense of it at all.

Then it dawned on him. He had forgotten about the planned two-week interval between the transmitted date and the actual date of the rendezvous on the twenty-ninth of October. Xenon still had two more weeks to get there! How could he ever . . . he felt ashamed at his mistake.

He needed to sort it out. It was clear he would have to scratch the conference. He needed to talk to someone he could trust. He wasn't sure about Ben Greenstone. As it stood, the ex-army Captain was the only one who knew of the rendezvous . . . but not the place, and only the approximate time. Not only had their schedule been tested, but the actual location of the rendezvous was now known. Xenon's cover had quite possibly been compromised.

The transfer was becoming far more complicated than he had ever expected. He felt terrible that it had put Mark in such jeopardy.

There were two more days until the end of the conference on Saturday, the fifteenth, but it did not seem to make sense to stick around the Adirondacks any longer. He needed help, and he wasn't sure that Greenstone was the one to provide it. But he wasn't out of options yet. John still had resources.

An old friend of the family, and alumnus of the school he attended, St. Michael's, in Hawkesbury, Ontario, lived in Montréal. Garrett Bennett was currently an appointee to the Department of National Defence (DND). He had earned the position, and his award of the Order of Military Merit three years before, in a successful naval rescue off Ellesmere Island, saving forty-six British submariners trapped below polar ice. He was a man who could be relied upon for both courageous action and decisive insight. And with his position in the DND, he would know if something unusual was happening up north. It would be good to have an insider who could explain things from the Canadian government's perspective.

All was not lost. John had been warned in advance that Xenon could be facing serious trouble on the mountain. The two of them still did have one element of surprise left in their favour. Their adversaries could not be sure exactly which day to expect them. It might be possible to make that work to their advantage.

FRIDAY, OCTOBER 14, 1983

Garrett's home was nestled at the end of a quiet street in Westmount, its cut-stone façade executed in the best traditions of the Neo-classical revival. The morning was a chilly one, with frost coating the grass.

John was greeted enthusiastically by the Bennetts, and they spent part of the morning catching up after a year and a half apart. Eventually, they moved into the living room, where a warm fire was blazing on the hearth. The maid brought in cups of hot mulled cider and generous slabs of warm, fresh-made ginger bread. Eventually, John and Garrett were alone, and John brought him up-to-date on Mark's adventures in New Hampshire.

When he finished, Garrett was quiet. He pulled the screen aside and poked one of the logs. "You say your nephew was kidnapped?" Garrett's voice held more surprise than question. "Do you have any idea as to the motive? The possible connection between Stillman Electric, QFR Nuclear, and the cabin is a puzzling one."

"Yes. It's a complicated story, Garr, and I don't know entirely what we're dealing with. John paused. He wanted to make sure Garrett got the message, without revealing sensitive security information. "It doesn't stop there. They landed in a remote area near Campbellton, New Brunswick—at an old, abandoned lumber camp or manufacturing facility. They call it Queboggin. Apparently, there was some kind of a meeting going on. A black town-car with a driver and a young woman inside were there just before he made his escape. There were other cars there, too."

"How long ago did all this take place?"

"Mark got to my cabin on Tuesday. He was kidnapped and flown to New Brunswick on Wednesday."

"Hmm." Bennett tapped the armrest of his chair and stared into the flames.

"What?"

"It may be nothing, but . . . you said Mark saw a girl there?"

"A young woman, yes. Why?"

"I don't suppose you read today's paper?"

John was puzzled by the change of topic. "Which one?"

"The Montréal Gazette."

"No, I haven't seen it. Sad to say, it's very hard to find any Montréal papers on newsstands in the States."

"Well, a girl from McGill was kidnapped Tuesday evening, right outside her apartment on Mount Royal. I was notified because her father is a nuclear scientist from Winnipeg. We were worried about possible political implications."

John was stunned. "A nuclear scientist? From Winnipeg? Is his name Roeloff Vanderstadt?"

Now John had Garrett's full attention. "You know Dr. Roeloff Vanderstadt?"

"I just met with him a month ago."

"Are you tied in with his project?"

John paused. This is where the ground he was on began to get shaky. "I'm not allowed to discuss it."

"I see." Garrett fixed John carefully with a stern gaze. "So tell me, what are you allowed to discuss?"

"Do you remember the three years I spent in Asia?" He was being careful now.

"Yes—before you and Sal were engaged?"

"Exactly. I was there on business for the U.S. Government. A courier is coming from Europe with information I need from my time there."

"And?"

"I think Mark's kidnapping may be linked to an attempt to capture the courier."

"A courier—who was coming to the cabin?"

John nodded in the affirmative.

"What would you like me to do?"

"Without informing the police, is there any way to check the license on the car that Mark mentioned? It's a small green Fiat, plate number HYG-365. I'd like to know who owns it. Second, at the camp in New Brunswick—the black town-car with the young woman in it. It was a six passenger Chrysler from the Province of Québec. Mark couldn't see the license number because of the snow. There were two other cars, an older model Plymouth, also from Québec, and a Chevy."

"This definitely looks like an out-of-province operation, either drug smuggling or . . ." Garrett gave John another pointed look. "Something like that. Especially with the connection to the U.S."

"I don't know. I just don't know. I called you because I need perspective on this thing."

"The trail could be getting cold, you know, John," Garrett stated flatly. "They may have already left the New Brunswick camp because of Mark's escape."

"That's very possible, Garrett, but I think we ought to try. Especially with the new connection to Mark and Dr. Vanderstadt."

"Do you really think his daughter could have been in the town car Mark saw?"

"I'd say it's possible."

"I will admit, it certainly puts a whole new complexion on things. Especially with this . . . connection of yours. I think we had better contact Dr. Vanderstadt immediately, and let him know we may have traced his daughter to New Brunswick. We should find out what authorities he has notified. We should also contact Mark, to check on his safety, and see if he has learned anything more."

"I hate to put Mark in the firing line—I'd like to get him back to Boston as soon as possible—but you're right. I'll see what he can do."

Garrett stood up and poked the fire again. John could see his mind working intensely. "Say, John, can I get you anything? I think I need a fresh cup of hot coffee."

"Sure, Garrett, coffee would be good."

Garrett rang for the maid, and in a few minutes, she brought in coffee and a small plate of cookies.

"The real question, Garrett, is what our next steps should be.

These incidents could be part of a much larger picture, involving national security for both our countries. That's really the main reason I contacted you."

"Yes, well. My own gut instinct is that, of the two companies that Mark found a connection to, QFR Nuclear is the more likely. First, because of the Québec license plates that Mark saw, and second because Gelda, the daughter of a nuclear scientist, went missing in Montréal."

John nodded, but his stomach tightened at the probable implications towards Philippe. He was still amazed at LeClerc's new position with QFR. Kidnapping just didn't seem his style. But how could he really tell anymore, with all the years that had passed? Maybe it was just wishful fancy.

Garrett continued, "Despite that, we don't necessarily want to spring the trap on QFR and its director, LeClerc, until we know positively who his associates are and what they're up to. Until they show their hand, the fewer locals chasing these individuals, the better."

"I think you'll get the same reaction from Vanderstadt, even though, sadly, his daughter may be at risk."

"I understand, John. The fact that Vanderstadt could be involved makes it very serious indeed. I'll get right on it and try to open up some connections for communication." Garrett stared off into the fire for a while, lost in his own thoughts. After a minute or so, he roused himself. "Can you stay for lunch?"

"No, thank you just the same, Garr," John said, rising. "I've got to get back. I need to take a deposition at eight-thirty, Monday morning." John took his coat from the closet.

Garrett laughed. "You do cover the ground, old buddy. Are you still driving that old Porsche?"

John smiled. "It's parked outside."

Garrett laughed and shook his head grimly. "I wish we didn't have to meet under such urgent circumstances. Let's stay in touch. If this thing is linked, we will want to coordinate surveillance with our governments' intelligence at the highest level. There could be a great deal at stake. Please let me know how you make out with Mark."

Outside Garrett's home, the red Porsche was waiting. Though John's eyes were set toward Philadelphia, his mind thought back to his childhood friend, and how he had managed to get involved in something so dire.

8

Jean Claude, known as Number 2 within the secret Parti 17 Separatist movement, was a man in turmoil.

He knew he had incurred the ire of Philippe LeClerc, his boss at QFR Nuclear and Number 1 in the Parti, over the events of the weekend in New Brunswick. He did not like to be at odds with LeClerc—not because of his technical position as LeClerc's inferior, but because they had worked together, had shared similar goals, for so many years. But it was no longer so.

It was regrettable that non-politicals had to get involved, and that his relationship with LeClerc had to take a hit, but Jean was hardened enough to take it in stride, and chalk it up to the costs of the mass revolution. There were winners and losers, and individuals were expendable.

LeClerc had proven he was not devoted enough, that he did not want the Parti to go all the way. The Parti had stagnated in the past few years, and something had to be done to get things moving again. Martin Drapeneau seemed to be the man to do just that.

It had been on Drapeneau's suggestion that Jean had moved against Gelda Vanderstadt. It had seemed like the perfect plan—just the edge that the Parti needed. He had followed those orders to a 'T', and he expected to be praised when the Parti's new European arrival reached North America.

Martin Drapeneau was a shadowy figure—as much an enigma to Jean Claude as he was to anyone.

Jean recalled his first meeting with Drapeneau in divided Berlin, back in the sixties, when he was stationed with a Canadian unit in West Germany. Though Martin used to make much of his French heritage, Jean could tell his primary loyalties were toward the East, and to the Warsaw Pact agenda in Europe. Multi-lingual, he liked to crack jokes in Russian and German, as well as French.

When Jean was off-duty, Martin occasionally invited him out to some German bar or other. With Drapeneau's clandestine ring of associates, talk ranged from European politics to the Marshall Plan, from management and labour in basic industry to military strategy and foreign policy—even to the location of American bases overseas. The discussions were serious, and gave Jean a sense of participation in something bigger than just being a member of an occupying military force.

After Jean Claude's tour of duty in Europe was over, and he returned to Canada, Drapeneau kept in contact with him in closely typed letters once or twice a year. These letters were treasured by Jean, and he kept them in a bureau drawer. He responded with news of Canadian politics, student movements, labour negotiations in the ports, the electrical unions, the Québec Libre struggle, and information of a general nature designed to impress the foreigner.

This pattern continued for years, and Drapeneau in turn put Claude in contact with other leftists from both north and south of the U.S. border. It was a beneficial relationship that had affected Parti 17 for years, even if LeClerc had not realized it.

When Drapeneau announced he was planning to come to North

America in October, Claude got excited, and wrote his mentor asking if there was anything he could do to prepare for his arrival.

Drapeneau responded that the daughter of a prominent nuclear scientist was a graduate student at McGill University. It would be useful to the internationale if this girl could be taken as a bargaining chip to prevent the escalation of the nuclear arms race between East and West. Claude was told she might even be won to their cause.

Claude did not devote much thought to the request. He had recruited a number of young radicals through his contacts in the Electricians' union and the sports club he sponsored. It seemed like an easy assignment.

Through one of the young, impressionable members of his sports club, a kid by the name of Dionne, he learned that Gelda Vanderstadt lived only a few blocks away. It seemed like a piece of cake to pick up Mm'selle Vanderstadt where she was most vulnerable—outside her apartment on Mont Royale.

In his mind's eye, he even thought it would be a feather in his cap to take her to the Queboggin meeting and present Philippe with 'un fait accompli'. He had not expected to get that strong a reaction out of the QFR leader. Then again, if that young New Hampshire man hadn't upset everything by escaping, maybe LeClerc would have taken it better.

Only a week before the Queboggin meeting, Jean had received another letter from Drapeneau. It asked if there was a way he could check out a mountain cabin in New Hampshire. Apparently, a meeting with an agent from Europe was supposed to take place there. This was an extraordinary request, and Jean felt that Drapeneau was giving him a chance to prove his worth. Once again, Martin Drapeneau was introducing him to bigger and better things, and Jean didn't want to disappoint.

However, he was already committed to picking up Mm'selle Vanderstadt. Since Drapeneau had requested the observation be a long-term thing, Jean figured he could get another of his recruits to watch the cabin for those few days that he would be away bringing Gelda to Queboggin. He had a young engineer named Charles Bourget, at the Laval plant, undertake the task. Another of Philippe's employees, Yves Bonnard, had a light plane, and Jean asked for his help in transportation. Yves was often requested to do little favours for Parti 17, and since Philippe was already in that area anyway, Yves had promptly filed a flight plan for the nearest airfield in Lebanon, New Hampshire.

But it had all gone wrong. Jean hadn't expected them to actually find anyone at the cabin—and neither had they. The young hiker was obviously being nosey, so he couldn't fault them for bringing him back to Queboggin for questioning. But the darn kid escaped. Claude himself went out looking for him, with Yves and a few others present for the Queboggin meeting. In the freshly fallen snow, they had had no luck.

Now, Jean needed guidance. Everything he had felt so confident about at Queboggin had fallen to pieces. In his last letter, Drapeneau had included his arrival date—he should have gotten in to Canada late last night or earlier this morning. But Jean had no way of knowing how to contact his mentor, and he became more and more anxious. What was he to do? The phone's sudden ringing jolted Jean from his musing.

He scrambled for the receiver. "Qui est à l'appareil?"

"Bonjour, Jean."

Jean was taken aback by the brusqueness of the gravelly voice. "Ah, M'sieur Drapeneau. Welcome to Canada! How was your trip?"

"Look, Jean, I'll meet you in the park across from your house in ten minutes." The line clicked.

Apparently he was impatient to get down to business. Jean shrugged. It was a long trip from France. He would be impatient too.

At the park, he found Drapeneau waiting. Jean was eager to get the events of the past few days off his chest. After a detailed explanation of the events leading up to Queboggin, he paused to allow all of his news to sink in. He expected some guidance, and at least a little praise for his efforts.

What he got was another thing entirely. "Bon Dieu, Claude! You imbecile. Why would you let that man escape and give Gelda to LeClerc? I don't have time to deal with a crétin like LeClerc."

"Philippe is the leader of Parti 17, Martin. If these events are to benefit the Parti at all, then he—"

Drapeneau's low growl cut him off. "You still don't get the point, do you Jean? This business is not about you, Jean Claude, or your precious Parti 17. It is beyond that—beyond Québec, or Canada. The purpose of holding Gelda is to shut down NATO's access to information that Vanderstadt is presenting in Brussels this June. I need to have him under my thumb. If Gelda gets extinguished in the process, so be it. You have got to understand, we are playing for keeps. We will stop at nothing to achieve this goal."

Claude turned pale. This roasting by Martin was far worse than LeClerc's. He had not counted on murder. He swallowed hard, but made no comment.

Drapeneau continued, "We still have time. Threats alone may be sufficient. I think I can salvage this. But whatever you do, do not— do not—try anything like that again. Follow my direction, or do nothing. Understand?"

Jean agreed, rather sullenly. This was not what he had expected at all.

"Now, can you give me this Philippe LeClerc's telephone number? Private home and office, please."

Jean wondered what had suddenly shifted Drapeneau's tone, and said just as much.

Martin responded."I have an idea on how to deal with those that meddle in what should not be their business."

Jean cringed. He had thought, with the arrival of Drapeneau, he could bask in his mentor's approval. Now, he was facing fear of arrest for another's threats. He did not know how to stop the train of events that he had started.

9

Mark was restless. Saturday was the third day he had stayed at Dr. Freebury's home, just south of Kedgwick. He was scheduled to go back to the hospital in Campbellton on Monday to get more x-rays of his shoulder; it had taken the brunt of his spill.

It was not a separation, but a cracked collarbone that was of concern. His arm was in a sling, but even with that and the medication, it was painful. The blow to his head was also serious, but the doctor said once the swelling went down, he should be out of danger. It would take a lot of rest and some time for the cut to heal.

Mark had briefed his uncle on the situation at the camp at Queboggin. Uncle John had been very pleased to hear about the flight log and maps. Mark had already forwarded them to him by mail. He had also cautioned going to the police about it right away. There was something more behind it all, and Uncle John wanted a chance to figure things out at his end. He seemed worried about someone he knew having connections to QFR. Mark didn't know what that was about, but he hadn't been keen on going to the authorities on his own, anyway. He didn't know how the Canadian RCMP would react to his story, especially how it pertained to his crossing of the border.

His uncle said any additional information would be welcome, but cautioned him to be very careful. "Once they learned that you had escaped, they probably cleared out of there, pronto. Nobody wants a kidnapping rap!"

Mark would need transportation to return to Queboggin, to do some more investigating there. He found there were buses going from Campbellton to Edmundston regularly. They held promise. A schedule confirmed he could make it to the camp from Kedgwick, though he would have to hike a mile to get to the village bus stop. Dr. Freebury had a busy day with appointments at his clinic. A return bus would be passing by between two and three. Mark did not want to bother the doctor with details of his excursion. He left a note saying he planned to return by six o'clock.

Boarding the bus in Kedgwick, Mark was soon well past the Cody farm. The motorcycle was currently sitting, un-repaired, in Dr. Freebury's garage. At the unmarked road where the driver let him out, there were no tracks visible across the field. That was a good sign. There was still the risk that the Frenchmen were still up there at the camp, but it was looking less likely. Still, he would have to keep his eyes open.

With temperature in the mid-thirties, the melting snow was about ten inches deep. He was glad he brought a ski pole for his strong arm; there was less pain in his shoulder during the day, and it was good to get some exercise.

He hiked nearly a mile up the road before he came to the point where he started the motorcycle. In spite of the unspoiled snow, he was nervous about approaching the buildings. He looked for places to take cover in case he was surprised.

He was relieved when he saw the building abandoned. There were no cars in the parking lot, and the plane was no longer in the field.

Looking to where the black town car had been parked, he wondered what had happened to the girl—she had not seemed much older than he. Her involvement in it all was still a mystery.

The lock into the production facility yielded without too much difficulty. He made his way up the stairs, and was glad he had brought a flashlight. The upper room ran the full length of the building, and was lighted by a few long windows just below the eaves.

There were scattered chairs, a table, a curtained-off area with cots, and a large trash bin filled with newspapers, cartons, cans and debris. Several kerosene heaters with Coleman lanterns were placed strategically throughout. It easily had been a meeting of ten or more people.

Mark was about to start rifling through the debris in the trash, but thought better of it. Police detectives should be in charge of the investigation. They could lift any fingerprints and see where the evidence pointed. He must leave the scene undisturbed.

He wandered over to the curtained area. There were no blankets or pillows on the cots, but it was obvious the meeting was meant to last more than a day. He saw a silver object at the end of one of the mattresses.

He couldn't help himself. Pulling a handkerchief from his pocket, he picked it up to examine it. It was a ball-point pen, with a chrome cap and the words, 'INS-Manitoba, Winn.' printed along its length. It seemed out of context, so it might be a clue. He put it carefully in his pocket, still wrapped in the handkerchief.

Not much else was of interest in the building. The site itself wasn't anything spectacular until he thought of the plane. A private airfield would have its uses. He decided to leave and check the shed. He refastened the entry door as best he could.

It had been colder inside the building than out, and he was glad to be in the open again. The sun was bright, and chickadees were flitting among birches and low brush at the edge of the field. He made his way through the snow to the shed. It would be almost impossible for a plane to take off with snow that deep. The shed was unlocked and the padlock missing.

There, in the shadows, stood the plane, intact and ready to depart. He looked in his jacket for something to write on. The plane's wing markings and the serial number of the engine matched the log book. With the pen, the log book and maps, and descriptions of the cars, it was time to return to Kedgwick and report the findings to his uncle. This was good fortune indeed!

10

The Can-Am Line's motor vessel L'Aventure laboured westward in the North Atlantic. It was to be one of the last voyages of the venerable craft, due to competition from the airline industry. Heavy following seas, spawned by counter-clockwise winds, emanated from a hurricane eight hundred miles away near the Azores. Louis had come up from his tourist cabin, amidships and two decks down, to get a breath of fresh air. The smelly oil fumes from the engine room, mixing with cooking odours from the crew's galley, had given him a headache.

The dining saloon on the main deck was deserted, except for a waiter at the bar polishing glasses. With difficulty, he opened the door leading from the companionway to the deck outside. A strong rush of air passed around him to the interior of the ship. His face felt the wind-driven spray coming over the deck as the ship rolled and plunged into the next wave. Although it was about three-thirty in the afternoon, the sky was dark with scudding clouds and occasional rainsqualls coming from the northeast.

He pushed his way forward on the lee side, past tightly covered waterproof hatches, to the heavy bulkhead protecting the foredeck from the storm-tossed ocean. The green sea rose and fell, and at times came up through the narrow ports of the glistening anchor chains. The anchors, canted and lashed to the hull below the bulkhead, must have weighed several tons apiece.

Louis was grateful for the thick knitted sweater underneath his yellow slicker. He pulled the string of his hood tighter around his chin. The white tops of long combers passed under the ship from the stern to the port side as the ship entered another trough, stretching as far as the eye could see to the western horizon. Though temperatures had been mild when he left Le Havre, they had now passed the Gulf Stream and were starting to experience the effects of the Labrador Current sweeping down the west coast of Greenland from the Arctic. The sea, overcast and rain-swept, would improve; it could not be much more than another day before they entered the Gulf of St. Lawrence.

A slight figure in a green raincoat and a wide-brimmed waterproof hat tied around her chin struggled with the door from the dining room. She lurched to the side rail as the ship rolled to port. The woman wrapped her bare hands securely around the iron rail, but Louis could tell the force of the gale was testing her strength. He paid scant attention, other than questioning if it was smart for her to be on deck in the storm. He searched instead, toward the lighter sky on the western horizon, for any change in the weather.

He became conscious that the young woman had made her way forward and was standing only feet away, gasping for breath. He glanced quickly and was surprised at her youth. A damp strand of hair crossed her nose and covered her left cheek. She opened her mouth to speak, but the wind was too loud. He stepped closer and cupped his ear. All he could manage to hear was ". . . storm." He smiled and nodded, and turned away again. The woman moved to the relative protection of a ventilating funnel bringing warm air up from the crew's quarters below. She sat on the curb and stared at the painted steel deck plating, shivering and lost in thought.

A huge wave swept forward from the stern along the starboard side, cresting close to the railing. A heavy, grey, spray-plume of sea-water lifted into the air, crossed the bow, and struck both of them with a drenching icy shower. They were soaked head to foot. Louis' pants and shoes were damp, but protected by his long slicker. The woman, wetter than he—her raincoat in no way adequate for the weather—looked up in stunned surprise.

Louis held out his hand to help the woman to her feet, grasping her slender, icy fingers. "It would be wise for us to go inside," he said, in smiling French above the storm. "Unless we want another quick repetition of that experience."

She nodded and gulped, perhaps likewise not being able to hear his full sentence. At the entrance to the companionway, he held the door for her and she thanked him quietly.

Once inside, in the way of polite conversation, he asked if she would care for a cup of coffee.

She quickly replied in broken French, "Oh, non merci—not now! I am so wet. I must go and change my clothes." She ran a hand through her elbow-length hair, a nervous gesture, it seemed to Louis. "But yes, I would love a cup of coffee afterward. May I come back in ten minutes?"

"Mais certainement!" Louis laughed, and then bowed. "Vous êtes Anglaise, non? I will look forward to it!"

When she left, he looked down at his trousers, and though the legs were damp, he felt there was a good chance they would dry out. The saloon was empty, and he took a seat at a small table near the forward windows. He was pleased to feel the heat of a steam pipe that ran continuously along the wall under the window line.

The waiter came over from the bar to ask what he would like. "I am expecting la Mm'selle to return in a few moments. When she comes, may we have a pot of fresh coffee and cream . . . des petites patisseries? Les Anglaises—elles les aiment!"

The waiter smiled, bowed, and turned on his heel.

The passenger liner continued pitching and yawing with the following waves, but a brightened sky in the southwest indicated they were moving out of the rain that had covered their voyage the last four days. Louis had heard that the large fogbank they had experienced was due to the mixing of the warm Gulf Stream with the colder Labrador Current. Fortunately, icebergs were no longer a threat this late in the season.

He expected L'Aventure to have two more days of sailing. They would reach the Strait of Belle Isle, north of Newfoundland, in the early morning, and then it would take a day and a night to voyage through the Gulf of St. Lawrence past L'Ile d'Anticosti and the Gaspé Peninsula, to the Port of Québec.

In a short while, the young woman returned. This time she was dressed in warmer clothes: a skirt, a plain grey wool jacket, and a heather-coloured cardigan sweater.

Louis rose from the seat by the window and stretched out his hand.

"You are very kind to invite me," the woman said. "My name is Hélène Vodrey . . . and yours?"

"Je m'appelle Louis Xenon, Mm'selle; I am very pleased to make your acquaintance." He helped her with the chair and then joined her at the small table.

When they had settled in, the waiter approached with a tray of cups and pastries, and a silver pot of coffee.

"Oh my!" said Hélène, obviously delighted.

"So, how do you like the weather?" Louis asked.

"I'll be glad when this trip is over."

"May I ask where are you going, Mm'selle?" Louis poured himself some of the coffee, ignoring the cream and sugar, then filled Hélène's as well.

"Merci . . . I am returning to the Maritime Provinces, to visit my parents."

"Oh, and where do they live?"

Hélène looked down shyly, stirring her coffee. "In a small village, called Baggs' Inlet, on Nova Scotia. It's south of Sheet Harbour, north of Halifax."

Louis nodded his head. "And where are you coming from now?"

"I teach at a very small school for girls, 'The Brackley School for Young Women' in Oxfordshire. We have a trimester break that lasts until mid-January. I am making use of the long holiday."

"Très interéssant!" Louis replied.

Hélène picked up a small pastry. "And you, M'sieur? What is your background?"

"I am a retired military man. I was in the Army."

"Oh?" Hélène looked up once more. "And where did you serve?"

"In the Far . . ." Louis caught himself. She was so open. It was easy to be caught up in her honest expressions. But he did not want to reveal too much of his experience to this young woman. "Well, farther south. Actually in Algérie and North Africa."

"When did you retire?" She seemed honestly intrigued, more than just making small talk over coffee.

"About seven years ago. I live on the northeast side of Le Havre."

"You do? My mother comes from Dieppe. My father met her after the war. He was in the British Coast Guard during the invasion of Normandy."

"Ah, yes, c'était une expérience très formidable!" He shook his head.

"And, M'sieur Xenon, why are you going to North America?"

"It is a vacation. I am going on a fishing expedition in Québec. I hope to explore the headwaters of the Péribonka, above the Savanne River."

"Oh, that's interesting. I have an uncle who fished there many summers of my youth."

The conversation turned to details about life on board L'Aventure, travel in general, world events and Hélène's experiences at Brackley.

Louis was amused by the young woman's enthusiasms. He had grown a bit less active in the routine of the last seven years. In his late forties, grey hair was accumulating around his ears. He did not feel the same level of motivation he had when he left the army. Still, he felt it might have been due to the lack of new incentives.

The horizon grew darker as the afternoon waned. The long combers grew less distinct and the waiter adjusted the over-head lights. More staff had arrived. They were busy laying out silver and glassware in preparation for the first dining room sitting at five-thirty.

"Have you made plans for dinner?" Louis offered.

"No, not actually," Hélène said, "I sit at table twelve, second sitting, starting at seven-thirty."

"Aha!" Louis said, "I would enjoy it—If you will allow me, I would like to make arrangements with the Maître d', for a table for two—at the same time?"

"Oh, it would very nice. I'd like that! Thank you; you are very kind." She blushed. "I . . . I think I should leave now, so I can get ready."

"Oh, non, non, non! Don't do anything special, Mm'selle. We are just two sailors on this ship."

Hélène laughed as they stood up. He could tell that on this voyage, she had not received many invitations from nice gentlemen, and he felt obliged to make her feel at ease.

After escorting Hélène to B-Deck, he returned to his own small tourist quarters below, on Level D. He pulled a book off the shelf and settled into a chair between the bed and the closet. His view through the porthole showed the heavy seas were continuing.

His mind kept wandering back to Hélène. She had seemed somewhat depressed when she first came on deck. Louis wondered what he could do to cheer her up. He had spoken to the Maître d', and secured a table by the orchestra.

An hour and a half later, he changed to a dark jacket and grey flannel slacks and went to the promenade deck. The bright lights cast a festive air about the saloon, although he knew that certain passengers still suffered from mal de mer in their staterooms. The sea had calmed somewhat. There was a sliver of clear sky on the horizon.

He looked around the floor and saw a few guests still with coffee and dessert plates from the first sitting. Waiters were turning tablecloths and laying out new silver for the second. He went outside for a few minutes to get some air, and determine if there was any detectable change in the temperature.

The air was fresh in his face, but the seas had subsided a little, and the long combers were not as threatening. He was on the leeward side, keeping as far from the railing as he could to avoid getting wet.

Ahead of him, he noticed a man peering through the windows into the dining room. He was dressed in a dark coat, but something about him was unsettling. The man shifted stealthly to the next window, to get a different view of the room. He was obviously trying not to be seen, and yet was very intent on the every move of the guests entering and leaving the dining room. Louis studied him carefully for a moment, and then realized, to his horror, that it was none other than M'sieur Drapeneau!

Why would Drapeneau be on board? He could only think of one answer, and it explained why the disreputable younger man was interested in Louis' departure. Drapeneau was a player in the counterintelligence game.

Louis' heart sank. There was no place for him to hide. He would be on board for at least two more days, and Drapeneau would be able to follow his every move.

Louis stepped quickly back out of the light, into an alcove. Drapeneau might know where he was, but Louis wasn't going to let him know that he knew of the European's presence. He would continue to play his chosen role, of a man on vacation, and then catch Drapeneau unaware when it came time to leave the ship.

At least Hélène's presence would add some authenticity to his guise as an ex-Army NCO on vacation.

That said, he needed to get back to the table immediately, so that Hélène would not feel he had set her up.

He turned carefully and made his way around to the windward entrance, so that Drapeneau would not know he had been seen. The wind caught Louis' hair and dampened his jacket, but he was otherwise intact when he returned to the table. Hélène had not yet arrived. Louis was grateful that a raised planter partly screened the tables next to the dance floor. At least he wouldn't have to stare directly at Drapeneau during the meal.

He had just taken his seat when Hélène appeared at the far door, chatting with the Maître d'. At first he saw only a vision, a stunning young lady with dark hair and white skin in a longish pink dress, looking over the crowd. Then she recognized him and came toward the table. He rose from his chair, acutely aware that he was one of the only passengers with someone so beautiful as his dinner guest. Many heads at other tables turned to make the connection.

"Mm'selle—vous êtes ravissant ce soir—you look extremely attractive tonight!"

She smiled at him, the first time he had seen her with a truly confident expression. He sensed her natural shyness, which likely made her uncomfortable meeting people for the first time.

Louis, himself, felt shy with her unexpected transformation. Louis began to feel much less at ease, and at the same time, more protective of this beautiful and vulnerable young woman. He had not had the same emotion for many years.

Hélène sat down and commenced the small talk typical of a schoolteacher from a young ladies' school. But Louis began worrying. Drapeneau raised a new dilemma. It might not be all that easy to dismiss the threat that he posed. If he was an intelligence agent, then how far was he willing to go to get the negatives, and the information they contained? Could Hélène herself be in danger?

Not noticing his discomfort, Hélène was chatting about the possibility of the Channel Tunnel between France and England. "My friend Zoë is all excited. She thinks it will allow many Londoners to shop in Paris—on weekends!"

"Oh, is that so?" Louis was polite, but found himself only half-listening. He was weighing the necessity of disassociating himself from Hélène, in order that she not become involved. He could not ignore the possible hostile counter-intelligence capabilities embodied in his fellow boarder. Louis had only known Martin Drapeneau since his arrival at L'Auberge des Trois Normands, a few years after Louis' retirement, but Louis had an increasingly uncomfortable feeling that perhaps Martin knew much more about Louis than he had revealed.

Hélène picked up her purse, freshening her lipstick. She paused halfway through, lowering her hand. "Is anything wrong, M'sieur Xenon?"

"Non, non, ce n'est rien, Mm'selle. I just saw a man I do not like, and find it unfortunate that he is on board."

"Oh, I am . . . sorry." Her confusion vanished with his explanation, and she returned the lipstick to her purse.

Louis brought his eyes to the young woman's face. There she was, in the absolute prime of life—and then there he was, involved in some dark and devious enterprise. It seemed a crime to trouble her any more. Even though he didn't feel like it, he felt he owed it to her to try and be as bright and gay as the occasion demanded.

The waiter arrived with their order, but Louis paid little attention to the food. Unfortunately, he found himself still worrying how he could possibly protect this young woman. Every moment they spent together they proceeded further on treacherous ground.

After dinner, they walked back to the ship's cocktail lounge, where they found comfortable chairs. The setting was more intimate, and they had less chance of interruption. Drapeneau had disappeared.

The conversation led to Hélène's childhood and her father's career. Her account of his retirement with her mother, the descriptions of the small village, and their farm with horses by the sea charmed Louis. Abruptly, she said, "Tell me about your youth in Algeria, your father's farm—what was it like?"

Louis vividly remembered the sun-drenched days in the early 70s, close to the mountains, when he visited his brother's family who kept a low profile there. There was tremendous Muslim resentment against former French colonials. To Hélène, he mentioned only the positive memories, to make his career in the army sound routine. He had no desire to have questions raised about his true experiences in Algeria, and subsequently elsewhere in Asia, as an intelligence officer for the French government.

It was almost nine-thirty when there was a lull in their conversation. The faint music in the lounge was overcome by sounds of the orchestra beginning to warm up next door. The low frequencies of the bass section reverberated through the floor.

Hélène stood up. After all the excitement, it was time to retire. Louis offered to take her back to her room.

She smiled and thanked him when they reached her door. "I had a wonderful evening, M'sieur Xenon."

"Mais non! The pleasure was all mine," Louis said. "Will I see you on deck tomorrow?"

"I have an appointment in the morning at the hair salon, but I may show up after lunch." Her eyes twinkled.

Louis bowed. "Then I will look forward very much to seeing you again, Mm'selle!"

She nodded and he departed. He was thoughtful as he retired for the evening. This was their next-to-last night onboard L'Aventure. He wondered what the morrow would bring.

SUNDAY, OCTOBER 16, 1983

Louis got up early the next morning, and went on deck for his constitutional. The sky was clear, and there was a brisk, cold breeze from the north. On his right, he was able to detect the low profile of the mainland of Labrador, and to the south, there was a land mass he presumed to be Newfoundland. A freighter, bound for Europe, was silhouetted against the coast.

Xenon took in a full draft of fresh air and swung his arms backwards and overhead to expand his chest. He cast his eyes to the southeast. The sun was rising over a low-lying bank of fog on the distant horizon. It would be a beautiful day.

He looked forward to seeing Hélène, but understood that further contact held risks. He needed to warn her, and yet not reveal anything that might prove useful to Drapeneau. If she was ignorant, then Drapeneau would see no need to use her for information.

Overnight, he had come to the conclusion he should explain to Hélène he had 'business' that extended beyond the trip north to the Péribonka. He could only hint, indirectly, that Drapeneau might be involved. By early morning on the seventeenth, they would arrive at the Port of Québec. He felt Hélène should disembark quietly from L'Aventure, as early as possible, and hurry to her flight to the Maritimes. He would tarry on board as long as possible, to keep Drapeneau pre-occupied.

The end of their voyage was at hand, and each step was critical. In spite of everything, he was eager to get back to dry land himself.

Louis spent the morning in his cabin, poring over the maps he had brought. He had to memorize a potential escape route. After the staged 'accident' on the Péribonka, he could not carry much with him besides his money belt and the negatives. He was still uncertain how to elude Drapeneau if there were any serious pursuit.

By ten, he was hungry. He went first to the breakfast buffet and then out on deck. Standing at the stern, he tossed pieces of orange peel into the sea. Alert gulls and terns swooped down to investigate the scraps bobbing in the ship's wake.

Out of the corner of his eye, Louis spotted movement behind one of the ship's large ventilation funnels. It might have just been another passenger seeking shelter from the wind, or maybe . . .

He heard a startled voice and a slight thump. "Excuse me, M'sieur."

Drapeneau's voice. Another passenger walked on deck, straightening his hat, knocked askew. Quick footsteps followed, back inside the passage to ship's quarters.

Louis waited until the slow count of three, then left the rail. He popped the last of the orange in his mouth. Now it was his turn to do the watching.

Louis entered the passageway and stopped just inside the door. There were a few other passengers about, but he didn't see Drapeneau. But no one was on the stair to his right, either. Most likely, Drapeneau also travelled tourist class.

Louis strolled down the passage. When he caught sight of Drapeneau's back, he slowed his pace. The younger European never seemed to notice Louis.

Louis followed him all the way to his quarters—on the opposite side of the ship from Louis' own. Drapeneau entered, and Louis paused. Once there was no one else in the corridor with him, he pressed his ear to the door to listen. He heard the sound of typing. His investigations of the morning were now creating even more unanswered questions. It was most disturbing.

Hélène sat in a deck chair facing the sun when Louis found her. She brightened visibly when he came into view. She had been watching a shuffleboard game, and was wearing a short-sleeved, white dress. As Louis approached, she shaded her eyes and smiled. "You made it!"

"Yes, I had a quiet morning in my cabin." Partially true, at least. "Did you sleep well?"

"Very well! It's good to get away from all that fog and those heavy ocean swells. The storm was pretty rough!"

"Bien sûr! It's turned out to be a lovely day. I wish the whole trip was like this!"

Louis pulled a deck chair next to hers. Hélène ran a hand through a lock of her dark hair. It seemed extra lustrous to him, and he noticed her perfume. She appeared in high spirits.

"I spent the morning with seven women in the Salon de Beauté. I heard all the gossip on the ship. The conversation there was mostly about the eligible men on board." She smiled winningly at him. "You scored quite highly."

Louis laughed, but was embarrassed. He hated it when people drew attention to his bachelor status. "And?" Louis reluctantly allowed her to elaborate.

Hélène's eyes sharpened. "Were you ever married? Do you have any children?"

"Mais non, Mm'selle! Why do you ask?"

"Well . . . you're quite good looking . . . I think, it would be very natural!"

"Trés naturel, bien sûr, mais . . . I once knew a girl while I was in the Army, but the distances were so great. We couldn't see each other often. She met a man from Lyon, and they got married."

Hélène made a long face, but he could see she was sympathetic. Louis felt he needed to change the subject. "Would you like to take a walk around the promenade deck?"

"Sure! Let me put on my sweater."

She took a knitted white cotton sweater from the back of the deck chair and covered her shoulders. They were in the lee of a large lifeboat, but when they stepped beyond its protection, the cool breeze from the north struck their faces. The wind had freshened from the morning. Sea gulls following the ship rose and fell in a familiar pattern in the bright sunlight. Louis could almost reach out and touch them.

"What will you do when you leave the ship?"she asked.

"Well, I'll do some sightseeing Tuesday, and Wednesday I fly to Chicoutimi on the Saguenay, where I will join my guide. We will take a float plane, with other members of the expedition, up north from there." He had planned every detail, but there were still loose ends.

Hélène stopped and turned to face Louis. "Forgive me, but you do not seem very relaxed for a vacation. Are you sure you're going to be all right?"

Louis looked at her quickly, and then away again. "Miss Vodrey, I have to tell you something. This trip to Canada is not completely about a vacation. I also have some business. You know that man I mentioned, whom I do not appreciate being on board?"

"Yes," she responded cautiously.

"I know him as Martin Drapeneau. I think he is following me. There are a few reasons why I think he could be doing so, and they lead me to believe that he may be a very dangerous man."

Hélène's face clouded.

"I want you to promise one thing when you leave this ship. Do not dawdle or try to say good-bye to me. Try to be safely on your way home, as soon as possible, tomorrow morning. I am going to stay on board until the last minute to distract him. I do not want anyone to follow you."

Hélène swallowed hard, and Louis could tell that she had serious new questions now that troubled her.

He continued: "Miss Vodrey . . . Hélène . . . please do not worry about me. I believe this man is possibly an agent of a foreign power, and is trying to interfere with information of importance to the Canadian and U.S. government." That was all she needed to know. Hopefully it wasn't too much. "If you are questioned by anyone, just say the last thing you heard from me was that I was planning a fishing trip to the upper Péribonka."

"Why didn't you tell me that you work for the Canadian government?"

"I don't—it's just some unfinished business left over from when I was in the army. I have to take care of it while I'm here."

Hélène stared out over the edge of the ship. Louis could see the thoughts turning over in her mind. "Why don't we just drop the subject and enjoy the last day of the trip?" he said. "I won't see you tomorrow."

Once more, Hélène swallowed. Perhaps she would rather just leave his presence now. He wouldn't blame her.

"Are you going back to France after your trip north?"

Louis couldn't answer. The less she knew of his plans, the better.

Her eyes widened slightly, and she nodded.

For many minutes, they stared at the wake of the ship spreading wide to the horizon. They were leaving their stormy passage from Europe further and further behind.

Louis looked down at her fine, delicate hands. The knuckles had a slight blue tinge where she gripped the railing. "You look cold!" Louis instinctively put one of his hands over hers.

Hélène smiled weakly.

"Let's go inside." Louis guided her across the promenade, to the raised threshold of the companionway door leading to B-Deck. She brushed his shoulder with hers as she stepped onto the carpeted floor. The warmth inside was welcome. They walked up a few stairs and down the hall, past staterooms and into a small lounge. It was about two o'clock. Louis paused. "Would you like some tea or coffee?"

"Actually, I've been hoping to read for a while," Hélène said. "I've found a good mystery book in the ship's library. Do you read much?"

"Yes, I do. I would like to join you, but I have preparations for tomorrow I must make. Do you have plans for dinner?" He couldn't help but ask.

"Well, it's the final evening. There is only one sitting at seven-thirty. I think it's supposed to be formal."

"It sounds like fun." Louis was tentative, but couldn't give up his last chance. "Would you like to meet again?"

"Yes, I'd like to very much." She smiled brightly at him.

"W-wonderful, Mm'selle! I'll arrange for the same table."

"I'll see you there."

Louis looked at her for a moment. He wanted to thank her for trusting him, but hesitated. Instead, he pressed her hand in his, and went down the hall toward the lounge.

"Oh, M'sieur Xenon," Hélène called after him. "By the way, you don't have to address me as 'Mm'selle' all the time; you can just call me 'Hélène', and I'll answer!"

Louis blushed and answered, "Oh, pardonnez moi! You also, Hélène, please, just call me Louis!"

She smiled at him, and softly closed her door.

Louis looked at his watch. He had forgotten that he had had no lunch. Louis hurried past the purser's office and down more stairs to his cabin on D-Deck.

He had not seen Drapeneau since the previous night, and felt ill at ease, knowing his Auberge des Trois Normands nemesis was somewhere on board. He decided to check back at Drapeneau's room for the second time.

Drapeneau's cabin was number D-23. The hall was empty. Louis stood quietly outside the door and tried to listen, over the usual vibrations from the engine room and the twin propeller shafts. Yet, once more, the intermittent sounds of someone typing a letter were the only sign the room was occupied.

What was going on? Could Drapeneau be communicating with his contacts in North America—or perhaps Europe? It was a puzzle, and Louis would have given a lot to know the answer.

He rubbed his chin, and took the connecting passage to his side of the ship. If Drapeneau was not going to show himself, then Louis would not bother to try to raise him. Louis had a lot to do before morning.

At seven-twenty, Louis went back up to the main promenade deck and the dining saloon. More passengers were showing their faces than earlier in the week. They seemed eager to get off the boat. As Hélène mentioned, the five-thirty sitting had been cancelled, to make the later event better attended and festive.

At each table, there were candles and a bottle of champagne on ice. It was not long before the guests started filling the room, and the waiters scurried around to seat the ladies. The Captain and First Mate made their appearance in white uniforms, and Louis looked around anxiously for Hélène. He soon spotted her coming from the foyer. This time her dark hair contrasted with a light blue satin gown.

She looked lovely, as before. He rose from the chair and hurried over to her side. "Pardonnez-moi, Hélène, mille fois! I forgot to get you some flowers."

"Oh Louis, it's all right. Look, I have a lovely corsage right here."

Louis saw a beautiful cluster of gardenias attached to a sash around her waist.

"Oh my, it's lovely. Where did you get it?"

"The Captain sent them around to all the ladies' state rooms shortly after you left."

"Aha!" Louis laughed. "Now I know why he's so popular."

Hélène blushed, but he hoped she understood that he was only teasing her.

They heard a tinkling of glass, and a hush spread across the room. The Captain rose at the main table, a smart figure with his tanned face and gold-encrusted white uniform. He smiled at everyone, thanking them for choosing L'Aventure. With a final 'Bonne Chance!', he lifted his glass, smiled again to them all, and sat down.

Amid the clapping, Louis' gaze passed to the guests on the Captain's right and left. Louis paused, hands poised mid-clap. Drapeneau sat at the Captain's right.

Louis clutched Hélène's hand. "Look! Do you see him?"

"Who?"

"Drapeneau! He's next to the Captain—on the right side."

"Oh, that man. He doesn't look so bad."

Drapeneau was engaging the Captain in conversation, and while they watched, the Captain and Drapeneau both laughed.

"Do not underestimate him. He is very intelligent, and always plays the part of someone low on the learning curve. That is how he catches up with you, and tries to gain your confidence. He has as much character as a snake!"

Hélène frowned. "Well, I will certainly look out for him. I don't like reptiles."

Louis smiled ruefully, and put his hand over hers to reassure her. Fortunately, their table was several yards away from the main table, and Louis and Hélène were able to turn themselves so they were no longer in direct line of sight.

The waiters brought appetizers, then soup and salad. Hélène felt the need for something light, and Louis, partial as he was to fish, chose the salmon.

Their conversation had been general, though quite formal. Hélène did a lot of staring up at Louis from across the table—he wasn't sure whether to feel pleased or embarrassed.

"You haven't told me much about your long-range goals!" she said suddenly, searching his eyes.

"Future? I don't make my plans very far ahead—and you?"

"Well, I enjoy teaching in England, but eventually I would like to get married, come back to Canada, and start a family."

"That seems fair enough." Louis winced inwardly, however. Marriage was still a sore subject for him.

The dinner, with all its courses, lasted about two hours. They engaged two other couples at a nearby table in conversation. One came from Alberta, and the other British Columbia. Both were planning to continue their trip west by VIA Rail.

As they finished coffee, Louis was surprised to note that Drape-neau had left the Captain's table, and was nowhere to be seen. Louis was wary, but, at the moment, could see no reason to leave Hélène.

The tables were being cleared and removed from the dance floor, and members of the orchestra began tuning up.

Louis asked, a bit hopefully, "Would you care to stay for the dance?"

"Yes," Hélène said with a smile. "Very much so—but, if you don't mind, I would like to freshen up first."

Louis rose, and helped Hélène with her chair. He watched as she made her way to the ladies' lounge. There was no doubt that she was beautiful. She seemed much younger than her thirty-three years.

Louis made his way past the tables to the promenade deck. A large group of men were laughing and talking by the railing as the western end of L'Ile d'Anticosti loomed low on the horizon to the south. The smell of cigarette and cigar smoke was thick, but Louis had given up tobacco when he left the Army.

He walked first toward the stern, and then to the bow. There was no sign of Drapeneau. He must have retired for the night, possibly to continue his correspondence.

The breeze outside was fresh, but chilly, and Louis was glad to go inside again. Once the orchestra struck up its theme song, there was a general rush from the promenade. Not all the music was Ameri-can. The band members were European, and Louis recognized some popular Latin tunes playing currently on Paris radio.

After wending her way through the crowd, Hélène arrived breath-lessly in the middle of the first number. "You wouldn't believe the line in the ladies' room. I'm lucky I made it out alive."

"Typical!" Louis laughed. "I don't know why they never make them large enough."

They stood side by side for a moment as Hélène placed her purse in the chair. She looked at Louis and he nodded, holding out his hand. Soon, they were in the middle of the floor, just as the first number ended. Hélène was surprisingly light in his arms. Her hair brushed against his cheek and he noted for the first time a scent of gardenia that matched her corsage. Women were most resourceful.

They danced for almost an hour, through a series of waltzes, fox-trots, polkas, and cha-cha-chas. They sat down to a booming twist.

"I've had it!" Hélène laughed, her face flushed.

"Me too. May I get you a drink?"

"Oh, Louis, I think not. Tomorrow is a big day. I better go to my room!"

"Well, I guess this is it." Louis was more than a little disappointed. "It's been a lot of fun."

"It really has." Hélène looked at Louis searchingly.

"May I escort you to your stateroom?" Louis asked.

"Yes, please do."

They walked very slowly, hand in hand, down the carpeted corridor.

"Louis?" Hélène turned to face him. "If you decide to stay in Canada for a while, after your fishing trip—if you would like to—I would really love to have you come visit my family in Nova Scotia. We live only an hour and a half north of Halifax. I think you would enjoy meeting my father."

Louis could see that this invitation from Hélène was more than just casual, and really a plea. Her eyes were bright with expectancy, and their time together had gone a long way toward dissolving his own normal tendency to shun such a relationship. He was reluctant to commit, and yet he found it hard to disappoint her.

"Hélène, it's been wonderful meeting you . . . I can't tell you what my plans are, but if they do change, or if I feel I have enough time to visit you, I will certainly call. How long will you be at home?"

"About three months. I have to return in time for the new term in mid-January."

"I should know before then. Please be patient. I'm not sure how it will work out. Do you have a telephone number where I can reach you?" Louis pulled out his little black book.

"If you need to look it up in the directory, my father's name is William Vodrey, and we live in Baggs' Inlet. The house number is on this paper. I really hope you can come." She presented him with a small card. She had obviously thought this out beforehand.

Louis was touched, and found that he did not know how to say goodbye; the young woman in front of him was so gracious and unaffected. He felt awkward, but decided to go ahead anyway. He leaned forward and kissed her cheek. "Au revoir, Hélène, be safe."

"Au revoir, Louis—Please take care of yourself too." With her eyes on his face, she placed her hand on his arm, and then closed the door.

It was over.

The morning was clear and bright. The M/V L'Aventure was already at the dock when breakfast was served. Louis went to the dining room for fruit, coffee, and a roll and returned to his room. Starting at six a.m., cargo was being unloaded from the holds, and at seven-thirty, the first passengers were allowed to start disembarking.

Noontime came and went, but Louis remained in his room. The sounds of passengers and crew in the corridors diminished and, except for occasional footsteps on the deck above, the silence of the ship took over. It was almost two-thirty before Louis ventured from his room, carrying two large suitcases. The corridor and companionway were empty.

He hoped, with all his heart, that Hélène was well on her way to Halifax before Drapeneau had a chance to go looking for her.

Louis found a taxi that took him to Château Frontenac. He would fly to Lac St. Jean and Chicoutimi early Wednesday morning.

His room on the seventh floor had a fine view of the river and the city in the waning sunlight. After taking a brief rest and freshening up, Louis decided to visit the historic streets below the hotel. They catered to the tourist trade, but Louis admitted the port had the flavour of certain districts in Le Havre. To stretch his legs, he walked along the waterfront—salt water mixing with fresh—it carried the same brackish scent of the breezes at L'Auberge des Trois Normands.

A small boîte-sous-terre on a narrow street to the west had empty tables and chairs on the sidewalk. A delicious fragrance of garlic, wine, and butter wafted toward him. He was reminded that he had not enjoyed anything substantial since breakfast, and it smelled too delicious to resist. In the dining room below, after ordering a grilled steak marinated with a cabernet and mushroom sauce, he picked up a newspaper lying on the chair next to him.

The headlines mentioned NATO, and word that Casper Weinburger was on his way to China. There was on-going editorial comment about the Soviet Union's attack on a South Korean airline. It did not sit too well with Koreans in Toronto, who demanded immediate retaliation. In protest, all Soviet flights into Canada and from Cuba were suspended. Louis sighed as he skimmed the last pages and folded the paper again. Would the unrest never end?

Just then, le steak arrived, and he set to, hungrily.

When Louis left the restaurant, it had grown quite dark; there was an afterglow in the clear sky to the west. The breeze coming off the harbour cleared his head. He walked slowly back through the narrow streets, crowded with pedestrians, and took the "funicular" to Dufferin Terrace and the hotel.

As he entered the passenger elevator to go his room, a man entered behind him and stood in the corner of the car. Louis did not pay him much attention. He looked over once when they approached the seventh floor. He caught his breath. "Drapeneau! What are you doing here?"

"Never you mind." Drapeneau pulled his right arm out from behind him, revealing a handgun he'd had tucked away. He cocked back the safety. "Keep on moving straight into your room."

Louis took a steady breath. It wasn't the first time he had had a gun pulled on him. He slowly moved to his room door, and pretended to fumble with his key at the entry. Drapeneau remained patient.

As the European followed him into the room, Louis stepped behind the door and slammed his hand down on Drapeneau's wrist. The gun discharged, but went skittering across the carpet.

Drapeneau dove toward the gun, but Louis leapt on top of him.

His opponent's head hit the bedside before rebounding off the floor. Louis had him thoroughly pinned to the ground. He wrenched Drapeneau's left arm behind his back, nearly dislocating the younger man's shoulder.

Drapeneau cried out in pain and dropped the gun, which Louis scooped up in his right hand.

"What do you think you're doing, M'sieur Drapeneau?"

The agent said nothing, gritting his teeth against the pain. He had obviously underestimated Louis' strength and experience.

"On your feet, you scum."

The younger European stood; a chore, as Louis kept a firm grip on his arm. Louis motioned him to the door.

Drapeneau hesitated long enough to return a well-aimed kick at Louis' groin.

Clutching the gun, Louis fell to floor, curled in writhing pain.

Drapeneau glanced back at him momentarily, but before Louis could shoot, ran down the hall to the fire stairs.

A bell started ringing. Someone had turned on an alarm. Louis staggered to his feet. He would have a lot of explaining to do, but it was obvious 'someone' had tried to rob him.

Hotel security was able to access videotapes of passengers in the elevator and fire stair, and determined Drapeneau was not registered at the hotel. Louis turned the gun over as evidence to the police, and paid for damage to his room.

Louis' credentials were checked, and his arrival in the port the previous day noted. Management apologized, and said they would exercise better screening procedures to prevent unregistered guests from accessing the upper floors.

Drapeneau had escaped, but now Louis was confronted with a major decision. Should he go north on the expedition to the Péribonka? Drapeneau had obviously been following him. Waiting for his chance. He had failed here, but Louis worried about Hélène. How often had Drapeneau seen her with him?

The answer was obvious to Louis. His opponent had made the first move—it was Hélène and her family who needed protection now.

Early the following morning, Louis contacted the tour guide office in La Baie and cancelled his flight to Chicoutimi. There was a cancellation fee for both, but it was a price he was willing to pay.

Then he went to Barclays, and drew out a sum for his expenses during the next weeks. A travel bureau at the Frontenac had a schedule of train service to Halifax, but the next one would not get him there for two days.

Dismayed, he began looking at plane schedules, and found a departure at Québec Airport for twelve-fifteen p.m. That would give him time to call Hélène, and give her a bit of warning as to his change of plans.

Despite the dire circumstances that drove him, Louis felt like a weight had been lifted from him as he reached for the telephone.

11

Hélène sat on a large stone, watching the water rush back and forth between rough pebbles on the small beach below the bluff. It was a quiet place, out of sight from the farm or any other human habitation. It was almost a quarter mile from the horse pastures of her home, down a rough path lined with wild roses all the way to the stony shore. The gentle wash of the salt tide was soothing to her soul.

She had been home for only a day, but was already adjusting to the rhythm of her parents' life. Her dad still liked to get up at six o'clock and spend time in the barn with the animals and farm equipment. Her mother would make the beds after breakfast, and do a little cleaning before settling down. If it were harsh weather, she would read or sew; if it were pleasant, she would go outside to spend her morning in the garden or take the Percheron mare for a brief canter across the fields.

Before lunch, once or twice a week, her parents would drive to Sheet Harbour to get groceries and the mail, or go to the hardware store. Her parents were running just such errands today. Since the morning was sunny and warm, Hélène sought the fresh air coming off the ocean.

In spite of the joy of seeing her parents again after almost a year, and re-bonding with her beloved horses, she was struck by a strange new sense of dissatisfaction, which had not even taken form until she disembarked from the M/V L'Aventure. Where was she going with her life? She enjoyed teaching at the Brackley School, but was it a dead-end job? In spite of her good friends, she did not want to spend the rest of her life there. Was it time to move on?

She sat for a long time, tossing stones into the small wavelets that came ashore. She did not know if it was a question of depression, or just feeling sorry for herself, but she was not sure which way to turn. The brief contact with Louis had given her a taste of something new, the companionship that might be possible between two people. Each could share the past, the present, and hopes for the future. Was that what she was missing? Her heart ached for an answer.

The simple rhythms of the ocean, the warmth of the sun, the fresh salt breeze coming up the coast, and the quiet beauty of the rocks and fir trees in that place, began, slowly, to calm her fears and restore certainty. Her life so far had been eventful and happy. She would not change any of its details, even if some were painful. It was her life, and she had to make the most of it. The shadows from the bluff above swung gradually around so that the flat stone on which she was sitting moved from sun to shade. She remained for a while, but the cool breeze off the ocean became uncomfortable, and she rose to stretch her legs. She walked up the beach to where waves splashed against a rocky ledge jutting out into the water, and then turned down to a pile of driftwood that had come in on winter storms. She noticed a small white skiff anchored near the far shore.

She turned back to the stony path, winding up to the fields above. The sun-warmed rocks provided shelter from the breeze. The scent of wild rose, bayberry, sea heather, and juniper alternately filled the air.

From the top of the bluff, she could see the barns and greying clapboard walls of the house three fields away. Candy and Jet, two of her parents' horses, grazed not far from her path. When she held it out, Candy came over and nuzzled her hand for a lump of sugar. Hélène paused to pat and smooth her chestnut flank.

Walking back through lush fields, from gate to gate, she reached the farmyard just as her mother and father arrived in the Jeep Laredo. They smiled at her, expectantly.

"Did you have a nice morning, dear?" He mother asked.

"Yes, I spent it on the beach until I got cold." Hélène helped pull some of the groceries from the Jeep. "There's a white skiff anchored across from us on the opposite shore. Do you know who they are?"

Her father answered, "I think they are a couple who've bought some property on the peninsula. They like to go exploring."

Hélène started to help her mother prepare lunch when the phone rang. She picked it up. A man's voice asked for "Miss Hélène Vodrey." It sounded so familiar . . .

"Louis?"

"Oh, hello Hélène! I thought you were your mother."

"Louis! I-I didn't expect to hear from you so soon. How are you?" She fiddled with the cord on the phone, purposefully ignoring her mother's raised eyebrows.

"Well, not so good, Hélène; I had to cancel my trip to the Péribonka."

"Oh, how sad, Louis. What happened?"

"A change in plans. I will have to go to New Hampshire on the twenty-sixth."

Hélène's breath caught for a moment. Then it all came out in a rush. "Well, why don't you come here?"

"That would be very nice." His agreement was immediate. Was that why he was calling? Had he wanted to come see her so badly? She had thought it a slim chance when she had handed him her parent's number. Her heart bubbled up into her throat.

"Yes, I'll ask my parents—just wait one minute." She put her hand over the speaker. "Mum, I met this very nice man on the boat coming over. I invited him to visit us in November, but now he's had a change of plans and can come right away. Would you and Dad mind if he came now?"

William and Marie shared a look. Hélène knew it was because she had rarely brought home any male visitors. Normally, she would have felt embarrassed, but she was just too excited. And didn't she deserve to enjoy someone's company once in a while? She was thirty-three, after all.

William smiled, and Marie nodded. "Please tell him he's very welcome," her mother said.

Hélène spoke again, "That will be wonderful, Louis, when will you arrive?"

"I can take a flight to Halifax that lands at three p.m., Atlantic Time."

"Great, Louis, we can plan on supper at home! I'll see you at the airport!"

They hung up. All the anxiety she had been experiencing had disappeared. Her heart sang.

Her mother paused in her preparations. "Hélène, you look so different. Who is Mr. Xenon?"

"Oh Mother, he's a very nice gentleman, whom I met on our voyage from Europe. He's French, from Le Havre. I think you and Dad will like him a lot."

Louis took his handbag and exited the DeHavilland twin turboprop plane along with the other forty-seven passengers. The overcast afternoon sky was a welcome sight. He walked to the arrivals lobby while the baggage handlers unloaded freight from the plane's storage compartment. He had brought warm clothing, but most of his gear was left at the Frontenac, pending his return on the 26th.

As he approached the exit gate, a slight figure stepped forward, and he recognized her.

"Hélène!"

"Louis!" She rushed forward and he kissed her lightly on the cheek.

"Did you have a long wait for the plane?"

"No, I just arrived. I drove direct from the coast."

Louis was surprised again at her youthful grace and the excitement in her hazel eyes.

"And how are your parents?"

"They're both fine, and can't wait to meet you. Would you like to get something before we head back to the inlet?"

"That would be great. For some reason, I'm having difficulty getting the engine noise out of my head."

They went to the cafeteria, where Louis ordered an iced cola for himself and Hélène. He found a table for two near the front and helped her remove her coat. She was dressed in tan corduroy slacks and a mixed brown leather and corduroy jacket. Her dark hair, gathered in the back, was complemented by a plum-coloured turtleneck jersey.

"So, you flew in safely yesterday morning?" He smiled at her, trying not to show his concern. "Tell me, Hélène, did you have any trouble getting home to Baggs' Inlet? I was really worried about you."

"No Louis, none, but I did feel a little let-down once I got home. It was after the excitement of the trip. You'll see what I mean when you get to the farm. It's very quiet here."

"Believe me, Hélène, I'm looking forward to it. I can use some peace and quiet."

Hélène paused at this. "What happened with your trip to the Péribonka?"

"Oh, I just . . . didn't plan for all the contingencies, it seems." He didn't want to go into details and worry Hélène. If she hadn't seen any sign of Drapeneau, all the better.

"Contingencies?" She stared up at him, not easily dissuaded.

"Well . . ." Louis sighed, giving in. "It was my friend, M'sieur

Drapeneau. He was not too happy, and we did not part on good terms."

"Are you in trouble?"

"No, but he is! Be very careful if you ever see him." Louis paused. "In fact, I hope you never do."

Hélène gave a worried frown at this, but didn't push the subject.

Louis paid for their sodas, and they went to the parking lot. They stowed his bag in the Jeep Laredo, and Louis noted dirt on the fenders. They were headed out into the country for certain.

It was almost one hundred thirty kilometres through the heart of the peninsula to the farm, mostly inland, with occasional glimpses of fresh water lakes.

Driving into Baggs' Inlet, Louis could see that it was more a hamlet than a village. Only one small dock and four or five homes at the head of the inlet were visible, with several farms peeking over the hills on higher ground.

Once off the main highway, Hélène drove the Jeep on a sandy road through low coastal reed grass, beach heather, bayberry and sand willow wetlands; over juniper, cedar, and scotch pine forested crests and gullies, and finally up a steep gravel driveway to the farmhouse itself. The buildings had a warm, lived-in look, offering shelter to those that sought it.

Near the end of a fir-mantled promontory with lush grassy meadows, the Vodrey farm was situated with beautiful views of the inlet and ocean. A dirt road stretched past it to low woods overlooking the mouth of the waterway. Louis could not imagine a more isolated spot.

"The winters here are not too pleasant, but Mom and Dad love the privacy, and the chance to live their own lives away from the city."

With grassy meadows still green and neatly mowed, there was a sense of order and care about the place. It was early afternoon when they arrived and low, cloudy skies were threatening showers before evening.

"Let me show you our horses before we go inside." Hélène said excitedly.

Louis left his bags in the Jeep, and they walked over to a door at the back of the run-in shed next to the fenced pasture. Louis noticed the fresh, dry straw on the floor and the smooth corners of the wood doorframe where the animals had rubbed off sharp edges. Two chestnut Arabians and a black Percheron were in the lower field on the bluff above the water's edge.

"Which one is yours?"

Hélène's eyes brightened. "The smaller Arabian on the left—her name is Candy. My father's is George, the large gelding, and my mother's is Jet, the Percheron mare. We keep them here year-round. The grass is wonderful for them."

Louis could see copper strands in Hélène's dark hair reflected from a bright spot low in the southwestern sky. There was love in her eyes for the three swift-footed creatures.

They bolted the barn door and turned toward the house. Louis retrieved his bags from the back of the Jeep, and followed Hélène up the path from the driveway. She knocked on the door and a small woman with grey hair and a warm smile opened it a moment later.

"I was watching you when you drove in," she said with a sparkle in her eye. "How are you, M'sieur Xenon? Welcome to the Vo-drey Farm."

Louis smiled broadly. It was interesting to see the daughter's like-ness in her mother. She wore a printed, blue cotton dress under a cable-stitched white pullover. Her hands were red and damp from scrubbing vegetables for dinner.

"Oh, please call him Louis, Mother. We want him to feel at home." Hélène hung her jacket in the hall closet and took Louis' overcoat from him.

"You have a beautiful farm here, Mrs. Vodrey. It reminds me very much of the west coast of Brittany."

"Yes, m'sieur. I was born near Brest, and we lived in Dieppe, until

I met my husband."

"Oh, did you? Now I know why you like being near the sea."

"Yes, I met William toward the end of the war—that was a long time ago." She paused a moment and then continued with a smile, "The guest room is upstairs in the back. You'll have a nice view of the ocean from the window. There is a small lavatory at the beginning of the hall, and there are guest towels hanging on the door. Hélène, why don't you show Louis upstairs?"

Louis manoeuvred his suitcases up the two bends in the narrow staircase, following Hélène. The shiny paint on the treads reflected light from the dining room.

The perfume of hand soap in the lavatory permeated the second floor hallway. There were storage closets flanking a long, hand-tied rag runner extending to a low doorway at the end.

"This used to be a pilot's house in the 1800s, when people were shorter." Hélène laughed, and opened the door to the guest room.

They stood there, the light impact of raindrops on the roof and the ever-present moan of wind at the windows breaking the silence. The ceiling sloped to conform to the roofline, and through curtains, Louis could see grey mist and rainsqualls coming off the ocean. The water was rough, with white caps where the waves entered the inlet.

Louis placed his bags on top of an old trunk and admired the hand-woven coverlet at the foot of the bed.

Hélène had her hand on the bedpost. There was a soft halo of light around her head from the lamp in the hall. At that moment, Louis felt like he was on the edge of a swiftly moving stream. He glanced at Hélène's trusting eyes. He wanted to sweep her into his arms.

"Hélène?"

"Don't say it." She put her fingers on his lips. Louis held her close. Her perfumed hair pressed against the weathered stubble of his cheek.

They were quiet and listened as the wind drove patterns of rain across the wooden shingles. Louis took Hélène's hands. "I'm glad you invited me to meet your family."

She gazed at him for a long time, and Louis could see tears in her eyes.

"Me too," she said. "I'm so glad you've come."

"Children, it's time to get ready for dinner!" Mrs. Vodrey's voice interrupted from downstairs.

They smiled, and went downstairs to join Mrs. Vodrey.

William Vodrey came inside a moment later through the kitchen door, and washed his hands in the sink. Louis could see from the hall he was short, but powerfully built. He had a cheerful manner and, when Hélène introduced him, a strong handshake. Louis liked him immediately.

They sat down around the oval table in the dining room. It was crowded, with Marie Vodrey's best china on linen placemats. As Louis looked from mother to father to daughter, a feeling he had not known for many years overcame him; he felt like he was in a home.

After two helpings of the delicious boeuf bourguignon, Louis had to push himself away from the table. The conversation brought out Mr. Vodrey's experience during WWII as a captain of a vessel in the British Coast Guard, and later as a pilot in the merchant marine. Marie Vodrey told some funny stories about her village when the Allies first arrived.

After coffee and fruit trifle, and a few more stories of life in France and North America, Louis could barely keep his eyes open.

"You look sleepy, Louis." Mrs. Vodrey said.

"I didn't rest very well on the plane, and I guess it's catching up with me." He certainly didn't want to mention the activities of the previous evening.

"Well, it's probably time for all of us to go to bed. You've had a big day, Louis. Hélène, do you think eight-thirty is a good time for breakfast?"

"Sounds fine with me. Louis?"

"Très bien, merci!"

His warm comforter and soft pillow were in sharp contrast to the flight from Québec City. He remembered a faint pine fragrance pervading the room and the glow of a nightlight, but that was all.

In the morning, he woke to the sound of pans rattling in the kitchen, and the savoury smell of bacon. It was a signal to get up.

Fog and a light drizzle outside kept the sky grey. Through the window, he noticed bands of silver in the lower pasture where the grass was holding moisture. Louis saw a slight figure moving toward a chestnut coloured Arabian at the edge of the bluff. It was Hélène, in a waterproof jacket, talking to her horses—a quiet, pastoral scene that Louis held close to his heart.

For the next several days, Louis slept late in the morning and went to bed early. Hélène showed him all her favourite places and, when the weather was sunny, they would walk, read, or just chat. She even convinced him to ride Jet (with her mother's permission) out to the rocky point where the Atlantic met the mouth of the inlet.

Fun bubbled up wherever he went with Hélène. At low tide they searched among the rocks for seaweed and harbour seals. They laughed when the surf grew high with the incoming tide. Louis was impressed with the power of the waves. Somehow, they were different from those on the coast of France. It may have been the light, the temperature, or the fresh smell of the pine forest mixed with the bayberry, peat, and grasses of that windswept place. Something primordial and untouched attracted him, and he began to understand the urge that drove Europeans to endure great hardships to come to the new continent.

The two were turning to leave, when suddenly the bow of a freighter, miles up the coast, emerged from beyond the far side of the narrow inlet.

"That ship is specially equipped to carry liquid wood pulp to Japan," Hélène explained. "It's cheaper to make the paper over there."

In the afternoon, they reversed course and rode the few miles on the winding dirt and sand road to the head of the inlet. A few of the farms had more paint on their buildings than others, but white was the colour of choice. Again, the smell of the spruce and pine was perfume to Louis' senses.

When they reached the tiny dock, they noticed a few small dinghies tied to the pilings. There was only one sailboat at anchor in the small harbour, and it was battened-down with tarps against the breeze and cold weather.

"There won't be many sailing days left this year!" Hélène said, brushing the hair away from her face. "It gets too cold, even for the fishermen who can stand a lot; although, there are still some trawler fleets that go out year-round. It's a tough life for them."

Atop their horses, Louis and Hélène stared the length of the inlet to the wide ocean beyond, drawn by the ceasless sound of waves against the shore.

The following two days, Louis helped William Vodrey re-fence one of the two pastures bordering on the forest. Mr. Vodrey had cleared the land during the summer to expand the pasture and sell some of the lumber to a local sawmill. It was not a large area, but the farmers were in a constant battle to reclaim land taken out of production. It rapidly became overgrown and reverted to woodland. It was remarkable that this coastline had been populated and cultivated for centuries, and yet the mark of man still remained indistinct.

MONDAY, OCTOBER 24, 1983

A number of days later, Louis awoke abruptly in a cold sweat. He had a strong sense of foreboding, like something had gone terribly wrong. Was it some event in the past that was returning to haunt him—possibly from the years he had spent in Algeria? Was it a premonition of some evil to take place in the future?

He remembered the cries of innocent villagers as the army searched for terrorists outside Algiers—he hated to recall the experience. A dark emptiness surrounded him in the room. In spite of all the past happy days at Baggs' Inlet, he could not shake the feeling. He lay in bed, unsettled, trying to rationalize and control his emotions until daybreak.

The experience stuck with him as he prepared to leave his bedroom in the morning. It left him sober and ill-at-ease. He busied himself with preparations for his departure the next day, but it did nothing to improve his mood.

For a while, he debated whether to include the pistol in his rucksack, but finally, reluctantly, decided against it. He had not had the chance to apply for a permit that would allow him to take it across the border, and the immigration authorities and police might not prove to be sympathetic to his situation. He would have to take a chance and go without it.

Really, Drapeneau would have to have extraordinary resources to be able to pin-point Louis' location now. Was there really any point in trying to pass undetected into the United States? Louis thought not, but to be sure, he would try to carry a very low profile. He had already obtained a tourist visa to visit the U.S. before he left France. It seemed best to take a flight back to Québec, and then bus it from there. He had in mind to purchase a bicycle for the last miles to the Jason Head region near the White Mountain National Forest. He took his warmest clothes, preparing to camp outdoors if necessary.

The weather had turned colder again, and there was a threat of snowfall in the mountains. He needed to think of purchasing matches and dehydrated food to sustain himself in case of emergency. From what he had heard, some New England villages had no stores of any kind, and that meant securing provisions in advance.

Saying goodbye to Hèlène and her family was the toughest part of all.

Hélène and Louis made their way eastward through the heart of the peninsula, over a twisting, two-lane road toward Enfield. The farmland, covered with light snow, was beautiful, and the spruce and fir plantations stretched for miles. Understanding how the economy worked was going to be one of Louis' challenges in this new land. Already, he was starting to consider the possibility of applying for a work permit to prolong his stay.

Hélène was largely silent on the trip, and Louis looked at her several times to see if she was happy. She seemed to be trying to hide it from him, but as they drew closer and closer to the airport, he came to the conclusion that she was not.

This was unexpected, and he struggled for the reason. He was sure he had been trying to do the right thing for her, but perhaps he had over-intellectualized it all. Perhaps he had been too logical, thinking more of the process and himself than of Hélène. He felt, somehow, she seemed to be missing the spontaneity that she had expected and hoped for in their deepening relationship.

They were approaching a village and he noticed a small sign advertising 'The Victorian Cottage: Lunches 11:00 a.m. – 3:00 p.m.'

He decided now was a good time to speak up. "The plane isn't scheduled to depart until quarter after two. Should we stop here for a bite?"

Hélène seemed to cheer up a little at the prospect.

The tiny restaurant was next to a small, unfrozen pond with sloping lawns leading down to steps that parted a crescent of shrubbery close to the water. Two cars were already parked in front of the inn.

They were welcomed into the cozy dining room by the hostess, who was also the owner. She showed them seats for two next to windows overlooking the pond and gave them the luncheon menu. Both their meals were surprisingly good. They took coffee afterwards.

Louis stretched out his large hand and covered Hélène's. "I want you to know, I've had a really wonderful time staying at your home with you and your parents. You have made me feel most welcome. Whatever happens in these next weeks—you should know that I have really appreciated it."

"But Louis! Is—is anything wrong?" She looked up at him with worried eyes.

"No, no, certainly not," he said. "Unfortunately, we live in a very difficult and dangerous world. We cannot act irresponsibly; each of us have certain duties to perform. But earnestly, I believe, that in between, we are supposed to experience the free and simple beauty of life, which is also always there; I want very much to spend that time with you."

Hélène nodded slowly as he spoke, but still appeared uncertain. Liquid glistened in her eyes, as if she was holding something back. "I'm sorry; I don't think I know what you mean." The tremor in her voice turned the statement into a question.

Louis reached into the inner pocket of his coat and brought out a small, heart-shaped locket on a fine gold chain. "This was my mother's. She died shortly after the war. I'm sure she would approve me giving it to you. It is part of a promise."

Hélène gasped. Her hand was shaking. A silent tear had started down her cheek, but her face lit up from within. "Louis? Are you sure?"

"With all my heart, Hélène; I want you to have it." He leaned across the table to help her with the clasp.

Twenty-five minutes later, they were in Enfield at the Halifax International air terminal. The Jeep was standing next to a noisy land cruiser. Diesel fumes enveloped them as the driver and an attendant unloaded bags from the storage compartment for arriving passengers. Louis put his arms around Hélène's long coat and kissed her. They stood for a full minute, each reluctant to part. He knew he was facing danger.

Before he left, Hélène asked him, "When will I see you again?"

"I can't say, Hélène; this next part of my visit may be difficult. As soon as I find my way clear, I'll give you a call. Remember, if you ever encounter anyone who looks like Drapeneau, avoid him at all cost." He was sad to have to say it, but it was necessary.

Louis pressed her hand to his lips and waved to her as he went inside. Hélène had tears running unchecked down her cheeks now; he hoped they were of happiness.

From inside, he watched her drive the Jeep back onto the highway. As she faded from sight, Louis made his way, reluctantly, to the flight departure gate.

12

Louis shook the snow out of his socks as he sat on a fallen tree trunk near the highway, east of North Godwin, New Hampshire. He had manhandled his bike off the road to the edge of the woods, and was contemplating a snow-covered lane a mile or so up through the fields to the trailhead above. He would have to hide the bike and proceed on foot. He had not expected the snow so soon, and wondered how it would affect his climb to the rendezvous almost twelve hundred metres above the valley floor.

He had spent the night in Benton, at a small inn on the outskirts of the village. The proprietress had smiled when she saw the rucksack tied over the saddlebags on the back of his machine.

"You're a brave man to be venturing out at this time of year in a rig like that."

Louis responded, "C'est naturel, but what can I say? Of course one must go where one must go." and he had smiled back at her.

After a decent breakfast, Louis had set off again. The roads were clear, and even this morning he had made good progress. A certain amount of slush on the road was melting fast, but there were about fifteen centimetres of new, wet snow in the fields. He was glad that the day of his meeting with Craig Durrand had finally come. He did not wish winter to be fully established before he finished his mission.

He thought again of the dark dream he had experienced at Baggs' Inlet. The war in Algeria still haunted him, but the morning light and fresh air of the mountains today helped push bad memories into the background.

He put on a clean pair of long, dry, heavy wool socks from his pack and tucked them around his pant legs to just below the knee. He was wearing only a light jacket, because he knew his exertions would have him perspiring in no time when he started climbing.

The pack was heavy. If Craig was delayed, it contained extra sweaters, cap, gloves and food rations he might need.

He had not traveled far up the lane before he decided that two poles would be handy for stability in climbing. He cut saplings and trimmed them to length. He thanked his lucky stars that he had not let his physical condition deteriorate too rapidly in his retirement.

He reached the trailhead about a hundred fifty metres above the highway. An opening from the upper fields allowed a backward glimpse at the village of North Godwin. A narrow path with signs was visible across the clearing, and he made his way in that direction. The sun was out, and, in the field of bright snow, he felt as if he was in the Atlas mountains of his youth. After quickly checking the USGS map in his case, he followed the path and began climbing up through the maple and beech hardwoods.

Two hours later, the trail broke out of the forest. For the first time, Louis was able to appreciate the panorama before him. With the much higher summits of the Presidential Range to the east, and the Green Mountains of Vermont some eighty kilometres to the west, he began to understand why 'New Englanders' were such a hardy breed.

He had been labouring hard. The fresh snow here was over thirty centimetres deep, and the surface was powdery in the colder temperatures. The air seemed thin, and he had to stop every few moments to catch his breath. Although the sun was out, snow weighed down the branches of balsam fir, spruce, and juniper, and plastered the face of aspen and birch saplings on either side of him.

The trail was indistinct at times in the lower woods, and he had to back-track more than once around snowy thickets and over fallen tree trunks. His boots were still dry, but the heavy wool socks he wore were coated with snow up to his knees.

The white peaks of the Presidential Range arranged themselves in succession some forty to fifty kilometres away. Their white caps showed distinctly the limit of forestation on each. Louis knew he had a way to go. The trail curled up to the timberline, and then onto an exposed saddle. Once there, he would have to double back to a small pond, some distance off the trail, to the grid mark he had made on the map.

It occurred to him that this entire adventure was a reckless enterprise, with such tenuous lines of communication. What if Craig was not at the rendezvous as planned? What if the grid coordinates were in error? What if?

He paused on the mountainside, struggling with his doubts. His entire life had been filled with risk. Craig Durrand had taken a major risk in giving him the negatives. Louis had only heard limited details of Craig's subsequent capture, but had been delighted to receive the first postcard from him, to learn that he was now safe.

Even his new friendship with Hélène was a gamble. If he pursued the relationship much further, it could require a major change in lifestyle and goals. Old habits would have to be supplanted by a new concern for another's well-being. A life together would become a shared responsibility. He wondered how she would think about such matters.

These thoughts filled his mind as he turned once more to the trail. He would have to be careful. As trees grew scarce, trail blazes were less frequent, and it would be easy to wander off in the wrong direction.

Up to this point, the weather had been perfect, but he worried about a distant bank of clouds looming in the north-west. He climbed over a series of ledges as the terrain became more open. The vista of the two snow-covered peaks that made up the summit, one slightly higher than the other, was a breath-taking sight. Only an occasional scrub fir or low-lying juniper now found shelter in the lee of the large granite outcroppings. Snowdrifts, in places, were waist deep. Clouds now filled the whole horizon. It soon became overcast, with light snowflakes beginning to fall.

Near the saddle, he found a trail marker on a post, almost buried by snow. He saw that his path branched at right angles from the trail that continued to the far peak. There were no other landmarks. It was still late morning, but the wind had risen and he was eager to find shelter. He faced away from the stiff breeze and referred to his map again. Two small ponds lay about a quarter mile to the south. The rendezvous was at a point beyond a ridge, rising to the west of the upper pond.

Passing through the saddle itself, the terrain closed in to form a small valley, with stunted birch and poplar nestling in the hollows. The sky darkened; the snow fell in earnest now. He could barely see the upper slopes beyond each side of the trail. Below, to his right, the dim outline of the surface of the small pond formed a flat depression in the snow.

He was deciding which way to skirt it, when a shot rang out. A bullet whizzed by his ear. He instinctively dropped full-length into the snow.

Would this be a deer hunter, firing off at random movement? Or, worse, was it someone trying to intercept him and the negatives? Vivid scenarios started playing through his head. He regretted not having his pistol, but it was far too late for self-blame. He waited quietly, for what seemed a half hour, but there was no follow-up.

He got cautiously to his feet, and proceeded down the trail—much more alert this time. A dark cliff rose close to the pond on the right. He circled the pond to the left, where hummocks of reeds bent over with snow. He hoped enough ice had formed to prevent him from getting his feet wet. He found no footprints. Perhaps it had been just a hunter, his shot travelling farther than expected.

The rise to the west of the pond was covered thickly with pine and spruce, and though the canopy formed a degree of shelter, the slope of the grove was steep.

He struggled for a hundred yards, his heavy rucksack a burden. The poles were of no use, because he was on hands and knees as often as his feet. He finally abandoned them. He hoped against hope that John would be there when he arrived, because he had put every ounce of strength into reaching the rendezvous on time.

It was close to noon. At the top of the rise, the grove thinned, and a stand of beeches surrounded a clearing that contained an old log structure. The cabine. He had made it. The front porch faced the glen.

As Louis entered the clearing, a new shot rang out. A stabbing, burning sensation tore at his upper right arm. He grabbed it with his left glove, and a warm, dark sticky substance covered the fingertips.

He stooped down, instinctively. This was more than just some hunter. He had to get to shelter. He looked about him as he ran to the porch. Though the door appeared locked, he found the hasp and staple loose and was able to enter and close it behind him. He had to secure his position. Neither shot had been deadly, and from the echo, they were taken at long range. But how long would it take for his mysterious shooter to arrive? A numbing pain began to replace the burning sensation in his right arm. He could not move his fingers or elbow. He had to act quickly.

There were two small windows on either side of the only door.

He put two benches in front of one to protect against a shot from outside, and tried to move the table against the other; it was too heavy for him to lift. Instead, he pushed it against the door.

Drops of blood followed him on the planked wood floor. He couldn't feel anything from that arm anymore. He had to stop the bleeding. The wound was mid-way on his upper right arm, and it was hard to get compression on the injury. He bundled a pair of socks from his rucksack, but needed something to hold them down. A quick glance about the room indicated there was nothing suitable. His own belt would have to do. Placing the socks directly over the wound, he cinched the belt tight enough to apply constant pressure. He was all thumbs trying to use his left hand, but it seemed to help.

He situated himself so he could look out the unblocked window. The snow was swirling and the sky was darker. He couldn't see far. What if this unknown marksman went after Craig? How could he warn him in time?

Minutes passed, and it seemed that conditions were worsening. No one came to the cabin. Was the shooter gone, or just waiting? Who was it that shot at him? Could it have been Drapeneau? But no, how could he have followed him? Would he have the coordinates?

Running his mind in circles wasn't helping. He fumbled in his pack for rations. It was a difficult process because of his bad arm. He considered a fire. There was dry kindling, but not enough logs for warmth, and it was far too dangerous to go out searching for firewood. Even if he had the energy.

He found old army blankets on cots in the bunkroom, and wrapped himself in them. He was already shaking. Louis recognized the symptoms of shock, and knew they were taking hold.

He had little choice for now. He would have to wait until morning unless Craig made it safely. If not, he might have to try to make his own way back to the village. If he could.

Louis loosened the belt and felt the wound. There was no sensation in his arm, except general aching numbness. Blood still oozed easily from his injury, so he retightened the belt a little.

He felt much weaker, with a growing sense of nausea. He would have to lie down. Again, he tried to wedge the table against the door; there was no real protection. In weakness and desperation, he pulled a mattress off a narrow cot and lay down by the fireplace. The pain came in waves. His shivering finally merged with utter exhaustion, and he lost consciousness.

FRIDAY, OCTOBER 28, 1983

John left Buckingham, Pennsylvania, for the White Mountains at seven-thirty on Friday morning. He drove his station wagon, which seemed more suitable for New Hampshire than the Porsche. The weather was unpredictable in the North Country. The forecast for New England was for light snow throughout the day. New Hampshire had several inches of snow already earlier in the month. He took warm clothing, boots, a rucksack, and cross-country skis in case the weather deteriorated.

He had reservations at the White Mountain Inn for the entire weekend. He did not know how Col. Xenon would feel, once the negatives were passed to Greenstone. He imagined the Colonel might want to travel, or do some sight-seeing—John would remain flexible on any account.

John wanted to be on the mountain in good time the next day to welcome the friend he had not seen since Phnom Penh. He knew the Major had been promoted to Lt. Colonel in recognition of his brave duty in the Cambodian capital. Xenon had put his own life in danger to ensure that as many French nationals as possible were evacuated from the city before the Khmer-Rouge took control

John reserved an adjoining room for Xenon on the second floor of the south wing, and spent most of the evening going over papers he brought from his office in Buckingham. He would drive over to Cauley in the early morning, to reach the cabin by noon.

He was discouraged next morning to find the access road from Cauley to the trailhead almost impassible. The new snow on the south side of the mountain was deeper than he expected. What if Xenon encountered difficulties approaching the rendezvous? He hoped the Frenchman could make it.

John drove the station wagon as close to the trailhead as seemed safe, but had to stop well short of the damaged bridge. He noticed Mark's abandoned VW, buried in snow, and he parked next to the road near the stream. The reality of Mark's trauma hit home, and reminded him to be on his guard. By now, Mark would be back home in Boston. John made a mental note to hire a tow truck to retrieve the VW, and have it serviced in West Cauley.

Considering all that had taken place, Mark had done very well. Garrett Bennett, through Dr. Vanderstadt, was able to confirm that Gelda went missing about twenty hours before Mark was brought to Queboggin, giving an adequate time lapse for the girl to appear at the camp. The doctor had received no other word from his daughter. Mark had given John his second report earlier in the week, verifying that the camp was abandoned, with the exception of the light plane still left in the hangar. Authorities determined the plane left Lebanon, New Hampshire on the day Mark himself was kidnapped. John had already forwarded the plane's log book to Bennett.

The most interesting thing Mark had turned up was some evidence on the recent occupancy of the camp. A ballpoint pen with the words 'INS Manitoba – Winn.' had left Dr. Vanderstadt very excited. He was almost certain that Gelda had picked up the pen when she briefly visited his Winnipeg laboratory over the Canadian Thanksgiving weekend.

Garrett told John he had ordered the two kidnapping investigations to be quietly coordinated at the level of the National Defence Department, so that the maximum amount of information could be gathered before the media was alerted. The pen was being analyzed in a government lab, and a special forensic team was sent to the site to look for other evidence. The New Brunswick RCMP were alerted to gather information on 'persons of interest' in a black Chrysler town car.

And to think, it had all started on this mountain. By ten, John had climbed well up the trail on his skis, and could begin to see some of the Green Mountains of Vermont in the distance to the west. Only a very few trees retained their leaves. It had been a beautiful, clear morning so far, but he noticed an approaching front on the northwest horizon.

In another three-quarters of an hour, he reached a large rockslide with ledges above. This part was difficult in any weather, but impossible on skis. He took them off, and, threading the poles through the ski bindings, managed to drag the skis behind with one hand while climbing with the other. The process was clumsy, and took a while to negotiate the icy ledges, but eventually he reached the top.

It was eleven am. The sun was behind clouds and the sky growing darker—the front was moving in fast. Wind from the northwest strengthened, and soon heavy snow began to fall in earnest. In the distance, John heard the crack of a rifle. He wasn't sure hunting was allowed in this area, but deer season was only three weeks away.

He re-fastened his ski bindings, and thirty minutes later was approaching the lower end of the passage to the saddle. He heard a second report, nearer this time. John grew concerned. Could it be a coincidence? But the nagging knowledge that someone might know the location of the rendezvous encouraged him to remove his handgun and tuck it within easy reach. He picked up the pace.

Soon, he encountered fresh footprints in the snow. Someone had crossed the trail in a hurry, toward Jason Gorge, from the direction of the spruce grove. The tracks were well below the normal path from the pond; the rapidly falling snow hadn't yet filled them in. Had Col. Xenon missed the rendezvous point, and wandered down the mountain? Or could it be someone else?

The Gorge trail was a tough choice in winter. He shook it off. Yet, suspicion aroused, John proceeded warily. He would have to consider all options. The cabin was first. If Xenon was there, then all was well and good. But if not, he could come back down and follow the tracks to the gorge.

He skied through deep snow as far as the pond, and was relieved to find prints with pole marks, almost filled with snow, coming toward him down the open slope from the pass. They headed up through the grove toward the cabin. John had little doubt that the Frenchman had arrived. Hopefully he was still there, and hadn't moved down the gorge.

He traversed back and forth up the slope through the spruces, and in a few minutes reached the clearing. The Colonel had abandoned his walking sticks, but his track led directly to the cabin. John was thrilled at the prospect of seeing his friend again.

Brushing snow from his parka, he shouted, "Hello, Colonel! Are you in there?" There was no answer. Stacking his skis on the porch, he noted the broken lock on the door. Mark had mentioned such from the break-in. "Colonel, are you okay?" Still no answer. Worry rose in John's chest.

He tried the door, but something blocked it from the other side. At his first attempt, he could only budge it an inch, but applying his full weight, he was able to squeeze inside.

The room was dark. John noticed benches blocking one of the windows. Then he saw the Colonel, sprawled near the hearth on a mattress. A pool of blood stained the floor and mattress cover. "Oh my God! You've been shot."

The Colonel was unresponsive. John checked his breathing. It was still regular, though weak. A belt held wadded fabric to his shoulder.

John loosened it slightly. There was a seeping of blood at the injury site, but clotting had begun. It was less than an hour since John had heard the last rifle shot. The Colonel must have been exhausted. Or fallen fully into shock.

Security was a big issue. Was there more than one marksman? John had only seen the one set of tracks to the cabin, but that didn't say much. Either way, his immediate concern was getting the Colonel to a hospital.

He needed to get some warm liquid into the Frenchman, to prepare him for the freezing cold outside. John put all the kindling in the fireplace and brought in a pot of snow from the porch. Louis stirred with a low groan.

"Colonel!" John said. "Comment ça va?"

The Colonel's voice was thready. "Pas bien."

"You've been shot."

"Oui, I couldn't see him." Xenon looked up at John, blinking his eyes rapidly, as if to clear his vision.

" I'm going to take you to a doctor. I'm making some hot tea for you."

"Merci . . ."

In five minutes, with some more wood, the pot was boiling, and John got tea and sugar from storage.

Xenon was not in shape to walk any distance. The cabin had a toboggan, which John used for hauling supplies in the winter. The trick was to make it comfortable and safe enough for the steep slopes. If the hunter was the man who ran off down to the Gorge, John doubted the man would remain at these heights in the continuing storm.

The Colonel had been watching his efforts. "Thank you for the tea—I feel much better. Mon ami, you have here a beautiful sled, but it will be dangerous on the steep parts. I think I had better try to walk as much as I can."

John glanced at the officer with appreciation. "Well, if you think you are able, that's probably a good idea." He retightened the makeshift bandage, and made sure the Colonel's head and shoulders were covered, his parka fully buttoned.

Checking around the cabin, John put things in rough order, secured the Colonel's rucksack and two blankets, and then slid the toboggan out into the snow.

While John fastened the door, Xenon folded the blankets as best he could. The snow continued to sift through the tree canopy. John estimated three more inches had accumulated since the Colonel arrived. His earlier tracks were almost obliterated.

They descended through the glen, and John was able to recover one of the Colonel's cut saplings to steady him.

Once beyond the ponds and on the trail, they had less interference from tree branches, but were more exposed to the wind-driven snow. No sign of the hunter's tracks remained.

On steeper ground, they walked together, but often John was able to pull Xenon behind him. He knew the Colonel was conserving his strength for the long haul, but there was also a race against wind chill. John hoped, beyond the ledges and rockslide, the Colonel would be more protected.

When they reached the ledges, the buffeting of the freezing wind was fierce. Happily, going down proved easier than coming up. The footing was treacherous, but they were able to slide feet-first on their stomachs over some of the surfaces John had struggled to climb in the morning. The sled and skis also provided a hand-hold, at times, to work their way over rougher sections on the tumbled rocks below. Their worst injuries were barked shins and elbows.

At the foot of the slide, John looked closely at the Colonel's face. The snowy ground provided enough visibility for the trail, but in the gloom, the Colonel's face looked pale. He needed rest. John hoped the belt was still holding.

"It's time to get on the litter, Colonel." John shook the snow off the blankets and wrapped them over the Colonel's head and upper body. The Colonel was relieved to sit down, but the toboggan was no feather bed. John tucked the blankets under the Frenchman and covered his face.

"Can you breathe?"

"Oui, merci."

"It's a pretty smooth trail from here to the car, so try to relax."

"Très bien."

The Colonel sat with his head on his knees, but John's work had just begun. He had four more miles to get to the damaged bridge. Fortunately, John's skis glided well through the powder, and Xenon's weight lifted the front end. Despite that, the frame still created a great deal of friction. John had to break trail through deep snow at every step.

After nearly a mile, he paused for a breather and checked the Colonel. The Colonel was asleep. John was panting, and far too over-heated. He took off his outer jacket and placed it over the Colonel's head.

John knew that time was precious. Louis' wound was still bleeding. There was no medical centre in Cauley, but he could get some directions to the nearest hospital there.

When they finally reached the stream, it was almost four. There was no way to bring the toboggan across the damaged bridge. John roused the Colonel, still groggy, but strong enough to lean on John as they made the passage.

John re-crossed the bridge twice to get his coat, skis and the toboggan. He put the blankets around the Colonel's shoulders, and they staggered the last half mile to the station wagon, looking like war refugees.

It was after two in the morning when Louis Xenon was released from Littleton Regional Hospital, ten miles north of Franconia, New Hampshire. Louis' wound was cleansed, the muscle sutured, and blood-flow stanched. X-rays showed the bone was grazed, but not fractured. His own first aid care had likely saved his life. The doctor advised Louis to drink nourishing liquids to replace lost fluid.

Accommodations at the hospital were limited. The doctor decided the Colonel was strong enough to return to the Inn. When Louis was leaving, he gave him medications and a prescription to relieve the pain. Doctor Lamson promised to visit Louis at the Inn on Sunday afternoon, so the Colonel would not have to travel again while healing.

John was dead tired as they made the thirty-five-mile drive back to the Inn. He called ahead, and the night clerk promised he would be waiting for their arrival.

There were still some serious questions about what had actually happened on the mountain, but conditions at the time made pursuit impossible. It had been a terribly long day for both of them.

Later, as John stretched out in bed at the Inn, he thought of Sal and Carl, and hoped they were both safe. Events at the cabin had taken an ugly turn. As soon as he got the negatives from the Colonel, he would contact Greenstone, make the transfer, and hopefully, that would be the end of it.

SUNDAY, OCTOBER 30, 1983

The travel alarm showed nine a.m. when John became aware of bright daylight shining through the curtains in the window. His back and shoulder muscles were stiff. He must have pulled something guiding the Colonel going down over the ledges. Thankfully, the bed had been very comfortable.

He got up and drew the curtains aside. The valley and mountainside had been blanketed with fresh snow, and the sky was cloudless.

After a fast shower, he tiptoed to the door of the adjoining bedroom, and listened to the Colonel's heavy breathing. John was satisfied the doctor's painkiller and sleep medication were doing their work.

He dressed quickly and went down stairs. A call to Sal confirmed she and Carl were all right. Travel plans were affected, so John would miss Carl's Halloween trick or treating event on Monday evening. "I'll try to give you an update on my schedule this evening, Sal," he said.

As he finished the call, guests were beginning to arrive in some numbers at the breakfast buffet. John helped himself, and requested a carafe of coffee, some rolls, and fruit for the Colonel. On his return, the Colonel was still asleep, so John got out his briefcase and resumed work on the CEANET brief.

It was just before eleven when he heard the Colonel running water in the bathroom. When he was finished, John knocked lightly on the adjoining door. "Are you still alive?"

The Colonel laughed. "Barely!"

When he entered, the Colonel was standing by the bed in his pyjamas. He seemed somewhat unsteady, but was smiling and extended John his left hand. "Good to see you, mon ami. I didn't think I would sleep so long."

"You need all the sleep you can get. The doctor will be here sometime after two o'clock. If you're hungry, I brought this tray up for you. I can heat the coffee in the micro."

"Merci beaucoup! I do feel sleepy, so I think I'll rest some more. Thank you, Craig, for your help." Louis did not mention it, but John could see the pain in his shoulder was really hurting.

"Of course, Colonel. And if you don't mind, my civilian name is 'John Thurmond'."

"Really? Okay, John." The Colonel nodded with a slow smile. "And you could do me a favour by just calling me 'Louis'. For security, I'm trying to down-play the 'Colonel' part."

John put the tray down in the Colonel's room and closed the door. He was impatient to talk to the Frenchman, but Louis' recovery was more important than anything else at the moment. He decided he needed a breath of fresh air, and put on a dark ski jacket with cap and gloves.

Outdoors, the sky was startlingly blue, the whole landscape a winter wonderland. The temperature was bracing, but not bitterly cold. He walked out the main driveway to the highway and back. The road was plowed, and the distance to the highway entrance only about a quarter mile. He admired the white trunks of birches weighed down with fresh snow, and wished they would thrive better on his property at home in Pennsylvania.

Above the Inn, curving down the mountainside, the highway was empty except for an occasional truck rushing by, splattering slush and salt. The full mountain range spread out in the foreground. On his way back, a grey Chevrolet sedan slowed just enough to turn off the highway, passing alarmingly close as he headed toward the Inn.

John wiped the splattered slush from his coat and returned to the resort. When he arrived at his room, he found Louis sitting up in bed and munching on a roll, with coffee on the side table.

"You didn't sleep very long. How does your arm feel?"

"I didn't sleep. The arm is sore, but it must have been my conscience—I kept thinking about these negatives. I better give them to you before anything else happens."

John smiled, relieved. "You're right, Louis. After all this effort, we don't need any more accidents." He took the small plastic envelope from Louis, and scanned each one of the nineteen exposures. The numbers on the sepia-coloured celluloid frames corresponded exactly to those he had spirited out of China.

"Thank you, Louis. Well done. I appreciate all your efforts to keep these safe. I am sure the scientists who are waiting for this information will say the same."

"Yes, thank you too, John. Without your mission, I wouldn't be in North America today."

John stood. "Well now, Louis, if you don't mind, I would like you to meet my contact, who got all this thing going. He was the officer at Ft. Sill who first asked if I was interested in working on a special project. I had no idea at the time he meant the CIA."

The Frenchman pursed his lips and shook his head. "Mais non! I have no objection. I am here as long as it takes to work things out."

"That's excellent. Ben Greenstone will be able to reimburse you for your full expenses, along with the negotiated courier fee. By the way, how are you feeling right now?"

"I'm rested, but a little stiff. I think some of the medication is wearing off. I can move my fingers, but the shoulder is pretty sore."

"Well, I'm glad you're getting the use of your hand back. The doctor should be here after two o'clock. Are you hungry?"

"Well, I have these rolls here . . ."

John waved a hand. "That's not good enough. Can you make it to the dining room?"

"Yes, I think so."

John helped Louis with a shirt and slacks, and loaned him a jacket from his own wardrobe. Standing by the window above the parking lot, he saw a man below, striding from the entrance toward a grey sedan, parked almost directly under Louis' window. The man put the car in reverse and sped toward the highway. It looked like the Chevrolet.

"That guy was in an awful hurry."

"Who?"

"It was a guy who came to the Inn while I was out for a walk this morning. He left the parking lot now with his wheels spinning."

Louis shrugged, then winced.

John shook his head, then guided Louis down to the dining room. "Say, have you had any additional thoughts as to who might have winged you with the rifle?"

"No, I don't. His first shot missed me as I came over the pass. I thought it an accident then, but he got me later as I was coming out of the woods at the cabin. I didn't see him either time."

"I wish we'd been able to follow his tracks. He headed toward the gorge, below Jason Head, but of course you were injured, and it was getting dark." He paused. "I think the cabin's location might have been compromised."

"M'sieur, I'm sorry, but I may have been responsible. On the voyage, I had the misfortune to be joined by a resident from my boarding house, named Martin Drapeneau. He boarded the ship at Southampton. I never had any direct contact with him while on board, but when I left the ship at Québec, he attacked me in my hotel room."

"Really?"

"Yes. He is a most unsavoury character. We were not on the best of terms in France. But this takes it beyond that. When I went to my room at the hotel, he surprised me in the elevator and pulled a gun on me. I was able to knock it out of his hands and recover it before he escaped."

"Do you know where he went?"

"Not a clue. I did notice on the ship that he spent most of his time typing letters below deck, and only appeared at meal times."

"Why do you think he may have followed you?"

"I think it's undoubtedly related to the negatives. Somehow, he has learned of my connection to you. He must be a sleeper agent, who was just waiting to pounce. However, when I flew east to Baggs' Inlet, I thought for sure I had shaken him for good. I have no idea how he could have followed me from there."

By this time, they reached the carpeted dining room, and took seats at a small table over-looking the snow-filled valley. A fire crackled nicely on the hearth of a nearby fireplace. John was hungry, but the Frenchman took a long time over the menu.

"So, you mentioned you went to Baggs' Inlet. That seems like a small place. Why did you choose to go there?"

"Yes. My original plan was to go fishing on the Péribonka. But there was no way I could do that after Drapeneau showed up in my hotel. He had seen me with a young lady I met on the boat, and I worried he might try for her next. She had invited me to her home in Nova Scotia and I decided to take her up on it."

John's eyes twinkled. "I hope you had a good time there."

Louis didn't appear ruffled in the least. "As a matter of fact, I did very much so. I want to go back as soon as I can after this."

The waitress came, and Louis ordered broiled lake trout. When the food came, John saw he had a good appetite. They worked their way through dessert and coffee.

"By the way, Colonel—Louis. I told you about my capture in Phnom Penh after I left the French Legation. But how did it go for you? Were you able to get away from the capital without trouble?"

The Colonel lifted his eyes to the window. John could understand it was a big adjustment to think back to the heat and dust of the Cambodian capital so many years before.

After straightening the knife next to his plate, the Frenchman answered quietly, "Well, the French helicopters from Bangkok shuttled into the legation's parking lot as long as the rebels gave them permission to land, but then word came from Pol Pot that the next helicopter to arrive would be destroyed on the ground.

"I gave my seat on the last flight to Bangkok to the headmistress of a Catholic girls' school. She had stayed behind as long as possible to counsel her young students' families. On the final day, when the legation closed and its remaining files were burned, I was able to contact my warlord 'friend', who guided me, and two other French officers, over-land toward Thailand."

John nodded slowly. He understood what such a trek, through enemy territory, was like.

"A month later, we finally arrived at a Thai refugee camp. Sadly, on the way we passed through several villages that had been ransacked and burned by the Khmer Rouge. It was unbelievable—the toll taken for any kind of resistance. After two weeks of processing at the camp, I was able to fly safely back to a French army base in southern France for debriefing."

Louis took a sip of water from the heavy glass next to his plate.

John asked if he had had further contact with associates at the Embassy.

Louis shook his head. "While I was still at the capital, our kind café proprietor, Ahn-malan Prabang—the one you met—was arrested unexpectedly by the Khmer Rouge in one of their very first sweeps. In spite of my attempt to intervene, Prabang's beautiful daughter, Soo Lin, was also taken, and suffered an unknown fate." Louis stared out over the window. "It just happened overnight! Thousands upon thousands of educated young people were rounded up, systematically brutalized, and eventually, murdered."

"Both Prabang and Soo Lin? I can't believe it. The whole thing is so . . . terrible." The word hardly seemed adequate. "What a colossal loss."

"Bien sur, bien sur!" The Frenchman's face was grave. "Mon ami, after this business on the mountain, I must say I am worried! I had a very pleasant interval in Baggs' Inlet, but I had some extremely dark thoughts when I returned to Québec. I think there is a very good chance someone knows who I am and knew about the rendezvous. We must remain on guard."

"You're absolutely right, Louis; I agree. Whoever the shooter is, he may strike again." John stared down at the sleeve of his tweed jacket. The nuclear fusion secrets may have traveled a great distance, but they still had not quite reached the people they were intended for.

It was approaching two o'clock, and time for the doctor to arrive. They rose from the table. Before going upstairs, John left word for Dr. Lamson at the front desk.

Back in his room, the Frenchman seemed a little weary. He changed into something looser, more comfortable, and returned to bed.

John felt the outline of the envelope in his jacket pocket, and tried to think of the safest place he could hide the negatives. They were definitely a liability. He needed to contact Greenstone immediately.

"If you don't mind, Louis, I'm going to try to call Ben Greenstone now. It may take a while to get through."

"Fine. I'll just close my eyes a little."

John could see the Colonel was starting to experience pain again. He closed the door, went into the next room, and sat down by the telephone near the window. A Buick pulled up at the main entrance, and Doctor Lamson stepped out.

John dialed the first number Greenstone had set up for contact, which he recognized as the main exchange at Langley. When he entered the correct code as well as Greenstone's extension, a pleasant voice said, "How may I direct your call?"

"To Mr. Ben Aaron Greenstone, please."

The phone clicked and then . . . nothing. He was puzzled. It seemed he had been disconnected. He tried to ring the operator again, but there was no dial tone. John got up and walked over to the connecting door to the Frenchman's room. When he opened it, he saw Louis staring directly at him. "Louis, is your phone dead?"

Louis blinked and then nodded to his right. John followed his gaze, and was stunned to see a dark-haired man in a grey jacket next to the closet, holding a pistol trained on Louis. There was something terribly familiar about his face.

Louis spoke first. "John, this is M'sieur Martin Drapeneau."

M' sieur Drapeneau cocked back the safety on his weapon. "Shut up!"

John was stunned. Where did he know this man from? How did he get into the room? Drapeneau moved menacingly toward the bed, and for a moment, John thought he would pistol-whip Louis.

Drapeneau turned to John. "I think you have something that belongs to us."

The gravelly voice was all-too familiar. John stared at him in shock.

"What? Do you not remember me, John Thurmond? Or, I'm sorry, is it Craig Durrand?"

A twinge of panic rose up John's spine. His interrogators from Malaysia. There were old scars, and yet . . . the younger of the two Russians, whom John had thought dead—was standing directly in front of him.

He struggled to get a grip on his emotions. At first, his words came out as choked coughs. Finally, he managed to say, "I thought I dealt with you."

"Oh, so you do remember me. Good. Because I could never forget you. You killed my chief, and left me to die. You were lucky you got away. But this man, he is not so lucky." Martin struck Louis' shoulder abruptly, and Louis cried out in sharp pain. "Now, which one of you has the negatives?"

John clenched his fists in fury. "Don't try anything foolish, M'sieur Drapeneau. You could spend a long time in our prison system here. We have a very special place that will suit you fine."

The Russian swung his pistol around and pointed it directly at John. "I think you are the one being foolish. We have a score to settle, M'sieur Thurmond; you may go out of here feet first."

John was thinking fast. If he could keep the Russian talking until the doctor arrived, maybe he could spook Drapeneau into thinking it was the police. Or at least get the doctor to call for help. "Just exactly how do you know about the negatives?"

Drapeneau grinned smugly. "Your friend, Dr. Spolchelnik, told us everything—we even got a first-hand description of you. How else do you think we found you in Phnom Penh? From there, it was easy to find your dupe of a contact." He shoved Louis' shoulder again.

Louis winced at the pain, but kept silent.

"We waited for you to contact him again, this time with more information. But we didn't think he knew anything about the negatives, let alone that he actually had them. I should have taken action years ago."

John felt a chill. He remembered Malaysia only too well, and knew exactly what kind of action Drapeneau was talking about. But they could still buy time, and it did not look like the Russian had any backup.

"I think you should know the authorities will be arriving soon, M'sieur Drapeneau." John said.

The Russian was sweating. With John's words, his head jerked abruptly and he glanced out the window.

"Yes, they'll be here very soon."

"Well, all right, M'sieur Xenon. Out of bed and into those boots." The Russian gestured toward the corner. The Colonel rose stiffly and, holding the back of a chair for balance, placed one foot after the other into the boots.

John took a steadying breath. It was characteristic of the Russian to pick on the weakest member to exert his will.

"Come with me. Quickly!"

There was a soft knock at the door. "M'sieur Xenon?" The doctor had arrived.

The Russian looked sharply toward John and hissed through his teeth, "One move and you're dead." He grabbed Xenon by the arm and pulled him roughly into the other room.

John waited a split-second, and then answered the doctor at the door. "Come in please." He had to get the doctor out of harm's way. Pulling the confused man inside the room, he was just in time to see Drapeneau and Xenon hurrying down the hallway, toward the rear exit stair.

"Wait here!" he shouted. John knew there was only one plowed road to the highway; he must stop the Russian at all costs. He raced in the opposite direction, down the corridor toward the main entrance lobby, nearly knocking over some guests on the wide, plush stairs. He yelled to the receptionist, "Call the police, quickly!"

Running out the front door and back toward the space where the station wagon was parked, John found the vehicle covered with snow. He unlocked the door, and had just started the engine, when a grey sedan rounded the corner from the back of the south wing, speeding toward him. He kept his feet on both the brake and the gas pedal; he had to time this exactly.

The wagon strained in reverse. He released the brake suddenly, just in time to back the heavy Ford directly into the driver's side of the sedan.

A horrendous impact tore the metal of the driver's door as the momentum of the station wagon pushed the small Chevy right across the narrow drive and into a snow bank.

John jumped out of the Ford. The sedan's driver's door was caved in. Drapeneau sat in stunned silence.

In the confusion, Xenon had managed to grab the Russian's gun off the front seat with his good left hand. Drapeneau tried to recover quickly, and gunned the car's accelerator, but his wheels spun on the ice, and the wrecked sedan remained stationary. The Frenchman kept the Glock trained on the Russian, poking him in the back of his neck with it. John heard his words, "Time to give up, mon ami; it's all over."

John helped with Louis' door while the Frenchman backed out, keeping the firearm trained on Drapeneau.

"Good job, Louis!" John helped to steady his friend. "You saved us."

People started milling about the front entrance, including Dr. Lamson. Louis was standing in his unlaced boots, wearing nothing but pyjamas. Nodding to the doctor, John took the gun from Louis, and told him to go inside and get warm clothes.

A crowd gathered under the portico, and guests were looking out the windows. The doctor returned with Louis to his room.

Drapeneau had stopped trying to extract himself from the wrecked sedan, and did not seem eager to be out in the cold. In the interval, up on the mountainside, John could hear the wail of a police siren on the highway. He waited patiently by the car with the Glock pointed at the Russian agent.

In minutes, the police patrol vehicle arrived like an angry hornet with its red and blue lights flashing. When the trooper saw John standing with the gun, he immediately called for back-up. The two-way radio crackled, and the trooper stepped onto the snowy pavement. He had his pistol drawn. "Drop the gun, please."

John complied, and the trooper retrieved the Glock with its seventeen round magazine. Examining it, the young trooper was impressed. "Pretty heavy artillery!"

"It belongs to the Russian." John said, pointing to the sedan.

"Both of you, keep your hands up, please. No false moves!"

In another ten minutes, two more squad cars arrived, and the young officer walked over to him. "I'm going to have to take both of you into custody. Please come with me."

When the Russian got out of the car, a second officer snapped handcuffs on both of them and directed them to the separate police vans. A third officer was taking statements from onlookers.

John said, "I would like to leave word for my partner. He's upstairs being treated by a doctor."

The young officer paused and looked at him. "Then I guess we'll have to take him in as well—I'll see you at the station."

John ignored the officer's affront and got inside the waiting van. Drapeneau was already in one of the other vehicles, looking none too happy. He said nothing and stared out past John toward the snowy countryside. The game was not over.

They arrived at state police headquarters a mile south of Woodstock, New Hampshire, and were placed under guard in separate rooms. The young officer was joined by a detective, and took statements from them as the detective listened and made notes.

John wondered what kind of story Drapeneau would try to pull off. It wouldn't be very hard to turn things around. It was just two peoples' word against another's. The wrecked Chevrolet and the

Glock pistol, with Louis' and his fingerprints all over it, were pretty damning evidence. The doctor would be a key witness here. John asked that he come to the station and give a statement.

It was a complicated situation. John and Louis weren't able to give all the information required of them, and as a consequence, their story appeared full of holes. The troopers could not be sure how many crimes may have been committed. To make matters even worse, two of the men they were holding were French citizens, and the third was a New Hampshire property owner. John knew they were not likely to be released until there was a full investigation.

But they didn't have that kind of time. John hadn't even been able to contact Greenstone; he had no idea how much Sal would worry once she heard about it.

John knew he was going to have to move fast, or the whole situation would bog down in a legal swamp. The priority was to get the negatives to Greenstone, and then maybe the old army Captain might be able to help address the problem with the troopers and Drapeneau. But he had to reach Ben first.

After some delay, the sergeant made a phone available to him, and once again, he called the number at Langley. This time, though, he got through.

"John. Good to hear from you. How is it going with the courier?"

John confirmed that he had the negatives, but that he was in State Police custody with the courier and a Russian agent posing as a French citizen. The courier had been shot, and two vehicles damaged. "We are being held for further questioning at the station south of Woodstock, New Hampshire, just off of Interstate 93."

"Well, you've got yourself into a fine mess, haven't you, John? I leave you alone for two months . . ."

"Yes, but this agent could be a high profile asset—he's the same guy who interrogated me years ago in Malaysia."

"Is that so? If it goes back that far, then they must still really be after that information."

"I'd guess that's the case."

"Look John, it's great that you've got the goods, but don't say another thing to the police pending my arrival. I'll leave now, and be there the first thing in the morning. Remember: not one word."

John spent a restless night in the cell. He was not able to speak to Louis directly, other than to reassure him that Greenstone would be arriving in the morning. The doctor's testimony had been extremely helpful, because it leant credence to their statements, but Drapeneau was a superb actor. He played the innocent victim for all he was worth.

Ben Greenstone arrived shortly after breakfast in the morning. He had driven the Mercedes to Vermont overnight, and yet looked impeccable in his dark suit. John was stupefied to learn from the police that Drapeneau had been released on his own recognizance later the previous evening, based on his travel visa and the fact his car had clearly been damaged by the station wagon.

What other sob story he told the police was unclear, but the gun had been in Louis' and John's possession, and John had not been able to comment on the reason for the encounter. Given that, all the suspicion fell on them.

When Ben heard the news, he was outraged, and let the officers, the detective, and anyone within hearing know what a colossal blunder it was, in no uncertain terms. He identified himself with the Department of State and the CIA, and demanded custody of John and Louis as contracting agents of the United States Government. The officers' eyes widened as they realized what they had stumbled into.

It took many phone calls to state and federal authorities before the police were willing to release the two into Ben's charge, but eventually they became apologetic.

Before leaving, Ben announced that any public comment would be considered a breach of national security, and result in dire consequences for the department. He made clear Drapeneau was a target of government inquiry, and that any and all information on his whereabouts should be forwarded to the Agency immediately. In the end, it was nearly noon before the three of them could get away.

Louis was surprised by how quickly it had all turned around. Whoever this Ben Greenstone character was, he could certainly get things done in a hurry. They had to return to the Inn, as John needed to pick up his things. The wagon and the Chevrolet sedan had been towed to a local garage, so John's CIA contact drove them.

Ben seemed in a hurry to get back to his office in Vermont. "We don't want a lot of questions, John. Just get your baggage, check out at the front desk, and return here. Louis should remain with me. We'll have some lunch, and you can make phone calls later."

Almost as soon as John left, Ben turned to Louis, questioning him about his trip and plans for the next weeks. He nodded solemnly all through, and when Louis was done, settled down comfortably in the driver's seat. From his demeanour, Louis assumed those had been the 'right' answers. Ben even went so far as to congratulate Louis on his efforts to date.

He seemed particularly interested in Louis' assessment of Drapeneau, and the threat to others that the Russian might represent. Louis was still amazed that the fellow boarder he had known for so long had dual identities, and had been able to conceal them so well.

"M'sieur Greenstone, I didn't like Martin from the start, but I had absolutely no idea he was the man who tortured John in Asia. When he first came to L'Auberge des Trois Normands in Le Havre, Drapeneau was recovering from injuries, but he was very quiet on how he received them."

Ben rubbed a hand over his face. "My instincts are that Drapeneau will immediately head for the Canadian border; the faster to escape U.S. jurisdiction. He must have some contact for outside help. I'm going to take you and John to the Northmont Centre in Chelsea,

Vermont. The CIA has resources there, which will be helpful in finding Drapeneau and bringing him to justice."

Louis was not all that reassured by Ben's statement. He did not know whether he and John would be the subject of further questioning, but he did share Ben's instinct that Drapeneau was long over the border.

John appeared, carrying his overnight bag and what was left of Louis' rucksack. "I have to make one more trip, and I'll be right with you."

"Well, hurry," Ben barked.

The next trip, John returned with Louis' things on hangers wrapped in his raincoat. Ben helped him put them in the trunk.

"I've got everything now, Ben. I called my insurance agent, and they will be taking care of the cars."

Greenstone shook his head. "It's only money, John."

John smiled at the sarcasm in the agent's voice. "Yes, but think about it, Ben. Louis is with us now instead of with Drapeneau! If Drapeneau had succeeded, we would have faced a real disaster, for everybody."

One half hour later, as they were crossing into Vermont, Ben pushed a button on the car's dashboard. A tray opened, with a radiophone connected to a concealed antenna. John shook his head. Ben and his communications. He dialed a number. "Agent 24 here. I need a report on a French national travelling under the alias of 'Martin Drapeneau'. He debarked about three weeks ago from the M/V L'Aventure, at the Port of Québec. He may have returned to Canada from the U.S. late last night or early this morning. The crossing could be anywhere from Ogdensburg, N.Y., east to Maine. He might also be travelling under a name with a Russian extraction. Timing is critical. Please get back to me as soon as possible." The phone crackled, and Ben clicked off.

Ben was travelling west toward Haverhill, New Hampshire. John admired the brightly coloured foliage near the road. He had to admit, Ben had just saved them from a very sticky situation. They could have been tied up there for days. He was starting to feel that his early mistrust of the gruff Captain had been misplaced.

They arrived at the Northmont Centre a little after two-thirty. It consisted of an isolated series of low brick buildings, well hidden by trees, and accessed by a curving, wooded entrance drive from the highway. A manned gate restricted vehicle access to the parking lot. There was no other indication that this was federal property.

After checking in, Ben showed them to two comfortable rooms at the rear of the complex, then led them to the cafeteria for a quick lunch. "No doubt you would like to contact your family, John? There's a phone in your room with outside lines. Louis, if you want to do any research, there's a library in building 'A' with lots of maps, reference books, and card index files. I'm going to give each of you a visitor card, which you should always carry with you for identification purposes. I want to get together with you again at five-thirty, before we have dinner. Let's meet at the library. All the buildings are linked with heated passages, so you won't have to go outside unless you want to."

John was eager to catch up with Sal, and also needed to call his office and explain his whereabouts. It had been a wild day. The spectre of Drapeneau on the loose was unsettling. He had no idea what Ben had in mind, or how long they would remain in his custody—for now, he was content to wait.

He apologized to Sal for having to delay his return, but said he would keep her posted. Carl, of course, had been disappointed, but his friend Jimmy had come by, and they went to a Halloween party in costumes together.

John mentioned the damage to the station wagon, but skipped the details. "I'll have to make some kind of arrangements to retrieve the car and equipment after it's repaired. Maybe the shop can deliver it for me to the airport at Burlington." Sal's van would need to fill the transportation gap in the meantime.

Louis took Ben's advice after leaving the cafeteria, and went for a stroll. Light snow lay in the woods, but not nearly as much as in New Hampshire. Louis reached the library through the system of corridors and, after presenting his ID, asked to see maps of both New England and the Eastern Provinces. The librarian directed him to a bank of oversized drawers, where individual maps were indexed by size, scale, location, and purpose. He was absorbed with the detail, and spent an hour following his journey through North America. The soreness in his shoulder persisted in spite of the pain pills. He wondered when he would be able to get the stitches removed. He still had Dr. Lamson's card.

At five-thirty, Ben appeared with John in tow. They went to a small conference room, where they sat in comfortable chairs across a narrow table. Louis wondered what this was going to be about.

Thankfully, Ben Greenstone wasn't the kind of man to beat around the bush. He started by explaining his role in John's mission, filling in gaps that Louis had only been able to piece together up until this point. Apparently, the negatives were already being processed, and had been labelled for view by only those above Top Secret classification.

Louis contributed what he knew of Drapeneau, and how he believed he had been followed. "But I do not know how he tracked me to New Hampshire," he admitted.

"He may not have," John put in.

Ben raised his eyebrows.

John proceeded to inform them of his nephew's kidnapping, and that he believed the location of the rendezvous may have been compromised. "It was our timing that threw things off," he explained.

Louis nodded. It had been his idea that any correspondence would not contain the correct date, and it seemed that had paid off in the end.

John's surprising story didn't end there, however. His nephew had found evidence at the Queboggin site that pointed to a nuclear scientist's missing daughter—the very same nuclear scientist who was assigned to work on the negatives that Louis had transported. The coincidences were beginning to pile up. After so many years, the French veteran had stopped believing in coincidences.

Ben took all the information in stoically, though annoyance crossed his face when John mentioned he had gone to the Canadian Department of National Defence on the matter. "Why was I not informed of these developments earlier?"

John response came carefully. "We did not receive this information all at once. We were feeling our way as facts became available. And I thought that, because Canadian nationals were involved, my contact would be the better choice for some insight. And he was. It was he who made the connection between Mark's kidnapping and the missing Gelda Vanderstadt."

Ben nodded approval, his mouth still a tight line. "On that note, Dr. Vanderstadt is scheduled to make a presentation on fusion-energy policy to NATO in June, and pressure on him, through his missing daughter, could be acutely embarrassing to both Canada and the United States. We would very much like this situation resolved, and quickly."

He looked carefully between the two of them. "Both of you have had more direct contact with Drapeneau than any other people currently available to our department. We need to get inside his mind and figure out what he is up to. With your permission, I would like to take you both to meet with Dr. Vanderstadt at the QFR Portage Lake Nuclear Plant on Wednesday morning."

John was the last to agree. He wondered how his wife, let alone his staff at work, was handling all of these sudden and unexplainable disappearances of his.

Ben nodded curtly. "Excellent. We will leave tomorrow morning. Seeing as QFR is also under watch for suspicions in both kidnapping cases, I am going to have to ask both of you to keep your eyes open. But don't reveal anything just yet. We don't want to risk spooking them."

John shifted uncomfortably in his seat. "As yet, we have no proof that it is all of QFR that is involved."

"Quite true. Another reason to keep things quiet."

The room was silent for a minute.

"Well," said Ben, stretching. "If we have covered everything, gentlemen, then I would say it is time for dinner."

13

In the morning, Ben gave the impression that he had already put in several hours of work and was eager to get going. Once underway, he seemed to relax, and fell quiet as he concentrated on the road. At the border, the Canadians gave them careful scrutiny despite all their papers being in order. They were looking hard at persons of French citizenry.

"Ben, how did you make out in the search for Drapeneau at the border crossings yesterday?" John asked.

"There was a car with a French citizen named Martin L. Drapeneau who passed through the immigration office north of Highgate Springs, Vermont, on I-89 at a little after two am, October 31. We are trying to get more information on Drapeneau from French authorities. Drapeneau was being driven by a certain Jean Claude, a Canadian citizen from Montréal, Québec. They had nothing to declare."

"I'll bet they didn't." John muttered. "Well, it raises questions: What is the link now between Drapeneau and this Jean Claude?"

There was a significant drop in temperature as they made their way northeast over narrow roads and through small villages to St. Pamphile, close to the Maine border. Much more snow was on the ground than in Vermont, and the roads were absent of any salt. The heavy Mercedes seemed to handle it with ease.

At St. Pamphile, it looked like the end of the route east as far as improved highways were concerned. Not far north of the village, there was a manned gate where several large tractor-trailers with loaded flatbeds waited in line. The condensed combustion air from the idling diesels rose in straight columns in the clear afternoon sky. A light blue QFR Portage Lake logo, mounted on a large illuminated sign, said:

L'ÉNERGIE DE L'AVENIR POUR NOTRE QUÉBEC
ENERGY OF THE FUTURE FOR OUR QUÉBEC

Greenstone cleared entry with security at the gate, but it was still over a dozen miles to the plant entrance. Ben explained that Portage Lake was a body of water straddling the U.S. border, with a steady up-stream supply adequate to provide necessary cooling for the nuclear reactors. Due to the environmental concerns of U.S. citizens, however, the plant's non-radioactive cooling water was not allowed to discharge back into the headwaters of the St. John River. Instead, it was pumped thirty-five miles north into the St. Lawrence River, causing an outcry from Canadian environmentalists. Because the pipeline was buried underground, however, the public's initial concerns ultimately faded.

Ben pulled in front of the administration building, and his passengers got out to stretch after the long ride. The tractor-trailers continued to a large service building in the rear.

The huge scale of the building structures could be estimated by comparing them to familiar objects like the trucks at their base; the two cooling towers were almost five hundred feet tall. From John's time studying nuclear energy, he knew a plant such as this processed nearly a million gallons of water a minute, although ninety percent was condensed from the steam and re-used. A cloud of condensation, that could be seen from miles away, formed many feet above the towers.

"It's certainly cold here." Louis searched for his parka in the trunk.

Ben said brusquely, "We can deal with that stuff later, when we locate our accommodations. Let's go in now!"

Once inside, they appreciated the warmth of the reception office. A clock said four-forty p.m. A few drivers were standing in line to get paperwork processed. It appeared that, due to the isolated site, overnight bunkrooms were available for them as well. Local employees commuted to the plant from adjacent villages.

Ben asked for Dr. Vanderstadt. The receptionist smiled at them. "Welcome, messieurs, the doctor and the Plant Director are in a meeting now, but he told me to expect you. Please sign the registry and take these visitor identification cards with you."

Ben thanked her. "Why don't you fellows go straight to the rooms? I'll bring the car around."

John's room was small, but tidy. Exhausted, he took off his shoes and lay down on the bed in his clothes. He put a call through to Sal. She had just returned from shopping with Carl. He told her what he could of where he was, and when he hoped to be home. She expressed concern at so much travel, and John could all but see the crinkle in her brow. He hung up wistfully. Tomorrow couldn't come soon enough.

At six p.m., the Plant Director joined Vanderstadt and Ben at the cafeteria and welcomed Louis and John. Though most of the conversation at dinner centered on Portage Lake, Vanderstadt was particularly interested in meeting Louis.

John began to get nervous about where this thread of the conversation might lead. The Plant Director had to be kept out of this particular loop. With a slight shake of his head, John interrupted with some pointed questions about Vanderstadt's work here at his laboratory.

Fortunately, the doctor seemed to agree with his meaning, and went along with the change in topic.

After a few more pleasantries, the Director left for his long commute home. Ben wasted no time. He turned to Vanderstadt, and handed him a set of the photos he had made from Spolchelnik's negatives. "You may want to look these over."

Vanderstadt scanned the enlargements carefully for some minutes with a gradual look of recognition and delight on the scientist's face. "The theories present here . . . why, I'm going to have to guard these with my life!"

Ben said, "You better, and you may have to." John smiled at the look the doctor gave. But John was starting to understand Ben; it was his way of speaking. He intended it to be funny, but things usually came out as a gruff imperative.

"Yes, well . . ." The doctor ignored Ben. He was used to the reactions of his U.S. partner. "Thank you all very much for this material. I know you've had to pay a heavy price to get it here. Our scientists will look forward to examining this in careful detail—honestly, I can't wait to get into it myself."

Vanderstadt smiled, glancing from John to Louis. "I wonder if, in the morning, you would like to take a tour through the plant? I can ask one of my staff to be your guide . . . Any interest?"

John sagged at the thought of more movement. He had seen that Louis' eyes were drooping, and he occasionally shifted his arm uncomfortably. It would take Louis some time to heal. "I would be very interested in seeing the plant, but let's do it in the morning. Nine a.m. tomorrow would be just about right." He looked to Ben and Louis, who both nodded.

Ben said, "You men can come straight to the cafeteria. I'll be eating early, but I also have some commitments. I won't go on the tour, but I'll see you at ten o'clock. Sleep well."

The two agents stumbled back to their rooms, barely able to keep their eyes open. They were both exhauted.

⊕

John joined the Colonel in the cafeteria in the morning. Louis had never eaten sausage and flapjacks before, but John urged him to try some.

"Mais, non, mon ami! Must one eat dessert before le pain et le fromage?"

"No, Louis, this is not dessert. These are what you need to eat to withstand the winter storms of North America. Here, have some butter and maple syrup to make it go down better." He enjoyed teasing the Frenchman, because he was sure that Louis would treat him the same way when it came to sampling snails, frog legs, ripe cheese, and other French delicacies.

Having readied themselves for the day, they proceeded to the information desk, where their tour guide, Miss Robinson, awaited them.

"Do you mind commuting here every day from so far away?" John asked her.

"Not at all, m'sieur," she said. "It is a good job, with security and pension. Some of my friends come from much further away to work here."

She handed them a copy of the same pamphlet they had received the previous afternoon, and pointed out the map on the second page. Different colours indicated the different types of buildings. Major transmission lines extended beyond the electrical sub-station at the generating plant. These arched overhead for miles to the horizon.

"There are a little under a thousand employees in total," she explained. "QFR is one of the largest employers in the region."

John noticed six more flatbed tractor-trailers lining up inside at the delivery bays. "You have a lot of truck traffic at this facility!"

"Yes we do. It goes on day and night. They are planning to bring in a railroad spur, but the matter is still being negotiated, and needs lots of approvals."

At the main building, they entered a locker room, where each received an orange suit and hardhat with protective visor. The suits and helmets all had large numbers on the back, for easy identification.

A guard at the door checked their visitors' cards before allowing them to pass. In a sealed corridor, a second guard scanned each of them with a Geiger counter. He then permitted them to walk along a platform at the edge of what looked like a large swimming pool.

John peered down into the deep water, and noticed a faint greenish-blue light emanating from large rectangular containers in the centre of the pool. Other darker objects lined the bottom on the near side. They were headed into a special secure section, where the doctor's experiments were being conducted.

A door opened across from them, and two workers in orange uniforms, one with a three-day beard, passed in front.

Louis tried stopping one of them. "Excusez moi, s'il vous plait. What is that big crane used for?"

The first worker stared directly at him. John noticed his intense blue eyes just as Louis exclaimed, "Drapeneau!"

Drapeneau, disguised as he was in his uniform, appeared just as surprised to see Louis. His eyes widened, but then he immediately ran toward the outer locker room.

Louis cried out loudly, "C'est Martin Drapeneau, et un accomplice!"

"Call security!" John yelled to their guide, and raced after them.

The other worker followed Drapeneau full-tilt toward the exit. John could see through the glass that the two had left the building, and were running through snow to the huge service building a hundred yards away.

A moment later, a big ten wheel tractor, without the trailer, pulled from the end of the building, spouting blue diesel exhaust. It headed directly for the two-lane main entrance road.

Louis caught up to John. "Security is on the way."

"They've left the building. We need to call the front gate."

They scurried back to where their tour guide was conferring with security, and relayed the news. "The front gate?" One of them responded. "But that's miles away."

Louis threw his arm in the air. "Call them anyway—these are dangerous men."

John was dumbfounded that Drapeneau had followed them to Portage Lake. Had he not realized that the negatives would have been passed on by now? He looked about the enormity of the plant. Then again, perhaps it had been Vanderstadt himself who was Drapeneau's target.

When he was certain Louis was okay, he looked at his watch. It was quarter to ten. "Come, Louis. We must go back and notify Ben and the doctor."

They quickly returned their uniforms and equipment to the locker room, and arrived at the main reception desk just as Vanderstadt and Greenstone finished their meeting.

An officer from security appeared at the desk, and explained that the tractor had parked at a siding, just before the entrance gate. Two men had jumped out, and ran behind the kiosk to a blue sedan waiting on the other side. Security contacted the provincial police to stop and hold the men for questioning, but it looked like Drapeneau and his accomplice had made an escape. The security van was not supposed to leave the property.

Vanderstadt was disgusted. "Well that's great! We've just seen a perfect demonstration of lax measures, which are supposed to be designed to prevent this type of threat. We need stronger procedures, both operational within this plant and with local authorities." He looked at Greenstone and muttered, "Ben, I think we need to go into a closed session on this immediately."

Ben nodded, and Dr. Vanderstadt turned to his assistant. "Miss Robinson, thank you very much for your help this morning. I'll be back in the lab after lunch."

She smiled sympathetically and left for the laboratory.

The doctor pointed down the hall. "There's a small room near your dorms on this level. I think we will be more comfortable there." He led them down the carpeted hallway to an office at the end with a view of the lake.

Dr. Vanderstadt slumped into one of the seats. "This thing is turning into a nightmare. How did foreign agents get so easily past our security?"

Louis stopped to place a hand on the doctor's shoulder. "He is very good at this sort of thing. I myself have only just realized that I have been duped for years by this man."

Vanderstadt nodded slowly. "What concerns me most are his intentions for being here."

"He appeared quite surprised to see me," Louis put in. "With that, I don't think John or myself were his targets this time."

Greenstone nodded. "Most likely, it was you, doctor. He must be getting considerable help from other operatives."

John frowned. "On that note, we might have to consider QFR's involvement once again."

Vanderstadt sighed. "Yes, Garrett Bennett filled me in on that suspicion. The seeming involvement of the QFR director, Philippe LeClerc, in that operation is a most peculiar and serious discovery. Since we are in a QFR facility, this knowledge jeopardizes the very existence of our research here, and the future of our collaboration with QFR. We need to go into this subject carefully."

"There has been some other news regarding that," Ben put in quietly. His tone had John's full attention. "I established contact with Garrett this morning. Through the Civil Aviation Authority, Bennett has determined that the Cessna, used to transport Mark from New Hampshire to New Brunswick, belongs to Yves Bonnard, a pilot and employee of QFR at their Cité des Mélèzes plant. The flight plan clearly shows a trip to Lebanon, New Hampshire. However, the return plan was filed to Charlo, New Brunswick—not to the camp at Queboggin. There was no follow-up report of any emergency landing."

"Such things can lead to quite the problem for a pilot," Vanderstadt said. "The Aviation Authority does not take kindly to such indiscretions."

"So we have yet another connection to QFR," John said quietly.

"So it would seem." Ben's face was grim. "Since we have found frequent connections between these cases, I would like to propose that Roeloff and I coordinate all incoming information with your friend Garrett Bennett, who has proven to be both knowledgeable and discrete."

It seemed to be the most logical course. Privately, John decided to call Bennett, and give him a head's up on the proposed meeting. He wanted to mention his own personal sensitivity about drawing the net too tightly on LeClerc. He wanted to respect LeClerc's situation; at least, until they had gathered more conclusive evidence.

"One last thing," Vanderstadt added. "You should all know that my wife and I have involved the Montréal police with regards to Gelda's disappearance. They found evidence that led to a delicatessen near her home. The proprietress, Marie Dionne, confirmed that Gelda had left there that previous evening. There were no other witnesses, except a younger brother who helps Miss Dionne run the store." Dr. Vanderstadt looked down at his clasped hands. "That is the last we have heard of Gelda . . ." The doctor seemed to sink into himself, and no one was inclined to interrupt his solitude.

The meeting broke up. Louis and John got stiffly to their feet. John took one more look out at the placid waters of Portage Lake. There was a dark band of evergreens on the far shore. The bright, over-cast sky and silvery surface of the lake was in such contrast to the deep, dark, and cold water underneath. The chill of the room made him shiver.

After a quick lunch, they said goodbye to the doctor, and wished him safe travel back to Winnipeg. They re-packed their bags in Greenstone's car, and headed out the road to the main security gate where the abandoned tractor, with engine idling, still sat a hundred yards before the kiosk.

Ben lifted his radiophone, and left a message for the doctor suggesting he have the truck checked for fingerprints on the steering wheel and door handles. It would be important to start building a case against the two intruders.

John sat in the back with Louis' parka and rucksack next to him, while Louis enjoyed the passenger seat. Louis' eyes constantly scanned the forest on either side of the road. John hoped that, after this, the Frenchman could finally begin to relax and enjoy his visit to North America. The large burden of his responsibilities had been transferred to others.

By four-thirty that afternoon, they reached the underground parking garage at Château Frontenac. Ben invited them to have dinner before departure to their various destinations.

John had to arrange his return to Bucks County. He called Sal to confirm arrival in Philadelphia, just before midnight. Sal was bringing Carl to the airport, so they could drive home together. John eagerly looked forward to returning to his family. It had been six days.

Ben asked Louis to give him a summary of expenses. They found a quiet alcove in the lobby, and reviewed the list that Louis had copied onto notepaper. After converting French francs to Canadian dollars, and Canadian dollars to U.S. dollars, they finally agreed on a figure that was fair. On top of that, Ben added a generous courier's fee, and wrote Louis a cheque for far more money than Louis had seen at any time since he retired from the French army. He was most pleased.

When John returned from the travel desk, Ben rose from his seat. "We have an early seating in the Empire Room."

An hour and a half later, they concluded the delicious meal in a private room, elegantly served by the staff. As they sipped coffee, Ben asked a waiter to bring out a package that he had passed earlier to the Maître d'. It was long and thin, and enclosed in a cardboard cylinder. He presented it to Louis. "It comes with a carrying case. This is your reward for being willing to be Drapeneau's target."

The present was unexpected, and Louis was embarrassed.

"Don't worry, Louis," Ben said, "John and the doctor have chipped in on this one too."

Louis carefully peeled back the wrapping paper, and then peered inside the end of the tube. He found the tip of the most expensive fly rod on sale in the Frontenac sporting goods store. A waiter brought out the carrying case and a wicker creel containing a beautiful, state-of-the-art line and reel. Louis stared at it all for a full moment. "Mes amis! C'est magnifique! I am honoured by your generosity!"

"You deserve it, Louis." John added. "This is supposed to make up for your trip to the Péribonka. It's been a long time coming, but with your patience, goodwill, and God's grace, Louis, we finally made it." He clapped Louis on the back. Louis noted that it was rare for his friend to show such emotion.

The three of them stood up. John had to catch a cab to the airport, and Ben had a long drive to New York State's Finger Lakes.

John turned to Louis. "What is your plan, Louis?"

"I will be in town tomorrow. I have to go to the bank, get some things from my hotel, and go to a clinic to get the stitches removed from my shoulder. In the evening, I'll be taking a flight to Halifax, Nova Scotia." He handed John a slip with the Vodrey number.

"Ah, right," he said. "Your friend in Baggs' Inlet?" John smiled knowingly.

They went to the coatroom where their bags were checked. Ben shook hands warmly with each of them and took the elevator down to the garage.

John gave Louis his own home phone number. Together, they walked down the adjacent stairs to the lower level. "Look Louis, you and I need to stay in touch. If you need anything, please let me know. This world can be a rough place if you don't have allies—Really."

Louis nodded and grinned, "D'accord, mon ami!"

John gripped his hand firmly, smiled, and went to the line of cabs standing by the lower lobby entrance.

Louis waited by the curb until John's cab left. He was on his own once more. Somewhere along the rugged coast of Nova Scotia, Hélène was waiting for him. More than ever, he looked forward to seeing her again. The past sixteen days had been a struggle, but he knew the first chapters of his visit to North America were over.

Part II

LAC TAMARACK

STORM FRONT

In the dark stabbing cold void of night,
when crystal cracks, and the grey sunless dawn
casts doubt that anything will live
through the day,

Men's souls are tried,
and an anxious God
asks why the Arctic was made.

CDB Jr.
1994

1

Philippe was in a fury the morning after he returned from Queboggin.

Wednesday night, he could not apologize to Gelda enough, and had offered to transport her in his private jet back to his offices in Lac Tamarack. Though she had been hesitant at first, she had finally agreed when he assured her he wanted to return her personally to her family. She could call them and explain her sudden disappearance as soon as they had access to a phone when the plane arrived at his headquarters.

Philippe wanted to put off involving the police until Gelda was safely home and emotions had calmed down—on both sides. Their eventual involvement was inevitable, he supposed, but that was Jean Claude's own fault. He had made his bed. He would have to lie in it.

Philippe had been very quiet on the flight to Lac Tamarack. He brooded about the stupidity of Jean's latest move and wondered about its origin. Jean Claude was one of his most senior contacts in Parti 17. Philippe had pretty much handed him the managerial position of the Laval substation; Jean effectively controlled the Montréal Parti membership. But this was a huge departure from the Parti's general strategy. It must have its roots somewhere. Was it a power grab, on Jean's part, trying to assert authority? Kidnapping was an extreme measure; it was like a declaration of war on the establishment. Philippe could not let Jean's actions set an example for the Parti. They could only expect swift retaliation from the government.

And he certainly didn't want this getting into the news. He had a company to think about. Jean was still his employee—at least, for now. If the media got their claws on this, QFR would be dragged in the mud right alongside Jean Claude. The publicity would shatter everything they had worked for.

When he arrived at the plant in the morning, Philippe was still fuming. He strode into his offices, Gelda trailing quietly in his wake. He gave a curt nod to Suzette, his personal secretary, when she looked up, startled, at his entrance.

"Oh, Philippe, there's a very insistent . . . My, who's this? Gelda! How did you sleep?"

" Hi, I slept very well, thank you. I was wondering if I could make a call to my father . . .?"

Suzette put her hand on Gelda's shoulder, but her questioning glance was for Philippe.

He shook his head. "I'm sorry—not now, Gelda. Could we wait a little?" This was not something he wanted to deal with now. He would, eventually. As part of his 'kitchen cabinet', Suzette was someone he was in the habit of discussing strategic moves with before taking any dramatic steps.

For now, he had to focus on the doldrums of business. "Sorry, Suzette. You were saying?"

"Oh. There's been someone needing to speak with you since I got here. After his third call, I put him on hold on line one."

"Thank you. If it's important, I'll just take it now."

Philippe strode into his office, not bothering to close the door. He tapped the phone once for speaker. "This is Philippe LeClerc."

A gruff voice responded. "Hello, M'sieur LeClerc? How are you feeling today?"

Philippe raised his eyebrows. He did not recognize the voice at all. "I'm sorry, do I know you?"

"Yes, M'sieur LeClerc; I understand you have custody of a young woman. A certain Gelda Vanderstadt?"

That got Philippe's attention.

"What?" Gelda entered the room on hearing her name.

"Now, I wouldn't do anything silly, like trying to contact her parents or the police—it would be most unfortunate for everyone concerned if you did. Do you understand what I mean, M'sieur?"

How had anyone known about Gelda? That certainly wasn't Jean Claude's voice on the phone. Or anyone else who had been present for the Queboggin meeting, for that matter. "I'm sorry; I do not appreciate crank calls. Next time, do not waste more of my time, or I will have to call the police."

"Then let me make myself perfectly clear, M'sieur. You live on Place Belvédère, in Montréal. At least, when you are not at your offices or QFR plants. But your family is there. As to Mademoiselle Vanderstadt, her father is a very prestigious scientist in Winnipeg. It would be . . . unfortunate, should anything happen to them."

Gelda's hand went to her mouth. Her eyes were wide.

"Who is this?"

"Let's just say I'm your reminder. So remember: take good care of Gelda. Keep her close. We'll stay in touch!"

The phone clicked off and the line was disconnected.

That afternoon, everyone was still in Philippe's office. Suzette had taken Gelda aside to reassure the girl and keep her calm. Gelda demanded answers from Philippe. He gave them to her. The whole long story of Jean Claude's idiocy, including the injured young man who had escaped into the night. It was a nearly fantastical tale. Considering the overheard phone call, Gelda could not question any of it.

"What do you want to do next?" Suzette asked. "Do you really think this man can make good on his threat? I mean, if you can get the police involved . . ."

Philippe answered, "I don't know. He knows where I live. Where Bethe and the children are. And we have no idea where he could be calling from; who he could be working with. How he even got this information . . ." Philippe had his suspicions, though. Claude was going to hear it.

"Honestly, Suzette, I want to know that my family is safe. I want to see with my own eyes that they are in no danger—and get them some protection. Then, maybe then, we can proceed."

"I agree, M'sieur LeClerc." Gelda looked at the two of them with a cool expression.

"Excuse me. I-I do not want to risk my own family's safety, let alone yours, when you have tried to do so much for me."

Philippe nodded. After hearing that last phone call, she refused to call her parents. Philippe wished he had been able to record it. Maybe then, he would have some solid evidence . . . that didn't implicate him in this whole mess.

"Would you be willing to do that, then?" he said. "Be willing to stay here, with Suzette for the time being? I'll go to Montréal tonight. Maybe I can come up with a plan. I'll spend the weekend with my family, and see you on Monday."

There was a sense of inevitability in the room. They could only do one thing at a time.

"Look after Gelda, Suzette," Philippe said. "Make her feel comfortable. If this works well, then maybe we can do something to get her home soon."

When Philippe reached his cul-de-sac in Westmount, he was unusually subdued, and more than a little on edge. He was pretty sure his wife, Bethe, noticed the change, though she didn't ask the reason. Philippe couldn't blame her. He tended toward mood swings when the pressures of his office became intense.

That first afternoon passed well, and Philippe was specially attentive to Binne and Paul. The nanny expressed her surprise, but didn't push the issue. The children were in high spirits, and temperatures were moderate in Montréal. By Saturday, the warm sun just called for a stroll in the beautiful fall weather.

Philippe, Bethe, and the children walked down Summit Road near their house. There were few cars in the area; everyone felt at ease.

Philippe was holding Paul's hand, and so felt him jump when a screeching sounded from behind them. A blue van raced down the street toward them. Philippe pulled Paul out of the way just as it swerved, almost hitting the two of them.

Binne was so scared that when she ran to the curb she tripped, and fell on her knee. Her mother, nearly as panicked, checked to make sure she was all right. She pulled out her handkerchief to cleanse the dirt from the small cuts.

"What do those maniacs think they're doing?" Philippe shouted, staring down the road after them. He had not seen who was driving, let alone a licence plate.

Paul was shaking.

"My, God, they scared me." Philippe said. Paul looked up at this assurance from his father.

Philippe put his arms around the shoulders of the two children as they walked quickly home.

The incident had everyone rattled, and though Philippe went to bed early, he couldn't fall asleep until well into the night. Bethe was downstairs.

He woke up to his wife's shout.

"Philippe!"

Thrashing out of bed, he was down the stairs before he fully comprehended what was happening or where he was. Bethe's shout had brought the butler as well.

"The-there was someone in our yard." Bethe stared out the sunroom windows like a woman afraid of what she might see. "Sneaking through the grass. I think he was peering in at me!"

Philippe immediately ran out to investigate. There was no sign of a man in the garden, but when he went around to the front gate, in the distance he saw a dark blue van pull away from the curb.

Philippe returned, to reassure Bethe there was no one in their yard. Any longer. He did not add that the two incidents might be connected. He did not want to try and explain that to Bethe right now.

In the meantime, he instructed George to keep a careful lookout for trespassers, and to call the police immediately upon there being any suspicious activity.

Breakfast wasn't even made when the phone rang.

"It's for you, sir."

Philippe got up. "Bonjour, Philippe LeClerc speaking."

"If you know what's good for you, M'sieur LeClerc, you'll watch your step. I would be very, very careful."

And the phone line clicked.

Philippe set the phone down carefully. He quickly excused himself, and strode to the upstairs sitting room. He had to get to the bottom of these incidents. He closed the door sharply, and dialed Jean Claude's apartment in Outremont.

"Jean! What the hell is going on? Are you trying to kill my kids?"

"What? What do you mean, Philippe?"

214

"The van. The blue van. Threatening phone calls, and someone spooking around my property this morning."

"You're not making any sense, Philippe. Just calm down—what happened?"

Philippe poured out his anger with the details. "What's going on, Jean? Are you trying to get back at me for Queboggin? Gelda's in a good place and she's being taken care of."

"No, Philippe, of course not. I don't know what you're talking about. Honest!"

Jean did not seem exactly sincere in his concern, but Philippe let it pass. It might be that Claude was secretly happy that he was having worries.

"Well, Claude, just remember: if anything gets out of line, I'm watching. More than ever, I think that picking up Gelda was the stupidest thing you've done since I've known you."

With that, Philippe hung up. He felt like screaming inside.

Philippe LeClerc returned to Lac Tamarack on the earliest flight he could Monday morning. It did not take long to get Gelda and Suzette together. First, he asked how Gelda was holding up.

"I am well, M'sieur. Suzette has been keeping me company whenever she can. And your family?"

Philippe frowned, and summarized the disturbing events that had transpired over the weekend. He wasn't sure at first how much to tell them, to worry them, but in the end, everything came out.

Gelda was the first to speak. "That . . . that doesn't look good . . ."

"What can we do?" Suzette, practical as always.

"I don't know."

Gelda sat in a chair, staring off at the corner of the office. She was obviously a girl in over her head.

Suzette glanced worriedly at Philippe. "Apparently he knows where you are and, thus, can guess at where Gelda is."

"What if he comes here?" Gelda was still staring at that corner.

"What do I do? Run? I don't want someone like that after me." Her voice rose to a shaky pitch.

"No, it's okay—we're not going to let that happen," Philippe said, in what he hoped was a reassuring voice. "We aren't . . ." he trailed off. What were they going to do?

Suzette tapped the desk as an idea hit her. "I have an idea."

2

Hélène stood when the flight's arrival was announced. The plane was full, and there were quite a few along with her, awaiting the new arrivals. She began playing again with the locket around her neck that Louis had given her. She hoped things had gone well for him.

She searched the stream of people who emerged.

"Hélène!"

"Bonjour, Louis!" There he was, as steadfast as always.

He met her half way and caught her up in his arms. It wasn't a gesture she was familiar with, but she found that she liked it.

"I have missed you, ma chère."

It was not even two weeks. Eleven days, in fact. It seemed longer.

He started walking out of the airport, fingers wrapped in hers. He was moving slowly, carefully, like he was tired.

"How did your plans go?" He had been specifically quiet on those, and she wasn't sure how far she should pry. But something about them had affected him.

"It was tough, but successful. The mission was accomplished.

There are some loose ends, though—we're still not sure about Drapeneau. He's a most elusive guy."

That was certainly not all of it. Hélène looked deeply into his eyes. She could see kindness, pain, fatigue, a certain skepticism, but a strong craggy resoluteness in the Frenchman. He seemed to have aged a little.

Did she want to know all of it?

After two days of rest, Louis began to feel like himself again. On Sunday afternoon, the temperature was close to freezing, and an overcast sky hung above the coast with a threat of new snow. Louis was restive, and felt the need for fresh air. He asked Hélène if she would like to walk to the point, where the inlet met the coast. After an early lunch, they bundled up in warm clothes and headed outside.

The sandy tracks of the access road continued beyond the entrance to the Vodrey farm. The horses were bedded securely in their stalls, and they struck out on foot for the point a mile away. When out of sight of the farm, Louis took Hélène's gloved hand in his, and they made their way over the twisting humps and ruts in the road toward the ocean.

Occasionally, views of the inlet showed white caps on waves not sheltered by the land. Louis was surprised at how much time the walking required compared to their ride on horseback. As they neared the ocean, the breeze freshened, and their stay at the point would have been abbreviated had not Hélène brought a book of matches in her parka pocket.

"We have picnics out here in the summer. We could try to make a fire from driftwood, if you like. There's a nice protected spot above the beach; I think we can get out of the wind."

Like children, they began to search for the gnarled and bleached driftwood branches cast up along the shore. With dry, brown seagrass and dead twigs from brush nearby, they soon had a merry blaze behind the protective rocks.

"We're going to smell like 'old smokies' when we get home, but Mum won't mind if we have to put our stuff in the laundry."

Louis sat down on a weathered plank in the sand next to Hélène, and leaned his back against the stone. It was good to relax. The breeze toyed with the tassel on his cap, but basically, he was warm underneath.

He put his arm around Hélène and held her close. It made the breezes less chilly. "This is fun," he said. He pulled a small package of tart Jujubes from his breast pocket. "Would you like some?"

Sharing candies, they sat in silence, listening to the wind and watching sparks from the fire as it glowed and settled in front of them. Hélène leaned her head against his shoulder.

There was no shortage of wood, and at times, the fire was almost too warm.

"It would be nice if we could just stay here forever, and not have to worry about what the rest of the world is doing," Louis said wistfully. The stress on him had been intense the past few weeks.

Hélène agreed. "Why does life have to be so complicated?"

Louis thought for a long time about what she had said. "Maybe that's what we have to do—strive for simplicity." It was becoming a deeply held conviction for Louis, and he could tell the idea resonated with Hélène.

As they looked at each other, he could not resist kissing her. He held her tenderly as the wind played with the grass and the breeze blew fine granules of sand into the folds of their heavy jackets.

"Hélène," he said, "I'm so glad you have invited me to be here with your family."

On the fourth day, without hearing from Ben or John, Louis decided it was time to take the initiative and check in. He knew their silence was more an attempt to let him rest than keep him out of the loop, but he was anxious for news. Just knowing that Drapeneau was still out there left him on edge.

He didn't want to worry the Vodreys, or give away any classified information, so he hinted to Mr. Vodrey that he wanted to go to Halifax to check train schedules He also wanted to ask John what he thought about job possibilities in America.

It was arranged that Hélène would take the Jeep, drive Louis to the VIA Rail station, and do some Christmas shopping while he made phone calls.

They arrived at the train station around ten in the morning, and Louis was in high spirits. They planned to meet at eleven-thirty, at the station waiting room, and then go to an early lunch.

Louis made his way inside the VIA terminal and picked up a schedule of train departures and arrivals. It wasn't just for appearances' sake. He knew he couldn't stay at the Vodrey's forever; and he certainly did not want to outwear his welcome. He was uncertain of his next destination, but he wanted to have all the schedules at his fingertips.

With them in hand, he returned inside to a bank of telephones. Since they were on Atlantic Standard Time, it would be nine-thirty in Pennsylvania, and John would be at work. Thankfully, John had given him that number as well.

John was more than willing to bring Louis up to speed over what had occurred in the last week. It seemed Greenstone, Bennett, and Dr. Vanderstadt had been collaborating on many levels, and John now referred to the three men, with some humour, as 'Tri-Force'. Louis thought the name had a ring to it.

Sadly, Vanderstadt still had not heard anything from his daughter, and no one had been able to find any trace of Drapeneau. It seemed as if both had vanished into thin air.

Louis mentioned, hesitantly, that he was exploring the possibility of spending more time in North America, and had been thinking about finding a stable source of income. John thought it was a great idea. He did not know what line of work to suggest, but said he would certainly give it some thought. Fortunately, Louis' Army pension would continue to be paid to his account.

Suddenly, Louis froze. He had been looking through the glass doors of the telephone booth. The panels faced toward the waiting room, which was starting to get crowded. A man with a newspaper walked up to the stand containing the train schedules—the very same that Louis had recently vacated. Louis had a full view of his face, only partially shielded by a hat.

"Louis? Are you still there?"

"Mon Dieu, John. Il est ici. C'est Drapeneau—c'est M'sieur Martin Drapeneau!"

Hélène had dropped Louis off only a block or two away from a department store where she wanted to pick up a few items for herself and her mother. She asked herself why Louis would suddenly want to leave? Had it been something she said, or was he just bored? Of course, with her invitation, there had been no time limit implied, and maybe he had something else scheduled, but it had been so nice to have him around. He was always considerate and polite. She felt depressed just thinking about the possibility. How could she get him to stay, without appearing too desperate? Maybe her mother would have some advice.

That reminded her that she had a purpose in coming here; her mother had asked for some new wool. Hélène had thought, while she was here, to buy some material and make a new dress for Christmas. She knew the style she liked, and had been able to save a pattern from a catalog her mother kept.

Maybe she could invite Louis back for Christmas? Maybe that was the answer.

She made the purchase, and moved on through the store, thinking she could get Louis a nice present. What do men like?

An hour later, Hélène was still undecided. She was in the men's department, and trying to decide between a wallet and a briefcase.

Both suited his personality, but one might be considered over-kill. Why was it so hard to shop for men?

Time was running out. Louis would be waiting for her by now. She decided to go with the briefcase—it was the more useful of the two.

It was another five minutes before she walked out of the store and down a few blocks toward the station. She passed a restaurant— someone was cooking onions—then a small store with a display of children's toys.

She paused to look at a wooden train in bright colours, and next to it, a teething ring with small pink and blue plastic rattles. She had a sudden, strong impulse to go in, but then it came to her, very much like a private revelation. . ." There is no doubt about it; I am deeply in love with Louis. If he asks me, I will marry him." This was a first experience for Hélène, which she was not sure how to handle—it was a discovery she wanted to share with her mother.

Louis cringed and turned away from the window. He whispered into the phone to John. "He's here. I just saw him walk into the waiting room. He's only about twenty feet away from my booth."

"Drapeneau? What are you going to do?"

"I don't know! I'm stuck here—but my friend, Hélène—she's arriving any minute!"

"Don't panic, Louis. You don't want to draw attention."

"You're right. But she'll be a target too!" Louis took a deep breath and angled his face away from Drapeneau and the crowd. "I'll have to sneak out."

"By all means, Louis. Don't let him see Hélène. Get out of there fast, and give me a call back as soon as you can."

Louis hung up, and peered sideways through the glass at Drapeneau. He was dressed in a dark suit, as any businessman, and he seemed unconcerned as he leafed through a newspaper.

Louis collected his change, gloves, and the packet of schedules.

He stood up carefully in the cramped space. The Russian agent was facing the door to the main terminal and intent on his newspaper. Louis opened the door and slipped to the side behind a column.

Why was Drapeneau here? Why was he that intent on targeting Louis? The Americans had the film. The deal was done. Was it a grudge against him, or something else?

One thing was for certain—Louis didn't want to wait around to find out. He had seen it many times before—ignorance was something that got good men killed. He would have to take action.

From the pillar, he took careful steps to a coffee shop by the station.

He chose a seat with its back to the wall, where he could maintain surveillance of the newsstand and the customers around it.

He didn't have to wait long. Drapeneau had found what he wanted in the pamphlets, straightened his grey felt hat, and moved at a brisk pace out of the station. Louis waited a moment, then rose from his seat to follow. He hoped Hélène would still be busy with her shopping. He had to figure out what Drapeneau was doing in Halifax, and if she or her family were in any danger.

He followed Drapeneau down a few streets, and soon realized they were headed toward the port. Martin looked at his watch once, and placed the schedules in his jacket pocket. He never faltered in his route. He seemed to have important things to do.

Cold rain blew in Louis' face. The street grew more care-worn as vacant stores and warehouses substituted themselves for the fashionable shops around the station. Louis could smell the familiar, brackish scent of harbour water. Trucks and vans were parked at all angles along the industrial thoroughfare. The hulls of merchant ships, secured by heavy hawsers, rose from the docks along the quay; Drapeneau was in his element.

The Russian agent had not turned around once to see if any were following him, but Louis kept a respectful distance anyway.

Coast Guard ships were located across the harbour at the military depot. Two small destroyers, an icebreaker, and a sea-going tug were at anchor. Louis was surprised at the variety; they passed ships from Britain, Latin America, the Mediterranean, Panama . . . but where was Drapeneau going?

At the end of the docks, a lone ship swayed on the breaking waves. It was a long, grey, low-hulled craft, with a high forecastle and multiple booms aft. It was separated from the others by a hundred yards of open paving. The wharf extended at right angles at the end of the thoroughfare.

Louis strained his eyes to read the name on the bow. Baltisheski something. . . he couldn't make the rest out, but his eyes moved to the stern and he recognized the small red Hammer and Sickle flag of the Soviet Union. It was the "Baltic Star", a Russian trawler, with a mass of electronic surveillance radar and radio antennae mounted over the wheelhouse.

Drapeneau didn't miss a step, but walked up to a Port Authority vehicle parked alongside, presented papers, and shortly after, was escorted by a sailor up the gangplank to the ship. Someone from the bridge had authorized his access.

Louis leaned against a dock piling. Inside, he could bet they had all kinds of shortwave communication, capable of keeping contact with political officers across the globe. Drapeneau was likely receiving orders straight from the Kremlin.

The temperatures were not pleasant, and the wind and rain continued in intermittent gusts. Twenty minutes later, a figure appeared on the gangplank, and Drapeneau started coming Louis' way. It was time to make himself scarce.

He walked back along the pier toward a Norwegian ship offloading large pallets of frozen fish. He moved behind a truck as the agent passed, and continued to follow Drapeneau toward the station at a respectful distance.

It was ten after eleven, and the over-cast sky was getting darker. Drapeneau pulled the schedules from his pocket and checked them again. He tapped them in his hand. He looked at his watch, and then picked up the pace. He was headed back to the station.

When they entered the terminal, Drapeneau went straight to the ticket master's counter. He stood for a few minutes, talking to the agent, and then plunked down money for rail fare.

Louis followed Drapeneau as he went through the gate and down the steps to the train departing for Montréal. He was riding in the coaches. The dozen sleeper cars ahead were being prepared for the long transcontinental trip to the Pacific Coast. Once again, Louis thought of the vastness of Canada.

Drapeneau was carrying no luggage. It seemed that this would be an ideal time to alert Tri-Force, specifically Garrett Bennett, and put a tail on the Russian when he got off the train. The train only stopped at certain stations, including Montréal, before heading west.

Louis went immediately back to the phone bank and called Garrett's residence in Westmount. Louis left a message describing Drapeneau and the scheduled time of his arrival in Charny and Montréal. Louis then called John and brought him up-to-date on the story. John was greatly relieved to hear that Louis was okay.

"You left me hanging in the air—just waiting to hear back from you. I didn't know if you'd been wiped out."

"You were right—it would have been very dangerous for Hélène. I thought it best to follow him, and figure out just what he's up to on the east coast." That reminded him. "Hmm—you know? I'm sorry mon ami—I have to go. Hélène is probably worried."

He hadn't realized it, but a considerable amount of time had passed while following Drapeneau. He was supposed to meet her for lunch nearly twenty minutes earlier.

He hurried out into the street, the wind pulling at his coat. Which direction would she be coming from? Then he saw her arrive on an opposite corner across the intersection. He raised his hand and waved at her, trying to get her attention.

Though she was wearing heels, she hurried across the street to him. "Louis! Oh, I am so sorry I'm late. I didn't see you at the station, so I thought to check back at the car, but then . . ." She trailed off, looking up at him. "Are you all right?"

"Yes," he said. "Just an . . . unpleasant shock." He held out his arm to her, trying to appear jovial. "Come. Let's go where it's safe and dry."

Martin Drapeneau left the coach cars of the VIA train after travelling from Halifax to Moncton. The next stop was Miramichi, New Brunswick, although he did not want to go that far. His instructions were to stay at a farm in the rural outskirts of Moncton where other Soviet agents, operating in the north and east, found safe haven.

Today he had received coded orders from General Zuloff to continue to disrupt any and all preparations by U.S. and Canadian authorities for the June NATO summit. He must specifically target the proposed discussions on fusion research. The information from Dr. Sergei Spolchelnik was in American hands, but Martin was determined to show the North Americans there was a price to pay for it.

He had to make up for his failure in the White Mountains. Though he had been able to put a scare into Louis Xenon, he still needed to settle the old score with Thurmond. He had underestimated the two. From the encounter at Portage Lake, it was clear that Xenon and Thurmond were coordinating with Dr. Vanderstadt and others in the government. It was unfortunate he hadn't succeeded in reaching the doctor himself.

In the coming month, Martin planned to return to Montréal to clean up matters with Jean Claude. Claude had been somewhat helpful, but at heart, he was a weak man. Martin would have to meet LeClerc.

It was important that Claude introduce Martin to Philippe. In person; not just his impromptu phone messages. LeClerc had a reputation for being the hard-driving head of Parti 17. He was also very independent-minded. He followed his own vision for the future of the party, and was not likely to be subservient to directions from Moscow. If Zuloff wanted to disrupt NATO's fusion research capabilities, it was a colossal blunder for Claude to turn control of Vanderstadt's daughter over to LeClerc. It was critical that they re-align the circumstances of her captivity to get direct leverage on her father.

So far, Claude had been useful to Martin as a conduit of information about the situation in Québec and QFR, but the man had made blunders in the past, and was prone to personal ambition. He was occasionally helpful, but not totally reliable, and that was a problem.

The Russian needed to rethink and regroup for the next steps. He needed to spend time with Claude to analyze Parti 17's organization, bring fresh blood in, and toughen it for the struggle to come, They would have to weed out the weaklings and strengthen the organization's information-gathering capabilities. Indeed, Claude and LeClerc themselves were obstacles, but for now, they might still be manipulated.

Drapeneau knew the Canadian and U.S. governments were on the lookout for him. Zuloff wanted to get things going. Claude had mentioned LeClerc's annual New Year's Eve party. It could prove useful.

The cell would have to move strategically and with force to embarrass and discredit LeClerc, take over the Parti, and seize control of Vanderstadt's daughter as their main bargaining chip. Careful planning, logistic support, secure sites of operation, as well as trained manpower, willing to follow orders without mental or moral reservation, would be required.

Perhaps it would be beneficial to move to Montréal even sooner.

It was unwise to become dependent on Claude for necessary initiatives. There were a few . . . strategic matters he had to take care of there, anyway. One could never be too careful.

3

It took the rest of the day for Louis to shake the uneasy feeling the appearance of Drapeneau had brought upon him. He had realized something, however. Already, his connections here far outweighed the few he had made in France. He cared deeply for Hélène and her family, and he hated to think of his 'visit' ever ending.

After dinner, when they had finished the dishes, Louis and Hélène went out to the stable to be sure the horses were watered and comfortable. The wind had been steady nearly all day from the northeast, bringing a bout of colder air with it. A few wet flakes of snow were in the air.

They were spreading clean straw on the floor and putting fresh hay in the mangers. It was a simple chore, and Louis found his mind turning to the ideas that had been brewing in his head. "I've been reviewing my plans for the coming days, and I have been thinking I need to make a change."

Hélène looked up quickly. "Really?"

"Yes. My retirement in Le Havre has been pleasant enough, but as they say, it's not going anywhere. I've thought about it quite a lot in the last weeks. The atmosphere here is so invigorating and fresh; I think I'd like to find a job in Canada, and start something new. There's an opportunity to be creative here."

"Oh, Louis, that's wonderful!" She was obviously pleased. She dreaded the thought he might be leaving soon for Europe. "What will you do?"

"I think, first, I'll go back to Québec and look around a little, and then slide down to Montréal and see what the city has to offer. I am travelling by bus this time. I'll get a chance to see the countryside."

Hélène nodded, more seriously. "How long will your search last?"

"In the two major cities, I don't know. If I don't find something there quickly, then I'll have to work out some other strategy. Of course, if I do get leads outside the big metropolitan areas, I'll try to follow them up as well."

"Have you considered Halifax?"

"Yes, but your Dad says the big cities have better potential."

"It might be worth a try though."

They fastened the stable door and walked back to the house. Flakes were beginning to accumulate in the grass next to the path. The wind had not diminished. At the steps to the front door, Hélène took his arm again. She had been smiling constantly since their conversation amongst the horses.

After Louis said goodnight to Hélène and her family that evening, he had a strange feeling of awkwardness. Yes, he wanted to find a job, but realized that an underlying cause of his unrest was Hélène herself. He had grown more and more fond of her in the recent weeks. He remembered her bright smile and the snowflakes in her hair as they came indoors from the stable.

The companionship they shared felt so natural, and yet he knew it was unfair to encourage her further until he had sufficient resources to support her. His meagre army pension simply would not suffice for two people.

The same reasoning applied to her parents. William and Marie were wonderful, but Louis felt that their blessing could only be unreservedly extended if Louis was fully responsible and prepared to adequately support their daughter.

The next morning, Louis packed his bags before he went down to breakfast. It seemed the family had been expecting something to happen. Marie had prepared soft boiled eggs and homemade croissants with wild blueberry preserves. Louis appreciated her kindness.

He announced his plans to go to Québec over the breakfast table. From her parent's reaction, Hélène must have already shared the news with them. Though she had been excited last night, Louis noticed that Hélène had hardly touched her plate.

He was thanking her parents for their hospitality when she looked up at him. "Louis, if you ever need a place to stay, until you hear from an employer, we'd love to have you stay here. Sometimes it takes quite a while for employers to get back to you. We'd especially like to have you with us over Christmas."

The look in Hélène's eyes was so imploring that Louis' heart melted. He would do anything she asked. "You are most kind to invite me, and yes, I would very much like to accept. It would quite convenient to be able to use your address for correspondence. Could I check on it frequently with you by phone?"

"Certainment, Louis," Marie responded. Louis appreciated how she had accepted him as a part of her family.

Louis folded his napkin and looked out through the dining room windows. He would like to stay at the farm indefinitely, but felt duty-bound to keep moving.

THURSDAY, NOV. 10, 1983

Louis' first days in the city of Québec were enjoyable. He did a day of sightseeing at the start, trying to get a feel for the provincial capital and its surroundings. He methodically explored job possibilities in the port area, but nothing really seemed to be the right fit. He knew that, to provide for Hélène properly, he could not just take a job as a labourer or a clerk. He needed to have enough income to support them both, yet he had to be willing to learn from the ground up. He would have to market his experience with the French legation and in the Far East.

After a brief time in the Québec area, he took the bus to Montréal. A job search was only part of the reason—he also wanted to check up with Garrett Bennett. He hoped his tip about Drapeneau had paid off.

Eight days later, Louis sat in the waiting room of Garrett Bennett's office. It was located in one of the nicer, traditional government office buildings on a busy street. Outside, snow continued to fall through the small, intricate branches of the hedge, onto the handrail of the steps and the branches of the white cedar next to the window. The bridging action of the snowflakes began to form a white cap that blanketed not only the hedge, but cars and the street as well. The early snowfall had choked arteries of traffic heading into the city, changing many of the residents' plans for the day.

Louis often enjoyed the snow, but found that the sight of it could not cheer him today. Apparently, Drapeneau had not been aboard the overnight train, at least, not by the time it had reached the Charney station, across the river from Québec. Louis could not explain the Russian's absence, other than that he might have left the train at any of the other intermediate stations. The man was adept at covering his tracks.

Louis could do nothing more than give Garrett a careful description of what the Russian was wearing when he boarded the train. Garrett had obtained a copy of the agent's passport, and Louis confirmed that the photographic likeness was that of Martin Drapeneau.

They spoke for a while on other matters, and Louis began to realize just how much the Canadian had become involved in their mission. He was also able to provide an update on Dr. Vanderstadt's missing daughter. Unfortunately, the search for clues as to Gelda Vanderstadt's present location had gone nowhere, but there was confirmation, through fingerprints on the ball point pen, that she had been transported to the same logging camp in New Brunswick from which John's nephew had been able to escape. Her initial disappearance had been here in Montréal.

"Why, yes," Garrett said in his easy-going manner. "A friend of hers, who runs a small delicatessin near her apartment, was the last to see her; so we know she arrived in Montréal after she left the Vanderstadts'. Her friend was quite distraught, and unfortunately unable to provide any more information as to what happened.

Louis asked for the location of the shop anyway. He was interested to see what he could learn of Gelda from her friend. He had an uneasy sense of responsibility regarding what had happened to the girl. Perhaps, if only he had realized what a danger Drapeneau was earlier, much of this could have been avoided.

After a friendly farewell, Garrett saw him to the entrance door and Louis was back on the street. He suddenly realized that Garrett had spoken excellent French during the entire interview.

The snow swirled down thickly. Louis was not wearing a hat, and his hair was soon soaked. He headed northwest to the street near McGill University where Marie Dionne's delicatessen was located. When he found it; the rich aroma of coffee led him inside.

A small door bell rang as Louis went in to look around. He was attracted to the array of imported delicacies that Marie had on display. She smiled at him with a friendly "Bonjour," when he entered.

Louis picked out a few small things that Hélène and her family might enjoy and then went to the counter and ordered a medium coffee.

"Oh, just help yourself, m'sieur, the coffee is free! C'est gratuit!"

"Très bien! Merci beaucoup!" Louis responded.

A young man with tallow-coloured hair came from behind the curtain, carrying sliced meat for the refrigerated case. "Jacques, will you see if the soup is ready?"

Jacques went back behind the curtain, now carrying a tall pot with lid. He looked about seventeen years old, and did not seem too inspired with his work. Louis wondered if he knew Gelda, or had known anything about her disappearance. Would the police have thought to pay much attention to him? It might be important. Louis left with his purchases for now—he was not the only one in the shop, and it was getting busier with the after-school rush.

Louis was thoughtful as he rode the bus back to his hotel. Peering out through frosty windows, Louis could see pedestrians scurrying home from their office jobs, waiting for traffic to pass; thousands were seeking the warmth and shelter of their homes after a busy week.

Some days later, John gave him a call to catch up on Louis' job search. Things had been chugging along, but Louis had not heard of anything positive as of yet. He hadn't really expected to, this early in the game.

"You sound like you could use a break," John said. "How would you like to come with me to Ottawa?"

"Ottawa? What's going on there?"

"I have a ten am meeting with the Maritime Transportation office tomorrow, but that shouldn't take too long, and then we might do some sightseeing." John's practice frequently brought him to Montreal to consult with Canadian firms.

Louis' interest was aroused. He was getting tired of the daily routine of the city, and welcomed a break. "That would be very pleasant."

"I'm staying at Hôtel Richelieu. If you come over to our small restaurant up on the top floor, 'The Tower' serves a decent breakfast. You can meet me at seven, and we will get underway by eight. The weather is supposed to be nice. Maybe things will thaw out a bit."

Louis was delighted. "Thanks very much, John. I'll see you in the morning."

Louis got up early, and checked the possessions in his small room. The paperwork on his desk was beginning to mount. He locked the door securely, and took a bus south to the Richelieu.

It was five minutes to seven when he arrived at the restaurant on the 19th floor. John, looking freshly scrubbed, arrived in the elevator at the same time.

"You're early," he said cheerily. "I think we need some coffee."

They found a seat at the windows, and admired the view as the sun rose over the city. On a happy note, John asked Louis, "So how's the job search?"

"Pretty good. A firm asked me to come back in for a second interview on the twenty-fourth. They're looking for a point man, with some experience in Asia. They want to put Asian corporations in touch with engineering and manufacturing consultants here.

"Will it require travel back to Asia?"

"Not too much, but a little. I don't think it will be bad; I enjoy travel, and I'll get on with people better if I'm not associated with any government or political ideology."

"So I take it you will not be returning . . . to France?"

"Not at this point. No, I don't think I want to go back to France. I—well John—I think I've fallen in love."

John smiled. "You do seem to have connected! I am glad things are working out between you and Hélène."

"They are, but I've put off asking her to make a commitment. I didn't think it was fair to her. At this point I'm still trying to figure it all out, to get a job and settle in here, but it's coming very slowly."

"Don't worry about it too much, Louis. When you know it's the right time, it will happen. Just be patient." John looked at his watch. It was nearly eight. John had to get to his meeting.

The snow banks all but concealed cars as they passed around the circle at the Maritime Transportation office. There was little truck traffic.

John returned shortly, as promised. After a brief lunch at a bistro in Hull, they drove to the National Gallery. John introduced him to original works by 'The Group of Seven'. Louis enjoyed how the artists managed to capture the romance of the Canadian North.

As they walked from room to room, Louis was surprised at the outpouring from John when it came to art, but he also saw it as an expression of strong emotions he himself had felt along the deep, forested corridors of the maritime peninsula. The artists showed great perception in a variety of ways, some in painting such simple things as leaves in a brook, or a distant mountainside.

The drive back to Montréal took about two hours, and darkness had settled over the city as an unending stream of commuter headlights faced them in the outer suburbs. By the time they parked the Porsche at the Richelieu, it was time for supper. They had dinner nearby at a good Italian restaurant, just a few stops away in the Underground City.

Nursing their espressos, John asked, "So what are your next moves, Louis?"

"Hélène has invited me back to Nova Scotia over the holidays. I'm hopeful the interview will pay off tomorrow. If it does, I will start next Monday."

"That's excellent, Louis. In the meantime, I know of something that might help you out. Ben and Dr. Vanderstadt say they want to put you on a payroll—I'm serious, Louis. I told them you have limited income, but they think you have a very important role to play here, and they want you to be available, when you can, to help us with Drapeneau. You should keep track of all your expenses, and if you don't mind, they would like you to move into the Richelieu so that we can all coordinate more easily. I know this is a change, but its central location makes it easier for communications, meetings, messages, etc. Would you mind?"

"No, mon ami, not at all. Merci! The Richelieu is a lot closer to McGill and l'Université de Montréal, where I use the library, and it will also improve my bus transportation."

"Good! I'll register you to start tomorrow, and you can charge all your meals and services to your room number. Don't worry about room and board; we'll take care of it while you're in Montréal."

Louis could not believe his good fortune; he had been conserving funds he received from his courier fee, but they were steadily diminishing. Maybe things would work out with this new direction in his life.

4

WEDNESDAY, NOV. 23, 1983

Louis spent his last night in Quartier Latin. The transition from army life, to a civilian pensioner, to a businessman, was not smooth, and he was having to adjust at every step.

After lunch, he checked out of the hotel, and moved his belongings to the Richelieu. His room was on the tenth floor, and had a great view of Mount Royal. He called Hélène to tell her about his new quarters, and she was as pleased as he. He mentioned the 'Group of Seven' exhibition in the National Gallery.

"Oh, Louis, I studied 'The Seven' when I was in school. You mean you had a chance to see the original paintings? I would love to have been there." Hélène was enthusiastic about art, and Louis made a mental note to visit the gallery again, this time with her by his side. They caught up on other news, as they did frequently, and then said good bye. He would call when anything new developed.

As weeks passed, in addition to his employment search, Louis made a habit of visiting Marie's Delicatessen frequently. He was slowly learning more about the proprietress and her brother, Jacques.

After his fourth visit, late in November, he had thought to mention Gelda and her kidnapping. Marie got quite upset on the subject, and even Jacques stopped to listen when they were talking about her last visit. Neither had heard any news on the progress of the investigation. Marie listened intently when Louis relayed what he had heard about her being traced to the Maritimes.

Louis was especially glad to see that he had piqued Jacques' interest. He thought it would be easy to relate to the younger boy. He learned from their accounts of the days following the incident that Jacques had been, in fact, ignored by the local police. Louis thought this odd. Was Gelda not his friend as well?

At the hotel, he had been trying to think of the best way to approach the young man, when he picked up the latest Montréal Gazette. An article boasted that the Montréal Canadiens were firmly holding the position of second in their division, and had a game against Toronto the following Saturday . The consierge said there were still tickets available at the Montréal Forum. He ordered two centre-ice seats.

Marie and Jacques would be busy in mid-afternoon, preparing food for the evening rush. He wanted to catch them before that, so he left fairly early that morning.

Marie was arranging the display next to the cash register when she recognized and greeted him.

"Bonjour, Marie," Louis said. "When I'm outside your store, I smell that coffee, and I just can't resist coming in."

Marie laughed. That was the start to most of their conversations.

Jacques came through the curtain from the kitchen. He looked at Louis briefly and nodded his head. He put some bread in the bin at the sandwich board, and then looked around to see what else was missing on the counter.

Louis decided this was his chance. "You know? I have a problem. I'm new to Montréal, and I have two tickets to see the Canadiens play the Maple Leafs next Saturday afternoon—but I don't have anyone to go with."

Jacques looked up from the counter, but Marie spoke first. "I'm sorry, I don't—I can't, but Jacques—would you like to go?"

Louis glanced at Jacques, and tried to look as receptive as possible. Jacques stared at him, weighing the offer, and then shrugged his shoulders. "Okay, I don't mind." He tried to appear disinterested, but Louis could tell he welcomed a chance to get away from the deli.

"Excellent," Louis said. "The game starts at five, so on Saturday, I'll come by at four o'clock. You'll have to show me how to get to the Forum by game time."

Thursday was a cold, dry day. Louis had obtained a second interview with the consulting engineers. They had been particularly interested in the emerging manufacturing segment of the Southeast Asian economy. They questioned him about Thailand, Taiwan, Indonesia, and Malaysia, and Louis was glad that he had travelled and read extensively about these markets and could speak with authority about the people, languages and culture of the major population centres.

When he returned to the Richelieu that evening, he was bursting with anticipation. It was early for their weekly phone call, but he wanted to talk to Hélène anyway.

"Guess what, Hélène? I got the job!"

"Oh, that's wonderful, Louis, when do you start?"

"Next Monday, in Laval."

"Well, I hope you get evenings off."

"Hmm?" That was an odd thing to mention.

"Surprise!" Hélène sounded giddy. "We plan to visit my aunt and uncle who live in Granby, Québec, and we thought to take the chance to come see you in the city."

"Really?"

"I was going to wait until we were on our way to tell you, but, well, I guess I'm not very good at this."

"No, really, Hélène, it will be wonderful to see you."

They spoke well into the night about Hélène's more distant family—Louis was a little nervous that he was already getting the chance to meet them. He supposed it made sense, but the prospect was daunting.

When they finally did hang up, he realized he hadn't told her about the hockey game. It seemed like such a different part of his life. He deeply wished the whole kidnapping episode was over.

Saturday morning, Louis went into a sport store and bought himself a jacket with a Montréal Canadiens logo. He was amazed at the store's great variety of sport apparel.

At four o'clock, he showed up at Marie's. Jacques was ready in a navy blue hood with gloves and boots. They said goodbye to Marie, and Jacques directed Louis easily through the correct bus routes that would take them to the arena. The stands were not yet filled, but the crowd was building and noise level increasing. They went to their seats above the Toronto bench.

In the first period, Maynard dominated play, and action was mostly on Toronto ice; the goalie made some spectacular saves. In the second period, a total of three goals were scored, and Toronto was leading two to one at the buzzer.

By the third period, the capacity crowd started to get nervous, and the noise level doubled. Montréal began to draw penalties, but LeFèvre was able to score a second time, and the game was tied.

In the last twenty-five seconds, their best Canadien left winger finally left the penalty box, and the team made another rush on the Leaf's goalie. The two defencemen fell to the ice, and LeFèvre pitched headlong over them, sliding into the cage. But he didn't have the puck; he had dropped it backwards to Ray LaBlon, who drilled a bullet into the upper right corner. The game was over, three-two. The crowd went wild, and Jacques said it was the best game he had ever seen.

The event ended at seven. Louis asked Jacques if he would like something to eat; there was a pizza place directly opposite the main gate, and their throats were rough from cheering. Soon, the hot cheese and cold colas worked their magic. Louis said, "I see you like hockey."

Jacques said, "Yeah, I played varsity in high school until dropping out to help Marie—I really miss the game."

Louis asked Jacques more about school, what subjects he enjoyed, and if he would be interested in going to college.

Jacques was uncertain, but warmed to the friendly questioning; Louis had the impression that not many took a personal interest in his situation. Louis felt that Jacques had missed the normal companionship of his father, and they slipped into a thoughtful silence as the subway swept from brightly lit station to station.

5

Dinner with Hélène's family was a pleasant affair. Her parents had chosen a small restaurant near the theatre, and everyone was in good spirits when Louis arrived at the table. William's younger brother, Henry, looked almost identical to the older. The two rose from their seats and welcomed Louis with hearty handshakes.

Her aunt said, "Hélène tells me you were the answer to her prayers when she met you on the boat!"

They all laughed. The comment was meant to be kind, but Louis saw Hélène cringe. Louis vowed privately not to share their inner-most thoughts so openly with friends and relatives.

Afterwards, the others left for a production at the local theatre, providing an excuse to leave Louis and Hélène on their own. As soon as the couple left the restaurant, they fell into each other's arms. They had not been alone together since Hélène had dropped him off at the bus terminal in Truro, back in early November.

Louis watched the snowflakes falling on Hélène's dark hair and thought how lucky he was to have her beside him. "I couldn't wait to get out of that place, but your uncle and aunt are both very nice."

"Yes, they've really made us feel very welcome." Hélène smiled up at him. "We spent the whole day exploring local shops while you were at work. They have them both above and below ground here."

"Yes, Montréal is truly amazing." Louis was nervous about what he was about to do, but this seemed about as good a time as any. He put his hand in his pocket—it was still there. He had managed to find a simple gold and jeweled engagement ring during the week and he earnestly hoped she would like it.

"Hélène?"

"Yes"

He cleared his throat. "I too have been doing a bit of exploring this last week. I went into a small 'bijouterie' and this gift seemed to have your name on it."

He handed her a tiny white box with a white ribbon.

"Oh, Louis!" Hélène untied it with trembling fingers.

When she opened the box, he bent down to one knee."Hélène, would you willing to be my—my wife?"

She looked deeply into his eyes. "Oh, Louis, I thought you'd never ask! The ring's so lovely . . . I most dearly want to marry you—I've wanted to since we first met!"

"Really? Oh ma chérie, you've made me so happy!" He picked her up and gave her a kiss and a big squeeze. She was breathless when he set her down.

"What about your parents?"

"Well . . ." Hélène looked bashful. "I told my Mum, if you asked me, I'd say yes."

Louis grinned widely—he was so relieved.

They walked for a time, hand in hand. "When do you want to get married?" he asked after a while.

"As soon as possible."

"At Baggs' Inlet?"

"I'll have to work on it with Mum and Dad—if only we were closer to Montréal . . ."

It took a long time for each of them to recover from what had just occurred, but when they finally reached the car, Louis' jaw fell open. "What happened to the Laredo?"

Hélène laughed. "Surprise, surprise! The old car was great, but Dad felt it was time for a larger one. He got a good trade and a real bargain on the new Cherokee. Wait 'til you try it." Hélène insisted that Louis drive, and it was his first experience with an automatic shift.

They drove to Cité-du-Havre and the loop around the 'Habitat' apartments. After viewing Safdi's popular residential complex, they parked close to the water's edge. Looking across the harbour toward the twinkling lights of the major office buildings downtown, the lighted Cross on top of Mt. Royal gleamed faintly as snow melted on their windshield. It was almost as though, while sitting warm and snug inside, they were watching the view from their own apartment living room. Their lips met again and sealed a promise for the future that neither of them had expected a few months earlier.

Informing Hélène's family produced a flurry of activity. They agreed to the idea of an early wedding. . . Louis was just settling in to a new job, and it would be a good time for the two to start searching for their own place to live.

Even Hélène's young cousins got excited about her 'fiancé'; the girls could not stop giggling about it. Louis wondered how they seemed to start taking an interest in weddings at such an early age.

They decided on the guest list; Louis wanted to invite his new friends, the Dionnes, and asked John to be his best man. Hélène was not able to invite those friends she had in Europe, but still had many connections in the provinces from her school years. The family decided to hold the wedding in Valcourt, near Granby, as it would be easiest for both the new couple and their guests.

The idea of visiting and arranging with a priest was the hardest for Louis. "You know, Hélène, I haven't been to Mass in over twenty years—I wonder how the Father will take it."

Hélène replied quickly, "I wouldn't worry about it, Louis. Many people have difficulties in their lives that take them away from religion. The teachings of the Church set out a pattern of how one should treat one's fellow man. Beyond that, I think we have to work out the details based on our own experience."

Louis found comfort in those thoughts. "I hate to jump through hoops just because someone tells me to." But in reality, it was not quite that simple.

"Hélène, following Diên Biên Phu, after my officer's training, I was deployed in the French national government crackdown accompanying Algeria's war for independence. French settlers known as Pieds-Noirs, ex-army officers in the OAS, and Muslim rebels of the Front de Libération Nationale, and Armée Libération Nationale, were all caught up in revenge killings and terrorism that took thousands of innocent lives.

"I was with the French army under General De Gaulle, trying to maintain order. Questions of right and wrong were blurred as we struggled to fulfil our respective missions. I have been troubled for years by memories of this terrible period; they haunt me to this day. I have nightmares and sweats . . . I can only feel guilty for what I have done to innocent people."

Hélène took his hand. "Louis, all I can say is, at that time you acted according to your conscience. Please don't worry about this meeting with the priest. If he accepts us, it's great. If he doesn't, it's okay; we'll keep going until we find somebody who will." She gave him a kiss. "In the meantime, thank you for telling me. I think it is very important that we have open communication; please, never feel like you cannot talk to me about these things. I don't want there to be any secrets between us."

Louis shifted uneasily, and wondered how far this issue with Drapeneau had to go. He had never been torn before as to whether to keep that kind of government information away from others close to him. Perhaps it was a good thing he was finding a new career. This would all be over soon, and he and Hélène could get on with their lives.

In the following week, Hélène and her mother made arrangements for the printing of invitations, a reception room and caterer, endless calls to friends and relatives and, of course, the selection of and fitting of a wedding gown. Hélène was radiant. Every dream she ever had imagined was leading to this moment.

In Montréal, they signed a lease to rent a small house not far from a Metro stop. Almost a hundred years old, the house had a bay window on the driveway side allowing a limited view of the street and the back yard from the living room. A dark stained cherry staircase connected the first floor with the second. Upstairs, a large bedroom, a smaller guest bedroom with separate bath, and a tiny room suitable for an office, sewing room, or an infant's bedroom, needed furnishing.

Amazingly, it all seemed to be coming together on its own.

SATURDAY, DEC. 17, 1983

Hélène and Louis were married at the Cathédrale du St. Eustache in Valcourt on a cold, blustery weekend, near the middle of December. John drove up with his family a few days before to spend time with the couple. The day of the ceremony, the parking lot was full.

The luncheon reception following the wedding was held at the Granby Inn, and staff handled the catering. After the bride and groom departed, the celebration for the bridesmaids and ushers, friends and family, continued until five p.m.

John helped to collect the newlyweds' generous gifts, and delivered them to their home at Rue St. Denis, across the river from Laval. He knew they would be spending a few nights at a resort on Lac Memphremagog for their honeymoon, but then going immediately to Hélène's family home in Baggs' Inlet for Christmas. John hoped fervently that they could enjoy this time. He knew what it was like to be away from those you loved, and the idea that he might have to be the one to separate them pulled at his heart.

FRIDAY, DECEMBER 23, 1983

Louis' new offices were closed for the holidays, so Louis was able to join Hélène at her parent's for the festivities. The newlyweds were hard to separate. Hélène's enthusiasm for the season only increased with Louis' presence at Baggs' Inlet

For the first time in many years, Louis felt a real sense of homecoming while at the Vodrey's farm. Any nagging sense of unease quickly left him.

Evergreen decorations added their fresh fragrance throughout the home. A wreath was hung on the door, and Mr. Vodrey enlisted Louis in selecting a suitable Christmas fir for the parlour. Overnight, the tree was decorated with lights and ornaments, and a bright red skirt around the base of the tree began to be covered with presents.

On Christmas Eve, the ground had a fresh cover of white snow, twenty centimetres deep, and it was still coming down. William Vodrey set up the plow on his pickup with Louis' help. He regularly plowed for the neighbours as well, and it wasn't until evening that they returned.

Dinner that evening was accompanied by some of Hélène's mother's tapes of her own favourite French language carols. The conversation frequently paused as the beautiful strains of the music and the choir pervaded the house.

Christmas morning, the family slept late, tired from the excitement and preparations of the previous week. Despite the holiday, chores still had to be done before and after breakfast. Louis considered the tidy discipline of the household a good omen. When they returned from the farmyard, the sitting room doors were opened and the beautiful, festive scene spread before them.

Three hours later, all the presents had been distributed, and the coffee pot was empty. Louis was given a beautiful black 'Samsonite' briefcase by Hélène and her parents, and Hélène loved the embroidered French lace blouse that Louis had picked out for her. That morning, Hélène wore a lovely new dress made of dark blue wool, gathered at the waist. A narrow V at her neck accented her image. It was elegantly tailored, and suited her dark hair and white skin perfectly. She had made it herself. Louis noticed she wore the fine gold locket he had given her.

He complimented her with a kiss; "You look beautiful," he said.

She answered, laughing, "We strive for simplicity!"

The afternoon was spent reading, writing belated thank you notes and cards, and relaxing by the fire. It was such a contrast to Louis' previous solitary existence.

The cold temperatures continued in spite of the sunshine. Louis and Hélène enjoyed being together as much as possible, making cautious but careful plans for the future. Hélène needed to explore the possibility of teaching somewhere in metropolitan Montréal or its suburbs. Hélène was insistent that they now had to start considering their future with regard to their joint budgets and schedules. This was a new thought for Louis, which he couldn't help but appreciate.

Despite all the joy of the season, Louis still held very serious concerns about Drapeneau. If he were to return to Halifax, he did not want Hélène to be anywhere near the port. Louis made sure to check in on the Russian trawler every chance he could, which was rare thanks to the deep snow. However, his holiday with the Vodrey family was so perfect, he just kept putting that dark cloud aside.

Eventually, their vacation had to come to an end. Louis needed to get back to work, and Hélène admitted that it would be good to settle into their new place. It had been a long week. Louis had begun to think of the Vodrey household with real affection, and for him, there was reluctance in their departure.

After a pre-dawn breakfast on New Year's Day, Hélène's parents drove them to the airport at Enfield. Louis and Hélène said tearful goodbyes, but now, finally united, they were ready to return to the world at large.

6

Suzette Dunne was busy in the kitchen on the first floor of the Executive Lodge. Overlooking Lac Tamarack, it had a panoramic view. Yves Bonnard, one of the employees at the offices of QFR, had brought in supplies from the plant commissary and she was making a tray of lunch to take upstairs.

It was the day after Christmas. Though she was not religious, Suzette felt somewhat depressed that she was stuck in Cité des Mélèzes while Philippe and other executives celebrated the holidays in Montréal.

She and Gelda had remained up north at the Lac Tamarck QFR plant. They hoped that they could keep Gelda out of reach of any harm, but still close enough to Philippe and QFR that they could intervene if necessary.

Suzette knew she had volunteered for a high-risk responsibility, but someone had to be with Gelda, to ensure her comfort and safety. If not, the future of Parti 17 could be in jeopardy. So far, they had received no more threats pertaining to the safety of Gelda's family, but the girl still did not wish to risk anything by returning to Montréal.

Yves stuck his head in the door. "I'm going to the garage to check out the van. I think it needs oil. I'll be back in twenty minutes."

Suzette nodded. She had needed someone else to help her out with Gelda's care, and they had to pick carefully to avoid arousing suspicion. Yves was a pilot and general handy man. He was, specifically, not interested nor involved with Parti 17. They could trust his loyalties.

What to do with Claude was still in the air. Philippe could not reveal what No. 2 had done, nor did he want to be rid of him—so long as he was in sight, Philippe could account for his actions.

Suzette suspected that Claude was actually relieved to hand responsibility for Gelda over to LeClerc. The storm of media attention his action had gathered surprised him. He obviously had not thought through the implications of the girl's kidnapping.

Suzette lifted the tray and went through the pantry to the service stair. When she reached Gelda's room, she knocked to give warning before entering.

Gelda sat by a window, absorbing the noon sun. Slightly above the southern horizon, it brought only a few hours of daylight to Cité des Mélèzes during January. Almost twelve hundred kilometres north of Montréal, the Lac Tamarack plant was locked in snow and ice during the long winter.

Gelda greeted her pleasantly, and they enjoyed lunch together. The young woman had been surprisingly patient with her new location once LeClerc took responsibility away from Jean Claude. Suzette was grateful for the improvement.

They talked about a variety of things over their lunches, and the topic of schooling came up. Suzette admitted that she had been a lot wilder than Gelda in her school days, and told her a little about the protests she had attended.

"It was a world where the rich and powerful had gone amuck with things like Napalm, Agent Orange, and the bombing of civilian targets in Vietnam and Laos," Suzette explained. "When French Canada overwhelmingly supported us and the U.S. draft evaders, I decided to join the 'Québec Libre' movement. It was a chance to help secure independence for the province. I left college, and came to Montréal to join the protests there."

"Is that where you met M'sieur LeClerc?"

Suzette hesitated. She did not want to go into the details of Parti 17. The threats against Gelda might be because of her father, but bringing politics into the mess would only complicate matters. It wasn't what the Parti stood for—she didn't want Claude's example to colour Gelda's opinions of them further.

Apparently Gelda had noticed her unease. "It's okay, Suzette," she said. "I know M'sieur LeClerc also supports the protestor stance— that's what the gathering in New Brunswick was about, right?"

Queboggin. Suzette wondered how much she had overheard while she was there. "Yes. But Jean Claude's actions . . . I think there is something more behind them."

"Or, rather, someone." Gelda shuddered.

Suzette nodded, remembering that sharp voice over the phone. "Yes. Violent acts such as this . . ." Suzette shook her head. "It is not something that we stand for."

"I think, I would like to speak more with M'sieur LeClerc on such matters."

Suzette smiled, standing with the tray. "Hopefully, soon you will."

"By the way, we got a card from Philippe. Inside it said, Dear Suzette and Gelda, Season's greetings, from the Le Clerc family." Suzette laughed, "Well, at least we were not completely forgotten!"

SATURDAY, DECEMBER 31, 1983

Philippe LeClerc parked his car inside their large garage and released the latch on the trunk. He had just been to the liquor store to replenish the bar and pick up some chips at the deli, in preparation for their New Year's party. It was primarily Bethe's affair, but he had invited a few of his close friends and some associates from QFR.

Philippe planned to spend most of the evening at the bar downstairs; his wife could have her whirl upstairs with the balance of the guests. Fortunately, their young children, Binne and Paul, were both on the top floor with the nanny. With lots of games and TV, they would be safely out of the way.

He was upset by the year-end corporate reports starting to come in from all divisions. It seemed regulators were trying to make it almost impossible for the corporation to breathe. To top it off, the stupidity of Jean Claude at Queboggin continued to enrage him. Both his, and Gelda's, family had been put in danger. Was it because of this new delegate that Claude kept talking about? Who was this guy, Drapeneau, anyway?

Philippe was not leaving anything more to chance. Though he and Jean had partnered together a long time, he no longer felt he could trust him. He had briefly spoken with Jean on a number of occasions since, and though he was civil, his loyalties seemed to have shifted.

Bethe rounded on him as soon as he came through the door. "Where have you been? You were supposed to be home at three o'clock. The nanny planned to take Binne and Paul to the puppet show, and you didn't even call."

"You didn't tell me."

"It doesn't matter!" Bethe's voice was rising. "You were supposed to be here at three. Binne and Paul are both crying. You know the nanny can't drive."

Philippe shook his head, but said nothing. If anything further went wrong, he was going to go out and shoot somebody. Why did these stresses have to be added on to all the ones he already had? "I actually came up to tell you that Claude is coming tonight, so make sure to have a place setting for him." It was better to keep him close, where Philippe could keep an eye on him.

"Oh, him? Philippe, why do you invite these people? They don't even fit in with any of my friends. All they do is drink and stare."

"He's a part of my company. If other executives can come, then so can he."

"What about Suzette?" Bethe's voice had lowered to a surly tone.

"She has to stay up north this year."

"I'm surprised Suzette isn't coming. She follows you around like a shadow; she spends more time with you than I do."

This was a sore spot between the two of them. Philippe knew Bethe was being purposefully spiteful. His expression closed down. "Do you want me for anything more now?"

"No, but don't you go anywhere. I'm going to need you to greet guests at six-thirty."

Philippe looked at his watch. It was four-thirty. Maybe he would finally have a chance to read that Environment Department report from Ottawa. Suzette had been driving him nuts about it.

He went to his study on the second floor and stretched out in the leather armchair next to the radiator. Looking out the window, he could see the dark sky. It was still snowing. He pulled out the thick, blue-bound report and thumbed through the first pages. They were merely introductory, but the repetition of words like 'violation', 'negligent', 'inadequate protection', and 'ignoring requests' jumped out at him. The Director of the Enforcement Division had written the cover letter himself. He used the word 'mandatory compliance' three times in the last paragraph.

Philippe flipped to Portage Lake. Except for some comments about proposed construction and revisions to the security system, they got a clean bill of health. Apparently, Vanderstadt and the plant director had stayed on top of all but some very minor environmental requirements. This was good. He wished he had more men of their calibre.

He was beginning to draft a full response when the door bell rang. Philippe looked at his watch and swore. It was quarter to seven. Bethe was going to be sure he heard about this.

Philippe dutifully greeted and guided the succession of guests into their home. The decorations in the house were splendidly festive; Philippe had to hand it to Bethe, she sure knew how to make the house look beautiful at the last minute. The caterers were supplying the guests with appetizers and drinks, and most of the QFR crowd were gathered by the hot hors d'ouevres.

"Please everyone—dinner is served. You may take your places in the dining room."

Under the crystal chandelier, in her floor-length satin evening gown with ivory beading and lace embellishments, Bethe was a stunning image of haute couture. With a slight nod to Philippe's business associates, she glided in amongst her friends and led the party to the next room. The time for dinner had come, and Philippe brought up the rear.

The waiters opened the sliding oak doors, and the blaze of candles, glass, and silverware made the guests murmur in appreciation. They were all seated at one table, twelve per side, with Bethe at one end and Philippe the other. Most of the QFR folk had gathered at Philippe's end, but still, there was no sign of Claude.

A five-course dinner was served and the pitch of the conversation rose as the effect of the drinks took hold. At one point, Philippe caught Bethe's eye at her end of the table. He raised his glass to her—she smiled and lifted hers—but that was about the extent of their communication.

The meal ended with an exquisite crème brûlé served in ramekins. The orchestra began tuning up in the ballroom and played light after-dinner music for an hour while the guests took a break and the ladies retired upstairs. The men went down to the bar, and soon the air was thick with cigar smoke. The Canadiens were ahead in the hockey game, and controlled the puck well.

Philippe was going upstairs to coordinate with Bethe on the next phase of the celebration when the doorbell rang. Philippe went to the door. Jean Claude and a tall stranger with swarthy complexion stood on the porch outside.

Jean Claude spoke before entering. "Philippe, may I introduce my friend, Martin Drapeneau, our delegate from Europe."

Philippe was taken aback. Drapeneau stood there, not smiling, his steel blue eyes drilling Philippe and then, scanning the foyer and stair, they shifted to Bethe. Philippe had a sudden impulse to slam the door in his face.

Cold air swirled inside while the two arrivals stood on the threshold.

"Please—please come in." Claude walked up to Philippe and whispered to him, "We've got to move Gelda."

This seemed outrageous and rude. Drapeneau's face betrayed no trace of emotion. "What do you mean?" Philippe's voice was rising.

"Just what I'm saying—we have to move Gelda." He glanced at Drapeneau for reinforcement.

"Says who?" Philippe was determined to get to the bottom of this. "Well . . ."

"Gelda will be much more secure with us." Drapeneau said, in a gravelly voice.

Philippe tensed. He knew that voice. He stared at Drapeneau.

The tall stranger straightened his back and met Philippe's gaze. His expression did not change.

This was the man who had threatened him. Threatened his family. And Jean Claude had brought him here. Rage overtook Philippe. "You, m'sieur, are going to leave. Now. I never want to see you here again." He hoped his voice did not come out too shaky.

"First, let me repeat my friend's request." Drapeneau reached into his jacket, about chest height, and pulled out a handgun. It was dark, with no metallic gloss. "We need to see, and move, Miss Gelda Vanderstadt."

Claude winced, and shrunk away from his associate.

Philippe froze. Then he straightened with a huff. "She is not here. And you, m'sieur," Philippe began to raise his voice, "are not welcome here." They had kept to low tones, to not alert the other guests. Now, Philippe thought, he needed witnesses. "Think carefully. There are a lot of people here. None will take kindly to seeing a weapon in my home." He paused to let that sink in. "So get out."

The interloper looked about him, and nodded his head. "Very well. I'll go; but be careful, M'sieur LeClerc, be very careful. You may see me again."

With that, the dark-faced man turned brusquely to leave.

Philippe grabbed the back of Claude's jacket. "Not you."

The door closed loudly. Philippe was trembling. He was sure he had done the right thing, but Drapeneau had challenged him directly. He knew he had to protect his house and assert control of the organization. He made an effort to pull himself together. "Jean, I'd like to speak with you. Privately."

Sullenly, Claude followed him into the kitchen. Philippe shooed away the last of the caterers. Claude looked longingly at the large pans of leftovers.

"Claude, we've worked together for a long time; there's no easy way to put this—you're fired."

"What?"

"It's over. Drapeneau is the last straw. I've given you every opportunity to shape up, Claude, but when Drapeneau comes, as a guest, to my home, and threatens me with a gun, it's over."

There was a silence as Claude considered the implications. "What do you mean by 'fired'?"

"You can go to your office tomorrow, pick up your pencils and clean out your desk. I'm appointing a new manager for the La-val sub-station."

Claude winced. At fifty-five, a drastic change like this was not easy to handle. "Does this have anything to do with Gelda?"

"What do you think? Of course it has something to do with Gel-da! And that kid from New Hampshire. And the threats I received from your new 'friend'."

"I didn't know he'd go that far." Claude's voice took on a whiny tone.

"That's right, Claude, you didn't know, and you got him involved anyway. Now look at us! You have no idea the damage you've done—and not just to the Parti. What the hell were you thinking? It doesn't matter. You can turn in your badge, and if I ever see you, or your friend Drapeneau, on QFR property, I'll have you both arrested."

The old Marxist appeared shaken. They had known each other for twelve years. Philippe didn't know how Claude could do such a thing. To threaten the company, the Parti, his family . . .

"I'm sorry it's come to this—"

"I am too, Claude, but you've got to decide who in blazes you work for."

"Drapeneau won't like it . . ."

"Tell him to take his hat and head back home. Jean, you yourself can leave; and don't plan on coming back."

Philippe handed Claude his coat and watched as he left. He took a huge breath. Things weren't over yet.

Philippe found Bethe on the ballroom floor. The orchestra was play-ing a light waltz. It seemed appropriate to take her hand.

"Where have you been? We had to start without you."

Bethe's harsh whisper had Philippe upset, but he tried to look cheerful. The two of them whirled around the perimeter of the room. "Bethe, something has come up. I have to leave immediately. I'll probably be back on Tuesday. I'm sorry I can't stay to the end of the party."

"Oh Philippe!" Bethe had difficulty keeping her voice down. "How can you do this to the children and me? The one night of the year when we should be together, you go off to that damn plant. What is wrong with you?"

Unfortunately, they already had the attention of a few of the guests.

"I am doing it for the family. There's no other way; otherwise, I'd be here. Believe me, Bethe, I'm sorry."

Bethe sputtered, then huffed. She refused to look directly at him for the rest of the dance, and quickly excused herself afterwards.

Philippe didn't know how to deal with her, or the situation as a whole, but could waste no more time. He went up the servants' stair to the top floor. The TV was on, and the nanny had Binne and Paul watching the ball poised to come down in Times Square. There were toys and games all over the floor.

"Happy New Year kids, I love you."

The children ran over him, giving him a far greater hug than he could earn from Bethe.

"Papa, we wanted to go to the puppet show, but you didn't come."

"I know, it's sad." He looked at the nanny and shook his head. "Hi—I'm sorry—I'll try to make it up to you."

He turned to the children again. "Good night Binne. Good night Paul. I've got to go back up north tonight."

"Oh Papa, we wanted you to play this game . . ."

"I know, but Papa has some business he has to take care of."

"Come children!" The nanny took their hands. Philippe nodded a quick thanks to her and patted his children on their heads.

Reluctantly, he closed the door.

It was a little after four a.m. when Philippe touched down at Lac

Tamarack. The airfield, maintained by Cité des Mélèzes, was located half the distance from the city, and about three miles from the plant. Due to heavy corporate traffic, it was convenient to have the airfield close by, and QFR had its own hangar with two Lear jets available on a twenty-four hour basis.

Philippe's mittened hands gripped the leather-bound circumference of the steering wheel. The powerful heater provided warmth to the van's interior as he crossed the snow pack on the pavement. He went out the main airport gate, and turned west toward the plant looming on the skyline. The cooling towers emitted their usual plume of steam, and high-pressure sodium lights on the surrounding buildings glistened faintly on the snow. The air was crisp and clear, but the sun was not due to come above the horizon for another five hours.

Philippe settled in at the Executive Lodge, where his body cried out for sleep. His mind, however, was still in tumult. Things were only getting worse. What did this latest move by Drapeneau mean for Gelda? For his family? When sleep did come, it was far from restful.

Suzette was in the habit of going down to the breakfast buffet each morning and picking some preferred breakfast items for herself and her young charge. Gelda was supposed to be kept separate, where others were unlikely to see her, but Suzette thought she at least deserved some company. Yves stayed in town, and only came up about once a day, if they needed him.

So when there was a knock at the door after breakfast, Gelda volunteered to let Yves in. Suzette heard her shocked voice from the entryway. "M'sieur LeClerc!"

Suzette left the dishes where they were and joined Gelda at the door.

Philippe stood there, looking like he had gotten very little sleep. "I am sorry for the intrusion, but something has developed . . ."

For the next half hour, they settled in the living room while Philippe described the disturbing events of his New Year's party, from Drapeneau showing up, to firing Jean Claude.

"Will this not . . . complicate things?" Suzette asked. "If we are not able to watch over Claude?"

Philippe held out his hands helplessly. "I'm sorry, Suzette, but I had to do it. There was no other way. I can't continue to give him access to my home and company while he associates with that, that man."

Suzette dropped her head into one hand. "Well, it certainly makes things clear-cut. He'll probably try to take the Parti membership with him, but I don't think it will be anything near a majority."

Philippe looked sharply at Gelda.

"It's all right, M'sieur LeClerc. I was able to guess at a few things when Jean Claude first captured me." Gelda crinkled her nose in distaste.

Philippe sighed, and turned back to Suzette. "You're right of course, and if he does, I hope he takes the lunatics with him. Good riddance!"

Suzette was not so confident. That the Parti should split apart seemed extremely unfortunate. She would, no doubt, lose a lot of her old friends as a result. It was going to be a tough wound to heal—if it was even ever possible.

Philippe tapped the table pensively. "I can't help but wonder, though; what is going to be the impact on us, on our organization? Claude has set an example of violence and radical action. It's a disaster!"

Suzette stared out the far window, cocking her head thoughtfully. "I think we have to get back to the original principles of Parti 17. What do we stand for: revenge on our enemies and seizing power at whatever cost? Or do we stand for justice, equality, fairness, and support for the people of Québec? I think it's got to focus on the latter. If we don't, we're just going to have an endless escalation."

The room was silent for some minutes.

"Do, do you think that they will try looking for me here?" Gelda's voice was tremulous.

"I think we have to have a plan." Philippe said. "It is entirely possible that Claude or Drapeneau will come up here. I've kept things quiet on my end, but we don't want to give anything away. I came up to see if you were safe, and then warn you both that we have to be extra cautious. We can't let them guess at your location."

"It's really the long-range picture that concerns me the most," Suzette said. "Where do we go from here? What do we do? We can't keep you up here forever." Suzette dropped a hand on to Gelda's shoulder.

Gelda nodded, smiling at the older woman.

Philippe was thoughtful. "I get your point and agree, but how do we implement it?"

"Perhaps we can think of some way to contact Dr. Vanderstadt discreetly. Gelda says he is a strong man."

Gelda nodded again. "He is, but it is the rest of my family I worry about, too: my mother, my younger brother. They will not be able to protect themselves if something goes wrong. And what about your family, M'sieur LeClerc? Your business?"

Philippe stared off, not responding. Suzette sympathized with the director. She knew how long he had laboured to make Parti 17 a party of strength. But he had become tired of late. The traces of grey in his hair were turning whiter, and the veins on his temples more pronounced. He needed to find some help soon or he was going to break.

Eventually, he said, "It is a risk, but I think we must try something. I'll see if I can get our side of the table squared away, and try to hint to your father where you are." Philippe sighed, and rubbed his temples. "The only question is, how?"

7

On Tuesday, Louis stopped by Marie's to pick up some soup and pasta salad for lunch after a morning with a client.

Jacques came up from the basement, as usual, to say hello. As Louis was leaving, he asked if he could speak privately with him.

This was unexpected, but Louis wanted to make the most of it. "I can't stay here right now, but do you have any time after seven this evening?"

"Yes, our customers are mostly gone by then. Marie can handle the shop."

Louis was not sure that this was totally true, but he relied on Jacques to work out the details with his older sister. "Well, maybe we could get some supper at 'Chez Mon Cousin', down the street. It seems to be a nice place."

When Louis came back to Marie's Deli at seven, Jacques was ready. Louis could see Jacques had put on a clean shirt and tie under his sweater, but he wore the same blue outer jacket. He was eager to leave the store.

Outside, the air was crisp. The sky had been overcast all day, but only a few flakes were falling. The forecast was for ten centimetres of snow. It was three long blocks to the restaurant, and Jacques and Louis were thoroughly chilled by the time they arrived.

The restaurant was full, but not crowded. Most students were doing last minute studying before leaving for Christmas vacation. The smell of "un bon potage" emanating from the kitchen was delicious. They were shown a booth in a side aisle, and Louis sat so Jacques could have a view of the street.

Louis waited until after they had gotten settled and ordered before raising the issue at hand. "So what did you want to discuss?"

Jacques hesitated a little. Something was obviously bothering him, but it seemed like it was a large step for him to talk about it.

"You know my sister . . . Marie?"

"Yes."

"She took over the shop from my mother. I started working there two years ago, when her previous partner left to get married."

"Yes?"

"Well she has been lonely since then, and Gelda Vanderstadt has become a good friend."

"I see." That much had been apparent to Louis' observation, but he kept on like it was all new to him, hoping to encourage Jacques.

"She has been very sad since Gelda disappeared."

"I can understand that. How do you think it happened?"

"Well . . ." He squirmed in his seat. "I didn't know, okay? I only had guesses, at least until Christmas time."

Louis was interested. Neither of the siblings had mentioned anything before this. "Why don't you start at the beginning?"

"Okay." Jacques was slowly unfolding his napkin. "I belong to a sport club. One day, after shooting some pool, we were sitting around watching local TV news, and the Mayor of Montréal announced his decision to support 'Parti Québécois' in the coming election. This sparked a debate in the club.

"One of the owners, M'sieur Claude, is a strong supporter of Separatism. He launched a vigorous attack on the Prime Minister. He was quite convincing. With some others, I asked how I could help."

The napkin ripped, and Jacques abruptly set it down, putting his hands in his lap. "Then, when M'sieur Claude found out where I lived, he became very interested, and said Miss Vanderstadt had an apartment nearby. He said he wanted to meet her; that she and her father would be able to help our cause." Jacques shrugged. "But it's not really something you want to tell people about, you know? I suggested I call him the next time Gelda was in the store."

"And did you tell him when it was?" Louis kept his voice curious, not wanting to sound like he was accusing the boy of anything.

Jacques nodded. "It wasn't until two days later that we found out she was missing; it was in the papers." Jacques looked down at his hands. "When the police came to question us, we were surprised and very worried. I didn't make the connection right away. When I did, I asked M'sieur Claude about it, but he said he hadn't had the chance to see her yet."

"But now you are worried that may not be the case?"

"All was okay until this last weekend. On Sunday, M'sieur Claude and a stranger came to the store, and asked if the police had questioned us. We told them exactly what we had told the police. M'sieur Claude was very nervous and upset. He did not seem natural. His friend was a tough guy, and threatened us. He said that if we mentioned anything about Gelda, to anybody, we would be . . . be eliminated. He pulled out a gun, and said he would be watching the store."

Jacques looked back up at Louis. "You've spent a lot of time around us, and invited me out before. I don't think he'd be worried about you . . ."

Louis saw where this was leading. He could tell the police, if Jacques couldn't.

"What name did the stranger give?"

"He didn't. He was tall—about 180 centimetres, with dark hair and a heavy beard. He had a French accent—from France, not Québec."

Louis nodded slowly. Things were starting to add up. "I think I know this man. His name is Martin Drapeneau. You are right. He is very dangerous."

Jacques leaned back in his seat, instantly wary. "How do you know this?"

Louis sighed. "Listen, Jacques, it's a long story. But I am working with Gelda's father, Dr. Vanderstadt, on a project of his." That was the best way to put it, without giving away too much information. "He is very worried about his daughter, and I thought to check out where she was seen last."

"That's why you've been at our shop?" The hurt was plain in Jacques' voice. As was something else—suspicion.

Louis paused, and nodded. "At first. But I did not know that Drapeneau had gotten involved with you and your sister. He is a dangerous man, and has shown up a few times, trying to stop Dr. Vanderstadt's work."

Jacques was starting to look worried, glancing around the restaurant. "Is that why Gelda is missing?"

"I believe so."

Jacques went quiet, and Louis knew the boy would be wondering how far he could be trusted. "Please, Jacques. It is very important that we find her. Can you tell me more about M'sieur Claude? How long have you known him?"

"Just since I joined the club last spring."

"What does this man do, besides being a part owner of a sport club?"

"He is the Montréal manager of an electric company. He works for QFR, you know, the big nuclear utility."

This came as a major surprise to Louis. Another connection to QFR. "I'd like to meet him."

"You would?"

"Yes."

"Well, it might not be easy. He only comes around from time to time, when the other owners are present."

"Do you know where he lives?"

"Somewhere in Outremont, I think."

The waiter interrupted to bring them their meal. Louis had not realized so much time had passed.

When their server left, Louis leaned across the table. "Thank you, Jacques. This is a very important thing you have done. You may have given us another lead to finding Gelda. And I am going to try and get some protection for you and your sister, all right?"

This settled Jacques somewhat. Louis ensured that he finished his meal, and they walked back through the falling snow to the deli. Marie and Jacques had an apartment over the small store.

Louis said goodbye to Jacques, promising that he would see him again soon. For now, Louis had to talk to Garrett Bennett.

WEDNESDAY, JAN. 17, 1984

Jean Claude sat with a lighted cigarette in his small living room in Outremont. The air was close, and the furnace set very high. That was fine, as it matched his mood; he wallowed in anger and hatred, all directed at Philippe LeClerc.

How could the pompous upstart fire him? His association with Philippe went back years. Their party loyalty had proved an early bond. Claude knew that Philippe had provided him a comfortable job within the organization, appropriate to his abilities, but he resented the way that young LeClerc grew his electrical company into a major metropolitan corporation.

Claude, personally, thought that he deserved more than the meagre position that he held. Was he not there from the beginning, giving the company its first legs? And now, with his firing, LeClerc stood in the way of Jean advancing further in the corporate world. Where else could he turn to seek power and influence but in Parti 17?

After losing his job in such a humiliating fashion, Claude felt detached and aimless. In his mid-fifties, it was not easy to start a new career. He stayed in touch with some of his early contacts, who passed on the latest gossip of the plant. It was with a sense of grim determination that Jean decided to use this information against LeClerc. Jean now knew that Gelda was being held at the Lodge, but he also knew security there was tight. Any visit to Cité des Mélèzes held risks. He had forwarded the information to Drapeneau anyway. Since his rejection at LeClerc's home on New Year's Eve, Martin Drapeneau had occupied himself with organizing his own following among Claude's acquaintances and others in the Montréal area.

There was a sharp banging at Jean's apartment door. Jean grumbled, but got up to answer it.

Martin Drapeneau burst into the room. He wasted no time. "You know where Gelda is? Why didn't you tell me sooner?"

Jean huffed, and took another drag of his cigarette. "I just learned about it myself. Relax. Finding her wasn't the hard part. Figuring out how to get to her is."

"For you, maybe." Drapeneau started pacing Jean's small apartment. "We need to put the pressure on LeClerc, and we need to do it now. We need to scare him, get him to slip up somehow . . . or maybe just get him out of our way."

Jean didn't like it when Drapeneau started thinking along those lines. Every time, it ended with Jean in more trouble. He said the first thing that came to mind. "How about we get him arrested?"

Drapeneau stopped, slowly turning to face Jean.

"Or at the very least get them looking at him closely." Claude tried hurriedly to defend his idea. "Something to grab people's attention, and make life difficult for LeClerc."

"And how do you propose to do that?" The sarcasm in the Russian's voice was thicker than sour vichyssoise, but only half as smooth.

Jean shrugged. "Call in a tip. Anonymously. I could use a pay-phone, and say I'm a QFR employee that doesn't want to get in trouble. If I say I've seen a girl matching Gelda's description at Lac Tamarack, he'll be arrested, or at the very least detained for questioning. It would blackball Philippe's branch of Parti 17. I don't know if it would strengthen ours."

"Probably not, but it is something. Call it in. Just don't mention anything about Lac Tamarack. I mean it. We don't want the politsiya getting in our way when we extract Gelda."

Drapeneau stared off, eyes flickering. Calculating. "Make the call. I'll leave now, get the lay-down of the place. I'll expect to see you and Bourget there in ten days."

Drapeneau strode for the door, as suddenly as he had entered. He stopped at the threshold. "Don't disappoint me." And he was gone.

Jean Claude stayed in his seat. His mouth was open. Lac Tamarack meant real risks. Were they ready for it? He felt like he'd just been used as a punching bag. Why did this keep happening lately?

8

SATURDAY, JANUARY 21, 1984

John sat in an easy chair by his window on the fourth floor of Hôtel Richelieu. Below him, two young boys were playing soccer in the park across the street. The ground was dry enough to keep them from getting muddy. Oak leaves in the grass blew across the pavement, accompanying the laughter that buffeted up to his window. Their energy and innocence reminded him of Carl.

It took his exhausted mind time to process the scene and move on to other, more important matters. He had driven from Pennsylvania the previous evening after work, arriving at the hotel in the wee hours. He had only had the chance for a few hours' sleep and he was supposed to be meeting with Tri-Force in two hours. Big plans were afoot, and he needed to be a part of them.

John was concerned about Tri-Force. The fusion reactor data had long since been forwarded to the proper hands. However, it might be months, or even years, before test data would show any positive results. So what about Gelda in that time? Every day that passed was critical. What was her state of mind? They could be pretty sure she was still alive—otherwise, Drapeneau would have no leverage over the doctor. But even that was a hope, at best.

Drapeneau himself was an issue. With him at large, could anyone be secure? Louis and Hélène were happy in their new apartment, but how long could that continue?

John had enough experience with the Russian to know the situation was precarious. Images of those terrible days in the jungle flashed before him: the intense equatorial sun beating down on their fetid tent site; the muddy ground; the metallic scent of blood in the air, including his own . . . he shuddered in a sudden chill. In the process of his escape, he had killed the other interrogator—thought he had killed them both. Considering what they had done to him, they had it coming. Even so, to take the life of another human being . . . he was desperate . . . it had all happened so quickly . . .

Enthused shouting from across the street indicated that one of the boys had successfully scored a goal. It broke John's reverie, and he got a grip on himself. He knew that being tired, and not having a clear insight on the next steps, generally led to a state of depression. He had faced the feeling before. But he didn't have time to deal with that now; there was too much ahead of them to be done.

Not the least of which, in his mind, was ensuring that Gelda's safety would be considered in the coming conflicts.

John picked up Mark from the Pierre Elliott Trudeau Airport before heading to Garrett Bennett's office. He had arranged last week for his nephew to join him in Canada, in order for him to provide an official statement regarding his temporary capture in New Hampshire. He was glad Mark was willing to do his part in helping the case.

They wove carefully through the streets of Montréal, and met Louis outside the doors to Garrett's office. Louis also had a younger friend with him. John recognized him from Louis' wedding. Jacques . . . something. He was maybe seventeen, and wearing a Canadiens hockey jacket. He had extremely light blond hair, was cheerful, but not very talkative. John wondered why he was there. Garrett had said new information had come to light. Was it because of Jacques?

After Louis made introductions, John couldn't help but rib his friend. "You've put on weight, Louis, since I last saw you. Married life must agree with you."

Louis chuckled, and went along with the joke. "Messieurs, I think it is because I am transitioning from a lobster and sea-food diet to one containing more 'champignons bourguignons'."

This got a chuckle from the younger men, at least, and the ice was broken. Louis, still smiling, held the door open. They all entered the warm offices gratefully.

Bennett's office was on the first floor. The oak door opened, and the imposing frame of the chief assistant to the Deputy Defence Minister appeared. His craggy face welcomed them inside. "Come in, come in, gentlemen. Good to see you."

John entered Garrett's office for the first time. It was a pleasant, paneled room, with ground floor windows on the street and photos of Garrett's various naval comrades and Arctic scenes. It brought home to John just how valuable an ally his friend had turned out to be.

The secretary brought in more chairs to seat them all. The other two legs of Tri-Force, Ben Greenstone and Dr. Vanderstadt, were present.

The doctor was almost as tall as Garrett, but his lean and wiry frame, tanned face, and auburn hair indicated that he also was an outdoors man. His labs were not his only outlet. Ben was as reserved as always, but he examined the two younger men carefully as they entered the room. Mark and the other were talking hockey in an animated fashion.

Garrett served coffee, but quickly turned to the serious matter at hand. "Gentlemen, I would like to welcome you to Montréal; I am pleased you could come at such short notice. I don't need to tell you how urgent our efforts are here. We are moving things forward, collecting official statements, and I am very pleased that Louis Xenon has come with M'sieur Jacques Dionne of Montréal, a possibly crucial first-hand witness to the conspiracy."

Jacques squirmed in his seat at the introduction.

"Thanks to Jacques," Garrett continued, "We have been able to put both a name and a face to another conspirator in this endeavour; one Jean Claude, an employee of QFR."

John winced inwardly. Another connection to QFR. Things were not looking good for Philippe.

Ben shifted in his seat, reaching across the desk. "I do not know if everyone here knows exactly whom we are dealing with, so I have brought photographs of Gelda, Jean Claude and Drapeneau."

John looked at them carefully. Drapeneau was the only one of the three that he recognized.

When he passed them to Mark, he immediately flipped to the one of Gelda. "Yes, that's her. The girl I saw at Queboggin." He looked up at Dr. Vanderstadt. "She looked fine then, though maybe a little scared."

Dr. Vanderstadt nodded, lips tight.

"I think," Ben said, "it is time for the statements, then." He twisted in his seat to look at Garrett. "During that time, the rest of us can discuss what this information means for us, and where we are to go from here."

Mark frowned, but Jacques nodded slowly in understanding.

Garrett led them each to secure rooms, an attorney waiting to record the official account of events. John clapped Mark on the shoulder for reassurance before he left.

Dr. Vanderstadt was the first to speak after Mark and Jacques left. "Mark's information about Queboggin has helped us to a degree, but we seem to have hit a dead end. The RCMP and Civil Aiviation Authority have been to the site, and examined the plane there and taken fingerprints where they can. Gelda has been confirmed as being present at the site." The doctor's gaze swept out to the window. "But the trail ends there."

Ben cleared his throat. "It's good to note that we found a number of other prints at the site—they have been filed for future matching. The plane has been searched and tested for the possible importation of narcotics, with negative results. We do not as of yet have a connection between it and Gelda, but Mark's statement stands with regards to his own kidnapping."

"The plane's owner was an employee of QFR, was he not?" Louis asked. John himself had been reluctant to bring the subject up.

Garrett nodded. "He is. We have delayed moving against him because of the lack of evidence at this time. Mark's kidnapping has not been officially documented, so before we had no authority to do so."

"But with the connection to QFR, can we not now put pressure on the pilot?" Louis pressed.

Garrett looked to Dr. Vanderstadt, who slowly nodded. "It is time, I think, to move against QFR. Despite my reservations, it seems they are involved, at least in some way."

"We have been getting regulatory offices to slowly put pressure on QFR," Garrett said. "I think now is the time to come down on them on a broad front.

"We should confiscate that Cessna aircraft," Ben added. "Take it apart if we have to—put it in storage. That should cause the owner, Yves Bonnard, to complain. If he does, we can check it out. If he does not, we know he has something to hide. But it will create pressure, either way."

He slowly met the eyes of each of them. "The NATO summit is coming up. The personal pressure Gelda's kidnapping places on the Vanderstadt family is enormous. The U.S. stake in fusion research is in the order of billions of dollars. The program must not be held hostage to the whim of a few crackpots. The kidnappers have not shown their hand yet, but they have made major blunders. We need to tighten the screws until they make their demands."

John nodded. Even he had to admit that this was the best course.

Garrett leaned forward in his armchair. "Ben and I have been on the same page regarding this one. Considering the frequent connections to Philippe LeClerc and QFR Nuclear, we have been keeping an eye on each of the company's plants. The Captain of the Sureté in Cité des Mélèzes' has been reporting regularly to us on any unusual activity by key people at QFR's main administrative location, Lac Tamarack."

This had Doctor Vanderstadt's attention. "Yes?"

"He actually keeps track of most of the residents of the entire town, including visitors."

"Yes?" The impatience in the doctor's voice was palpable.

"He called me Thursday—I have since asked him to re-verify the information. There is a new face in town, and it closely matches none other than Martin Drapeneau."

"No!" The doctor jerked up to his full height. "I can't believe it— all this time, and he's been up there?"

"No, only recently. Apparently, Drapeneau was able to hire a private commercial pilot to fly him up north. We spoke to Captain Lavan, and he has surveillance tapes at the Cité des Mélèzes airport showing Drapeneau arriving there."

"Where has he gone?" Louis got the question in before the doctor.

Bennett turned to Louis, a frown on his face. "Captain Lavan was not able to verify immediately. He knows Drapeneau is in town, because he was spotted at the Company Commissary trying to purchase supplies, and later at both a small grocery store and a hardware outlet. Both merchants verified his ID from the police photos they were shown. But once again, sad to say, he's dropped out of sight. They think he's there for the long haul, because he purchased lots of groceries and items to fix a heater."

The doctor was curious. "Has he made any kind of connection to QFR?"

"None that the Captain was able to verify. It may be that Drapeneau is staying out of sight on purpose." Garrett leaned back in his chair. "Anyway, the long and the short of it is, I think we need to start having a more substantial presence at Cité des Mélèzes. Fortunately, this time of year, the rail connection closes down, and there is no available transportation from the vicinity other than by air. Air traffic can be monitored very closely. This means Drapeneau may have been able to get into the city easily, but there will be no way for him to get out without being apprehended."

"If the Sureté have not been able to find Drapeneau yet," John asked, "Will they even be able to? We do not have the kind of time it may take them to search." John nodded to the doctor. "Nor does Gelda."

"Quite right," Garrett said. "With his other responsibilities, Lavan will be stretched thin to mount a serious search for a man with Drapeneau's training. I'm thinking in terms of offering federal assistance to supplement the Sûreté officers that Lavan has at his disposal. This is a natural outgrowth of the doctor's meeting with the government in Ottawa. Conspiracy and armed threats by a foreign national are federal crimes."

The doctor nodded. "Yes, we have had discussions along those lines. As with them, I do want to insist, that if there is to be any direct contact with QFR's administration, I would like to be a part of it. I still believe I may be able to help stabilize the process."

John agreed, and was glad that the doctor was willing to resolve things peaceably. "I think the time has come to force the issue with Drapeneau and LeClerc. We have got to get to the bottom of who is holding Gelda."

Garrett stared at the carpet. "Yes . . . It may be time for you, Doctor, to fly north, and be available to us if we get to a stage where negotiations are required. I will assign a military officer as your personal aide, so you have protection the whole time that you're there."

Turning to John, he said, "What can you tell me about Drapeneau in this situation? We are slowly putting him into a corner. But I don't want to assume that will be the end of it."

John set his coffee down. He didn't want it to shake. "It won't be. He is a dangerous man. There is very little he won't do." He knew that from experience. "We will have to be very careful—and not just for our own sakes. If he does have Gelda, he isn't the sort of man to be hesitant about causing serious harm." That was as gentle as he could put it, considering Dr. Vanderstadt was in the room.

As it was, the doctor's hands were clenched tightly. He didn't look up at the others present.

A sharp knock on the door made all of the men turn. Garrett answered it. A secretary stood there, Mark beside her. He had finished his statement.

"I'm sorry, Mr Bennett. I know you stated you had not wished to be disturbed, but I think this call for you is important."

"Thank you." He looked back at the gathered men. "I won't be a moment."

Mark joined them back in the room, settling into the far corner.

The room was quiet until Garrett returned in a rush. "That was one of my contacts in the RCMP. They recently received an anonymous tip, from a suspicious employee who thinks Gelda Vanderstadt is being held by his employer, Philippe LeClerc."

Stunned silence met that blatant statement. Ben swore. "Great. Just what we need."

"Is this not a good thing?" Louis said. "It is not true confirmation, but it does reinforce our suspicions."

"The reason we were avoiding local authorities is to prevent attention. They are like a sieve for information—even if we try to keep it quiet, this will likely reach the media, and within only a few days at that."

"What if this panics Gelda's captors?" Dr. Vanderstadt was frantic. "What might they do to her?"

"We have to move now." Garrett nodded to John and Louis. "I'm sorry, but I think the doctor needs someone with him who has a intimate knowledge of Drapeneau and his mindset. Can you join us?"

John considered his schedule, but nodded in the affirmative. Fortunately, the next stage in the court case was weeks off. He could take some time off.

Louis hesitated, then set his jaw. "Hélène may not like it, but I need to see this through. Drapeneau tracked the negatives through me. I won't see anyone else hurt because of this man."

"He's not the only one that you and Gelda have to worry about."

Everyone turned to face Mark, startled.

He stuck his hands in his pockets. "Drapeneau has other people working with him. I've seen most of them. Those two that went to the cabin in New Hampshire were looking for Louis, yes?"

Ben's mouth was tight, but he nodded.

"So I'm going."

"Absolutely not!" Ben snapped before John could voice his own concerns. "We are involving too many civilians already. We don't need a college kid with no training getting involved.

Mark opened his mouth to protest.

"I don't want to hear it," Ben said.

Vanderstadt frowned. "So, if we are not investigating that route, what can we do?"

Garrett took off his glasses. "I have asked my department for permission to assign a small, highly-trained federal detachment, platoon-size, to help Captain Lavan in Cité des Mélèzes. The Captain said he can provide accommodations at his police barracks for them. It would also be handy to have the detachment available should the general security situation deteriorate. They can fly in on scheduled flights, in small groups of three or four, and integrate with Lavan's men. The whole approach is to go in quietly. We're also keeping a very tight watch on Jean Claude as well, to see how he moves."

Vanderstadt cut Bennett off. "But we don't know about Drapeneau's other accomplices. Mark is right. If Drapeneau only recently arrived in Cité des Mélèzes, and that is where Gelda is being kept, then there is someone else there with her. Mark is the only one who may be able to tell us who that is."

"I will stay out of the way if things show signs of becoming violent," Mark said. "I can just be available when we are investigating the plant. There are so many people about, I won't be in any danger."

Dr. Vanderstadt nodded. He could no longer sit still. "I have something else that might make it easier for everyone. It would generate way too much of a potential distraction to have our group move into Cité des Mélèzes on top of the soldiers at the local barracks. We don't want to draw that much notice. I would like to volunteer my plane. It can be converted from floats to skis, and has a capacity of six passengers plus equipment. If we fly up separately and establish a base camp at the north end of Tamarack Lake, it's within striking distance of the plant. We can easily stay in touch with Lavan by radio. When we need vehicle transportation, we'll call the Captain."

"It's not a bad suggestion—a kind of civilian component," Garrett answered. He was thinking it over. "It would give us flexibility without creating a stir among the citizens or employees. Can you stand the cold?" The arctic hero looked squarely at the doctor.

"My family frequently enjoys winter camping," Dr. Vanderstadt said. "If you can stand it, so can I."

"I am more familiar with a jungle environment, but I have plenty of experience in less-than-pleasant conditions." Louis wasn't going to let himself be forgotten.

John nodded agreement. Things were starting to move forward rapidly. They had best all be prepared.

MONDAY, JAN. 23, 1984

Suzette drove back to the Executive Lodge. It had been good to get out and about, if only briefly. She had just returned from a visit to the QFR offices at the Lac Tamarack plant. One of the other general secretaries had taken over her duties for Philippe, but it was still nice to be kept in the loop. Yves had stayed to keep an eye on Gelda, in case she needed anything.

She returned to the employee sitting room, where she found Yves in front of the TV.

"I thought you'd given up on soap opera." Suzette enjoyed teasing him. "Why don't you just find some girl, and get married."

Yves guiltily muted the television set. "I'm not sure there are any who would want me . . ." He trailed off and smiled weakly at Suzette; she knew it was just an excuse, and a poor one at that.

"Oh, come on. You'll never know unless you try. Anyway, a real girl would give you plenty of drama; and you're a person who needs a heck of a lot of it."

The two of them shared a chuckle.

"How's Gelda?"

"Nothing new. She returned those old magazines. Security came by at one-thirty to check the first floor windows, the doors, and the call system . . . it's all okay."

"Great. Oh, by the way—you've got some mail. Don't you normally get mail delivered to your post office box?"

"Normally, I would, yes." Yves' cheery demeanour had altered to a puzzled frown.

Suzette handed over the letter. It was return addressed as from the Civil Aviation Authority, Transport Canada. Maybe a licence renewal of some sort?

Yves deftly opened it up, and then groaned. "Sacré—" He bit off the rest of the word. He did not like swearing, or at least, what he considered swearing, in front of women. Whatever it was, it was serious.

"What? Yves, show me."

Yves limply held up the opened letter. Suzette snatched it, and glanced quickly down the printed sheet.

January 22, 1984

Re: Cessna Aircraft
Single Engine, 4 passenger
Serial Number: 07298034YH
Wing Markings: NHTK
Lic. No. 247CYH12

Dear M. Bonnard,

It has come to our attention that you violated Canadian air space by deviating from the flight plan for your aircraft and not returning to Charlo Airport, Dalhousie, NB from Lebanon, NH on Wednesday, October 12, 1983. Your aircraft has been impounded.

Please contact this office immediately regarding payment of fine and possible suspension of your licence.

Other charges may be filed by the Department of Citizenship and Immigration.

Very truly yours,

(signed)
Adam Rothberg
Director, Civil Aviation Authority

Suzette stared down at the letter. "What does this mean?"

"That I should have removed the plane and taken it to Charlo months ago," Yves said weakly.

"How are you going to explain it to the Authority?"

"All I can say is, I was forced down due to poor weather and darkness. I had to leave Queboggin in a hurry, because of the weather. I tried to call in, but the log books were gone. That young guy must have taken them. Queboggin has been snowed in since."

"Do you think they will believe that?"

"Probably not, but it may buy me some time. It's all true."

Suzette sighed. Queboggin again. When was that ever not going to come back to haunt them? She hated to see Yves involved.

From what Yves had explained to her, he got into real trouble when Claude wanted to secure the perimeter of the mountain cabin in New Hampshire. Yves knew that LeClerc would be in South Converse for the meeting, Tuesday, with Stillman Electric Corporation. He thought Claude had a legitimate reason for asking them to fly down on Thanksgiving to check out the cabin and its access points.

None of it was his fault, and yet he was taking the blame. "Do you want me to talk to Philippe about it?"

Yves straightened with a smile. "Could you? It might make things easier if I have confirmation from my boss as well."

"Certainly." Suzette shook her head. "Yves, how can you be so calm in a situation like this?" It wasn't even her plane, but her stomach was knotting.

"It's not hard. Whatever will happen, will happen—you just do the best you can with what you've got."

"I wish I had your confidence." She felt like she could use it in the coming days.

SATURDAY, JAN. 28, 1984

It was dark and rainy in Montréal when Louis looked out the window from their mall, rented home on Rue St. Denis. He had purchased a new rucksack, and it and his old duffle bag lay packed to the gills at the bottom of the stair. A parka was draped over the equipment, and his boots stood on the bottom step.

Hélène had busied herself over the last weeks with decorating the new home, and purchasing the hundred and one items so essential for a functioning household. Her parents bought them a beautiful new 'period' dining room table and sideboard with matching chairs.

Everything had been coming together so well. Hélène had also heard from the Superintendent of the Laval School District. The district needed a part-time assistant art instructor for one of their middle schools. Hélène was pleased to accept the offer, after an interview, and was thrilled with the opportunity to get her foot in the door and encourage the creative talents of young children at the same time.

Padding around in wool socks, Louis had breakfasted earlier with Hélène, and was looking over the list John sent him for a final check. There were some tearful moments earlier, but they had subsided. Hélène understood why he needed to do this.

"You and I have lived single lives for many years; we can probably survive a few weeks apart," she had said with a smile. "As for those painful memories, they may take longer to heal, but please keep on telling me each time they come. That's why I'm here. We can take on the ups and downs, the fears, together."

Louis looked about their new home. How lucky he was, months before, when she had first come out to brave the storm with him on the M/V L'Aventure.

John arrived in his station wagon at six, with young Mark Talyard in tow. Louis knew that John must be going through something similar. He had had to leave Sal and Carl time and again during the last few months. It was really a shame, and now Louis could truly empathize.

In transferring his things to the wagon, he was surprised to see, along with other rucksacks and duffle bags, two pairs of skis on the roof and snowshoes inside the vehicle. The scale of the operation was becoming evident.

John and Mark busied themselves in the driveway, re-adjusting the baggage, when it came time to part.

A pain tightened in Louis' chest as he went inside to say goodbye. Hélène stood at the foot of the empty stair, with tears starting to mist once again in her eyes.

Louis took her in his arms. "Be careful Hélène—be safe until I come back." Hélène could not answer. Again, he was conscious of how young she was. He hated to leave her alone. "I'm sorry, Hélène, but we have to do this. I love you. Please take care of yourself. I'll call as often as I can . . ." It was all something he had said before, but Louis needed to hear it one more time; a reassurance to himself as much as for Hélène.

For the last time, he held her close, her sweet-smelling, silken hair against his cheek. In a familiar gesture, she held out her hand to him as he went through the door—her fingers brushing his until they separated.

"I'll be back soon, ma chérie; it won't be long."

She returned a wistful smile.

As the loaded station wagon left their driveway in the first light of dawn, he saw her waving kisses to him until she disappeared from view.

Dr. Roeloff Vanderstadt had done an impressive job packing equipment and provisions in the cargo hold of his big, 600 horsepower

DeHavilland Otter. The officer that Garrett Bennett had assigned was already on hand and helping the doctor.

Louis investigated a number of large, thick containers with snap-down locking mechanisms.

The doctor noticed his curiosity. "Our food supply. We don't want to attract wolves or bears to our campsite. Food is scarce up north." In spite of all their equipment, there was still space left. "We still need to go over to the fuel dock, to get gasoline for the second part of our trip. It's very expensive up north."

With five men on board, the plane taxied over to the fuelling station, where a row of three drums were sitting. It took them another twenty minutes to load those on board as well. For safety, they had to carefully balance the fuel, passengers, and cargo. The doctor was very specific, and things had to be rearranged twice before he was satisfied.

Louis was curious. "Will we really need this much fuel?" Even with the lift, ramp, and trolley to help, the drums were heavy.

"Oh yes." The doctor slammed shut the last hatch, and began fastening down the locks. "Consumption varies greatly, based on wind direction, speed, load, and altitude, but for this trip, we will go through this and more. I'm budgeting twelve hundred air miles each way. We'll be refuelling at Moosonee, Ontario."

"That's near James Bay, isn't it?"

"Quite right. I am hoping it has frozen over by now—much of Hudson Bay does in the deep winter."

Louis nodded, taking a peek at the plane's under-carriage and the combined skis and wheels for hard surface runways. He imagined it would be tricky in the extreme to land such a craft on anything but the flattest terrain, usually the surface of a frozen lake.

After fastening their seat belts and getting clearance from the tower, the plane took off, making a wide arc from St. Hubert over Pointe-aux-Trembles and the St. Lawrence, toward the Laurentians. The noise from the single air-cooled engine was deafening, but to make conversation possible, they had earphones, with mikes and jacks connected to the pilot.

Flying northwest, the brown fields and grey forests beneath soon gave way to a few white patches of bare ground, and much larger regions of dark conifers and snow-covered lakes. They cruised at approximately three thousand feet, but were mostly below the clouds that extended up to the southern shores of James Bay. They encountered a few snow flurries near Montréal, but otherwise visibility was good.

Just before noon, the Otter touched down on the hard packed snow at Moosonee. While refuelling, they took a short break at the airfield's lunch counter, stretching after the four-hour flight. The break wasn't nearly long enough, in Louis' mind, before they had to take off again for Cité des Mélèzes.

The distant surface of Hudson Bay was locked in ice, though large, ice-free fissures showed where winds had exposed the salt water beneath. A snowy boreal forest covered the land surface. Louis began to appreciate the vast extent of the sub-arctic, stretching in patterns of dark and light to the horizon.

Louis knew very little about Cité des Mélèzes, other than that significant deposits of uranium ore had been discovered nearby. He assumed that the ore's extraction was a critical part of the plant's economic feasibility.

An hour later, they passed over the huge hydro plant at Radisson. It was approaching four-thirty when they touched down on Lac Tamarack.

The instant the skis grazed the deep snow, the doctor skilfully gunned the engine for extra power, and brought the tail down hard to compensate for friction in the front that would have toppled the plane over on its nose.

The props were revving at close to maximum RPMs as the doctor taxied the plane in a great arc toward the point of land where they were to make their camp near the north end of the lake. The men were happy to have reached their destination safely.

When the plane came to rest and the prop stopped turning, Dr. Vanderstadt ran through a quick shutdown procedure and lifted himself from the pilot's seat.

Louis unfastened his seat belt and flexed his joints, stiff from sitting in one place for so long. The others did the same around him, Mark on shaky legs.

They stepped out. Overhead, puffy, rose-coloured clouds stretched to the horizon in the southwest. Days and nights were far from equal, and the bright sun was well below the distant tree line. The clean air of the north was a lot drier than Louis expected, probably due to the cold temperatures. The doctor was business-like in encouraging his team to make haste. The extra fuel was left on board, but the tents, skis, and snowshoes were broken out quickly. There was even a toboggan for transporting supplies.

They made camp on the west side of the point of land, about a hundred yards up the beach from the shoreline. The snow was deep and powdery, and Louis had fun trying to master the art of walking in snowshoes. Trees in this area were stunted and sparse, grouped together where they found protection from rocky outcroppings and dips in the land. One such group of white spruce and balsam fir offered shelter as a wind break, and also material for insulating their ground cloths from the snow.

While the doctor's military escort contacted the Captain of the Sûreté, John and Mark got busy lugging supplies from the plane on the toboggan, and Louis helped the doctor with setting up the kitchen tent.

As predicted, the grey evening twilight soon deepened, and they all hurried to get the last of everything from the plane. Mark and John were only shapes moving around in the gloom.

The main tent was soon filled-to-capacity with supplies and equipment. Once everyone gathered around, they set up lanterns, and had some light to work by. Mark and John planned to occupy a two-man tent, the doctor would be in another with his bodyguard, and Louis would have his own tent.

New snow would bury the tents soon, so the trick was to be certain that melting snow was kept outside. Fresh white spruce boughs were the answer, and a liberal amount of these were put down as a base to provide insulation over the snow, before being covered with a waterproof tarp. They were soon prepared for the winter climate.

It was completely dark when John finished erecting his tent and spread out his sleeping bag. With his rucksack and duffle inside, he felt confident that he and Mark would have a restful night. The doctor had provided air mattresses, which made a big difference.

When John's eyes adjusted to the darkness, the white snow still gathered enough light to provide visibility between tents. When he returned to the main tent, the doctor was busy making stew. The smell made John realize how hungry he had become. They sat on packing cases, eating from their tin plates with eagerness. Afterwards, clean-up was quick, with hot, soapy water from a pot of melted snow on the stove. They had put in a lot of work.

"So what's the plan, Doctor? What's our first assignment?" John was eager to get going.

"Captain Lavan has been contacted, and told that we are on-station and operational," the doctor said. "I'd like to see how he's been making out with his detachment. I think tomorrow it would be wise for us to meet with the unit and get an update on their canvassing strategy. We will also want to have maps of the area ourselves. We don't want Drapeneau to escape this time. I don't want him to have the chance to do Gelda any harm."

"Mes amis, what type of armament do we have?" Louis, as always, brought realism into the picture.

John agreed with his friend whole-heartedly. He did not know if Drapeneau still had his Glock, but he was no longer willing to be out-gunned.

The doctor answered, "I've got two Savage deer rifles with scopes, and a small Mauser target pistol."

John patted his holster and weapon, lying on one of the crates next to him. "I've still got my 45; Louis, don't you have your 38 calibre police special?" Ben Greenstone had slaved hard through mounds of paperwork to rush specialty permits for John and Louis, allowing them to carry in Canada. Drapeneau's actions in New Hampshire had been enough proof for the protection of life authorization.

"Oui." His hand went to his belt, and he gestured to the doctor's escort. "But I hope that the Colonel has something heavier. This Russian doesn't fool around."

The Colonel laughed. "I do, but I didn't know I'd be joining a Special Forces unit."

John chimed in, "Don't worry, Colonel, we've been around the block a few times with this guy Drapeneau, and we know what to expect—I think it is the balance of the folks at QFR that we're a little unsure about."

Mark was standing by and said, "For the record, I am completely unarmed, and will have to keep out of the way—by using my little grey cells." He pointed to the wool cap on his head.

John laughed. "Oh, we'll have plenty of things for you to do, to keep you occupied."

The Colonel grunted. "You are here to identify those other than Drapeneau that may be involved. No more." Along with Ben, the Colonel had been quite against Mark's presence at the camp. John figured though, with what the boy had been through, he could handle himself.

Bit by bit, each of the men seemed to slowly lose their earlier energy. The day had caught up to them. The generator outside continued to purr.

The doctor stood after finishing with the last of the dishes. "Okay, men, lights out in ten minutes. We've got to save gas. Morning comes pretty soon around here, and we've a lot to do tomorrow."

John made his way back to the tent. The snow was deep, making snowshoes mandatory, even behind their treed shelter. Life in the icy north was possible, but progress slow. It required a lot of preparation just to accomplish a few things: to keep warm, dress, prepare meals, and get from one place to another. Things would not happen quickly; it was something they all had to get used to. After the long trip north from Montréal, he welcomed the chance to rest his weary bones.

Gelda was sitting on her bed at the Executive Lodge. There was nowhere else for her to be, really.

The low sun reached through the windows and warmed her hands as she practised knitting a scarf. She had no wool or needles, but she moved her fingers and imagined a ball of thread to occupy herself through the long days. Time was growing heavy on her hands, and she no longer took much interest in reading.

Further word of change was not forthcoming from Suzette. She was still friendly, but distant, and a sense of unease was always present.

The sun's bright disk approached the horizon among the branches of the tall larches outside, their dark tracery reaching her window. The lake had fallen into shadow. It would be much colder tonight.

Towards the south, she heard the distant sound of an approaching light-engine plane. She wistfully remembered her father's DeHavilland Otter, and the camping excursions that he used to take their family on. She missed home so much. Wouldn't it be nice if it was the Otter?

She stopped playing the game with her fingers and lay down on the bed, covering herself with a blanket. When would she be able to see her family again? How worried were they right now? But still, she didn't wish to threaten their safety; she hoped M'sieur LeClerc would be able to find a solution quickly.

As daybreak reached across the snowy landscape, Louis crawled out of his tent. It was eight-thirty; much later than he'd planned. The puffy clouds of the previous afternoon had given way to the light of a clear dawn. The air was crisp and frigid. John and Mark were up, and had joined Dr. Vanderstadt and the Colonel in the cook tent.

Mark laughed. "Here he comes now. We thought you had gone into hibernation."

" Messieurs, my body clock is tuned to the angle of the sun above the horizon. In the North, naturally, it falls later in the day." Louis could tell he was going to be the butt of jokes for the rest of the trip, but also knew that to weaken, in the face of the others' jibes, was to lose the battle completely. Joking right along with them eased things along well.

In twenty minutes, they finished their coffee and egg omelette, and began gathering their things for the day. Louis rolled up his sleeping bag, secured his tent door, and put the rest of his necessities in a rucksack to take with him. Making sure he had dry gloves and an extra sweater, he re-fastened the snowshoes to his boots.

Mark and John had looked at the map with Vanderstadt, and left immediately on cross-country skis to break a trail to the service road, roughly a mile and a half away. They had to cross the point of land and follow the shoreline to the north end of the lake. The doctor stayed to clean and secure the cooking utensils in the tent and make sure everything was put away for the day.

"I asked the Colonel to check the plane this morning. If you come with me, Louis, you can carry that battery case with you." The doctor wanted to be sure he had two-way communication with Captain Lavan at all times.

"What's the temperature this morning?" It seemed really cold to Louis.

"Oh, I'd say about negative twenty-five degrees—that's Celsius, not Fahrenheit."

Louis shivered.

"That's actually fairly mild for this time of year. Do you have enough layers?"

"Oui, I am ready to go."

They started out at a good clip. The doctor had brought ski poles, which he recommended for stabilization. The shoes and poles provided an opportunity for full body aerobic exercise, and Louis was grateful he'd had a good night's sleep. He trailed the doctor and his guard, the Colonel, but managed to keep up, and they arrived together at the service road.

Captain Lavan had arranged for a driver to pick them up at the turn-around, but he had not yet arrived. After a brief discussion, the men decided to make their way down the road to meet him. Louis could see the distinct advantage that John and Mark had on skis over those with snowshoes on this terrain.

When the police van arrived, they quickly removed their equipment and put it into the back of the vehicle.

It did not take them long to arrive at the barracks and be introduced. Louis appreciated the warmth inside. They soon got down to discussions of strategy used for canvassing the community. Captain Lavan took the floor. "We are sending four-man teams to inspect the outside of houses and interview the owners of those that live where Drapeneau was last seen. Hopefully, from there, we can trace where he went to next.

"In the meantime, we have set up a checkpoint between the city and the airport, manned by our men, with the backup that Garrett Bennett is sending us. All vehicles are inspected, and all newcomers to the city registered."

"Is that not a little obvious?" Louis asked. "What if Drapeneau panics?"

The doctor nodded, a frown on his face. "We do not want to push him, or Philippe LeClerc, into doing anything rash, like harming Gelda."

"Quite right," Captain Lavan said. "We are proceeding under the guise of a commonplace roadblock, checking for licences, impaired driving, and the likes. But each of my men will be on the look-out for this Martin Drapeneau."

John had remained silent, a troubled look on his face. Now he turned to Captain Lavan. "Have you mentioned anything about Drapeneau to the Director of QFR?"

The Captain shook his head. "Not yet. I wish to wait until we get the preliminary city search complete." He paused. "I have known Philippe ever since QFR broke ground for the nuclear plant here. I think he trusts me, as I do him. So far, I have not had an appropriate opportunity to meet with him in private."

Dr. Vanderstadt spoke out firmly, "Captain, this is actually one of the most critical questions we have in front of us at this time. We must know if LeClerc is supporting Drapeneau in any way, and what, if anything, he knows about Gelda's kidnapping."

The Captain sighed. "Very well. I will call the Director's office today."

9

Unusually perturbed, Philippe LeClerc lay sleepless in bed at the Executive Lodge. It was three o'clock in the morning, and the glowing face of his alarm clock looked like a red eye in the darkness. He did not know if it was the temperature of the room, or something he ate, or an aftermath of the long meeting he had with the other board members that same afternoon that kept him up.

The members had returned south in their separate planes, but the meeting had been like pulling nails out of an oak plank. There were objections to all aspects of the deal Philippe had negotiated with TransOntario. Some of the QFR board members had personal holdings with the company, and they wanted butter on both sides of their bread. Others were dead set against any merger at all.

Many things went through Philippe's mind, and he restlessly leafed through them as if he were picking up folders from his desk. Suzette's name kept cropping up. Was it right to continue to keep her with Gelda at the Lodge? But what other option did he have? He couldn't risk his family, not when he wasn't even there for them.

And what about the Vanderstadts? Was it better to put them at risk, or to leave them without knowledge of their daughter? He felt like his brain would explode.

A buzzer sounded on the side table. It was his personal telephone. Who could possibly be calling him in the middle of the night? A deep worried voice crackled over the wires. It was his Montré-al butler.

"Hi, George. What's going on? Are Bethe and the children okay?"

"Yes sir—for now. But I think this is really important, and deserves action right away."

"Why . . . What's happening?"

"I was reading the latest issue of L'Action Nationale, and—"

"What are they saying?" Philippe slumped back in his bed, relaxing a little.

"Yes, the wife and I were coming home last night on the Metro and I saw this article about you and QFR."

That got his attention. "And . . ."

"It says 'an anonymous tip was recently reported to the RCMP, and leaked to our sources'. The article claims that you and the offices of QFR have custody of one Gelda Vanderstadt, as an attempt to force your 'radical social views' on the scientific community, and block the coming European summit on nuclear energy."

"Oh no . . ."

"It's bad, sir. The article is painting you as some kind of a traitor, with ideals that betray Québec's national patriotism."

Thanking the butler, he sprung out of bed; but Philippe wasn't thinking about the company, Parti 17, or Canada. If Drapeneau found out, and thought that they were the ones to call in the anonymous tip . . . he paused, the phone line raised once more to his ear. Could Gelda have called in the tip?

He finished dialing Suzette on the house line.

His secretary's answer was immediate. "I don't think so, Philippe. She's not had access to a phone line. And I really don't think she would want to. She seems worried about her family, much more so than what's happening to her here."

"What a disaster. This will not only bring Drapeneau down on our heads, but the authorities as well." Philippe tapped his bedside table in agitation. "Could that have been his plan? Did he want that to happen?"

"Who?"

"Drapeneau! What if he called the authorities? To put pressure on us?"

"I don't know . . . it's possible."

"You know what? It doesn't matter. Either way, there's no time to lose. We have to move Gelda, and quickly."

"Tonight?"

"Yes. They'll assume that we have her on company grounds. She's no longer safe here. But we still need to be able to keep her close—I'll see if we can set her up in the Guest House, in town here."

"I'll have to let Yves know."

"Yes, get him to meet us there in about an hour. In the meantime, meet me in my suite. I'll get you a suitcase with two of my wife's overcoats—also a hat and scarf. Go wake Gelda and tell her we have to move her. Remember: be quiet."

Suzette hung up.

Philippe hurried to grab his robe. How had it come to this?

"Gelda . . . Gelda, wake up!"

Gelda groaned on hearing Suzette's voice, but moved anyway. She sounded scared.

It took a while for Gelda to understand what was expected. She had been in deep sleep.

"It's okay, Gelda, we just have to move you. Put your clothes on. We're taking a short trip. Pack your things in this bag, and put on the hat and scarf. It's cold outside. I'll be back in ten minutes."

For saying everything was okay, Suzette sure was in a hurry. She nearly slammed the door behind her, rushing down to the kitchen.

Gelda finished dressing, and started packing her things. The frantic rustling downstairs eased, and she heard voices.

"I'm going back to get Gelda; I'll only be a minute."

"Be quick as you can!"

The last was a man's voice, but she didn't think it was Yves. Gelda sat on her bed, her long blonde hair spilling over her scarf. Suzette entered in a flurry. She grabbed Gelda's suitcase, then stopped. "Do you have any pins?"

Gelda gestured to the nécessaire on the top of her bag.

"We have to make sure that none of this shows from under your hat." Suzette quickly combed Gelda's hair into a bun, and adjusted the scarf around her neck.

"Where are we going?"

"We're going to take you to the Guest House."

"Who's we?"

"Philippe is downstairs . . . M'sieur LeClerc."

"Oh. I haven't seen him since—"

"We have to be very quiet."

"Oh." There were huge questions Gelda was dying to ask, but the worry that etched lines in Suzette's face convinced her to hold off for now.

They tiptoed out of the room and down the hall to the main stair. M'sieur LeClerc was standing at the bottom, his tall frame blocking most of the doorway. For the director of a large company, he certainly was young.

"Good morning, Gelda." He smiled sympathetically, but it came out forced. He quickly placed her bags next to Suzette's in the back of the van.

Gelda looked up at the dark sky. The cold air stung her face. This was morning?

"Once we get to the Guest House, if anybody asks, I'm going to pretend you're Suzette's niece," M'sieur LeClerc said. "We need to move you quickly, but I don't want anyone the wiser. We're trying to get you back to your family as safely as we can."

The emphasis on these last words had Gelda questioning her guardians during the drive. Eventually, M'sieur LeClerc told her about the anonymous tip that the RCMP had received. Gelda expressed concern over her family, but there was nothing that could be done at this point. She had the distinct feeling that the QFR Director was not telling her the whole story.

As the van moved through the tamarack forest that gave the nearby lake its name, her eyes drank in the unaccustomed beauty of the white frost on the conifers caught in their headlights. Deep snow on either side of the road reminded her that she was much farther north than Montréal.

After two miles, they passed a manned gatehouse where a guard came out, smiled and waved them on. She was soon struck by the immense proportions of a huge building and two looming cooling towers that appeared on her left. Almost immediately, she saw lighted bronze letters on a low, concrete wall at the entrance drive, now almost drifted over by snow.

QUÉBEC-FERMONT-RAPIDE
LAC TAMARACK CENTRALE NUCLÉAIRE #3

They continued past the plant on a well-travelled road. Bright lights shone far to the left, with a few low buildings arranged around a small control tower:

Gelda read the sign, "AÉROPORT MUNICIPAL, CITÉ DES MÉLÈZES." She could see blue and white landing lights stretching out in the distance beyond the hangers.

A mile further, she began to see more lights in the distance, but suddenly the van slowed down.

"What's this? It looks like a road block." M'sieur LeClerc sounded puzzled.

There were police vehicles lined up on either side of the road, and two officers were checking the truck in front, which had just come from the airfield. When it pulled ahead, the officer walked up to the dark van. "Good morning, sir. Driver's licence please."

LeClerc pulled out his wallet.

"Very good, M'sieur. Please drive carefully."

As they pulled away, Gelda noticed that one of the parked police vehicles was filled with armed soldiers in white winter parkas. What was going on so early in the morning?

"Did you see that?" Suzette asked Philippe.

"I did indeed. Captain Lavan of the Sûreté wants to speak with me in the morning . . ." He shot a glance at Gelda and stopped.

Once again, she wondered what else these two weren't telling her.

The early pre-dawn transfer had gone smoothly. Yves was on hand, and had convinced the caretaker that 'Suzette's niece' was on the verge of collapse. The caretaker chattered away the entire time they were at the Guest House complex, and promised not to bother the new visitors unless called upon. Philippe ensured that Yves would visit the women twice a day. He would bring food, meds, supplies and messages as necessary.

A few hours later at his office, Philippe fought to collect his thoughts as the first staff began arriving. His world was imploding. He closed the door to his office and buzzed his secretary. "Please hold all calls. I'm going to be very busy today." He felt lost; Suzette was his sounding board, and now she was out of circulation.

He sipped hot coffee with the bun he had brought from the cafeteria. The first light of a grey dawn was beginning to show in the southeast. The sky was thickly overcast. He turned his chair to stare outside. A few fat flakes were caught in the light from his office as they drifted quickly down the heavily insulated glass windowpanes and built up on the sill. Normally, this would have been a good day.

There must be a way to get out of this situation with the press.

He would have to call Bethe at noon, and see if she and the kids were okay. And not just from Drapeneau. Extra security measures would need to be made, depending on how seriously the media were pressing. He might even have to notify the police—the neighbours would be going crazy.

Philippe's brain was racing ahead. At reception, no doubt, the switchboard was lighting up with calls from the south. Before much longer, the media would start flying in. It would be a madhouse. They could not let anyone but employees and suppliers inside the gates.

And then there was Lavan. The Captain of the Sûreté had scheduled a meeting with him this morning. Likely, it had something to do with that checkpoint business. Or could it be something more? If the media were already pressing him for information, what about the police? The Sûreté were separate from the RCMP, but if one heard news on the girl's kidnapping, it would likely be shared.

Philippe sighed heavily. There was no other choice; time had run out.

He buzzed his new secretary. "Geneviève, see if you can get Captain Lavan on the phone."

"Yes sir. We've been swamped with calls from Montréal. We even got a call from Toronto. The TV and radio stations are wanting information about something in the papers."

"I know, Geneviève, just tell them, 'no comment'. We'll release a statement later today." He would have to get his second-in-command, Ian McGuinness, to handle the press inquiries. Today, he needed to give full attention to Lavan—and Dr. Vanderstadt.

Drapeneau was an issue that would have to wait for tomorrow.

At quarter after nine, Captain Hubert Lavan arrived at Philippe's office. The Captain was a little under 170 cm tall, compact and muscular, with a dark complexion. His black uniform contrasted sharply with the informal civilian clothes worn by management. Curious staff peered around corners and office doors.

Philippe motioned Lavan in with a warm smile and shut the door firmly. "Welcome, Captain. Can I get you something to take the chill off?"

"No thank you, M'sieur LeClerc, I'm good." The Captain sat down. Philippe knew his formal tone was not a good sign. But then, this was a serious situation.

"Thank you for seeing me so early. I would like to bring you up to date on security measures in the Cité. No doubt you have seen the airport check point?"

"Yes, I was wondering about that . . ."

"It seems there is a felon wanted by authorities in Montréal, who has been spotted in town. A certain Martin Drapeneau."

Philippe stiffened. Drapeneau? Here? It was a good thing Gelda was safe. But how long could that last with that madman about? The Captain was watching him carefully, and Philippe forced himself to relax.

Lavan looked like he was about to say something else, but continued with his first thought instead. "He's wanted for attempted murder and forcible abduction in both the United States and Canada; including conspiracy in the Gelda Vanderstadt kidnapping case." He paused pointedly. "You may have heard of him?"

How had they discovered the tie to Drapeneau? Was now the time? The Sûreté Captain had set it up for him. Should he just announce it, out of the blue?

"Isn't Dr. Vanderstadt one of your employees?" The Captain was trying a different tack.

Philippe relaxed a little. "An associate, yes, but not an employee. He's the director of a laboratory at our Portage Lake plant, and is funded by grants from the Department of Energy, Mines, and Resources and Atomic Energy Canada. I respect the doctor very highly."

Philippe put his hand up. "Listen Captain, let's stop playing around. You want to know if I have had anything to do with Gelda's kidnapping, and if I know anything about Drapeneau's whereabouts—or if I'm trying to shield him. The answer to the first question is 'yes, indirectly' and to the second question, the answer is 'no'. Do you want some background on this?"

Lavan sat back in his chair. He had yet to close his mouth. He shifted uncomfortably, finally finding words. "You understand, Philippe, that anything you say can be used in a court of law against you?"

Philippe took the Captain's switch to his first name as a good sign. "Yes, I do."

"Do you want an attorney present?"

"No, I've already talked to my lawyers."

"Would you be willing to have this discussion recorded?"

Philippe hesitated. But he was in all the way now. "Yes, fine, Captain."

The Captain pulled out a hand-held tape recorder from his vest. He tested it, then pushed a button, setting it on the middle of the desk between them.

The Captain began, "Well, M'sieur Philippe LeClerc, why don't you start from the beginning . . ."

Thirty minutes later, LeClerc had completed the history of his involvement with the Queboggin incident and Gelda's kidnapping. He ensured that it was clear that Yves and Suzette were not involved until after Gelda's consent was given. Unfortunately, he had to implicate Jean Claude severely, but as far as he was concerned, Jean had gotten himself into that mess.

He also explained Drapeneau and his threats, both the implied ones and the explicit event at his New Year's party.

"Drapeneau kept proving that he was capable of what he claimed. I understand that this is a difficult situation, but it was for Gelda's, her family's, and my family's protection that we brought her here. She has agreed with the idea. But my lawyers still keep throwing red flags in my face. It seems the only possible outcome is jail time, big time."

"Well, Philippe, that's for a judge and jury to decide. They'll have to weigh it on the merits." The Captain tapped his pen on the pad he had been using for notes. "So the question I find I must now ask is: do you do know where Gelda is at this moment?"

"Yes, I do."

"And it is my understanding that she is not a captive?"

"She's only here on her own insistence."

"And do you think that you could convince her to be taken into police protection?"

Philippe hesitated. "I think so—maybe. She is very concerned for her parents."

"Well, her father is in town, as it happens."

Philippe nearly leapt from his chair. "Really?" That changed a lot of things.

"Well, as a matter of fact, he flew in here on Wednesday. I met with him yesterday, but our focus has been on apprehending Drapeneau."

"I certainly agree with going after Drapeneau, but, as I told you, he is a very dangerous man. He threatened me in my own home." And now he was in Cité des Mélèzes? How were they going to get out of this one unscathed?

"I know you're concerned." Captain Lavan folded up his notebook. "We know how dangerous he is. We have two civilians, both ex-military, with significant experience with him." Lavan leaned forward. "That is why we want Gelda under protective custody."

Philippe rubbed his face with his hands. "I'm definitely worried about Drapeneau. With the search going on, do you have enough men to protect Gelda?"

"Reinforcements are being flown in as we speak. By this evening, I am confident that we'll have both a place and protection for her."

"In that case, until this evening, I'd like to keep Gelda at the Guest House, where she is at the moment, for safekeeping. She's comfortable now, and well taken-care-of. Then her father can decide about the logistics of her release, how to deal with publicity, and everything else. I'm eager it not be a press festival. I'm ready to do all of this in her best interest."

The Captain sat back, considering. Philippe knew this was a big thing he was asking. Finally, he said, "Very well, Phillipe. I'll contact the doctor this morning. We're going to have to move quickly on this. Maybe he can meet with you here this afternoon."

"Right here would be fine."

Lavan stood up, sternly glaring down at Philippe. He was surprised by the officer's sudden change. "Because we need your continued compliance on this, and because it has been made clear to me that Martin Drapeneau must not learn what is transpiring, I am not going to arrest you here and now."

Philippe looked down. The tape recorder was gone—it had disappeared at some point during their discussion.

"But let me make this perfectly clear. A crime has still been committed. Under duress or not, you will still have to be held accountable. So consider this a house arrest. If I hear of you trying to leave these grounds, I will have to come down on you with the full force of the law. It will not be pretty."

Philippe reacted solemnly, all relief from having confessed the extent of his involvement evaporating. He glanced out at the thickening snow. The worst may have just begun.

⊕

A light snow was falling when Jean Claude and young Bourget flew in to Cité des Mélèzes on a small, chartered plane from St. Hubert, Québec. Once inside the heated lobby, a man with a dark beard greeted them, and they departed quickly in a rusty black van toward the city.

As soon as they sat in the van, Drapeneau passed them fake QFR Portage Lake employee I.D. badges. He had carefully duplicated them to look like originals, but the cards did not have the electronic wizardry in them that more sophisticated systems had. "We have to go through a new check point to get into the city, so pretend you still work for the company, but have been transferred."

The check point did not pose any problem for the three. The Russian had brought the same uniforms that he had used at Portage Lake, weeks before. Jean had his own.

When they cleared the barrier, Drapeneau turned to Jean. "So, did you call in the tip?"

"Yes I did. Even better, it was leaked to the press. I heard that one of the city's political magazines got a hold of it, and ran with the story."

"Excellent. That should put pressure on LeClerc."

Jean nodded, glad that Drapeneau was pleased. "There were many press people in the St. Hubert terminal heading north."

"Good. We've got to put the heat on LeClerc. We can't let this thing go cold."

It was snowing in light flurries when John woke up that morning. He looked out over the point of land and nodded satisfactorily at the snow-covered tarps providing camouflage for the plane and their little camp. Now, they were gathered for breakfast and to pore over the maps that Captain Lavan had given them.

Louis was sitting with these now, having laid them out on the folding table once again. John wondered idly if the Frenchman had taken their ribbing of him yesterday a little too close to heart. "At it already, Louis?"

"Ah, bonjour mon ami. Yes, I thought to get an early start on things. I was not the only one." Louis nodded towards Dr. Vanderstadt, who was pulling out supplies for breakfast.

John helped in preparation, and afterward, the four of them pulled out the marked-up maps once again while Mark did the dishes. It was nearly eleven am when the Colonel stepped outside to start up the radio for their morning communications.

"So, what are we supposed to be doing at this point?" the doctor asked. "Captain Lavan and his men have the town covered with the roadblocks and are investigating the houses near where Drapeneau was last seen."

"We have the capability to search more specifically," John said. "We're less obvious than the police."

Louis tapped the map, along the outskirts of town. "M'sieur Drapeneau is not just keeping himself out of sight to achieve his goals. In fact, he likes to have people underestimate him. I doubt he is staying within the city itself."

The Colonel waved Dr. Vanderstadt over to the radio. Apparently, the Captain needed to speak with him. He excused himself from the table.

"I agree, Louis," John said. "That man is able to survive in all manner of harsh conditions. I wouldn't be surprised if—"

"Really! She is?" the doctor's shout carried across the camp. "No, no of course I understand. Yes, I will be there as soon as I can. Of course!" He dropped the headset, leaving the Colonel scrambling to shut it down and get things back in place.

"Gelda's been found!" The doctor was moving as quickly as he could in snowshoes towards their parked gear and his skis.

"Really?" John said.

"Yup," Mark said, a big grin on his face. He was walking back from the radio as well. Apparently, he had been listening in. "It seems Philippe LeClerc confessed. He knows where she's being held, and is talking to the police now."

LeClerc's admission was big news to the three. Mark filled them in on what Captain Lavan had reported, as Dr. Vanderstadt was already making preparations to leave for the town, the Colonel in tow.

John was delighted to hear about Philippe's explanation of the events at Queboggin. It confirmed his long-held belief that Philippe would never intentionally harm Gelda or Mark, or even try to scuttle Dr. Vanderstadt's work. "I've always believed Philippe is a decent man—I just hope that Gelda's safe recovery will help him out of this legal swamp with Claude and Drapeneau."

Louis was looking at the map once again. "It also means that the Sûreté can crack down harder on our nemesis, Drapeneau. We will not have to worry about him or LeClerc harming Gelda. I think we should speak with Captain Lavan, and see what we can do to help."

"Quite right, Louis. Things are about to get a lot harder for M'sieur Drapeneau."

⊕

Before dinner, Jean insisted on being dropped off at Niko's Greek restaurant. He had taken one look at the Russian's cold, dingy shack and empty cupboards with nothing more than cans of beans, sardines, and instant coffee, and wanted out. Next time, he was going to do the shopping.

He waved off Drapeneau's concerns about being seen. He was not a wanted man. And he knew this city, having visited the plant many times. Most of the employees ate at the plant cafeteria. It was unlikely anyone at Niko's would recognize him; especially with the thick snow that was coming down now.

Drapeneau agreed to let him order take-out, while he and Bourget went to fill up at a gas station.

When Jean entered, he found a table in the corner by himself to wait for the order. He had been there five minutes when a voice, wheezened by age, greeted him.

"Hello, Jean! What are you doing here? I didn't know you were in town."

Jean winced. The caretaker of the guesthouse was a doddering old codger, who babbled ceaselessly to any fool who would listen. He wasn't technically an employee at the plant, so likely had not heard of Jean's firing. Still, he would have to think of an excuse.

"Oh, I'm . . . up here looking for a new apartment."

"In this weather? They say there's a storm coming, you know." The old man sat himself down without so much as a by-your-leave. "How are things at the plant?"

"Well, nothing much is new." He kept his answers short and hoped they would hurry up with his order . . . Maybe he could get away without causing a scene.

"Too bad. I guess we can't all have exciting times, like being visited by pretty young ladies."

"That so."

"I think you'll know them. Suzette Dunne and her niece, poor sickly thing, just moved into the Guest House. They've taken one of the nice, two-room suites; apparently, her niece needs special, full-time care. Suzette stays with her around the clock."

That had Jean's attention. Suzette? She was Philippe's loyal little lap dog. What was she doing away from him and the offices? And with a 'niece' . . . "Is that so?"

The old codger practically glowed with importance. "Yes, I took flowers to them both this afternoon. I hope Suzette's niece likes them. Poor child."

Suzette with a young 'niece' at the Guest House. That ought to put Drapeneau in a better mood.

Martin Drapeneau had some serious doubts about Jean Claude. He needed someone to back him up here in the north, but the idiot had already screwed up enough of his orders and Bourget was worse. Orders which, Martin thought, should have been simple enough to follow.

And now, to top it off, Claude was late. Martin didn't want to have to be waiting around in the van any longer than he had to. It wasn't the cold that bothered him, but the thought of being seen. It was getting difficult to move around without being spotted these days.

When Claude finally appeared, slogging up to him in the thickening snow with large paper bags, he seemed bursting with good cheer. Martin was in no mood for it. "Don't you have any better boots than that?" Claude was wearing low-cut, black Oxfords with overshoes.

Martin was disgusted. "Don't you realize you're in the sub-arctic? You're not just here to shoot pool and go to the movies." It seemed the man had the perverse thought that the less-prepared he was, the less responsibility he would have to handle.

His rebuke didn't faze the Canadian. "Not going to matter. Philippe thinks he's trying to be tricky—he's moved Gelda. I talked to the caretaker of the QFR Guest House in town. He's certain that Suzette Dunne just moved in there with her young 'niece'. Suzette is keeping a twenty-four hour watch over her."

This was a huge development. Who would have thought Claude was that capable? "What about the caretaker?"

"Oh, he's just a seventy-year-old busybody. No problem! Apparently, he has no other guests right now."

With a rush of new energy, Drapeneau responded,"Okay, here's the plan: we'll swing by the Guest House now, to see if we can tell what rooms they're in. Then—"

"Got it covered." Claude stomped the snow off his inadequate shoes and stepped into the van. "The caretaker said they're in one of the two-room suites; those are all on the second floor. I asked how well they were being taken care of, and he said they had all the amenities. That's the executive suite, saved for when other business-types come to visit the plant. West wing."

Good. Claude had been thinking. That would save them some time. "Is there a fire escape on that end?"

"Of course."

"Excellent."

"Will we pick them up now?"

"No, stupid. First, we've'vet got to get the supplies I've tucked away for just this opportunity."

A half hour later, the van crawled to a stop in front of an abandoned shack fifteen miles east of town, set back a hundred feet from the snowy banks at the edge of the road. The gravel highway was not plowed frequently, and used mostly in summer. Drapeneau must have spent hours shoveling to keep the driveway clear for the old Dodge.

Jean Claude was glad for the break, and carried their bags toward what used to be a front porch.

The Russian unlocked the front door, and a strong whiff of kerosene enveloped them.

Inside, the building was divided into four rooms, plus a small bath off the kitchen. A kerosene heater sat in the centre of the floor in what passed for a sitting room. The temperature could not have been higher than ten degrees Celsius. Jean could tell immediately that they were in for a rough time.

"Hey, come and give me a hand in moving these crates." Drapeneau signaled to Bourget to help him load two six-foot long crates into the back of his van.

Drapeneau had had over a week to do the practical work of fabrication, and Jean could see he had done a good job. He straightened his back with a crack. Drapeneau had a few other supplies stashed away in the shack as well: sleeping bags, another kerosene heater, more fuel, groceries, stencils, and black paint. Claude began to think that Drapeneau must be loaded, because the younger man was paying cash for everything. He wished he could borrow some for himself.

"All right, here's the plan." Drapeneau gestured Bourget to join them. "Once it's dark, we'll drive to the street in back of the guest house and park the van. We won't go into the lot. You'll take these heaters and gasoline, break a window at the east end, remove the caps, toss in the heaters, and douse the room with the petrol. Splash it good, and then throw in a match."

Bourget looked to Claude, who swallowed hard and nodded. He was a little shaken at the idea of arson, but they'd come this far. They might as well finish the job.

"Meanwhile, Claude, you'll come with me. We'll climb the stairs, set off the alarm, and you help the girls while I inject the sedative."

Claude felt sympathy for Suzette, but steeled himself. The party manifesto said: 'If society is serious about solidarity, the mass struggle for the ideals of the revolution must come first.'

"Meanwhile," the Russian continued, "in the confusion, we'll bring the girls out, Bourget will bring up the van, and we'll get out of there fast. You, Bourget, keep the engine running and wait for me. There can be no screw-ups! We've got to do this whole thing in under five minutes."

"Once we get out of this place, where and when do we go next?"

"You ask too many questions, Claude. You'll get out when I say you'll get out and not before." Drapeneau barked.

Jean leaned against the wall sullenly. He wouldn't have to ask questions if the Russian would just tell him the plan in the first place.

Perhaps Drapeneau realized this, for he continued gruffly, "I've contracted with a pilot to fly us back to St. Hubert. How we conceal the girls is another thing. That's why we've got these." He patted one of the crates.

"They're going to be alive, aren't they?" Claude recoiled at the idea of bringing corpses out of the north.

"They'll be alive, but just barely," Drapeneau said. "I have a drug that induces unconsciousness for about thirty-six hours. Our job will be to keep them warm enough so they don't freeze."

Claude remembered something. "We're going to have to watch the weather. There's supposed to be a big storm blowing in." If the chatty old man could be believed.

Drapeneau frowned, grabbing his gun belt. He started strapping it on underneath his QFR uniform. "Timing is going to be everything in this operation. But yes, grab some extra warm clothes. I want to be prepared if the worst should happen."

10

Suzette was starting to get cabin fever. She could sympathize with Gelda—she knew this experience was much worse for the young woman who had been kept inside for months—and not allowed contact with the outside world.

Yves had been a life saver. It was nice to finally have some company, and he was able to bring them a wider choice of magazines and novels.

But it looked like they might not be needed for long. Yves brought them news from the plant, and Gelda had been thrilled to hear that her father had come, and Philippe had actually talked with him.

Gelda asked Yves if she could send a message to her parents. Suzette had no objection, so Gelda spent the rest of the morning detailing her captivity, the events that led up to it, and how she had been treated. The letter was about five pages long.

"Would you like to read the letter, Suzette?" she had asked.

Suzette agreed, but had made up her mind to let Gelda speak frankly. It would do no good to try to edit anything now. She was surprised that Gelda's assessment was fair, and though there were rough spots when Gelda was afraid or lonely, she looked upon her treatment positively.

"Thank you for letting me read your letter, Gelda. I hope, for both of our sakes, you can leave the City of Larches soon."

They both laughed.

They had only had one visitor other than Yves. The caretaker had come by in the morning with a potted flowering plant and questions as to the health of Suzette's 'niece'.

The elderly gentleman just wanted to pass the time of day, but Suzette had all she could do to keep the lonely old man from coming into their room. She had been relieved when he had finally left.

Now, Suzette and Gelda sat in front of the television set in their suite. The sky had turned dark outside their rooms, and snow swirled off the roof, almost obliterating the view of the apartments across the lot. The newsman had a large map of Québec behind him, and pointed to the eye of a huge storm beginning to cross James Bay toward Kuujjuaq. There were heavy downpours between the St. Lawrence and Gatineau Rivers, though no icing had been reported. At Cité des Mélèzes, it was already snowing heavily.

"It's lucky we don't have to travel anywhere tonight." Gelda shivered. "It's nasty outside, and it looks like it's going to be a big one."

Rising, and walking to the other room, Suzette responded, "Yes, they said it should hit hard in another six hours."

Yves Bonnard had dropped by for a second time around two-thirty that afternoon. The news he brought was an update following the meeting of Dr. Vanderstadt and Philippe. They had decided to wait until the next day to move Gelda to police quarters, but in the meantime, a couple of officers would be watching the Guest House.

Gelda had been worried about the police being noticed, and Suzette was touched that in her letter she mentioned Philippe's family as among those that might be in danger if Drapeneau found out.

Therefore, at their insistence, the officers were to stay well back, and only investigate the most suspicious of activities.

Though Yves had no other news to give, his hearty manner was always welcome, and he stayed for an hour more to keep them company. Before he left, he told them not to hesitate to call if they needed anything.

When the door closed behind him, Gelda gave Suzette a sly grin.

"What?"

"Oh, nothing." The younger girl opened up the fridge, looking for something for dinner.

"Well, whatever this 'nothing' is, you certainly have an opinion on it."

"Yup." Gelda closed the door. "But maybe I think I'll wait and let you figure it out."

"Is that so?"

"Mm-hm." Gelda tried one of the cupboards. She paused, staring out one of the darkened windows. "Suzette?"

"Yes?"

"When this is all over, will I be able to . . . call you some time?"

"Of course."

This started a long conversation between the two women. They decided that, whatever happened regarding future events, they would remain friends.

Dinner became forgotten, until a loud clanging began to sound.

"What's happening?" Gelda shouted.

Suzette was shaken, until she realized what it was. "A fire alarm!" She could barely hear herself over the noise. "I don't see any smoke."

"Should we—"

A loud banging made both the women jump. A shout came from the other side of the door.

Suzette opened it, knowing that her eyes were wide. She was amazed to see two Portage Lake QFR workers, in full safety gear, standing in the hallway. The first shouted at her, "Let us in. Quickly!"

Gelda was already looking around the room rapidly for warm clothing, preparing to evacuate.

"Please put on warm sweaters as quickly as possible." Suzette could not place the tall dark man, but the second was Claude. Why was he here? Had he been hired by Portage Lake?

As Suzette finished putting her arm in a heavy sweater, she turned to Claude to ask him. She felt a sharp pain in her right shoulder, like being bitten by a wasp. "Ow! What was that? It really hurt."

"Hurry up! Hurry! We've got to go." Claude was insistent.

"But—"

The second worker grabbed Gelda's arm. "Come on."

Both were being ushered to the door. She heard Gelda behind her. "Ouch. What are you doing?"

The fire alarm continued to ring loudly in the hallway.

"I don't have my shoes."

"Don't worry! There's no time!"

The women were rushed bodily down the fire stair and out the exit door, into the snow. There was a van parked in the middle of the back lot. Flames were engulfing the east end of the building and the orange glare silhouetted the vehicle against the apartment buildings to the north.

A small, slight man came out of the fire stair and ran towards the main street, wildly waving his arms. "Help, help! Fire! Police! Help; somebody help me!"

Suzette wanted to stop and help the caretaker, but was pushed to the back of the van in her wet, stocking feet.

"Don't worry. We'll get you out of here." The man alerted another, sitting in the front of the van, to start the engine. "We'll take you someplace warm."

Suzette wondered where the officers were. Were they helping the caretaker? Or perhaps to put out the fire? Her thoughts were starting to feel mushy. And maybe it was the cold, but she couldn't move her fingers.

A few lights winked on in the apartments opposite the lot. Snow swirled across the dark space as the battered Dodge left the premises.

In her rush, Suzette was climbing over the packing cases in the back of the vehicle; Gelda followed suit. She was starting to feel really cold.

There were sleeping bags in the crates, and when the tall QFR worker suggested they get inside them, Suzette was only too happy to oblige. A numbness had started to envelop her arms. Her tongue felt like cotton. When the van lurched into motion, she asked, "Where . . . where are you taking us?"

None of the men answered. The tires of the van skidded, and she could hear the wipers trying frantically to keep up with the snowfall. In the distance, she heard a siren.

Suzette lay on her back in the soft bag. She had stopped shivering, but could not feel anything with her hands. It was almost as if she was floating in the darkness. She tried to speak out, but the words would not come. She felt paralyzed, and knew she was losing consciousness. She struggled to fight it, but it was too late.

When Philippe arrived in the courtyard on Main Street, Lavan's vehicle was waiting with emergency lights flashing. Fire trucks had deployed at both the front and the rear of the building and the whole east wing and much of the centre portion of the building were glowing, charred rubble. Sparks still rose high in the air. Amazingly, the women's apartment was still intact, though firemen battled the blaze in the roof structure. Water was at a premium in the sub- arctic, but a frozen glaze covered most surfaces.

When the alarm transfered to the police station, the Captain had allowed Philippe to be brought from the plant under watchful guard. He took Philippe by the arm, and guided him to the exit door at the west end of the building. From the vehicle spotlights, Philippe could see tracks all over the snow being freshly filled by the storm. Lavan said, "Someone jimmied the lock on this exit door. There was water and snow on the stairs. They must have gone in to get the women. There's no one in there now. They've disappeared."

"What?" Philippe was shocked. "I thought you had men watching this place?" He was shouting, and he knew he was drawing attention, but he didn't care.

"As soon as they heard the alarm, they ran over," the Captain said. "But things must have already been underway before then. By the time they got past the caretaker and into the women's room, they were already gone."

Philippe started pacing. "Well, thank God they're out, but we must find them quickly. Where can they be? Who do we have to help?"

A vehicle slid into the parking lot, skidding on the snow. Yves Bonnard ran out of the car. He left the engine running. "I just heard about the fire. Are the girls safe?"

"They're not in their rooms," Philippe said, "but we don't know where they've gone."

"How did it start?"

Lavan replied, "The caretaker said there was a big explosion in the apartment next to him. Then the alarm went off. When he went into the hallway, it was filled with fire and smoke.

He met up with my men, and made it to the women's apartment, but they were already gone."

LeClerc shook his head. The Captain's explanation was still inadequate. He wondered what might have caused the explosion. "Have you been down to the other end?"

"You mean where it started? Firefighters have been working on it, making it safe to approach."

Philippe looked over at the blackened walls of the building. "Well, let's take a look."

They had to go out onto the street again to reach the east end. The wood siding was still intact in places, blocking their view of the gutted interior. For structural reasons, the firemen only let them get so close. A faint smell of raw gasoline mixed with the smoke. The boards steamed as their flashlights swept across the chaos.

"What's this?" Yves carefully picked his way closer, and tapped some free-standing, twisted metal tossed nearby.

The Captain said, "Two kerosene heaters were removed from the building for evidence. The caps were off the fuel tanks. To top it off, they shouldn't even be here; the building has central heating. It's a clear case of arson."

Philippe's worst fears were confirmed. It had to be Drapeneau. But to do this, before the assigned officers could even intervene, the foreigner must have had help—where did he get it?

⊕

Far from the scene they sealed the lids. Martin Drapeneau took the keys from Bourget and told him to get in the back of the van. With both windows wide open and the heater going full blast, the van surged forward with its perishable cargo.

In his brief tenure with the regular Russian army in the Urals, Martin was an ambulance driver, and knew the tricks of getting a vehicle through rough terrain and drifting snow. He chose back streets, and avoided major intersections. The sound of sirens in the distance was muffled by heavy snow. He had scouted the city before Claude arrived, but there was no way to avoid the highway check-point just before the airport.

It was just after seven p.m. News of the fire would likely have reached the checkpoint, but hopefully no one yet knew its signifi-cance.

Martin turned to Claude. "Now's the time to look important." As an officer approached the van, Martin pulled out a fist full of invoices. "We're going to the airport with replacement parts for the Portage Lake plant."

The officer shuffled through the papers without reading anything. Looking in the rear of the van, he said, "How come you've got all the windows down?"

"The damn heater. The glass keeps fogging up."

"Okay, you're good." The officer nodded to him and Claude, and waved them through.

The van sped toward the airfield. Drapeneau allowed himself a thin smile. This was going to be easy.

At quarter to eight, the rusted van pulled in front of the low buildings of the municipal airport. Snow in high banks almost obscured the buildings, but pathways were well-maintained.

The large wet flakes that fell before had given way to a freezing light mist. It was making visibility through the icy glaze on the windshield all but impossible.

"We've got to go to the charter building on the right." Claude said.

Martin turned the van past the long QFR Lear jet hanger, and then on to the smaller private facility where charters were serviced. The lights on the building were out, and the gate locked. The parking lot was empty, but fresh tracks of one vehicle could be plainly seen heading west toward the main entrance.

It didn't look good. This was serious.

"Mike said he would be set to go at eight o'clock," Claude mumbled. "What do we do now?"

"Mère de Dieu! How do I know?" Martin exploded. Did that idiot expect him to have all the answers? "We'll wait a bit. We're still early."

A half hour later, nothing had changed. Martin had to stop himself from fuming. It looked like his carefully crafted plan was going to crash because of weather.

"I'm going back to the main building to try to find the pilot. Let's see what the damned story is." Martin muttered.

He drove back to the main parking lot, stopping between two smaller vehicles buried under forty centimetres of new snow. One car had very little on it.

"You stay here and keep the engine running. I'll go inside." He left his construction helmet on the back seat and pulled a knitted cap from his pocket. There was no point in trying to disguise identity now.

The lobby was almost completely empty. An attendant was standing at the Air Canada counter, and a baggage handler was putting some containers on a cart at the arrivals gate.

Martin went to the woman at the counter.

"May I help you?"

"Why is the gate to the charter service building locked?"

"All operations at the airport will close in the next fifteen minutes. We're expecting flight 252 from Kirkland Lake, Ontario, to be here momentarily. Severe icing conditions have cancelled all further flight departures tonight."

"There's a charter pilot, named Mike, who's been around here for the last couple of days. Is he still here?" Drapeneau was trying to restrain his temper.

"He might be with the air traffic controller now, but I can't guarantee it. The tower is busy because of the incoming flight, but you can probably get in after the plane lands."

Martin gritted his teeth. His options had evaporated. He could wait until the inbound plane unloaded, and then storm the tower with Claude to force the pilot to take off again with the larger plane and their cargo. But he was not sure if Claude would be tough enough to carry it out and the slower, lighter plane would be seriously affected by ice at low altitudes.

He also had no idea if the arriving plane would have enough fuel for a return trip. He doubted they could make it all the way to Montréal. An airport standoff at any destination short of Montréal would end their chances.

If they spent the night here, deteriorating weather would certainly make things even worse in the morning. He turned back to the attendant. "Thank you. I don't think I'll wait." In a controlled rage, Martin left the lobby. He was furious.

A dozen passengers disembarked from the newly-arrived plane as Martin joined Claude in the van.

"No luck! The airport's shut down. We don't have a choice."

"What are we going to do with our cargo?" Claude was a practical man, but not much good on suggestions.

"I think there's only one thing we can do. We've got to keep the boxes warm. We'll take them over to the QFR warehouse, and store them until we can get out of this miserable place."

Claude nodded nervously.

With the disruption the fire had caused, returning through the checkpoint to the city was out of the question. Everyone would be on high alert. A good factor was that Claude knew his way around the plant.

The heat from the stationary vehicle had melted the ice on the windshield, but it had started to snow again, this time with renewed ferocity. They could barely see the road beyond the end of the entrance drive, and their headlights were plastered with ice. Their only guide was a very faint luminescence in the sky, from the hundreds of high-pressure sodium lamps at the plant three miles away.

The further Martin drove, the thicker the snow fell. The wind whipped fresh powder off the banks of the highway.

"This storm is a mother. We won't be going anywhere tomorrow, either." Bourget's comment was unwelcome, but reflected the realities of what they faced.

The Russian's mind raced. He was trained not to plan too far ahead, when confronted with contingencies, but to be precise when dealing with the facts at hand.

"We're here!" Martin growled. Getting through plant security and into the loading dock area with their cargo turned out to be one of the few easy tasks of the night. He knew that would soon change. Once in the building, they would be persona non-grata. If they were caught, the game was up.

Claude seemed to be thinking along the same lines. "I don't think anyone will question us if we go to the cafeteria. They're open all night and, as 'guests', no one should hassle us. It's when we go through sensitive areas that there are a lot of check-ups. Heaven forbid we meet anyone we know."

"Well first, we've got to get these boxes safe, fast."

It took Drapeneau seven minutes before he could find anyone. When Claude finally heard him returning, he breathed a sigh of relief.

They were parked next to the concrete steps at the foreman's office.

"Not much traffic this time of night, what with the storm and all." The operator Drapeneau had found was a younger kid, and happy to help the stranded Portage Lake employees.

He was in a tee shirt, but when he looked outside, he did not hesitate to get down in the snow next to the van and help. He pushed the button for the nearest roll-up door and they put the two wood crates on the dock.

"I'll go get a truck."

"No, we can't wait." Drapeneau was quick to stop him. "We've got to keep these instruments warm. They're very delicate. You better close the door."

A strong wind was blowing frigid air inside the building. Jean guessed it was already at least negative twenty. With the door tightly sealed, temperatures began rising once more to acceptable levels.

When the operator returned with a lift truck, the two men had already lifted the crates onto a wide pallet. Jean was extra attentive to Suzette's. He was sorry she had aligned herself with Philippe, but maybe she could be convinced to switch sides. It was good she would be available to care for Gelda; Jean had a distinct aversion to the day-to-day care of anyone, let alone hostages.

He turned to the warehouse worker. "We'd like to store these crates about waist high, because we have to monitor them. Nothing should be placed on top. We may need to get them out quickly."

"Let's see . . . I don't have much that low . . . maybe over in aisle 17." He gunned the forklift, and Jean had to scurry to keep up. Aisle 17. How ironic. A lot of water had gone over the dam for Parti 17. Including these two women.

The crates secure, the three wandered carefully through the aisles, to the connecting corridor that would take them toward Administration and the cafeteria. Finally, Jean thought, maybe he would be able to relax.

11

John, along with Louis and Mark, hunkered down at the Sûreté barracks. Due to the intensity of the storm, Captain Lavan had invited the five from the Lac Tamarack outpost to spend the night there. But the barracks were far from restful. News of a disastrous fire at the QFR Guest House had everyone nervous. Captain Lavan told John that the Guest House was where Gelda had been in hiding, and there were strong indications that a carefully planned raid had been carried out by Drapeneau. Captain Lavan and Philippe LeClerc wanted to meet with everyone in the barracks situation room, especially those who had had contact with the Russian agent, and was prepared for an all-night session, if necessary.

The circumstances of their presence at Lac Tamarack had changed so suddenly that John was apprehensive about meeting his old friend again. He had not seen Philippe for years. Would he be able to recognize him? What was he like now? That painful past remained—would Philippe still bear a grudge?

Lavan and Philippe arrived in a flurry of energy. Despite the years,

John could pick out his old friend from the crowd of officers. He had the distinct impression that the QFR director was giving him and his companions careful scrutiny; John was not sure if Philippe had recognized him.

The situation room was packed. Lavan was sitting directly below the map, next to Philippe. Others, including John, Louis, and Mark, were in the front row. Most of Garrett Bennett's military men had been flown in before the airport closed down, and thus were present. Sûreté officers filled in the remaining spaces. Only the duty clerk was at the switchboard.

Captain Lavan made introductions among the civilians, briefly detailing their involvement in the case. Philippe did a double take when John was introduced. John nodded to him, and Philippe, with a puzzled look, smiled back.

Captain Lavan took a pointer and outlined the perimeter of neighbourhoods that the combined police and taskforce personnel had canvassed. He mentioned a few hot spots where further investigations were recommended. It was clear that the only routes out of the city extended to the airport and QFR property on the west and the highway to the local mining operation in Timmerman.

"Has anyone investigated in-bound traffic from Timmerman?"

Mark's unexpected query prompted a response from Lavan. "To date we have concentrated on the canvassing of local neighbourhoods, working our way out to the city limits. It probably would be worthwhile to check the highway to the Timmerman mines and see who has been using it. I'm not sure we can afford to man a full road block, however."

It was Louis' turn to add to the discussion. "We have been considering the idea that Drapeneau would avoid being in town altogether. He is more than capable of managing on his own in a remote location. Are there any abandoned or unoccupied buildings outside of town?"

Philippe was eager to consider this other option. "Let's check it out. If the canvassing will be wrapped up in another day, how many homes and buildings outside the city limits do you think remain to be looked at?"

"I'd say about twelve to fourteen."

"In the light of the current emergency, could we split off some people to check those out at the same time—to put a squeeze on Drapeneau?"

Lavan looked at his second-in-command, who nodded. "I think we can do that. We can pull men from the roadblock. All flights from the airport are cancelled until further notice. They had some bad icing out there. The temperature is only dropping, and the storm is apparently increasing from the northeast."

Philippe appeared significantly agitated. Though tension was high with everyone in the room, he couldn't even seem to sit still. John wondered how much sleep the director had been getting. Philippe continued,"And you've heard nothing suspicious from the airport? That must be the way that he means to leave."

After a nod from the Captain, one of the radio officers answered Philippe. "We got an update from the tower right after they shut things down. Except for the last flight 252 coming in from Kirkland Lake, all they had out there was a charter pilot assigned for parts transportation for QFR. No one wants to go out there in a storm."

That got John's attention. "Did you say a charter pilot?" If his difficulties in Asia had taught him anything, there were more ways than the traditional passenger plane to get out of a tight situation. "Maybe he was going to be transporting a little more than just parts. We should find out where he's staying in town, and get a full story from him. It may be a long shot, but Philippe is right—that's the only way Drapeneau and his friends can leave."

The QFR director nodded. "At least they won't be headed out of town anytime soon. But I am very concerned about the safety and condition of the two women. Where are they? If it's too much trouble to leave with them, will Drapeneau abandon them? Or worse? It is urgent we find them as soon as possible."

Discussions moved then to the deployment of officers and the division of resources that the Sûreté had access to. Snowmobiles were starting to appear a necessity, but were only provided to the troops with the highest priority—those searching the remote and outlying properties of Cité des Mélèzes.

LeClerc remained impatient, and continued to speak with Captain Lavan after the meeting had broken up.

When the Captain waved him away, he came over to where John, Louis, and Mark were still sitting. "Is this the John Thurmond I once knew—after all these years?"

John stood up and, smiling, extended his hand. "I wondered when the nickel would drop, Philippe. It's great to see you again."

Philippe shook his head, incredulous. "How on earth did you get tangled up with this thing? The Captain said that you have had personal experience with Drapeneau? He's bad news. How did you ever meet him?"

John introduced Louis and gave the director a very quick sketch of the Russian's past. "It goes back a long way, Philippe; neither of us have any love for Martin Drapeneau."

Captain Lavan walked up to their gathering. "All right now, Philippe, it's about time we got you back to the plant grounds."

Philippe appeared quite sober about this announcement, but nodded his assent. He turned back to John. "We absolutely must get together and talk. Can you come to our security building about ten o'clock tomorrow morning? I should finish the meeting with my managers about our new situation by then, and then we can continue to catch up from there."

"I'd love to. May I bring Louis and Mark?"

"By all means."

From there, it seemed, Philippe had to leave their meeting quickly. John worried about his friend. He realized he had not seen him outside of police supervision once since he had arrived. It made sense that not everything had been solved legally, yet. John could only hope that Gelda would be found, and soon.

Mark Talyard lay in a narrow bunk at the provincial police barracks. He had been awake for some time, tossing and turning. It may have been due to the two cups of coffee during the meeting, but he couldn't drift off. Whenever he started to sink into sleep, he heard a distant call in his subconscious: "Help. Help us—help!" It was like a bad dream.

In the morning, he had a tough time shaking the feeling, and the experience left him unusually solemn.

With his coffee cup in hand, he looked out the barracks window. In the grey light of dawn, the snow was coming down harder than ever. Plows had been working all night, trying to keep up with it. Louis walked up to Mark. "I'm glad the doctor has experience in this weather, because it looks like we're going to get some more. Mon Dieu, I've never seen anything like it." Mark could only agree, though in past years New England had had a good share.

Despite his quiet comment, Louis was beaming as he gazed out the window.

"Say, Louis, somehow you look different this morning. What's up?"

The Frenchman grinned. "I called Hélène last night. She was so excited. We may be having a baby!"

"Hey, man!" Mark said, "Congratulations! Pretty soon, we'll have a lot of little Xenons running around here." It really was wonderful news, and Mark was happy for Louis. He had come to like the Frenchman. But even when his uncle John entered and joined in their little make-shift celebration, Mark couldn't get those voices, calling for help, out of his head.

Dr. Vanderstadt was another solemn member of the party. He had remained silent throughout the meeting last night, and barely seemed aware of what was going on around him today. Mark thought that to have the hope of seeing your daughter again crushed so soon would be a devastating blow. He stayed with the doctor through breakfast, making sure he was eating and reassuring him that everyone was doing all they could.

When Mark, Louis, and John left for their meeting with Director LeClerc, Dr. Vanderstadt insisted on staying at the barracks. He wanted to hear the results of the police's search of the outlying houses, as well as to hear the account of the QFR charter pilot.

On the way to the plant, the others drove by the smoking wreckage of the Guest House. Charred wooden studs stood like gaunt fingers on raised foundations at the perimeter; nothing remained untouched by flame. The media was now broadcasting the news of suspected arson at the Guest House, though, fortunately, they had no knowledge of the disappearance of the two women. It would only be a matter of time, however. Luckily, things were slowed by the blizzard. TV crews could not come back until the airport re-opened.

The police vehicle's four-wheel drive had no problem in the snow, and though the going was slow, they made it to the Tamarack plant with no mishaps.

Inside the office buildings, tall windows overlooked the administration, maintenance and reactor wings. The twin cooling towers dwarfed anything close to them.

Director LeClerc was on hand to greet the party. He and Uncle John were proceeding to a conference room, but Mark had no desire to sit through yet another meeting. He knew his uncle and the QFR director had a considerable amount of catching up to do, but Mark didn't have all that much interest in the man. Not considering what had been happening over the past few months.

He had been told that the director had not been the one to engineer his kidnapping, but someone here had. Mark was uneasy with the idea.

He approached the last member of their trio. "Louis, do you mind staying out here with me? There is something I want to look into while we are here." It wasn't entirely untrue.

"Certainement, mon ami." Louis waved at John to go on ahead.

Although John gave them a puzzled look, he nodded and proceeded onward with the director.

"Now, what was it that you wanted to see, Mark?"

"Well." Mark shrugged. "I don't know if it will help much, but Uncle John said that the charter pilot was planning on shipping parts from the QFR plant. I thought maybe somebody here would know a little more about it."

Louis scratched his cheek. "That is a good idea, but how would we go about it?"

"Let's go to the Delivery and Shipping Office and see if they have paperwork for a shipment by air yesterday. If they do, maybe we can find out something about the pilot and who ordered what."

Director LeClerc had already given them some high-tech security tags, and they waved down an employee to escort them—but the answer at the office was negative. "We haven't shipped anything from the plant for a week and those were only small electronic parts back to a manufacturer for re-calibration."

Mark was persistant. "Something was either delivered to, or picked up from, the warehouse yesterday. Who would have those records?"

"Oh, well, then you'd have to see the warehouse foreman in Building C. Take the second corridor to the left and you'll find it at the very end of the connecting walkway."

They thanked their guide and said to him, "We can find our way from here."

After a brisk walk through the temperature controlled passage, they stopped at the warehouse foreman's office and inquired about parts deliveries.

"Why yes. Three men came from Portage Lake just last night, in fact. I'll get the lift truck operator who took in their equipment."

Through the foreman's window, Mark saw a van parked next to the concrete steps. Deep snow blanketed the van's roof, making it look like it had been there overnight.

The foreman returned with a young-looking warehouse worker. He was an amicable fellow, and didn't seem to mind the interruption on what he claimed to be a very slow day.

"Parts deliveries? Yeah, I had a couple guys come in at the tail end of my shift last night. Said their flight got cancelled, and they needed somewhere to keep the parts in the meantime." The operator shifted back on his heels. "Why . . . don't tell me you two are worried about the parts too?"

"Worried?" Louis asked.

"Yeah, the two of them were all specific about how the crates were supposed to be stored. Had to be real careful, temperature sensitive, all that."

"Is that their vehicle?" Mark asked, pointing out the window.

The operator squinted out into the snow. " Yeah, that's the one."

"We're here with some information their charter pilot gave us. Do you mind if we check out these crates?"

"Don't think I should be opening them up, if there's sensitive equipment, but we can check out their paperwork once we spot them." The young worker gestured for Louis and Mark to follow him. "That should also tell us who these guys were. Both were from the Portage Lake plant, so I didn't recognize 'em."

Mark hurried to keep up with their helper's lift truck. Maybe it was just all the weird goings-on lately, but something sure didn't sound right about these two men and their 'sensitive' machine parts. "How many crates did you say there were?"

"Two. Big ones, but lift-able."

They entered into the warehouse proper. The operator got his machine and led the two of them to Aisle 17, where he had loaded the crates onto a waist-high rack. Once again, he appeared confused. "That's strange. I didn't notice it last night, but these don't have a routing tag."

"Routing tag?" asked Louis.

"Yeah, telling us where it's going. Usually stapled to the top."

Mark was examining the containers. They appeared authentic, but the hand stencilling looked laboured, and maybe a little rushed.

The employee gingerly lifted the two crates from the racks with the truck, and Mark and Louis helped place them gently in the aisle. Worry gnawed a hole in Mark's stomach. The crates were six feet long—big enough for a person. 'Temperature sensitive equipment'? They hadn't actually stuffed the women in crates, had they? He thought back to Gelda's wide, frightened eyes, pleading with him to help.

He walked around the crates, still on their pallet. "It looks like each of them have holes at one end." Breathing holes, maybe? But if the women were in there, how come they couldn't hear anything? He turned to the forklift operator. "Quick, get a pry bar or something."

"What?"

Mark quickly told him about the women that had been kidnapped, and their possible connection to the charter pilot. The worker drove off in a hurry to fetch some tools.

Louis had his ear to the side of one of the crates. "I hope we're not too late."

The lift truck operator returned, with the foreman, and Mark took the offered hammer and pry. He noticed the foreman eying Louis' 38 police special.

"Better start at the opposite end, where their feet would be." Louis suggested. "Be very careful."

"I think I see a sleeping bag. It's a person all right." Mark was able to raise the cover enough to allow a handhold. With a few more deft twists of the pry, the other men moved in to help pull it away. The foreman and the operator were stunned at the discovery.

A girl with blonde hair lay on her side, motionless, eyes closed, but breathing very faintly. "She's alive. I think it's Gelda. Call the plant infirmary. Quickly! We better open the other one too."

It seemed to John that no time at all had passed before his visit to the plant turned into a beehive of activity. When Philippe got the phone call stating that Gelda and Suzette had both been found on plant grounds, his whole demeanour changed immediately. John was amazed to see how self-assured his old friend had become with authority. LeClerc exploded into action. "This is a CODE RED—All Building Managers are directed to meet in the Security Building in five minutes." Loud-speakers sent the order throughout the plant

John followed him to the Command Center where Philippe addressed the men.

"Plant security was breached between eight and eight-thirty last night. We have three suspects in the complex. It is urgent that these men are found without delay, quickly isolated, and incapacitated. They must be considered armed and extremely dangerous."

"The Security Managers of each building are to establish critical guard stations immediately, and report search progress at half hour intervals to Operations. If help is required to apprehend a suspect, suspend the search in your area and notify Operations here immediately. Except for essential tasks, the plant will be in a state of complete lock-down until the search of each building has been completed."

A limited number of employees were allowed through certain stations, each person's identity verified before they could pass.

The two women were still reported as unconscious, but LeClerc and John stopped by the Infirmary to see them and verify they were stable. Both Captain Lavan and Dr. Vanderstadt had been notified, and were on their way from the barracks, bringing Garrett Bennett's military contingent with them.

As John and Philippe approached the Infirmary, a man in a mid-length tan jacket ran up to meet them. "I heard they found Suzette. Is she all right?"

"Our medic is hopeful." Philippe said. "Yves, this is John Thurmond. John, Yves Bonnard."

John nodded to Yves, who held the door for the two other men. The name Bonnard rang a bell. Wasn't that the guy with the plane?

Louis and Mark were already there. "No one is allowed in yet," Louis explained. "The doctors still need to figure out why the women are unconscious."

John noticed that Mark was watching Yves carefully, with a puzzled look on his face.

"But they were not harmed?" Yves glanced at Mark. " Are you the one who found—"

"You!" Mark shouted.

Everyone looked at Mark, surprised at his outburst.

"Yes?"

"It's you! Uncle John, this is one of the men that kidnapped me."

Philippe paled. "No, that's not . . . exactly correct—"

"Mon Dieu!" Yves said, "The injured guy—from New Hampshire. It's you. You are all right? And kidnapped? Mais non! You were unconscious, injured, and we were taking you—"

"Like hell!" Mark's jaw was clenched in a grim line, and he advanced a step towards Yves. "Your 'friend' chased me in the dark, into the mill. I was only unconscious because I fell through the floor there. And then, you and he tried to lock me up."

Philippe stepped in between the two of them. John could only stop and stare. Louis was in the same boat, eyes wide.

"That's enough." Philippe said firmly. "That's not what was happening. Please, let me explain . . . "

Mark stopped shouting, his stance stiff and wide. He kept his fists tight to his sides, breathing hard. He glared at Philippe and Yves.

"Yves and Charles Bourget, the other man, brought you along from New Hampshire to New Brunswick, because they feared you were badly injured," Philippe said. "It wasn't right—they should have left you in town. But they acted without thinking. They were supposed to be coming to a meeting."

"Bourget said he found you unconscious," Yves said, palms spread wide. "I did not know anything about him chasing you."

Philippe nodded. "I am very sorry you got involved. It was Jean Claude, one of my . . . former employees. He said that this new friend of his, this Drapeneau guy, had asked him to send someone to check out a cabin in New Hampshire."

"He was after Louis, no doubt," John added.

Mark's voice was still tight, but he looked a bit calmer.

Now John felt he could start putting names and faces to the October events. "He might have told this Bourget to take or question anyone they found at the cabin, in case it was Louis. Or myself."

"And M'sieur Jean Claude," Louis said. "Wasn't he the one who abducted Gelda?"

Philippe nodded solemnly.

Yves looked back and forth between all the men in the room. "Crazy," he said. "I feel in over my head."

Mark sighed, visibly letting the rest of his anger go with it. "Don't we all."

Louis was glad when the women were finally declared stable. The medics were doing what they could to counteract the sedative given to them. Dr. Vanderstadt was inside with his daughter. Mark decided to stick around, at least until they woke up. He and Yves had reached a tentative truce over their shared concern for the women's recovery.

Captain Lavan had arrived at the warehouse about twenty minutes earlier. Lavan had coordinated with the Chief of Plant Security, and then wrapped yellow tape around the van and sectioned off parts of the warehouse as a crime scene. John, Louis, and Philippe LeClerc were with them now, walking through the aisles back toward the Administration wing.

Louis felt less anxious now; the girls had been found, and the worst of the pressure was off. But there was no way he could relax with the thought of Drapeneau and his accomplices wandering about the plant buildings.

As the group completed their inspection and approached Turbine Storage, Louis stared down the corridor. A man appeared from a door on the left, about a dozen yards away, and cautiously stepped into the hallway. When he saw Louis, and the group following behind, he turned on his heels and started walking rapidly in the opposite direction.

The man seemed awfully nervous. Louis wondered what would happen if . . . "Hey, Martin!" he yelled.

When Louis cried out, the man broke into a run and disappeared into another door on the left. Louis gestured wildly to the group behind him. An ear-splitting clanging of bells followed, and a flashing red emergency light pulsed at the entry. Louis pulled out his gun, and hurried to the doorway. He didn't enter—he would wait for backup.

He didn't have to wait long. John, Philippe LeClerc, and Captain Lavan followed with the Chief of Security and other guards in tow.

LeClerc shouted, "He's gone into the Spent Fuel Storage Building. Call the Command Centre. He turned to Lavan. "There's no way he can get out, except through the locked train-loading door to the outside. Tell your men to seal the corridor to prevent any escape."

John let out a fast breath through his nose. "We'll need an armed party to go in after him."

Lavan nodded. "How many of us have weapons?" Louis and John raised their hands, as did two Sûreté and one military officer among the guards.

"M'sieur LeClerc, that leaves you and the Chief out. You had better return to the Command Centre in case this thing gets ugly." Captain Lavan had his gun out as well, and gestured for one of his two officers to stay and watch the door. They were going in.

Martin Drapeneau was in a sweat and trembling. A deafening alarm bell was ringing, and he knew he was trapped. Five minutes earlier, he and the two others had left their mezzanine hideout next to the warehouse; a security inspection team was approaching the area. It was only a matter of minutes now before they would be discovered.

Martin told Claude to steal a truck from maintenance, and meet him at the airport charter service building at two o'clock. Martin wished them well, but knew Claude and Bourget would be captured. They just weren't competent enough. But, like all combatants, they were ultimately expendable.

His own chances for survival would improve without them, anyway. His life now depended on skills gained from his childhood on USSR's Kola Peninsula, above the Arctic Circle.

He had served with the Red Army in the Urals, a special forces unit in the mountain villages of Afghanistan, and as an agent for the KGB in Southeast Asia.

Later, convalescence in Le Havre had been the sole award bestowed by the Soviet Communist hierarchy for a career of dedicated service.

Now he faced a cavernous space, filled with ranks of gigantic, lead-lined, concrete casks for storage of spent uranium nuclear fuel rods. Each cask, when full, weighed over fifty tons, and was carried by a massive overhead travelling crane.

He supposed similar cranes connected the generator room, the pump building and the cooling towers. The casks were loaded, capped, and sealed at a station near the twin reactor cores.

He surveyed the space, dwarfed by the casks, knowing that any hiding space would rapidly be discovered by his pursuers. He looked upwards—the crane itself offered a vantage point from which to view the entrance. Plus, the lead and steel plating on the floor of the control cab offered much more protection than standing between the concrete casks.

He found a ladder on an adjacent sidewall, and quickly made his way up a dozen metres. He gingerly balanced along the catwalk to the great travelling mobile unit. The beam and hoists could be directed from a panel at floor level, but a master over-ride switch in the control cabin gave its occupant ultimate command, unless power was turned off.

He scanned the vast room for other details. The dim lighting revealed a metal railway, on columns opposite, used to support the far ends of the mobile cross beam. At the end of the building, there was only a single steel roll-up door, massive in height, permitting a huge secondary mobile crane to travel beyond and load casks on railway flat cars. There was no other door to the outside.

In what might only be moments before pursuit, Drapeneau tested the panel in the cab and found the crane's electro-drive mechanism smoothly responsive. Now the wait began.

He was well-armed, and had sufficient ammunition for a stand-off, but his real concern was getting outside. Did it make sense to shoot his way through the defences in the corridor and perhaps try to take a hostage? Or should he find some way to break through the roll-up door? No doubt there was a stop switch for the crane at the door opening?

Martin was examining the controls for raising the hoist, when the alarm bell stopped. The whole interior of the room was illuminated by the intense glare of high bay, metal-halide lighting.

There were few shadows anywhere, and he froze into a concealed position within the cab. Very cautiously, a door opened and two armed police officers entered, followed by the police chief and two others. Looking carefully, he was able to recognize Louis Xenon and John Thurmond. What a prize!

The officers, Xenon, and Thurmond spread out methodically to check the aisles between the casks. The police chief stared up to examine the superstructure supporting the mobile hoist. Martin knew that here the intense lighting helped him—with the glare, he would be difficult to spot. The chief raised a bull-horn to his mouth.

"M'sieur Drapeneau, the game is up. You might as well come out of hiding. There is no way to escape from this room. If you come peacefully now, it will be better for everyone."

Typical. And they just expected him to give in?

The officers spread out; Xenon and Thurmond were almost directly under the crane. The chief spoke again. "Hold your positions, men. I'm going up to take a look around." With that, he began climbing the metal ladder to the catwalk.

Martin knew that, once on the catwalk, the chief would have a direct view into the control cab, and the game would be over. Martin pulled the Glock from a shoulder holster beneath his bulky uniform. This was what he had practiced hours for. In three seconds, he raised the gun with a steady hand, aimed it, and squeezed off two rounds at the police chief. The older man cried out, clutching his chest, and fell eight feet to the floor.

Thurmond and Xenon ducked for cover behind a cask. Thurmond made his way over to Lavan. Drapeneau considered taking the shot, but knew his position had been given away.

Sure enough, the other officers began firing at the crane's cab. Whenever that happened, Martin re-positioned the crane toward the shooter, so that shelter from the casks was minimized, and the shooter exposed. The bright ceiling lights made accuracy for the gunmen below extremely difficult.

For a time, Martin was able to use his manoeuvring to thwart his adversaries, but he ultimately needed to break for freedom.

He aimed the crane, and started a one-hundred-metre run toward the railroad siding at the far end. He tested the knob for the great roll-up door. Chained shut for the winter, it would not budge. The shooters below spread out and advanced toward him. Switching to the hoist mechanism, racing against the six-to-one ratio of the support cables, he was able to lower the grappling hook a few inches. If he could only lift one of the empty casks near the far end, he might use it as a battering ram against the exit.

Martin aimed the hook at the lifting lug of an empty cask, and dragged it loose on his first pass. The cask swung like a slow-moving pendulum. It smashed through the portal as he braked to a stop, just feet short of the door.

The door jambs were badly bent, and the bottom seal displaced, but the resulting aperture was less than half a metre wide. Martin lowered an emergency rope to the top of the cask, then, dropping to the floor as the gunmen neared, fired three rounds from his weapon. His pursuers ducked for cover as he slipped through the narrow opening.

Despite the lack of direct sunlight, the blizzard snowscape was blinding. A suffocating cloud of dense ice crystals blew off the roof, filled his lungs, and quickly covered his QFR jacket in a damp, white coating.

The Russsian knew what to expect, and made quick strides to get away from the building. The waist-high depth of drifted snow made progress difficult, but he leaned forward and used his arms and legs to move westward, away from the door, bending low and then proceeding.

One hundred twenty metres from the roll-up door, Martin crouched, shielding his eyes from the dense snowfall. He was near a low copse of arctic willow, alder, and dwarf birch. No one was following, but it would only be minutes before a concerted search commenced.

His hands were cold, but the adrenaline of escape was providing the momentary energy necessary to overcome the effects of temperature. In minutes, he knew he would need gloves and more clothing. The van contained both, but, in full view of the engineering wing, he would have to wait until darkness before daring to approach the vehicle. Fortunately, he still had the keys.

Instinct told him to expect a search party any second; he had to hide quickly. Backing toward the stand of exposed brush, he covered his waist-deep track through the snow with his hands. Once within the willows, he tunneled among the stems of the bare branches and lay silent beneath a high, wind-sculpted drift.

Louis and John cautiously hovered near the opening, peering outside; Drapeneau was invisible in the swirling whiteout, his track already drifting in.

"I can't see him." Louis was obviously alarmed. "He can't have gone that far. Shall we follow him?"

John knew they would be vulnerable, twisting through the small opening. "Maybe we should get prepared and mount a serious search. He's going to be freezing out there in the cold."

They were both armed, but neither of them were dressed for the storm and who knew how far the Russian would be able to travel? The escaped agent would be rapidly affected by low temperatures and wind.

They hurried back to where they had left the other officers and Captain Lavan. John was worried about the Captain's condition. Lavan had been bleeding heavily; at least one of the bullets had missed his vest.

Sûreté officers had immediately moved the Captain to the corridor, and he was rushed to the Infirmary—John knew he would have to be taken to the local hospital to receive proper care.

They regrouped at the Command Centre, leaving other officers behind to guard the damaged door in case Drapeneau tried to return that way.

Two search teams were quickly assembled and equipped with cold weather gear. John and Louis joined the western team; the teams would meet at the door that Drapeneau had damaged.

The two squads, eight abreast, carefully examined snow for tracks as they converged on the Spent Fuel Storage building. Fine flakes swirled off the top of the huge roof structures, making visibility practically impossible. The new drifted snow was shoulder-deep close to the building, and only lessened by inches further out.

When the teams met at the roll-up door, they had discovered nothing. One of the platoon thought he saw tracks heading west, but the track disappeared and led nowhere.

"It's going to be difficult to capture him without dogs to find his scent—we're going to need skis and snowmobiles. This stuff makes pursuit almost impossible." The Colonel, who had joined the search, was discouraged. "It doesn't look good. He's on the outside, so he can threaten any part of the complex at will; but I'm sure he's also hurting badly with this cold weather. We'll just have to cut off all access to the plant, except the main gate. He'll have to either freeze or give himself up."

Jean Claude had to find a way out. He didn't know what Drapeneau had planned, but he was more than willing to let him fend for himself. The Russian had shown Jean nothing but scorn through the whole affair, no matter how much help to him Jean proved himself to be.

He and Bourget had to avoid the warehouse, and he quickly noticed that there was a lot of activity along the main corridors. No matter. He knew his way around the plant, and could successfully skirt high traffic areas.

Drapeneau wanted to meet at the airport, but Drapeneau had the keys to the van. That meant the two had to get off plant grounds some other way. Martin had suggested the maintenance section. There, large trucks were serviced, and snow plowing crews took breaks from their eight hour, round-the-clock shifts.

A big Kenmore plow, loaded with salt, had just backed in from the outside, and the door panels gleamed as the melting snow ran down and pooled on the floor. The driver went down five active service bays to talk with the dispatcher and get a cup of coffee. No one was watching the cab. Jean motioned silently to Bourget to get in.

Claude opened the bay's steel roll-up door before mounting to the driver's seat. The keys were in the ignition.

It was a simple matter to move the truck out into the snow. Once in the parking lot, Claude concentrated as he made a bee-line for the security gate. Passing under the canopy and slowing only slightly, Jean felt better to be leaving the plant. Snowplows passed through constantly. "Okay, wave at him. Look happy."

Just as he thought, the guard let them pass unchallenged. It would be a big surprise when they realized they were missing a truck.

Jean had three miles of highway before he reached the airport entrance. Drapeneau had said to meet him at the charter service building. Jean had many questions about that. Just what did the Russian agent have in mind? He stopped before the charter building gate. Nothing had been plowed in the lot, and deep snow obliterated all tracks. The building seemed just as vacant as the previous evening. Even at noon hour, daylight was growing dimmer as the storm intensified. Claude settled himself down to wait.

Two o'clock passed, then three. What if he had run into trouble? Maybe Drapeneau had been captured. Despite his increasing dislike for Drapeneau, Jean was willing to admit how dependent they were on the Russian for survival.

From time to time, he had to turn on the big truck's engine to keep warm, but as dusk fell, his hopes dwindled. The truth slowly dawned on him. They had been betrayed. Drapeneau knew, perfectly well, there was no one there to fly them anywhere. What had Jean been thinking?

Jean glared out at the howling wind bitterly. He thought of the sacrifices and humiliations he had endured to assist Drapeneau in his mission. But to be left like this, to be abandoned, was the bitterest pill of all.

His bad mood wasn't helped by his growling stomach. He had not had anything to eat since breakfast, and the cold was taking its toll. He decided to leave the truck there and enter the lobby. Vending machine food was better than no food. Bourget was sitting next to him. The young man had complained from time to time, but had long been silent.

They waded back through the snow, following the faint tire marks of the big Kenmore. Within the lobby, no attendants were on duty behind the counter. The only sign of life was light at the window of the air controller's office, up a short flight of stairs above the departure gate.

The lobby was certainly warmer than outside. Maybe they should just stick out the storm, and wait for the first flight to take off—to leave this place. Then, they'd be long gone.

Martin suffered in his snow cave. He knew his temperature had dropped to dangerously low levels. He kept his limbs as close to his chest as he could, managing to insert his hands back underneath the shirt of his baggy uniform and the extra clothing he had worn underneath. He placed the safety helmet over his face to form a breathing chamber below the loose snow. From time to time, he made an opening to the surface with his hand to replenish oxygen. He knew people had been buried in avalanches for over twelve hours and survived. At least the snow insulated him from wind chill.

The muffled noise of the search party was nerve-wracking. On the second pass, he felt someone's boots coming down right next to his buried shoulder. He was thankful when the search ended a half hour later.

As hours lengthened, his mind tired of weighing the possibilities of capture against the dwindling options for escape. He knew it would be hard to return to any buildings, now that he had killed or wounded the police captain. Drapeneau's thoughts went back to his own youth in a tiny fishing settlement, thirty kilometres up the coast from the arctic naval base at Polyarnyy.

Young Boris Kalnikov had been placed in a local Soviet youth camp by a dissolute father. The rigorous and brutal training that followed made his transition to the Red Army, at age sixteen, barely eventful. Boris grew to enjoy the painful treatment he was able to wield over fellow conscripts as he rose in rank.

It was only on his final return from Asia, a broken man with near-fatal injuries, that his government allowed him to visit his mother in Paris for convalescence. Because of illness, she had been forced to leave his father, and the frigid north, when Drapeneau was still a boy.

The KGB kept their eye on him constantly, and used his time in France, and his mixed French heritage, to their advantage. He had his surname changed to match his mother's side of the family; his first name sounded more French. His mother liked the name Martin.

He might only be able to look back at those early years in Russia with bitterness, but now in northern Canada, he had to draw on every ounce of training the Soviet arctic units had taught their troops. For years, during long winter months, they conducted war games along Finland's eastern border. Loud diplomatic protests from Finland in the United Nations met closed ears. Later, in Asia, the toughness he had learned in those early campaigns was legendary.

Stiff and chilled to the bone, when Martin finally decided to move, the storm persisted, and fine snow continued to swirl off the high roofs, coating everything, moving or stationary. He advanced along the railway siding in the twilight, his jacket solid with ice. The exterior building lights were bright, but fortunately, with no window openings on north and western exposures, he was able to reach the storage warehouse parking lot unobserved.

At the loading docks, the lot was still unplowed. Their van at the far end stood buried in snow. The engineering building was dark; all the staff appeared to have left.

He waded through deep drifts the full length of the loading

area, prepared to fall prone at a moment's notice. The warning tape around the van was obscured with drifted snow. Opening the rear door with effort, he found his parka, a wool cap, and, most importantly, gloves. He rummaged through Claude's things and found a fruit bar in Bourget's coat. The Canadian was long gone. Martin made the food his own.

Closing the door, he backed away from the van and covered his path carefully. It was a labourious task, but he didn't want to leave any clues that he was still in the area.

At the docks' end, he paused for breath, confronted with where to go next. His options were limited. He knew he needed shelter and food, but the QFR facility would be like an armed fortress. He had seen the extra military personnel on hand, and that could mean only one thing: the Federal government had become aroused, and was after him as well.

He thought the airport might still be vulnerable. Those on duty would not be prepared to deal with a man with no qualms about taking life But planes couldn't run yet, in this weather. And where could he go to, after that, with the Federal government after him? He couldn't request retrieval from Zuloff with nothing to show for his mission. No, he still had to do all he could to disrupt the coming NATO meetings on nuclear power.

To do so, he would have to strike at the highest-value target of opportunity; or at least, if he were to fail in that effort, maximize any possible collateral damage.

He hated defeat. This might be his final test.

And so, cold and hungry—as dangerous as a starving timber wolf, he turned his face westward.

At supper in the cafeteria, Drapeneau's escape was the news of the hour. Everyone was trying to get the facts straight, from where they thought he might be, to news of the rescued women's condition, to whether or not it was believed Captain Lavan would pull through.

John felt tired as he carried his tray to their table. They had secured the perimeter of the buildings that they thought would be at the most risk. There was still no sign of Drapeneau.

There was news, however, of the stolen Kenmore, which was a source of embarrassment to the Chief of Maintenance. But the time of the theft didn't match up with Drapeneau's escape. John sighed. They knew Drapeneau had accomplices, one of them most likely Philippe's old employee, Jean Claude. And they hadn't managed to pick up either of them.

Louis wasn't taking the situation any better than John. "The Security Chief thinks that Drapeneau is likely to freeze," he said. "But I highly doubt it."

John shook his head. "He's too tough; if there is a way to survive, he'll find it." If the jungles of Malaysia hadn't done him in, then a snowstorm wouldn't likely faze him. "Do you think he'll make a break for it?"

Louis frowned. "He is not the type to give up easily, our M'sieur Drapeneau. He followed the trail of those photo negatives for over eight years."

"And after nearly dying in the attempt the first time." John pushed back from the table. "So, what could he hope to accomplish now? Gelda is safe; he's got to know that we'll have the Infirmary guarded. And the negatives are long out of reach."

"I'm sure he's looking for a big target. So who is left?"

John stood, realization hitting him. "Not who—where."

"What?"

"Where would Drapeneau go to find a big target?" John leaned down over the table, tapping it for emphasis. "Where are people like Philippe LeClerc, Dr. Vanderstadt, or key military personnel likely to be staying?"

"The Executive Lodge. Mon Dieu!" Louis was standing now as well. "We'd better notify Command immediately."

The two men ran to Operations, leaving their half-eaten

meal behind.

At Operations, they were connected with Command and met with more bad news. "Dr. Vanderstadt is still with his daughter, waiting for her to recover, but M'sieur LeClerc has gone to the Executive Lodge for the night. His Chief of Security is in charge here, along with military personnel."

"I know it's only a chance that Drapeneau would try for the Lodge, but we have to warn Philippe." John was pacing the hall.

The officer tried to ring a call through. "No good—nobody is answering."

Louis shook his head. "It's the storm. We'll need to go out there and warn them."

The Chief of Security helped them put a small team together, a mix of military and police. There were only a limited number of snowmobiles available, however. The main group would have to wait longer for more of the scouting teams to come in from their search for Drapeneau.

There was no time for that. John and Louis left with two Sûreté in a police issue, four-wheel-drive van. First, they drove the short distance to the Security building, where they picked up their skis and rucksacks; then they headed towards the Lodge.

The road to the Lodge beyond the security gate was well plowed, and they arrived in good time. The snow still fell heavily, but it seemed to be coming more out of the north. The storm's low was well to the northeast, heading toward the southern tip of Greenland. A change would show up soon.

"Mon ami, I think, if I were Drapeneau, I would approach the Lodge from the rear. There is too much exposure out in front. Maybe that is where we should try to intercept him first—in the woods."

They stopped the vehicle short of the complex and the Sûreté went inside to warn the occupants. Louis had experience with close combat in jungle warfare, and John was happy to defer to him in the larch thickets surrounding the Lodge. "I hope you're right, Louis.

I'll follow you. I just hope we're in time."

With long smooth glides, the two veteran agents poled their way in a wide circuit around to the backside of the building complex. They only had the lights of the building to guide them. By now, Sûreté officers would be discussing the possible threat from Drapeneau with those inside. The only way Drapeneau could be truly neutralized was to determine what a highly trained Soviet agent would do in these extreme circumstances.

John knew surrender was not an option. Drapeneau had seen too much action as a Soviet advisor in North Vietnam and Southeast Asia. He had blood on his hands among the war-lords in the lead-up to the Soviet invasion of Afghanistan. John needed to think of Drapeneau as a man possessed by his mission. He would carry it out or seek as much destruction among his adversaries as possible.

The thought chilled him. John patted the 45-calibre pistol he carried over his jacket, but he could already feel that trickle of cold sweat running down over his ribs.

The new snow was almost waist deep in the midst of the tamarack grove. The wind only swayed the very tops of the tall conifers.

The Frenchman and the American carefully took off their skis and moved behind the rough-sawn siding of the boat storage shed. The silence of the woods was palpable. The only sound they heard was their own breathing—and the occasional distant creaking of a tree branch.

Maybe they had been wrong. What if they had overestimated the Russian agent? Perhaps the snowstorm had taken its toll, and Drapeneau was off somewhere seeking shelter and safety. Perhaps he really was willing to cut his losses and try to escape from North America.

After waiting silently for a half hour, Louis and John were suprised when they saw movement in the forest ahead of them.

Fifty yards away, a grey shape coated in white frost moved cautiously from the cover of a tall spruce. It positioned itself close to the edge of the opening. They were in the rear of a two-story garage behind the main building.

The snow dusting the man's form reflected from the outdoor lights of the Lodge. They saw him clearly at last. Drapeneau.

Louis signalled John to follow him, and drawing his 38 police special, made a wide, careful arc some thirty yards behind Drapeneau as he moved out of the woods.

John pulled out his own 45 and thought momentarily of Sal. Had it really come to this?

It was well after midnight, and Mark and Yves were still with Dr. Vanderstadt in the Infirmary. The doctor had been by Gelda's bedside all night. Her colour was better, and her breathing stronger, but she was still unconscious.

"Do you think she's warm enough?" Dr. Vanderstadt was always concerned about temperature. His wife, Mariéka, had been called hours before, but hadn't been able to fly in yet because of the storm.

The airport had news of different importance for them instead. A missing Kenmore had been spotted outside the airport charter buildings. They found Drapenau's two accomplices, Jean Claude and Charles Bourget, seeking shelter from the storm in the main lobby. At least Command now had the two suspects responsible in custody.

In the next bed, Suzette stirred and moaned, but did not open her eyes.

One of the night-shift nurses entered the room. "The effects of the medication are still wearing off. Gelda and Suzette will probably be unconscious for some time still. You should probably get some sleep."

Yves Bonnard sighed, and rubbed his eyes. Though at first Mark had had serious doubts about Yves' claimed innocence, watching him worry over Suzette had changed his mind. The pilot truly seemed to be a caring person. "She's right, you know," Yves said. "We should probably get some rest. That way, we can be on hand when they wake up tomorrow."

Dr. Vanderstadt was sitting next to Gelda. He took her slender hand in his and held it. Mark could understand why he might not want to leave. For a time, there was little hope of even finding her. Now cognition could return in a few hours. The doctor didn't want to miss it for the world.

The radiator made a popping sound as the heat circulated again.

"I guess, actually, it's the wisest course." The doctor wearily nodded his head. "I'll go get the Colonel."

"Come." Yves stood. "You're all to supposed to stay at the Executive Lodge. It's not far from here."

⊕

John held his breath as the Russian walked up to the clearing. Security lights were still on at the Lodge, and the complex was surrounded on all sides by thirty or forty feet of snow-covered grass that kept the forest from encroaching on the structures.

Suddenly, John froze. He saw what the Russian was looking at.

A Sûreté officer was sitting in his van, hidden behind and parked immediately to the east of the garage. The officer had a good view of the far entrance drive, as well as the rear service door of the house, and monitored all personnel entering or leaving. The Director was still under house arrest. The officer had ignored the woods in back of him.

The Russian pulled out his gun and was approaching the rear of the van, staying in the blind spot beyond the view of the mirrors.

From five feet away, he raised his gun to shoot the driver through the rear window.

Louis burst from the woods and fired two rounds at Drapeneau.

The Russian cursed, dropping to the ground.

The surprised officer immediately jumped from the vehicle and drew his weapon.

As John emerged from the woods, Louis rushed forward to cover the driver.

Momentarily, John saw Drapeneau's face. The Russian raised his arm, and fired two rounds.

He heard another report from a firearm. Louis leapt in front of John, returning fire. A Russian bullet sped toward its mark.

John had fired, but not quickly enough.

Louis slumped to the ground.

The young Sûreté officer took action, and placed his gun against Drapeneau's forehead. "Ne bougez pas! Drop the gun!"

Slowly, the Russian's gloved hand uncurled. The 9 mm Glock, with its seventeen round clip, fell into the snow.

John knelt down beside Louis, hoping against hope that he was all right. It was then he saw dark red blood leaching into the snow from a hole in Louis' temple.

When the QFR van arrived at the Lodge, following two Sûreté vehicles with flashing lights, the doctor and Colonel went directly inside.

Mark and Yves got out of the van, confused.

In the glow of security lighting, well past the Lodge, and the garage, they could see Sûreté and military officers moving about. Most had weapons drawn. The Russian agent, Drapeneau, was on the ground, favouring his leg. He had been hit at least twice, once in his upper thigh and once in his left shoulder. He swayed unsteadily where he sat, his wrists handcuffed behind him. Louis lay face down, sprawled in the snow.

John was kneeling beside the Frenchman, a blank look covering his face. In the hubbub, Louis remained in the snow. The significance of what had happened only began to sink in for Mark after the Colonel arrived from within the Lodge with Director LeClerc.

The Colonel checked the pulse of the Frenchman and verified he was dead. It was useless taking Louis to the hospital. They would have to call the coroner.

The Sûreté searched the Russian for other weapons, handcuffed him between two agents, and loaded him into a police van bound for the city hospital.

John did not speak to anyone. He stood up, stunned, next to Louis' prostrate form. Members of the Sûreté spoke in quiet tones, not wanting to interfere. It was obvious a valued man had been lost.

In twenty minutes, the coroner arrived and, in his professional but impersonal way, took a number of photos, collected data, and then, with the help of the police officers, raised Louis' inert body onto a stretcher to be taken to the city morgue to await disposition.

When the coroner had gone, John looked at Mark. Mark put his hand on his uncle's shoulder, and they walked together toward the woods.

"I have to get our skis," John said with a hoarse voice. "We'll need to check with the doctor to see what he wants to do with the plane."

Mark nodded. His uncle's mind was functioning on a practical level, perhaps only to keep from drowning in the dark waters that threatened to engulf him.

Mark kept his hand on his uncle's shoulder. He didn't know how else to help him.

Though others at the Lodge had tried to comfort him, the heartache of guilt and regret still overwhelmed John. He could not deal with it simply by talking. He had to extract himself and get away from people—he needed the long view. At last, John told Mark he was returning to the camp. "I'll probably climb to the lookout. I need space."

Mark hesitated, but nodded. "Be careful, Uncle John. It's still dark. I'm going to talk to the doctor and see if they need me. I'll be back in the morning. Can I bring you anything?"

"No, I'll be all right. I'll rustle something up from our supplies— but thanks anyway." John's voice sounded hard, like stone, even to him. He turned to the boathouse where his skis were stacked, and, moments later, set out to cross the frozen lake.

Lifting the skis that Louis had borrowed from the doctor to his shoulders, John felt a sense of emptiness that he had not experienced for years. He had been through so much with Louis, especially in the last month as Louis looked for work, and with Hélène . . . John felt sickened to think of her situation now.

In the darkness, he poled across the snowy expanse with his free hand, this time making a direct transit on skis to the point of land where the camp was located. He knew in his head that life must carry on, but his heart told him he needed to be alone, to turn around Louis' death in his mind and heart, so he could make sense out of it. So he could deal with it.

Not only had Louis volunteered to help John, years before in dusty Phnom Pehn when John's life was at stake, but he had safely protected the fusion energy intelligence for years in France. And then he had delivered it, as promised, to America. He had suffered personally at the hand of Drapeneau and, though in significant pain, repeatedly used his best efforts to help in the attempt to capture the agent.

And then, there in the clearing . . . Louis was hit, while John was spared. John could not find within himself the answer as to why. He knew he hesitated before using the 45. He should have ended the Russian's life right there.

When John reached the camp, the snow had stopped. The wind was still blowing, but he could see first light beginning over distant treetops in the south east. By noon, the sun would melt any snowy residue from the silver wings of the aircraft and their separate tents.

John put the doctor's skis in the plane and proceeded to consolidate Louis' belongings. He took a turn shoveling snow, working to clear the ramp for the Otter's departure. He tried to bury his pain by staying occupied.

It didn't work. He still felt an overwhelming sense of guilt. His mind went through a whole series of 'what ifs', asking himself what they could have done differently to avoid the terrible outcome.

Helpless, he went on his knees in the snow. He asked God for forgiveness; it helped to clear his mind. He was motionless for minutes, unwilling to move.

It came strongly to him that Hélène would have to be informed with great delicacy. Her fragile spirit might not bear the strain.

It was mid-afternoon when John returned to the cook tent. He forced himself to open some frozen hash and thaw it over a propane burner. The sun was shining, and long shadows crossed the snow. Nights and days were still unequal, and the sun did not reach high on the horizon. In the waning afternoon, he found other things to do, but glancing around their tiny outpost, he had a recurring sense of claustrophobia.

He needed to climb the ridge, to get above it all.

Though air temperature remained the same, the wind had dropped, and the pristine beauty of pink sky and clouds, the sun and snow-covered earth, foretold fair weather. Looking out over the snow, the clumps of white spruce and juniper, he saluted the determination of his wounded enemy. A lesser man could not have endured the blizzard, the effects of deadly cold from exposure, and still survived to exact the pain and suffering on others he had caused. He remembered, as if in a dream, the terrible month of torture in Malaysia. He wondered what Drapeneau must be thinking now.

To the northeast, the huge looming crowns of the twin cooling towers caught the last rays of the setting sun. Steam rose in the air hundreds of feet, and then drifted off into the shadows beyond the hill-top. The lights on the building below only hinted at the torrent of energy being transmitted over high-tension lines to the south and east, facilitating human industry and habitation for millions.

On the opposite slope, now cast in the grey twilight of evening, nature remained as it had for millennia: vast forests, frozen lakes, rivers and wetlands, a cornucopia of species of flora and fauna, of mammal, bird, and fish that flourished in the north. Twilight was deepening fast, and he was reminded he should report to Security at the plant. John skied carefully down the trail to his tent in the dark. Most of the clouds had disappeared. The moon had not yet risen over the landscape.

Turning back toward the lookout, John raised his eyes to the North Star and was struck in awe. Red, green, yellow, and blue pillars of light, rising and falling in a great glowing tower, converged overhead. He stood, gazing up at the northern lights. Louis, sadly, had been taken away from them. But new birth and death happened every day. Painful memory was a constant—but even it would fade over time. John knew he must pay back strength to Louis' young wife Hélène—in what-ever humble capacity he had, the same way Louis had given him strength in Asia, when he most needed it.

12

Light was the first thing that Gelda remembered, a soft, pink light, like the aura of dawn, coming through double insulated window frames and Venetian blinds. She had opened her eyes. It felt like she was in a dream. She was watching her parents, not able to communicate, but comforted by their presence. Her mind felt hazy. She tried to move her hand, testing to see if her new world was real.

"Mum . . . Dad? You're . . . here? What . . . what about the fire? Those people?"

Her first tentative words were barely audible, even to her, but her parents stood, appearing to hang on them.

"It's all right, dear, you're safe with us," her mother said.

"Did Suzette . . ."

"Yes, dear, she's right beside you."

Gelda turned her head slowly—it felt so heavy. She relaxed when she saw Suzette, breathing rhythmically.

The two young men had stayed outside when her parents arrived.

Her father said, "Everyone's been so very worried about you—

you're all over the news."

Gelda blinked. It was coming back to her.

Yves entered the room. "How's Suzette?" It took Gelda a minute to find him. She gestured to the other bed.

"Oh, I see—she's still asleep." He nodded to Gelda. "Glad to see you're awake now.

I don't know if you remember Mark—he's the one who found you."

"Mark?"

"Yes, he's been quite helpful," her father said. Mark was standing in the doorway.

"You may remember him," Yves said, kind of sheepishly. "We brought him from the States to Queboggin."

"Oh ... so that was his name ..." She was feeling very tired again. It was hard to hold on to words. She felt her father holding her hand in his. She drifted off into sleep once more.

FRIDAY, FEBRUARY 3, 1984

Hélène looked around the two-story house that she and Louis were renting. She could not wait for him to come home. She had written thank-you notes to the wedding guests for the lovely china, silver-ware, and kitchen implements they had been given.

While Louis was away, she tried to create a homey atmosphere that he would like. She had started making curtains and drapes for the bedroom, to match the beautiful quilt and comforter from John and his wife, Sal.

Hélène sat in her chair in the sitting room. The bay window, fac-ing south, overlooked the neighbor's hedge and garden. The bare branches of a lilac bush were moving back and forth in a stiff breeze at the corner next to the driveway. The sky was a uniform grey, with a portent of rain.

A small bird hopped among the branches of the lilac, looking for bugs, buds, or pieces of loose bark. Its short, quick movements showed how nervous it was to be so exposed. Hélène reminded herself to put thistle seed in the bird feeder.

This little fellow had a touch of yellow underneath, and his brown stripes were almost like that of a juvenile gold finch. It was a pine siskin, that lived year-round in this climate.

The doorbell rang. Putting on her slippers, Hélène rose to answer.

On the porch outside, John Thurmond and Garrett Bennett stood with hands folded behind them. John was wearing a dark suit. Bennett was in full military regalia, a formal uniform. Hélène was surprised to see two other soldiers, whom she did not know, standing a few paces behind the men. They, too, were in their military best.

A tightness formed in her throat. She forced herself to swallow. "J-John . . ."

"Hello Hélène," John said, "May I introduce Garrett Bennett of the Department of National Defence?"

"Hello Hélène," Garrett said. "I'm afraid the news we bring is not pleasant. May we come in?"

"Uh . . . oh . . ."

"Please, Hélène," John said softly. "This will be better if you are sitting down."

"Okay." Hélène backed out of the doorway. She would not panic. She would not assume the worst.

She backed all the way to the stair. "Won't you come into the sitting room?"

John and Garrett entered, closing the front door behind them.

"Hélène, I'm afraid we have some very sad news to tell you."

"Louis," she said "I-is he all right? Has he been hurt?"

"More than that, Hélène, I'm sorry. Louis was killed, in a heroic act to save our lives . . . He saved my life." John looked her in the eyes.

Hélène put her hand to her mouth in horror. She felt blood drain from her cheeks. She wanted to cry out, to wail, but for a full minute, she could not speak. Her shoulders shook under the weight of her crumbling spirit.

After a few moments of silence, Garrett began, in a low voice, to give Hélène details of the Government's effort to capture Drapeneau, the battle at the QFR plant, and the events leading up to the Russian's arrest at the Lac Tamarack Executive Lodge. Louis had played a critical role in all of Tri-Force's planning. He had extended himself to extreme efforts on numerous occasions to bring the mission forward—and now he had made, in the last moments, the final sacrifice to protect others.

Hélène sat still in shock. It had been too perfect—the time they had shared together. She thought of the moonlit snow at Baggs' Inlet, the storm-tossed deck of the M/V L'Aventure when they first met, the wedding in Valcourt, the fun they shared together in their first home in Montréal. She thought of the tiny signs of life emerging within her. Life that could no longer share the hope of a father's love throughout the years, to know only small photographs of a father the child would never know first-hand.

Hélène fought back tears, but also a sense of anger. Why did these men come into their lives and ruin everything? They had such a happy life planned together. It was so unfair. She couldn't look at John.

He tried to apologize. "I'm sorry, Hélène; we took Louis from you too soon. Things might have been different—he saved a young policeman's life, and mine too. It was very dangerous. I'm so sorry."

Sorry? Sorry would not bring her husband back. Hélène knew it was unfair of her. She knew John had tried to do his best. But her frustration welled up again and again.

"Go." The word came out soft, a bare flutter of breath.

"Hélène—"

"No. Please. Just—just go, John." She might as well have shouted them. She wanted to shout to the world.

John swallowed hard, and nodded. He carefully shut the door

behind him as he left.

Garrett remained, and extended the offer for Louis to be buried at the National Cemetery in Ottawa, and to be posthumously awarded the Star of Courage. Hélène's close family could be lodged in official government accomodations for the services, or stay with the Bennetts at their home in Westmount.

It was a very kind gesture, but it was far too much for Hélène to grasp at this point. Louis was gone. He had been hers for so very short a time.

Why was he always so duty bound to follow John's suggestions? What was the history that they shared? Louis was always so close-lipped about it; it must have been something classified. And what about Drapeneau?

Why, oh why, did Louis always try to be so brave? It was because gentle manliness and bravery were such a deep part of his nature. That was why she loved him. He was a rare person, and now he was gone.

She couldn't help thinking of his happy smile when he first arrived at the airport in Halifax. She was lucky to have known him, and share those last few months of his life.

If only he could be there for their baby. Oh God, please be with Louis.

Why did it hurt so much?

Garrett put his hand over hers. "My wife would like you to stay with us, the next several days, until all your family can be notified. You must understand that you and Louis have more friends than you can possibly imagine."

Hélène acknowledged the kind offer numbly. Her world, including all her personal surroundings, was turning to ashes. She only wanted to speak to her mother.

Hélène glanced out the sitting room window. She could see the little pine siskin, swaying back and forth as it balanced on a thin lilac twig. Then, it flew away.

Philippe's voice was clear,"I'm truly sorry, mon ami. Please pass on my condolences."

John nodded unevenly in response to the voice on the other line, then realized the caller couldn't see his movements. "Yes, Philippe. I will."

John had just finished relaying his trip back to Montréal, and Hélène's reaction to hearing the news.

John had faced injury, torture and death before, with friend and foe. The pain at such loss was excruciating. However, watching Hélène's reaction to the news was far worse than anything he had experienced. One moment, he saw a vibrant young woman: full of hope, love, and expectation. The next minute, there was disbelief, horror, frustration, and despair, as the shock of the news sank to deeper and deeper depths in her understanding. It would stick with him for a long time.

"What about things on your end?" he asked. "Is Drapeneau . . .?"

"He is in custody. His injuries are not serious, and will not delay a trial. We have ample physical evidence, as well as accounts from multiple persons; the case against him is strong. The only question that remains is how the trial will proceed."

John nodded again. The jurisdictional considerations affecting the case would take weeks to sort out; let alone how things would work out for Philippe and the others inadvertently involved in Gelda's abduction. John knew that the doctor and his wife were supportive of the stance that Philippe had taken, in keeping the Vanderstadts and their daughter safe from Drapeneau. He hoped things would work out for his friend.

John had a sense that Philippe and he needed to talk, one on one, about matters long past. Any friendship, from here on out, would have to be based on trust. Everything John said and did must help reinforce Philippe's confidence.

And yet, he didn't know what to say. Just like all those years ago, words just didn't suffice.

But he had to try.

"You know, Philippe, for years I have felt terrible about my mistake; about your grandparents not being able to visit Annette because of my carelessness. She was such a brave girl. I know it was a very long time ago . . . but, I want to know. Could you ever forgive me for that? Can you?"

Philippe was silent on the other end for a long time. "I know how you felt, John. It just hurt so much." He sighed. "We have all suffered from things in the past. And the pain remains; but I've had to learn, we have to be the ones willing to heal. To change."

They spoke a lot of Annette after that. And of John's own sister's death. Of Louis, and what Hélène now faced. And their families. They spoke for nearly two hours.

When they hung up, they had still not shared all their thoughts, but for John, a great weight had fallen from his shoulders. It was certainly not all dealt with, but it gave him strength to face the coming days.

⊕

In Montréal, the Bennetts fought hard to keep Hélène away from the media furor that had sprung up surrounding the events in Cité des Mélèzes. When the day of the funeral arrived, however, exposure to the public could not be avoided.

John and his family drove behind the Bennetts, who were escorting Hélène and the Vodreys. Despite understanding public interest in the Lac Tamarack events, John was amazed at the crowd surrounding the church. Photographers were taking pictures of Hélène, her friends, relatives, and the dignitaries as they arrived. Even the Mayor of Montréal and a representative from the French Consulate attended to show sympathy and support.

Louis' coffin was draped with the French flag, and the Colour Guard stood at attention as Father Simon pronounced the Funeral Mass.

After the ceremony, John spotted Jacques and Marie Dionne when Garrett came over to thank the siblings for their testimony. Tears openly slid down young Jacques' face.

Gelda Vanderstadt was so glad to see Marie that they held each other for a full minute. Marie had wept during the invocation and the public praise for Louis' services following Father Simon's eulogy.

Mark stayed by John's side through the ceremony, and John was grateful for his support. At the end, Hélène approached the two of them. "I'm sorry, John," she said quietly. "I know he meant a lot to you as well. I just want you to know, that I support the decision that Louis made to follow you up to Cité des Mélèzes. He wouldn't have had it any other way."

John was touched. He could only share in her sorrow with Mark, Sal, and Carl by his side.

A few more heartfelt words were exchanged, but John could see that events were wearing on Hélène. They parted not long after, and the four of them returned to the Richlieu for a quiet evening by themselves.

Louis' burial in Ottawa the following afternoon was peaceful by comparison. Louis' casket and bouquets of flowers, sent by well-wishers, filled the hearse. The cortège included only the closest family members and friends, although the senior LeClercs and Gelda's family attended. Earlier, the Vodrey's had gone to Rideau Hall to receive the medal from the Governor-General.

The weather was much the same as the previous Tuesday—the day John had to convey the sad news to Hélène. Blue sky alternated with puffy white and grey clouds from the southwest. A passing shower had dampened the ground and trees in the morning, but hardly any remnants remained of the blizzard that had pummeled the north the previous weekend. As the limousine containing Hélène, her parents and the Bennetts approached the gates of the cemetery, officials gave instructions to drivers for the sequence of the procession. Louis' casket was placed on a horse-drawn carriage before proceeding down the lane.

The burial plot was in a quiet grove, with simple grave markers reserved for those civilians of special distinction who had served the country. When the procession halted, a band played both the French and Canadian national anthems, and the official chaplain-in-charge blessed the departed and those attending. As the casket was lowered into the ground, the band rendered the beautiful strains of a Lutheran hymn.

"Now the day is over, night is drawing nigh / Shadows of the evening, steal across the sky . . ." John closed his eyes, letting the well-known words and music wash over him His breathing eased into the meaning of the song, and with it he wished Louis safe journey on the way ahead.

Hélène and the Bennetts departed with her family first, returning to the Bennetts' home in Montréal.

The Vanderstadts had made arrangements to fly directly from Ottawa to Winnipeg. Dr. Vanderstadt told John that Gelda's recovery had been overshadowed in the media for the moment by the sensational events surrounding the capture of Drapeneau. This was fortunate, because they felt they needed some quiet surroundings for a return to a degree of normalcy.

Before they left, John and Mark were able to say goodbye to the doctor and his family. Mark and Gelda had struck up a mutual friendship, and agreed to write each other at their first opportunity.

The doctor shook John and Mark's hands warmly. They had been through a lot together. The doctor, too, was deeply moved by Louis' sacrifice and said, "Somehow, we go around in our own little worlds, until something like this happens, and then we realize how deeply dependant we are on each other for survival. We've got to stick together. There's no other way. Please, let us all keep in touch."

It had been a tough five months for John's family.

With Mark off to Boston, and before their plane left, John, Sal and Carl had a quiet supper at an airport restaurant. John was relieved, at last, to be able to spend a peaceful night with his closest loved ones.

They were all ready to go home.

About the Author

The author was born in Oxford, England, in 1934 and attended Darrow School, New Lebanon, New York, and Phillips Academy, Andover, Massachusetts. He graduated in architectural history from Princeton University in 1957.

A commissioned officer of the U.S. Army Field Artillery Reserve, he attended Columbia University Evening School and Syracuse University's Graduate School of Architecture. For 32 years his professional responsibilities took him throughout the Northeast.

He lives with his loving family in Central New York.